A
BEAST
OF
MUDDY
BRAIN

Dear Andy

Verely — and my kit!

Charles Walter

12/06/08

A
BEAST
OF
MUDDY
BRAIN

CHARLES WALTERS

Acres U.S.A.
Austin, Texas

A Beast
of Muddy Brain

Acres U.S.A.

P.O. Box 91299

Austin, Texas 78709 U.S.A.

(512) 892-4400 • fax (512) 892-4448

info@acresusa.com • www.acresusa.com

ISBN 978-1-60173-013-8

Printed in the United States of America

Dedicated to

The memory of my brother,
George J. Walters, who wrote
Wir Wollen Deutsche Bleiben
(The Story of the Volga Germans),
and who inspired me to tell this story.

Acknowledgments

I have written this bio-history as a novel because the tempo and pathos of what has happened during one long lifetime becomes a statistic when reduced to mere facts and footnotes. Perhaps it will always be the role of the novelist to make the final statement for any historical era.

I cannot cite and thank the many who have facilitated this work. First and foremost, however, an Academy Award should go to Margaret Merrill, my star librarian at Virginia Tech, and to Ken Fousek, who edited the final draft for a writer with faltering eyesight. Gearld Fry and Ridge Shinn, the real masters of the Herbataurus breed, have educated a new generation — including myself — on herd genetics, as reflected herein, and Jerry Brunetti backgrounded some of the end sequences in this novel. Nor will the countryside soon forget the National Animal Identification System battle and the inspiration of Greg Niewendorp in the fight, which has yet to take its dying gasp. My wife, Ann, endured as she has through some thirty books, and Bryan Kight has earned a higher art degree for his cover design. The staffers at Acres U.S.A. again have exhibited the craftsmanship and professional excellence of a mature publishing company. Finally, my longtime associate Jake Voegeli was a valued adjunct in bringing a handwritten manuscript into print that people can actually read.

The People

The People is a beast of muddy brain,
    That knows not its own force, and therefore stands
    Loaded with wood and stone; the powerless hands
    Of a mere child guide it with bit and rein.

One kick would be enough to break the chain;
    But the beast fears, and what the child demands,
    It does, nor its own terror understands,
    Confused and stupefied by bugbears vain.

Most wonderful! with its own hand it ties
    And gags itself — gives itself death and war
    For pence doled out by kings from its own store.

Its own are all things between earth and heaven;
    But this it knows not, and if one arise
    To tell the truth, it kills him unforgiven.

— Tommaso Campanella
(1568-1639)

1

The high plains whimpered through the night, then settled into a silence you "most could hear." As the sun rose above the dust laden horizon a clean brilliance was promised for the day. When the people came out of their houses, a single thought became the acknowledgment they offered each other. It looks like a complete forage failure, they said, in dozens of ways and in several languages. The wheat fields surrounding the small towns established a little green, but it was covered with dust and made gray.

Jackrabbits ever on the hunt for their vegetarian diet stood still, as if to invite a farm boy's shot from a .22 long rifle. Horses and cows exhibited their ribs to passing trucks, which always kicked up dust as high as an animal's head.

It was only March, and the discerning eye saw only weeds. The most prevalent was the tumbleweed, the Russian thistle. Soon enough it would break away from its roots and march across the prairie like a member of the Coldstream Guard. Tumbleweeds ignored the rippled sea of grit, the oceanic waves of dust piled up along red wooden snow fences that caught little snow during the winter. Often the pile up of dust toppled the fences erected to protect the roads from snowdrifts and set up a tumbleweed ramp until the dust found a way to block the highway or the railroad track.

A small boy walked over the new carpet of dust that morning. You could hear him talking to the tumbleweeds, symbols of endurance when almost everything else had been scoured from the soil. He walked to a pileup that paved his way across a barbed wire fence separating a schoolhouse turned farmhouse from a pond, now dry and cracked into a jigsaw pattern. The old weeds tumbled across the dry bed, and the new ones made ready to follow the leader.

The boy figured there was something sacred about this plant. He had heard grownups call it a name that sounded something like the church tongue. The boy was ten years old, small for his age, and tanned because he rarely wore a shirt in summer. When a March wind picked up, usually before 10 a.m., his feathery blonde hair danced like a stage troupe, now covering his eyes, now sweeping back like a ripened wheat field. His eyes were what his mother called robin egg blue, and his skin was as soft as a girl's. He had no playmates on what Uncle Mike called "that God forsaken farm." The older brothers and sisters had clanned up the way large families do, and one older brother had gone away to seminary to study for the priesthood.

Grandpa said the tumbleweed came to Kansas with the arrival of the Volga Germans in 1876. "We brought it along with our wheat seed," the old patriarch said. So the boy figured it had something to do with the religion the immigrant people had introduced into their beloved country. It contained awesome rituals and Latin songs set to the music of the masters. The boy often sang parts of the High Mass and the Litany of the Saints to the family's pony, a strange chant that sounded like "Oh Robert Nobis" and a refrain, "Leave her on a stormy day."

It would be years before he would learn that the real Latin was *"Ora Pro Nobis, Libera nos, Domine."* Grandpa got scientific one night and recited the name of the spiny Russian thistle in terms of genus and species, *Salsola kali.* The next day the boy sang at the top of his lungs, *"Salsola kali,* leave her on a stormy day." He imitated the baritone voice of the rotund visiting Capuchin priest who intoned hellfire with the trap door open during Lenten services.

The high plains compared to the *Chernozem,* or black earth of the Russian steppes. The same crops flourished in both areas. Before the Volga Germans arrived, Kansas and the high plains had no Russian thistle weed, goat grass, Russian olive, corn cockle, or summer cypress. The boy's mother disliked corn cockle most of all. Stone ground with winter wheat, it made her bread taste rancid. The boy's mother had upbraided her men folk for failing to leave corn cockle behind.

Dad had his own pet antipathy, cheat grass, a thistle like weed that ruined his steppe by crowding out the calcium rich native pasture grass that once supported the world's biggest buffalo herds. It was said that on the high plains, as on the Volga steppes, the plants that thrived were weeds. The grand champion in the survival game was the Russian thistle. It had its aliases Russian cactus, salt wort, prickly glasswort, wind witch, but the name most people used was tumbleweed. There were other tumbleweeds of a different stripe, but Russian thistle was the real thing. You would find it in soils so dry it baffled the imagination how they endured. For a few weeks in a shower swept spring, the cows would eat these balls of vegetation. With warm weather, the plant hardened and set up like sawmill splinters, crowding out other vegetation. Then they broke from their anchorage and raced with the wind, dropping seeds that remained viable for years. Grandpa said some very educated men at Kansas State University had computed that a single tumbleweed plant could produce millions of seeds. Animal hooves and tractor lugs hammered them into the soil. Nothing helped the love hate relationship between Dad and the tumbleweed to grow as did the moldboard plow. It rolled the soil over followed by a disc or a drill and and left the soil undisturbed after that. Dad said seeds from a single plant could be used to populate a square mile if they all came alive.

The boy walked around the dry pond and across the berm that served as a dam for the now dry creek. On an outcropping of stone several feet above the vanished water level, a cluster of prickly pear sheltered a jackrabbit, a female big with babies. He took care not to disturb the lady rabbit and her family. From his vantage point atop an outcropping of stone, the boy could see heavy tractors in a neighboring pasture. Dad and Grandpa said some rich bastards were turning over even more "steppe fence" and tearing out stone fence posts that marked sections and plots tilled by tenants of absentee owners. There were big trucks with signs on the doors High Plains Land and Investment Co. The boy knew what the sign said, having seen it before, but he did not know what it meant. He heard his mother yelling, "Jim Bob! Jim Bob!" and so he started to run.

James Robert Neff was the name on the baptismal certificate on file at Sacred Heart Catholic Church, but to five brothers and sisters, and Mom and Dad, he was always Jim Bob. The Neff family, that is, Grandpa and Grandma and their parents had emigrated from Katherinenstadt on the Lower Volga late in the 19th century. They had brought along a cluster of relatives and enough children to populate a small village. Grandpa was the son of a legendary man named Kirghiz Jake. When land got scarce at a price the children of immigrants wanted to pay, Grandpa moved his family and numerous relatives further west. Most of the land was taken, so they became renters for the most part, often owning no more than the homestead. Only two of the Neff children were still at home. Joe Sam was off in Wichita. He had quit the seminary, worked part time while going to Wichita Business College, then landed a job at Southwest Kansas Stage Lines, now a bus company. Two older sisters, Catherine and Amanda, had joined a nunnery in Clyde, Missouri. Roy Lee was off somewhere in Colorado. He had left town with an Indian and a bunch of hobos in a boxcar.

One milk cow, two Percherons, and a small riding pony had survived the last year of dust storms. A dog named Rover always found a corner for storm survival, sometimes snuggling up to Jim Bob for comfort, sometimes breathing through a dampened cloth the boy held over the dog's snout. Rover was a mongrel pup, an unwanted animal someone had discarded along a country road. Jim Bob had found the half starved animal and brought it home, and he saw to it that Rover was fed and given water with the usual film of dust removed.

The house demanded dusting, scrubbing, and cleaning as soon as breakfast, oatmeal for everyone, was finished, and Mother remembered that there would be no oatmeal tomorrow. It was a scene played out all over the high plains. Even home canned food in the storm cellars was running low, and people looked to the heavens for relief and there was no answer. Men hoarded water and women conserved water, scrubbed clothes with homemade lye soap, and hunted jackrabbits and cottontails with single shot .22 rifles. Jim Bob was a crack shot. He was capable of taking a rabbit on the run, seldom missing.

As a boy of ten, it was his duty to have the cow serviced by the neighbor's bull, and to stand by when a stud stallion was brought in to breed with a mare. Before he was old enough to know better, he knocked a rooster off a hen with a stone. He thought he had killed the rooster and hid the comatose bird behind the chicken house. Mother saw him. "What did you do?"

"He was killing her."

"Don't do that again," Mother said. She did not stay on to explain. She dunked the comatose bird in a nearby stock tank. The rooster came alive, at which point the master of the flock was given his freedom.

Later on, Dad explained while a mare was being bred, "There's an egg inside her that the stallion has to fertilize so we can get a colt." The boy understood. Life on all the farms was glorious, but there was little anyone could tell a ten year old boy to explain why the country was dying.

Moving east of Ness County on the high plains, the normal 18 inches of rainfall became 27 inches at approximately the Topeka meridian, the imaginary line that cartographers call the isohyet. The tumbleweed could not stand that much rainfall, so even if the mobile weed rolled in that direction along the highways, scattering seeds by the billions, actual proliferation stayed in the bone dry territory. The poet Anselm Hollo once wrote that a tumbleweed looked like the skeleton of a brain. In Russia they had a word, *perekatipole,* literally "race across the fields." When the wind blew, the tumbleweed did exactly that. It lived to define the dust bowl. It seemed to say that the high plains would endure. It would endure drought and grasshoppers and dust storms in that order, but not in that order of importance.

The drought of the 1930s left a hidden scar on the psyche of the boy named Jim Bob. It was not the drought he would see as a grown up, when farmers complained and excused themselves for bad farming. It was a grinding dryness that stressed beyond endurance everything that grew. Yet the tumbleweed endured, and Jim Bob came to figure that he too would have to endure. As he toed the dust at the root of the plant, he detected the lifeblood being hoarded so that farmers had only a few days to turn the green plant into silage.

But no one seemed able to explain why the grasshoppers came. There were millions of them, perhaps billions and trillions. They settled on the roads to create a dangerous slime as cars rolled over them. In less time than it takes to pluck a pullet, both small winged and giant grasshoppers would make the green part of a corn leaf disappear. They could consume silk before it pollinated, eat every kernel off an ear of corn, and annihilate grass to the root level. On some Sundays at Sacred Heart Catholic Church in Ness City, hoppers would bite holes in the women's silk stockings. At home they chewed the curtains in the windows, and in the barns they made sizable dents in pitchfork handles. Not a leaf on the cottonwoods along the streams survived the onslaught of the plague. In a few days the bark itself fell victim to nature's own eating machine. The people did not understand, and the boy did not understand.

The hoppers took the fun out of the great outdoors. Every fence post became a living, writhing staff, and barbed wire took on the texture of living rope. There were that many grasshoppers end to end on the iron span. And yet the tumbleweeds remained unmolested. There was a government program to distribute poisoned bait, but the grasshoppers thrived on it. They seemed to spit out a stronger venom as one generation replaced the next.

If the grasshoppers ignored the Russian thistle, the Russian thistle ignored the dust storms. The dust storms followed grasshoppers the way a condor follows death. The boy Jim Bob did not understand, but it was his life's work to understand.

Grandpa's name was Xander. His name was really Jacob Alexander Staab, and he was 98 years old. Jim Bob walked about a mile to Xander's place to check on the old man now and then, to listen to his German words of wisdom. The boy's German was awkward, but his question was not. "What makes these storms?"

"God does this for his own reasons, probably to punish folks," Xander said. The old man tongued his pipe, fired the bowl and blew a perfect ring of smoke.

"Is being a farmer a sin?"

"I do not know what a priest will tell you," Xander said. "Plowing up so much steppe, yes, I think it is a sin." Xander continued puffing his pipe. The boy waited for the old man to say more. Xander's skin had the tone of a young man. He was a thin man, a careful eater who looked on meat protein as a condiment. He was muscular and tidy, and always wore a tie when not doing fieldwork. He had lost his wife two decades ago, and lived alone on the section next to the Neff farm, some of the time with an Indian helper and a hired white man.

He was remarkably alert when he talked to Jim Bob. He explained to the boy that God had installed magnets at the North Pole and at the South Pole. These magnets send ocean ice north and south and keep ocean currents forever mixing wind and evaporation forming weather on the small part of the globe called land.

The old man loved to blow smoke rings. He blew a half dozen, and then told Jim Bob that grass, not wheat, was the natural crop for the high plains. "Our people in Russia were farmers," Xander said. "We plowed, but we always left grass and we fed animals. We kept fish in the ponds." The old man liked to talk and he did not like to be interrupted. "The actual spawning ground for the dust storms," he said, "is small." Without breaking any speed laws, the local soil erosion official could circle it in a day. Tracking south of Ness County by way of Dodge City on Route 183 to Minneola, then moving southwest on Route 54, you'll go through Meade and Liberal, the gateway to the Oklahoma panhandle. The road maps show the highway intersecting Harker, Guymon, and Goodwell on terrain as flat as a well cooked pancake. Now you get on a lonely road to Stafford, Texas. From there, a state road takes you north to 287, back to the Oklahoma panhandle, then to Springfield and Lamar, Colorado. Then back to home territory. There, you have covered the heart of the dust bowl.

"We're two thousand feet above the sea," Xander continued. "The high plains run up to almost a mile above sea level. You have everything from Chernozem to blow sand. Some of our people are dumb as a bundle of straw. Just because they found natural phosphorus, potash and nitrogen, they thought it would last forever." He puffed his pipe some more. "Watch out. Too many people are educated beyond their intelligence." Then he added as an afterthought, "Learn to read the weeds."

He continued to talk to the boy. "The Volga-like Chernozem soil of the eastern high plains tends to become the dark brown soils of the western half of the area, with Colorado and New Mexico brown soil bringing up the rear, the latter not subject to wind erosion. Calcerous and sandy clays washed down the Rockies by glacial waters joined wind blown loess to make the area survive once upon a time, all because they had paramagnetic properties, but these had wasted away in time to intercept a dry cycle as dealt by nature's deck of cards. Paramagnetic soil particles attract, diamagnetic particles repel. The term of choice is flocculation, that property that causes soil particles to cling together. Flocculation is destroyed by long periods of drought."

Xander knew he was telling the boy more than he could absorb. But when the boy came around, it gave him a chance to talk to someone other than himself. His well thumbed Yearbooks of Agriculture and his volumes of Robert Ingersoll occupied most of the living room table.

"Son, here is a damn fool," he said, indicating the book by Ingersoll, "and here is the real truth." He gestured at a United States Department of Agriculture Yearbook, *Soils*. On another occasion, old man Xander explained, "There is nothing new about dust storms. The cycles discerned from tree rings tell us that dust storms have visited the area for periods of five or more years no less than twenty-one times between A.D. 738 and 1934. On the average, these droughts present themselves every thirty-five to thirty-six years. Some of the droughts lasted more than ten years and came every 55 years or so, much like the Kondratieff commodity cycle.

"Ah, but the tumbleweed has lasted through them all," Xander had said. And he went on to explain how some plants start from seeds every year and complete their life cycles in one crop. This holds true for the summer and winter annuals. The summer annuals actually germinate during every season except winter. They grow to maturity, cast off their seeds and die with the first or second frost. They have a root system that is simple in the extreme and produce an abundance of seeds. Pig weed is a good example of a summer annual.

Winter annuals come to life in the fall. They usually develop a small rosette of leaves and stay alive throughout the winter. Growth picks up in the following spring, producing flowers and showers of seeds. The next fall these annuals are dead. Shepherd's purse and mustard are good examples.

The perennials usually are more complicated. They grow from seeds or underground root particles, frequently from both. The roots often establish deathless properties, living on from year to year. In most areas the above ground part of the plant quietly passes away each fall and new growth issues forth in the following spring. Such plants almost always produce flowers and seeds each year. They grow in great circular patterns and defy annihilation with a diffuse root system. They creep all over the place. Lateral roots from bulbs give rise to still more plants above ground.

Garlic and white onions are outlaws. They reproduce by means of bulbs grown either above or below the ground, or from seeds. The dandelion, darling of the lawn, is in a class by itself. Still, it must be considered a perennial. It actually produces from seed, but is long lived because of its fantastic taproot system.

Biennials require two years to complete their cycle. Seeds germinate in the spring, a crown of leaves and feisty taproots are developed during the first year. They live through the winter and produce new stalks or stems the following spring. Later on, they flower and mature their seeds, this business being completed by the end of the second year. Good examples are weed carrot, millet and burdock.

For the purpose of crop production, astute farmers have come to view weedy guardians of the soil as nutrient thieves, as non-economic competitors to the commercial crop. In the high plains, "commercial crop" means wheat. Winter wheat was planted in the soil before any crispness came into the air. If the rhythm of showers followed its ten day to two week schedule, well tinted blends of wheat grass appeared well before frost and snow. Wheat asked for and needed snow, both for cover and as an insurance policy for amber waves of grain. Without frost, the wheat plant produced only foliage, no grain. Without moisture, it produced nothing.

Xander was well into the twilight of his life, and he knew it. The decades since his wife died saw him become as silent as a monk, but now he wanted the ten year old boy to know everything. He made the boy promise to read his books and papers as he got older. Once, before a big rabbit hunt, he had written out a message in exquisite German cursive script:

"When you get old enough to shave, put this on your person and memorize it. I am afraid the damn fools are going to turn to dangerous poisons to kill the weeds, especially tumbleweeds." Xander's message was simple in the extreme. "Each weed is keyed by the Creator to replace a specific deficiency in the soil."

He had whispered, and the people believed the unbelievable. They believed that the great American desert had returned. The only prosperous plant in the once bountiful land was the sunflower, a fence row weed that exploded superb color over a scorched terrain.

Xander Staab did not produce wheat. He believed in grass, so he produced forage first. He was an innovator. He was probably the first to sink down a deep well to tap the Ogallala Aquifer, a gigantic bathtub full of water several hundred feet under Nebraska, Colorado, New Mexico, the Texas panhandle, and western Kansas. He maintained a small lake to warm the water, then irrigated several acres of alfalfa to crutch his herd over any dry spell.

Xander's daughter, Eloise, was Jim Bob's mother. Another daughter had gone east and now taught school in the Mad River Valley of Vermont. His only son, Colonel Jacob Staab, had landed on the western slope of the Continental Divide. The two had quarreled and become estranged over the issue of Woodrow Wilson's war mongering.

Mother's voice drowned out the distant tractor noise of the corporation people ruining more steppe. Her "Jim Bob!" calls continued with staccato regularity. As the boy came within speaking voice distance, she said, "Your grandpa is here to give you a buggy ride." The boy dogtrotted to where she stood, and his mother gave him a quick kiss on the forehead. "Hurry now, Grandpa's waiting."

The boy and the older man took that ride, about four miles around in this section. They arrive back at the farm in the late afternoon. As dusk, come on, the boy stood up to jump from the buggy.

The boy dismissed all thoughts of Xander as he answered his mother's call, "Coming, Mom."

Xander asked, "Jim Bob, what about your brother Earl?"

Jim Bob said, "Not a word, not a letter."

Xander gave the boy a hug, a big hug. It was getting dark, too late to teach the boy about the enigma of a bull's horn, or the inventory of information he had assembled, and he sent the boy on his way.

2

In early May, the moisture was saved or hoarded, and flocculation failed again. Each wisp of wind claimed its share of the earth, and each vehicle on the road announced its presence with dust billowing behind it, and even paved roads sucked in soil from the ditches and off nearby snow fences that stopped little snow during the winter.

The Southwest Kansas Stage Line bus that made the run from Pueblo to Wichita passed through the dust bowl at speeds that sometimes reached sixty miles per hour. The vacuum it created announced its passage to grasshoppers and field workers alike, and attracted fine grit like a magnet. By the time the great vehicle parked in the depot stall across the street from the Kellogg Street offices, no one could read the sign on its door or easily identify the baggage on the rooftop carrier.

After the driver saw all the passengers and their Arkansas Gladstone suitcases, cardboard boxes with a string handle, really, off the bus, he slapped his visored cap against his right leg, and addressed the depot manager.

"I need to see Sam," he said. He meant Joe Sam Neff, the rate clerk and home office ticket manager. He added, "I'll be back in a few minutes." The driver was a six footer, tanned up to the white skin that indicated the perpetual resting place for his official cap. He walked slowly until the stiffness left his legs, passed through a door that needed lubrication, then knocked gently on the glass of Sam Neff's open door.

"Mr. Neff," the driver said, introducing his presence.

"Yes, come on in. Have a seat."

"I'm only going to take a minute," the driver said.

"What can I do for you?"

The lanky driver did not answer, and he did not take a seat. Instead, he fished a postcard out of his breast pocket. He handed the card to

Sam Neff. He waited for the silence he had installed in the office to be broken. He remained on his feet in case he needed to leave quickly.

Sam Neff took the card. "Have a seat, please!"

He read it once, exhibiting no body language, no surprise. Then he read it again. It was not an easy read. The card was wet. Perspiration followed the fabric of the driver's shirt until it came to the pocket that held the card, and the cardboard took over, moisture claiming a third of the card, the one cent postage stamp included.

"How did you get this?" Sam Neff asked. His voice was that of an interrogator, not that of a very minor clerk in a company that was lucky to be alive.

"This guy came up to me in Pueblo, a Mexican. He wants to know where he can mail a card for a friend." The driver paused. He knew he would be invited to continue, so he waited.

"Well, go on," Sam Neff said.

"I figured the Mex was sending a card to Mexico. I took a look at it. I saw your name and the company address. Hell, I'm coming back on the Wichita run." He waited for a response, and in a few seconds he added, "I really didn't read it just looked at it a little bit. Didn't make much sense to me."

"That's okay," Sam Neff said. "Thanks. I'm glad you didn't mail it. It'd probably take a week to get here, if ever." Sam Neff stood up to shake hands.

He did not wince under the powerful grip of the tall, even statuesque driver, who left as he had come. Sam noticed the back of the man's shirt, almost wringing wet. He watched him cross Kellogg Street and disappear through the glass doors of the bus station.

"Come," the card read. There was a map on it, twenty four miles east of the Pueblo city limits, then several section farms and a square house with a slant roof marked "X." The card was signed "Royal."

There was a p.s.: *"Ich hunger."*

Sam Neff reached for his coat, a garment he carried folded on his arm out of the Southwest Kansas Stage Line office, now that a blistering sun was melting the asphalt on Wichita's streets. He stuck his head in the office manager's door for an obligatory "Good night, Mr. Farr," but the office manager invited him in.

"Yes sir," Sam Neff said.

"Sam, I want you on the bus to Hutchinson Monday morning." It was an opener Sam had heard before. Usually it meant an hour long conversation replete with instructions repeated a half dozen times and the obligatory tag line that a written report would be expected within a week. This time the invitation to enter without knocking "and leave the same way," as the office manager put it, was as welcome as rain in a western Kansas dust patch. Sam told the man there was trouble at the farm. He wanted to take his own car and an extra day, without pay, of course.

"How long have you been here?" the boss asked. He knew to the hour how long Sam had been there. The date was June or July, 1929. Sam came recommended by a Wichita Business College, and he had never missed a day of work since then. In fact, no one dared miss a day of work since October 1929, not since the stock market crashed. No one had been hired by the bus company since then, and there had been dismissals. Sam had hung on through low pay and scare talk ever since. He had never asked for a day off and had even invaded scheduled vacation hours with home work, and the boss knew it.

"Is this serious?" the office master asked.

"It's my brother," Sam Neff said. He did not elaborate, and the way he said it, made the suggestion that it would be poor form for the office master to ask. "All right, but you're on expense account only on work days understood?"

Sam Neff nodded. He stood up and extended his hand. It was taken by a fishy handclasp. There were two other words. "Drive careful."

Sam "drove careful" out of Wichita, west on U.S. 54 until he came to the first after dark "EAT" sign along the highway. He had come a long way since he left the farm, vowing never to be caught dead doing farm work. He had left home at age 15. He allowed the local Priest to finesse him into seminary life, not so much because the spirit of God had commanded his soul and vision, but because he wanted to have done with a life that was going nowhere for his parents and family. Now, five years on the job, he wondered about his choice. He had been able to buy a used Chevy coupe with a rumble seat and he had sent home 10% of his wages to help out. He maintained a small apartment and was courting a girlfriend, but the times held little promise, so he stuck to his job and corresponded with Dad by mail.

As he tooled the four window Chevy down the paved highway, he felt a dampness under his arms and beads of sweat around his collar and on his forehead. The memory of Roy's postcard made Sam push the accelerator a little harder. He would cross the Colorado line as the sun came up if all went well. Darkness spared him the bleakness that unfolded as he drove west. Past Hutchinson he saw tumbleweeds dancing across the road and jackrabbits frozen in the headlights, both at regular intervals. The reference to hunger worried Joseph Samuel, Joe Sam to his brothers and sisters, Sam to his co workers. There had always been meat on the farm, jackrabbits the worst case scenario, side meat as a general rule, and often simply lard sandwiches.

As he drove, he remembered going to school with his brother. The walk to the old Mount Zion school was hardly more than two miles, and sometimes the pony was available to the eldest of the Neff tribe. Roy was three years younger than Sam.

Atop the family's pony, Sam rode with Roy hanging on, bareback of course. Often the boys carried a .22 rifle to school just in case a cottontail or jack furnished a target on the way home. Royal had been stuck with that appellation because he had entered the world as a blue baby and somehow survived. He had had a quick mind and performed well in the one room school, located at the cross section of two county roads. It was a site some of the children called "the high lonesome." There was not a building in any of the four directions.

The school grounds consisted of approximately three acres. Some of the space was devoted to a dirt floor basketball court, a softball diamond with a skinned infield, and two double station outhouses. Softball was the main sport. The school supplied no equipment. Each pupil had to come up with a glove and bat or borrow one. Only the oldest played on the baseball team. In practice everyone was needed and welcome. Sam smiled into the rear view mirror as he thought about it, sometimes speaking to himself. Girls not only played softball, they often excelled and shamed some of the undersized farm boys. Each Friday after school, Mount Zion played a team from a neighboring district. Each game was an occasion. Sam was ambidextrous and batted left handed. Roy was left handed and usually played first base.

The Ness City Sacred Heart Catholic Church operated an elementary school. A rare institution in Protestant Kansas, Sacred Heart tested its team at Mount Zion. With a large student body, it was usually no contest. Sam was benched one afternoon for playing too rough. It was then that Father Dennis sidled over to the bench for a talk with him.

It was the first of many conversations leading up to the closing of the deal. Father Dennis would help defray expenses if Joseph Samuel would enter the seminary in Cincinnati. He would provide the bus ticket and make the arrangements. He would be the pride of his county and his family. A bright boy should not waste his life on a farm that was too small to survive anyway. Sam threw up defenses. He was not sure he had a call. His parents could not afford any part of the venture. He had a hard time with Latin. The Priest fended off each argument, usually by talking in circles, or by defeating the objection with stirring portraits of the holy life Jesus gifted to only a few. Besides, there was no chance of further education. Great companies were assembling the land into a few strong hands. No student at Mount Zion ever left the school without a basic knowledge of reading, cursive penmanship and arithmetic. Peer pressure at Mount Zion matched and often exceeded that of life in the seminary, without the cynicism. The boys in Cincinnati had a saying: "They take young men, dress them like girls, and treat them like little boys."

As Sam's headlights swept the edge of the dust furrows in the road, three jackrabbits escaped the illumination through a hole in a red slatted snow fence. Grey soil was being replaced by the red berm of eastern Colorado. No wonder they named the place Colorado or colored red. Sam pulled over at a place with a three letter sign, "EAT". He filled his tank from the gravity fed pump, and waited to pay until the attendant finished emptying the glass tank atop the Socony vacuum apparatus.

"Ten gallons, a dollar forty," the pump man said. "You from the east?" The license plate said 1 407, meaning the car came from the most populated county in the state, Sedgwick County. There were over 100 other counties, each numbered according to standing population.

"Wichita," Sam said.

"Dry out there?" The filling station man asked, stroking two days growth of whiskers.

"Not like this," Sam said.

The filling station man waited a moment to talk. "I don't think there'll be much of a crop this year. We've had three dusters already."

"I guess the country's going to hell in a hand basket."

"Well," the gas pumper said, "it sure don't pay to keep the hours they want. You're only the seventh car that's tanked since midnight."

"Which way were they going?" Sam asked.

"East. Mostly east. You know that's funny. Down in Oklahoma most busted farmers head west, to California. Nope, our dust bowlers head east." Sam wanted to get back on the road. He ordered a hamburger, paid the fry cook and listened politely as the pump handler continued his commentary and interrogation.

"You a salesman?"

"No." Sam did not elaborate.

"Government man?"

Sam knew there was no escape.

"Yes. Soil Erosion Service."

"You can't help the farmer," the man went on. "They say supply and demand. Bullshit! If you're short, they import and import. I've got an uncle at the Port of Houston. Do you know what they're bringing in? Wheat, lots of wheat."

The man was on a roll. "I'm memorizing a poem about Roosevelt:

I curtailed crops when I felt mean,

I imported corn from the Argentine.

I double crossed both young and old,

And still the fools my praises told."

Sam walked to his car. The filling station man was still talking as Sam slid behind the wheel. "I got this straight from the horses mouth. You can take it to the bank. When he thought no one was listening, Mister 'R' told his flunky, What good is a constituency, if you can't sell it out."

Sam threw the Chevy into gear and peeled back onto the highway. The sun was using his car as a shadow marker on the road, one that stayed behind him, which it did until the shadow almost disappeared. Admittedly, he said to himself, learning Latin is a bit easier than handling a muck stick or a pitch fork, but there is even greater oppression when physical labor is removed, whether in a church school or a business office.

"I don't think Roy would have lasted as long as I did," Sam said to himself. He had lasted four years on the road to priesthood. It had come to him only recently what had happened. He had started asking questions for which no reply was forthcoming.

For instance, Moses said the law is easy to do. Good God, I remember the citation, Deuteronomy 30:11 through 14, more words than I remember. Jesus also said, "The law is easy to do and will remain in effect for all time." Matthew 5:17-20. Paul said, "No man can do the law. The law is abolished." Paul everywhere.

The instructor's eyes narrowed as he sought to answer all sorts of questions never asked. Talking in circles was a specialty, Sam concluded, for which reason he posed an even more difficult conundrum. In the New Testament there are two genealogies of Jesus' family. If you hold to the doctrine of Immaculate Conception, that means Jehovah impregnated Mary. In mammalian reproductive biology, the father provides sperm to the egg. If the father provides the blood to the infant Jesus, how did the female line's genealogy, and Joseph's genealogy, get in there? Now if the sperm supplies the blood. Stop. They had known that Sam was not a candidate they were looking for. The squirrel cage gets cranked up. It starts to squeak after all the grease is worn off.

"My son, accept Pascal's norm. Believe and you will come to believe!" the Director of Vocations advised.

The questions followed, but the answers did not, and yet Sam remained a spiritual candidate. He still went to Mass on Sunday and he was not going to upend civilization. It was enough that agriculture was being given the squirrel cage treatment, and his family was being ground down like corn in a 32 stone grinder.

Roy was out there somewhere, starving, if he had read the postcard correctly. He fished the crude map out of his pocket and started watching the odometer. The miles clicked off in packages of ten, and the section lines, fenced and unmarked, sailed by. Sam hit the brake, backed the Chevy a couple of rods, and made his turn toward an abandoned farmhouse a half mile down track. He was about 30 miles east of Pueblo. Roy was the smartest kid Sam had ever known. What in God's name was he doing here in a rundown farmhouse in the middle of nowhere?

Sam remembered a time at the old Mount Zion school. There was a Monday morning contest working arithmetic. The lower grade pupils were chosen to start the contest. Each pupil took a position at the blackboard that had covered the entire wall behind the teacher's desk. The teacher would call out an arithmetic problem that was applicable to the grade the pupils were in. The one who solved the problem first remained at the blackboard, and the loser returned to his or her seat. The pupil remaining at the blackboard had the privilege of choosing the next competitor. Only an upper class student could be chosen, never a lower class student. Roy was always the survivor at the blackboard.

Roy and Sam had roamed the fields together with a single shot 22 caliber 33 rifle. The rabbits bagged on the run or caught sitting helped feed the family. Short cartridges were used when the shot was close in. Those at a distance required .22 longs. The longer cartridges were more expensive and were used only when there was a need.

Sam pulled into the abandoned farmyard and sounded his horn. There was no sign of life. He mounted the porch and looked inside. The door was ajar. There was Roy on some old bedding, apparently too weak to move. An empty water bottle stood near the head of his makeshift bed. Roy had a week's growth of whiskers. He probably did not weigh 115 pounds. His eyes were sunken. It took only a moment to learn that he had not eaten in days, and very little before that. He had been unable to collect his wages from a farmer who also employed illegal Mexicans. "Let's go in there with a baseball bat and collect my wages," Roy said.

Sam took another look at his younger brother. "No," he said. "Let's get you on the outside of some food." They found an eatery on the road back to Kansas and paid the fee for a meal, hot water, and a bath. Tears welled up in Sam's eyes when he saw his brother disrobe for the outside shower. He looked like a refugee you would see in the newsreels at movie houses.

Roy ate sparingly before his shower, and afterward he downed a piece of pie. In the car he stayed wide awake, a fortuitous situation since Sam could hardly keep his eyes open. Roy talked. He had caught a freight train on the spot to Dodge City. He met a fellow named Marble. Together they had hopped the Santa Fe headed west to California where hobo billingsgate promised work. At Pueblo the yard bulls pulled him off the train while his companion named Marble escaped. The judge gave him three months, and when the sentence was completed the sheriff took him to a farm with the promise of employment, a dollar a day.

Roy worked thirty days before he asked for his pay. The farmer flew into a tantrum and told Roy to get out. He could go to hell if he thought he could collect for boondoggling and eating groceries without doing any work. Roy caught up with a Mexican named Martinez. "I didn't get his first name," Roy said. "He made the run to town to pick up laborers and supplies. I always kept some penny postcards so I could write home."

There was a long silence. Finally Roy spoke. "We heading home?"

"Yes," Sam said, his voice clear and distinct.

When Sam reached the first filling station in Kansas, a new calm settled over the two travelers. Colorado County Mounties ceased to be a worry, and 35 Kansas had no highway patrol. The road to Ness County was wide open, dusty and paved almost all the way. After a Kansas duster let up, the two found themselves wide awake.

"Roy!" exclaimed Joe Sam.

"Still here," Roy said.

"Let's go over what you wanted to tell Mom."

Roy stared straight ahead. "I couldn't find Earl Junior, that's all."

"Let's take it from the top. You left Ness City, how?"

"I walked. I took Half Moon, that ass half breed that hung around Xander's place with me. We walked and hitchhiked up into the mountains past Loveland clear up to Estes Park."

"I know that much. Mom got a postcard marked Estes Park," Sam supplied rather needlessly, he realized as soon as he said it. Roy did not say another word for a mile or two. Sam did not coax him. He knew Roy and his taciturn side. He would open up when he got damn good and ready.

"Ready" arrived when Sam swerved the Chevy to hit a jackrabbit, missing. "Don't do that," Roy said. "You're at least as tired as I am and you'll wreck the car."

Sam recovered his smooth glide over the road, and Roy began to speak. "The Indian left me at Loveland. I made it to Estes, then into the park, Rocky Mountain National Park. They were building stonework along Trail Ridge Road." He paused to let this information sink in. "The guys knew Earl. Apparently he was a stone man and they did not like to lose him."

"What happened?"

"Some railroad recruiters came along. They offered Earl more money. I guess they were building some railroad trestles down by La Junta. He signed on because they doubled his pay. That's all they could tell me." Sam knew there was more, much more. It came in a sort of a rush. "They gave him his passage to La Junta," Roy added, "at least that's what the Trail Ridge foreman said. He said, 'Why, hell, I wouldn't stand in the way of a fellow getting better money.' I guess it was government stuff, not the best pay in the world."

Roy then hitchhiked his way south to La Junta, Raton Pass, and into New Mexico. He found the crew on which Earl had worked. "Well, we got to a quitting point, so most of the crews were laid off," a foreman told Roy. "We wanted to keep Earl, but he wanted to go home. He drew his pay and he told me he was walking because the farm needed all the money he had. I told him that was dangerous, but he wouldn't listen. The last anyone saw of Earl, he was walking the tracks back north."

"That's it?" asked older brother Sam.

Roy nodded. There were stone fence posts along the secondary road that meandered north. Roy had helped set many a stone post. Unconsciously he started counting them, section after section. There was something soothing about the posts, but their silence would be ruinous to health if Sam stacked up the Chevy.

"Roy, what do you really think happened?"

Roy came back with speculation based on experience. "I wasn't about to walk alone from New Mexico. I hopped a lot of freights, and, Sam, it's brutal out there. You saw what happened to me?"

"Exactly what did happen to you?"

"I caught a Santa Fe freighter back toward Dodge City. Somewhere at a jerkwater the railroad bulls caught a bunch of us hobos napping. I caught an axe handle across the back of the head. When I woke up my money and wallet was gone."

"You get jailed?"

"Yes, but that wasn't all. Before the bull got to me, a big fellow in a straw hat and bib overalls fought back. Three bulls beat on him. It wasn't just a beating. The smallest of the bulls came at the big guy with an axe handle. He didn't try to hit him over the head. He grabbed the handle about a foot and a half from the end with his left hand and at the butt with his other fist. Then he ran it into that fellow, right in the stomach. The guy puked, crapped in his pants. He swallowed his tongue. They left him on the floor of the boxcar until he died. Then one of them hit me."

Sam said nothing for a while. He was getting a picture Roy would confirm as the secondary road crossed a highway and some very conservative signs announced the direction and mileage between towns. The day was sliding away and Sam soon realized he had been in the seat fully 20 hours with very few stops. Roy nodded off now and then. The last time he slept fully half an hour. When he awoke, Sam cautioned him not to state the obvious, it would kill Mom.

If Earl Junior left New Mexico with his pay in tow, the ex railway workers probably knew it. Sam doubted that any of the down and outers riding the rails dealt foul play to Earl. Mere assault and robbery might have resulted in a casualty, but then a body would have turned up somewhere along the tracks. No, that's probably not what happened. If Earl had encountered yard bulls. "Roy, that man in the boxcar?"

"Yes," Roy said, "I know what you're thinking. They turned me over to the local sheriff. A day later, a little owl eyed judge in a black Halloween smock gave me 90 days for vagrancy. While I was in jail one of the prisoners told me the bulls took that fellow's money and wallet. Later, one was on the detail that digs the graves. I think a coroner took a look at the body, and I was told the cause of death was a fall from a moving train." Sam said," No identification. No body."

"I don't think any of the hobos riding the rails got Earl." Sam repeated, "Don't tell that story and county jail?" He did not want to push now that Roy was opening up a bit. Dozing off seemed to have refreshed the younger man.

"They were real sons of bitches," Roy said. "Say the slightest thing or even make a facial expression and you get a stick or a kick in the shins."

"What did you get to eat?"

"Usually thin cabbage soup. That or beans that tore your gut out. It was mostly road gang work and boredom." Roy paused, then turned to Sam and gave him a penetrating look. "Sam, I'll tell you this, but you can't tell Mom or Dad. You can tell Jim Bob when he's a little older. Agree?" Sam figured he had better agree or a brooding silence would be all that would issue from Royal Lee Neff.

"Sure, Roy." He said no more.

"There was a trustee, an old Mexican. They had him mopping the office and doing chores. The first day he met me he froze like he'd seen a ghost. He crossed himself and said something like 'Jesus Christ' in Spanish. He backed away from me and avoided me for weeks, even when he shoved that slop into my cell. I think he referred to me as a ghost. He came into the shared cell to change a light bulb. I grabbed him by the collar. Did he think I had leprosy? I asked him. The poor fellow stammered and talked Mexican. One of the other prisoners started helping me. 'Have you seen this man before?' 'Si,' was all we could get out of that old Mex. 'When?' 'Six months ago.' 'Where?' 'Here. He look exactly like this gringo.'"

In bits and pieces Roy got the report he now relayed to brother Sam. The man who was a dead ringer for Roy Neff had been taken by two yard bulls while riding the rails. Apparently the freight train slowed at a place where there was no reason to slow. Railroad thugs hopped aboard, always gravitating toward boxcars with open doors. They surprised the unpaid traffic that way. Two of the bulls jumped this man who looked so much like Roy. One smashed him in the neck. The second bull hit the man across both shins, breaking one leg.

The trustee told what he knew and what he had heard. The prisoner was thrown off the car, handcuffed, and dragged to a waiting car. In the process he must have been kicked in the ribs. When he awoke in a county jail cell, he asked to be taken to a doctor.

"There ain't nothing wrong with you," he was told.

"I think I have a rib in my lung," the prisoner told his deputy jailer, this according to the turnkey.

"You don't know shit from Shinola. You just want to boondoggle." The ghost prisoner died that night. The doctor who came by said he died of pneumonia.

"What happened to the body?" One of the jailed men helping Roy with the interrogation appeared to threaten the old man.

"I don't know," the Mexican said.

The rough hands threatening his throat squeezed with dangerous force. "No, please, I tell you." The old trustee probably saw his life departing. He was shaking.

"He buried," he said. "He no name."

"No identification?" Roy asked.

"Si. No identification."

"No money?"

The trustee did not answer. "He buried in a county coffin." As Roy concluded his narrative, tears welled up in his eyes. Roy Neff was the spitting image of his brother Earl Junior. At Mount Zion the teacher often mistook one boy for the other. No wonder the harmless old jail trustee thought he had seen a ghost.

"Don't know," Sam said. "If that was Earl, then there should be closure for folks."

"The problem is, we can never find out," Roy said. "Christ, it would take lawyers and court orders to open that grave, if we could find it. That fat ass sheriff would stand in the way. Sam, we don't have the money, you don't have the money."

It was almost evening when the two weary travelers pulled into the farmyard. Old Xander Staab waved a salute to the Chevy coupe. At nearly a hundred years of age he was still walking the section road.

3

When dust reached New York and grayed the sky well into the winter, the nation's president and the government discovered the high plains. Sam Neff found long articles of exposition and analysis in the *Wichita Eagle* and *Wichita Beacon*, and he compiled the information that came his way. Recently, he had encountered a *Collier's* magazine article, "Land Where the Children Died." He found the issue displayed prominently on the same rack that featured John Dillinger, Baby Face Nelson, Pretty Boy Floyd and Alvin Karpis, public enemies 1, 2, 3 and 4. By this time Bonnie and Clyde had distinguished themselves by robbing a bank already closed by bankruptcy. It was the *Collier's* article, not the local papers, that convinced Sam Neff that the family should pull out and leave Ness County. Others were leaving for Washington and Oregon and California, even going east to the Ozarks for cheap land and ample rainfall.

Those with strong survival instincts hung on, or they hung on because they were too impoverished or old to move. A few like Jacob Alexander Staab were certain that the rain would come, that the great aquifer would be tapped and end this horrible drought, that the world would return to these wonderful acres usually green, then golden, with wheat. There were far off relatives forever sending brochures and reciting the same shopworn article which had caused Sam Neff to damn to hell all those who had insulted the prairies of the high plains.

Sam saw a short subject at a Wichita theater that confirmed the stories offered as print and text. It came styled *The Plow that Broke the Prairie Range*. It was issued by the Resettlement Administration with the imprimatur of Rexford Tugwell. Tugwell used his film to convince Congress that something should be done about the rape of the high plains all for the purpose of providing a surplus of wheat.

The Plow that Broke the Range was called a work of art on par with the still photography by Arthur Rubenstein and Dorothea Lang. The opening scene spoke out with a message that screamed louder than a thousand words. There it was, the prairie of yesteryear, a goodly slice of grass with a cultured English voice explaining how 40 million acres of high plains grass had covered the landscape before the arrival of settlers. The music under this fruitful scene was tranquil. As the plowmen arrived, the music grew louder. The screen showed the plow rolling the grass under furrow after furrow as it moved across the field. This was accompanied by music usually reserved for trouble in the streets.

Wheat began to grow. In time, clouds of dust rose towards blackened skies. The passage of time was depicted with a World War I era headline about soaring wheat prices. The images were intoxicating and mesmerizing, if not in the darkened chamber of the theatre, then out front in stills facing the street for the benefit of pedestrian traffic. Then the screen went black for a second or two. Now the skull of a cow appeared under a bank of dust. The image set up the announcement that 40 million acres of the prairie had been totally ruined by the plow with an additional 20 million acres badly damaged.

The buffalo were gone and the deer and antelope were not to be found. East of the Colorado line, a few coyotes and wolves survived because they preyed on jackrabbits instead of cows. Along the north fenced section of the Xander Staab farm, a red slatted snow fence ran in a half moon circle the length of a football field. It had been constructed during the last week with sledge hammers and baling wire, and had the earmarks of a corral. Half the circle was open. Beyond the section line, bits of greenery begged for life and the renewal of traditional rains. At a ditch near the terminus of the proposed rabbit drive arena was a dehydrated cow buried to her neck, probably overcome while trying to find the road during a recent black blizzard. When Sam and Roy drove the last half mile of dirt road, they wondered aloud if it was not a bit too late to save this year's crop. But both were too tired to wonder very long. They had not even noticed the absence of Rover, the dog, as they drove that last stretch of ungraveled ruts onto the Neff farmstead.

Sam could not remember the place ever looking this bleak. Even on this calm, late Saturday afternoon, the slightest breeze seemed to spawn little dust devils, as if to hint at a greater nemesis to come.

The farmstead was nestled in a dip of the prairie's flat terrain. The house itself had been a larger than average consolidated rural school before the area's population had shifted. It was now set up into rooms and set atop a full length basement with poured concrete walls. A special gangway allowed easy access to the bone dry yard and a debilitated plum orchard on a small bottom area near the equally bone dry pond. The cottonwood tree had been stripped stark naked by grasshoppers.

The basement served as a living room and kitchen. Adequate space had been set aside for the gravity fed furnace and storage bin for cow chips, the only affordable fuel supply.

The earlier classroom area had windows that touched your toes and leaped to the ten foot high ceiling. An attic space doubled as a spare bedroom. A crawl space above the attic contained a fantastic array of books left over when the building was moved several miles to the farmstead. There was no electricity or running water. The furnace that had been installed by the renovators did a more than adequate job of heating the single body structure. Sam Neff had last white washed the basement walls with a calcium slurry of mud mined near an outcropping of stone, sand, and white earth east of the barn and barely a stone's throw from the county road. There was a time when Sam, Roy, Amanda and Earl Junior played Annie Annie Over, a game in which a rubber ball was thrown over the roof. The team on the other side was to catch the ball, steal around the house, and tag one of the opposing players. The catch was on the honor basis. When rough play disturbed a side board, dry prairie soil poured out. It had been used as insulation between the outside side boards and the interior tongue and groove paneling.

No one met the car when Sam and Roy rolled to a stop. Merely stepping down off the running board delivered a moment of truth. In his mind, Sam compared the dry lawns of Wichita to this near moon landscape. Sam saw that only Mom's ingenuity and good taste had made the place tolerable. She had fashioned curtains for the odd sized windows. She had made slip covers for second hand furniture with printed feed sack fabric. When the pedal powered sewing machine was not creating curtains, fancy dinner towels, and table cloths, Mom was creating clothes for children, then for menfolk. Mom looked up when Sam and Roy entered the basement through the *"gang."* "Mother of God," she exclaimed. "You found Roy Lee." She was on her feet in seconds, showering both of the boys with kisses, tears and embraces. She was reluctant to abandon the task at hand.

"Dad," she called out, "get in here."

Then to Roy, "Where in the name of God have you been? You look starved."

"He is starved," Sam said. "The son of a bitch he worked for wouldn't pay him." Sam figured he would preempt the long explanation that was due by not mentioning jail and the near certain suspicion that young Earl was gone, no more to return.

Dad came in from part of the basement that had been sequestered as a furnace room and storage facility. Dad Neff displayed no emotion. He shook hands with both the boys as if he had just completed a deal at the Ness County auction.

Mom had not expected her oldest children and therefore merely surrendered her meal and Dad's plate to Sam and Roy. They ate in silence and rapidly, barely pausing for a word of conversation.

Finally Sam asked, "Where is Jim?"

"He's been gone all day," Mom said.

"Where's Rover?" Sam asked.

"She's out here," Dad said. "Jim says she's married a wolf that's been hanging around here." The two tired travelers each accepted a leg of chicken and a helping of vegetables. "That dog lives here, usually feeds off the scraps, then a while later she's off with the boyfriend."

"Jim Bob knows where she goes," said Sam.

Mom turned to Sam, looking him in the eye. She adjusted her glasses and dried her hands on a well worn apron. She had been a stunning beauty when she married Earl Neff and set up homemaking, a proposition confirmed by the sepia picture on the couple's dresser. She had a vision then, children setting up farm operations on earnings from eggs and cream furbished and refurbished by wheat checks promised to make that dream a reality. It was that faltering dream that interrupted sporadic attempts to get more information on where Roy had been, and what ever happened to young Earl. And so the conversation jumped back and forth and it was all irrelevant. Roy was too tired to talk, could not talk, in fact he fell asleep at the table. Dad picked up his 110 pound body and deposited him on a bunk near the furnace room door.

The boy Jim came in, and Mom furnished him with some food. He started to tell Mom a bit about Rover, but it soon became clear to him that he was to shut up, keep quiet, and say little or nothing.

"It came down to this," Earl Neff admitted to Sam when it was getting close to total darkness. Earl Neff wanted to get to the point. Often he did not observe the obvious, mainly that the boy Jim Bob was wide awake and halfway listening behind the water reservoir tank of the cook stove. "We've lost our lease on the Bonny Grady land. We won't have even half the acres for a crop next year."

Sam factored his Dad's pronouncement into the full range of facts and 50 possibilities. He had grown up when there was a fair chance of prosperity. The wheat crops were abundant and priced right. There was always excess grain to feed a fair flock of free range chickens. The creamery check always gave the family a fair amount of cash. When he went off to study in the east, there was always a little egg money from home. That same help had sent him through business college.

But Sam was the last child Mom and Dad had been able to help. Roy had had no place to go and had not found a job in three years. The two girls escaped to a convent, a fact that caused Dad Neff to chafe. Young Earl alone had found work, but now he had vanished without a trace. Sam thanked his parents for the support they had given him, and now he stood ready to share his meager earnings.

Wheat had priced out at $4.00 a bushel during the era in which President Hoover promised two chickens in every pot, a car in every garage. The last harvest of 160 acres had fetched no more than 17 cents a bushel. The commodity reporting service had it at 25 cents a bushel, but that had figured out to be the price at the terminals, not at the tailgate of the wheat wagon. "If we don't make a crop this year," Earl Neff said, "then what?" Earl Neff was a small man, always in perfect physical shape, his brown eyes full of humor and determination. During the halcyon days of prosperity he was known as a practical joker. He elected to distill wheat whiskey. He did not drink, but he liked to bartend at funerals and weddings, specializing in extra large shots. But the humor departed with the arrival of hard times. Some of the Volga German farmers blamed *der schlecter Woodrow Wilson*, the evil Wilson, for causing wheat farmers to overproduce. But the Wilson haters could never explain why wheat had plunged to where it had little or no economic value.

Always a student of history, Sam tried to supply an answer. He had been watching commodities on the Chicago market, keeping running tabulations, and matching events with prices. "You can blame some of it on the Reds."

"The Communists?"

"Yes, on Stalin," Sam said.

Sam went on to explain that when the Red tyrant had confiscated all the seed wheat from the Ukraine and the Volga Republic, he had dumped it on the world markets priced "to arrive." The shock value had sent wheat reeling. "For 17 and 25 cent wheat," Sam said.

"But that's a one shot deal, one year. We've survived even the worst markets."

Mom served one last round of coffee and went to bed. She had hardly said a word during the hours her husband Earl and son Joe Sam had talked and argued and solved the pressing problems of the world. Her mind was on her missing son and she believed she was being told less than the truth. The boy Jim Bob was still snuggled with Rover behind the iron range, ears wide open. From the conversation, he discovered there was meanness in the countryside.

The scope of that meanness took on a new dimension once Mom went to bed. Joe Sam pulled out a magazine article and read it aloud. It told of 40 million acres destroyed and implied there was no road back. "Forty million acres," Jim Bob said almost out loud. "That's a bunch."

Sam raised the conversation from the mundane to public policy. "This man, Rexford Tugwell, is like God Almighty in this administration," he said. "It was in the papers in January, 1934. Tugwell is predicting new regulation for land control. Listen" and he started to read. "'Government will control all land, public and private. Land that cannot be operated effectively under private ownership will be assembled into a few strong hands under government license, so to speak.' He's not talking about subsistence farms in Arkansas. He wants government say so on land that produces all storable commodities: wheat, corn, grain sorghum, rice, cotton, tobacco and rye and so on. Talk about Reds! You're going to be completely controlled."

29

"How much more control can they have? " Dad Earl said. "Hell, they can yo yo prices from zero to even less if they want."

"Listen" Sam said, and he started to read again. "'We have depended too long on the hope that private ownership can control and operate for the benefit of society as a whole. Present acreage reduction is only a stop gap.'"

"What does it all mean?"

"I've kept in touch with the farm expert at the seminary, a confidant of Monsignor Luguti."

"The subsistence farming priest?"

"That's him. Here is what's coming down the pike. They're going to try to control acres, the idea that supply will dovetail with demand to up prices. This gets a little hazy, but they're going to try to control foreign exchange with a government fund, so the grain trade won't get snookered in trade deals."

"Joe Sam, you're losing me."

"Well, consider this. Mr. Tugwell and Mr. Roosevelt are working together, taking privilege with the Constitution."

"Meaning?"

"Meaning all of storable commodity agriculture will be treated like a public utility. Those worthy of survival will be kept alive with subsidies, the rest will simply die off. The 160 acre wheat farm is to be starved out."

It was a little more than Earl Neff could digest in one sitting. It was well after midnight when Dad Neff discovered Jim Bob hiding behind the reservoir tank of the big iron stove. He had fallen asleep. Sam admitted he could not stay awake much longer. Even smoking Wings cigarettes, one after the other, did not help. When he got up, he pushed the wooden chair under the table.

"These dusters will pass," he said, "but they are being used to see to it that you can't survive. With a decent wheat price you could have paid for the homestead and even some additional land. Don't blame it on Joe Stalin, these are Chicago numbers. Last year we imported wheat and corn. In fact, we'll be importing an equivalent of ten U.S. wheat crops this decade." And with that, Sam worked enough numbers to extrapolate year by year. Sam concluded with a summary line, "Now do you see why the last harvest from 160 acres fetched only 17 cents a bushel? You didn't even get the 25 cents a bushel they paid on the exchanges."

"If we don't make a crop next winter, then what?" Earl Neff asked. He extended his hands as if to hand sign, "Who knows?"

"I don't know," Sam said at last. "Everything is changing. It is obvious to me they don't want people on the land. I don't think the trades want family farmers."

"Man, if we don't kill off some of those rabbits, they'll eat away the entire crop," Dad said. He wanted to change the subject, but didn't know how. "And if we don't get rain," he added, "the rabbits will starve with the rest of us."

Mom arrived in the kitchen in her nightdress. "Aren't you ever going to get some sleep?" she asked Earl and Sam. She and Sam exchanged kisses, she on his cheek, he on her forehead. Neither said a word for a moment, then she said, "We'll talk tomorrow." Tomorrow came after breakfast with two eggs, bacon, homemade bread and coffee.

Noontime saw Sam's car looking like a giant tumbleweed rolling down the soft earth country road. The small talk was of hard times, Roy's inability to find work, and finally the ever threatening Kansas dusters. "Look Dad, I'm a numbers man. I find current trends and I follow them. In the case of the bus company, we want to transfer money from one pocket to our pocket in return for a service."

Dad said, "You're talking in circles, like a Jesuit."

"Well then, try this on for size. In terms of quick projection, I calculate that it takes only 1 or 2% import to scuttle the price of wheat, creating the world market price. Joe Stalin taught them that. So when they can lower the world price, they can buy the entire crop at a worse than disaster price. That's the long and short of it. Dad, you won't get a crop this year. If the dusters win next spring, you'll starve here."

"We're not moving," Dad said. "We've had tough times before." Sam did not argue.

Sunday disappeared in a wink, clear and golden and dry. Mom asked about Earl Junior, and the answers came back as monologues about riding the rails and working for a skinflint sugar beet farmer. She mumbled to herself something about either Roy knowing something, or he did not. Late that afternoon, the family agreed that Roy should return to Wichita with Joe Sam. "Mom's too tired to nurse and feed him back to health," Joe Sam argued, and the elder Neffs finally agreed.

They all went to bed early that night. The run to Hutchinson would require quite a few hard driving hours, and the return to Wichita even more. Sam said his goodbyes that night, gave Jim Bob a friendly slap on the rear, and kissed Mom on the forehead.

"Rover is getting a little heavy," he said to Jim Bob.

Mom left the room. She was saying something to herself. Jim Bob did not hear all of it, but he picked up the last few words, "the people is a beast of muddy brain." He shrugged his shoulders and went to bed. He could not make heads or tails of it.

4

By midsummer, when the combines should have been filling hoppers with clean grain, all the while belching straw into the stubble of recently cut wheat plants, the daytime temperature held at 105 degrees or more. Men looked for signs of a cloud in vain, and all they saw was a ball of brass so red hot, it commanded instant rejection of the sight.

Men cursed the heat and the sun and the dry earth, and women prayed for rain. The Volga Germans made novenas, lit candles, and recited rosaries until the mantra of despair filled the churches and living rooms and bedrooms.

The men and their women did not see the sun as the ultimate capitalist, the source of all revenue. They did not even understand how sunlight, through the agency of chlorophyll and the mechanism of photosynthesis, trapped that solar revenue, joined it with water and a few earth minerals to deliver several pounds of new commodities, new wealth for every man, woman and child each day of the year.

They looked to the soil for nature's bounty. That soil had been years in the making, and when nature was secure with a climax of grass atop, the pioneers made ready for the harvest. They turned the grass upside down, giving microbes a flush of new food. Decay sent carbon dioxide into the canopy of crops, weeds, even trees along the rivulets of water called streams. The farmers harvested their bounty, plowed again, seeded again, often fertilizing with manures, rarely with the salts that science offered as a challenge to nature. They did not think of solar revenue or ask God for the one thing only God can bestow.

They did not realize that their world had become unbalanced, biologically, physically, economically. Nature and nature's evolution have decreed that atmospheric carbon requires a sink via the stomata of green plants. Over the centuries, all plant forms gobbled up carbon dioxide the way a funnel cloud gobbles up grain storage bins. Now the dusters were telling the high plains that the carbon cycle had run amok. As tillage and cropping destroyed the organic matter complex of the soil, the carbon-oxygen cycle became complex. Not one plainsman understood that the grand design called for carbon dioxide to be sucked in by plants, installed back into the soil, and traded off for oxygen. Hardly anyone reasoned beyond this crop, this year, this bottom line. Clearly, the carbon missing in the soil puts the carbon in the air on the other side of the equals sign.

There was a time, which ended in the late 1870s, when the organic soil content of most soils was at 3 to 8%. By 1934 this load had all but vanished for some 40 million dust bowl acres. Tractors capable of pulling gang plows, combines capable of harvesting whole sections in a day, seeding equipment that rioted across the countryside like a Mongol horde, all suggested that grass had become superfluous, and farmers once known as yeomen were an anachronism. Organic matter and humus were destroyed with reckless abandon. The small farmer, content with his egg money and cream check, no longer belonged, the pundits said. In the wake of Wilson's War, collapsed wheat prices, and now inclement weather, the self sufficient farmer found himself annihilated by forces he could not comprehend nor battle against. A few wise old men understood that when moisture and temperature are correct for plant growth, they are also correct for soil macro and micro life to degrade higher life forms. Uninhibited decay activity releases an abundance of carbon dioxide, much more than all animal and human life account for. Carbon dioxide is simply heavier than air. It finds its residence near the ground and under plant canopies. Energy from the sun separates the carbon from the oxygen. Carbon is then used to manufacture carbohydrates, which are food and energy for life. Released oxygen is then freed to be a catalyst for utilization with food and energy.

Those same old timers have come to reason that when sunlight becomes too intense, plant stomata close down and carbon dioxide intake is restricted to the epidermis of plants. Leaves bleach out. This is the cycle that eluded an entire generation, setting up migrations, penury, even revolution.

Yes, succulent plants take in water, but they still pull carbon dioxide out of the air to create carbohydrates. They then exude through the roots to feed microorganisms in the rhizosphere. Up to 80% of the carbohydrates a plant manufactures are sent out through the roots to heal the soil. This release into the soil creates carbonic acid that combines with soil minerals, making them ready for plant uptake.

School men examined these points and filled journals that farmers did not read with articles that even other scholars rarely read. Talk about transpiration and loss of minerals in the soil, and the eyes of both farmer and corporate man glaze over. Tell them that fully 99% of the water a plant pulls from the soil is lost into the air, and they say, "So what!" "So what" became a cloud of dust over all of Ness County that year, a winter calm setting in before the next spring storm.

As technology and greed and errant economics conspired to lay a leaden glove on the high plains, humans were not alone in vacating the scene. Sportsmen sought in vain for coveys of quail or runs of pheasant. Except for durable blackbirds and red wing hawks or a rare carrion feeder, bird watchers saw no exotic creatures, the robin and barn owl excepted. Even the migratory birds heading for Mexico and Central America swung wide of the dust bowl. The deer and antelope were gone, as were the fox and the predatory wolf, the last considered exterminated. It was not, of course.

There was at least one solitary wolf that roamed Ness County. The Indians called him El Diablo. Hunters had nicked him with everything from 45/70 Marlin deer guns to buffalo rifles. He had been cornered in what passed for a box canyon in Ness County, but cleverly survived. El Diablo ran a harem with feral dogs, and apparently had the intelligence to avoid taking down calves. This last would have brought the wrath of a veritable vigilante committee down on him. Food was never a problem for El Diablo as he went about the business of survival.

As with soils, microbes, carbon dioxide, and the natural nitrogen cycle, the jackrabbit was out of sync with the predator population allowed to live. And so the wheat grass fed the vegetarian rabbit, and the rabbit fed the omnivorous wolf, and the primitive appetites of townsmen with rifles fed on the ogre that legend had created.

The sun continued to dispense its revenue, and when the crop was gathered in, production times price meant income. When there was no production, the price did not matter. There was no income. When production was bountiful and there was no price, there still was no income. None of the equations was working out. It was a failure to be reckoned with, to be understood, to be reversed. But the great men in posh Washington offices did not understand, the economists did not understand, and most of the farmers did not understand.

5

A few months after Sam Neff had returned Roy to the farm, then taken him away again, it came to Jim Bob that something very serious was afoot. Mom and Dad often conferred in low voices. Always a heavy praying woman, Mom took to reciting several rosaries a day and crying a lot. Roy had gone and come back again, now full of stories about riding the trains here and yonder, meeting professors and professionals in boxcars, men who had lost all hope of finding work. Roy became adept at digging yard wells, and he conferred insight and knowledge on Jim Bob. Jim Bob, in turn, became a practiced Indian. He found he could track animals when Rover took leave with hardly a growl.

Jim Bob suspected that Rover had married a wolf. He saw the wild one come along approximately the weekend Roy came home. After one of the milder dust storms, he saw Rover join a pack of wild dogs that hung out near Grandpa Staab's farm. Included in the pack was a creature of slightly different distinction. His face had the shape of a pointed shovel. His coat was black with a few touches of gray. The animal was slim yet muscular, not at all run down like a junkyard dog.

Rover really was a rover. That night when Sam and Roy drove in, Jim Bob was away from the house because of Rover's penchant for, well, roving. She had taken up with a small pack of abandoned dogs, unsavory characters, said Dad Neff, but nature's own just the same. They extended invitations to frisk and play. You could always tell the winner, if that is the right word, or the rejected in the game of love. Dogs did not mismatch the way humans do, finding partners twice their size, or having pets that could not make it on their own. There were no less than four of the unclaimed or wild ones that came along while Rover was in estrus, all of them marking fence posts and trees with their urine, all of them within a few pounds of each other. One was a wolf, El Diablo, Jim Bob figured.

The boy suspected a courtship proceeding in the dark. It started this way. There were rabbits aplenty. Rover liked to chase them, always holding back as if to avoid catching up with her prey. When smaller prey came into her canine cross hairs, she initiated the chase, but abandoned it when her quarry reached the safety of a tree or brush pile or hole in the ground. Rover had rank. She did not hesitate to pull it, even on Jim Bob, her titular owner. When Rover failed to catch her prey, El Diablo stepped in and did the honors. Among canines, as among human beings, rank has its privileges. This means rank selects rank for mating. In the small pack that drifted in and around the Neff homestead, sometimes taking a hen, the creature of male rank was this wolf. Feral dogs knew this. Their offspring knew it, too. A wolf in wheat country was a rarity, its habitat having been destroyed as a hideout. El Diablo obeyed the Biblical injunction to increase and multiply.

Jim Bob feared for the wolf. He knew grownups had marked the animal for extinction. Jim was cleaning the stalls for Dad's two Percherons when he noticed Rover and the wolf meeting, probably not for the first time. The conception took place two weeks later. Rover took the stand of a dog in heat. Her feet were planted firmly. Her tail went up, then to the side, ears up. She invited the wolf. The wolf came forward and mounted her. Her spasm was that of a virgin, but her feet stayed planted. The act was completed rapidly, accompanied by little more than a short yelp. Her mouth stayed open, ears were laid back. Rover smiled a dog's smile. By the time it was over, Jim Bob's knowledge had come a long way from the day he had knocked a rooster off a hen. He counted the days as he watched Rover enlarge and make ready for the blessed event.

During the pregnancy, Rover kept up her wandering ways. She could be seen from a distance loping alongside the wolf, resting now and then, and eating prey. They would return to the farm and drink from the trough under the windmill.

When the day for delivery arrived, Rover became restless. The gunnysack bed prepared for her seemed to confine her, so she begged to be let out. The father of the pups about to be born, the alpha leader of the entire canine community, lurked about the place, never craven, never groveling, but deferential to the human population he respected and feared. Once outside, she made for the creek bank and privacy.

Jim Bob followed at a discreet distance. Within minutes after reaching her previously established nest, out came the first pup. It was dark brown and was followed by a black one, then gray and black, with the fatherhood of the wolf stamped in their faces. The terror of the new mother evaporated as each new pup emerged, each receiving an assent from mom herself. She almost doubled up to clean her vulva. She pulled the caul from each newborn. Her canine teeth cut the cord, and her instinct bid her to swallow it and consume the afterbirth.

Each delivery, four total, was attended by the same primal ritual. When Rover's task was completed, the human requirements of hot water and towels were unnecessary. Jim Bob watched with awe. At a recently achieved age of 11, he knew he was not to intervene. The nest was so well camouflaged, Dad Neff could not see it even after it was pointed out to him.

The alpha male had selected it, guarded it, supplied it with food. The surroundings were merely concealed, and the prairie acted like a curtain conferring privacy on the mother's den.

Jim Bob saw the wolf return to the den, arch his back, and deliver a copious amount of vomit to the young ones. They fed on it hungrily and the wolf indulged himself in a wolf's version of therapy, this being only the first installment on an animal vow to cherish and obey and to take responsibility for the family.

At breakfast that Sunday morning, certain rules for the family were established in the boy's mind. The boy told his mother about the pups, about the obvious concern of the wolf for his family.

"Mom, do animals have a soul or a religion?"

"They are creatures and I'm sure God gave them their rules." She went on to explain that instincts govern, that you can not expect a chicken to reason or exhibit morals in the same way man has been ordered to behave. The boy had heard the coming lecture before, but this time Mom seemed more reasonable than ever before. "You know about cards Roy and Dad like to play? You know about things? Well, God trumps the catechism and the Church. That makes the Ten Commandments the law above everything else. You know the Ten Commandments."

She said nothing for several minutes while Jim Bob ate the two eggs he almost always got for breakfast on a Sunday morning. He drank his glass of milk, and Mom came over to him, rubbing her hands on the shopworn apron she wore.

There was a philosophical calm in her face this morning, as if her thoughts had suddenly delivered comfort to cancel out a measure of stress. "Son," she said, "there's one other thing you need to remember. We have a family law. Your Dad and I live by it. I recommend it to you because I think it covers the Ten Commandments and the will of God. Everything else you hear is just elaboration."

Jim Bob waited. His eager look and silence assured Mom she had his full attention. She said, "Keep your agreements and stay out of other people's business."

The boy repeated the charge to himself a dozen times that morning, and he went to bed that night returning to Mom's conversation. Keep your agreements and stay out of other people's business.

But the family's business was also his business. He had heard Sam tell Mom, "He doesn't believe it, but he has to get out of here." Did Sam mean Dad, and was he talking about leaving the farm? The boy felt guilty because listening in on grownup conversations had become a hobby.

"Mom, those pennies Mr. Roosevelt is throwing around won't keep you," was another fragment the boy had overheard.

"I know that," Mom had answered.

"We're not made for relief," the oldest son had said.

"I know that, too," Mom had answered. Mom had looked at Sam just as the discovery that the boy was listening became evident. "Sam, what in God's name are we going to do?"

Before Sam left for his Hutchinson assignment, Jim Bob had picked up another fragment of conversation. "Jim Bob has to get an education," Sam said. "It just isn't going to happen out here. If Mount Zion doesn't fold, he might get eight grades, but he needs high school. There isn't a prayer of that happening with what you can make off this farm with reduced acres."

That was all he heard. The boy wondered aloud, "God educates the wolf. Rover knows instinctively how to have pups. The wolf got his education the day he was born." It was all a puzzlement.

He did not mean to get into other people's business, but you had to be blind, deaf, and dumb not to notice brochures from Oregon arriving in the mail, Roy off again hopping trains, returning with grim news about bums riding boxcars, unemployed, and word from the elevator at Bazine that wheat prices were likely to stay low for 1935. Rover's absence was more than noticed by Dad Neff.

"Where the devil is that dog?" he finally asked the boy. "I don't think she's coming home," came the reply. Jim Bob started talking fast. "She married a wolf and they have a litter of pups," he told Dad that day.

"Well, it don't matter," Dad finally responded. "They can't survive."

The boy responded quickly, "I think they will. The wolf is feeding them. Rabbits, I think."

"You saw that?" Dad asked at the time. "Son, you're getting mighty foolish. That wolf can turn on you if you get very close. You stay away, hear me?" The boy started to say more, but did not.

6

The boy was up at 6 a.m. that Sunday morning to walk the half mile to the secret den occupied by Rover and her wolf husband. The temperature was near 90 degrees well before 10 a.m. The sun had no clouds to penetrate, so it hung there like a molten ball of brass. The dust under the boy's bare feet was almost hot, and yet it felt comfortable. The new litter of pups was lively and hungry. From a distance he could see them nuzzling the nipples of the dog and then come to attention when the wolf approached to disgorge juice and little hunks of meat for the hungry tribe. The provider seemed to take particular pride in feeding his family. With equal pride the dad wolf had helped Rover fashion an artful den protected by prickly pear and curtained by prairie grass that hung like a screen from an outcropping of sand.

The boy stayed on for a few minutes, then dog trotted back to the farmhouse for the breakfast Mom would be serving.

"You've been out to see the pups," she said.

The boy nodded. "They're really feasting," he said.

"It doesn't matter," Mom said. "They can't make it no way, and that Rover is a fool taking up with a wolf." She served the boy his scrambled eggs and returned to the stove. The firewall hid the glow of half burned charcoal. "When you've finished eating, fill up the stove with some cow chips," she instructed Jim Bob. Then she picked up her subject again.

At age 11, the boy was ready to hear some truth, and of late Mom often talked to the boy, largely because conversation had all but died between Mom and Dad. She sat down with her son and said, "The reason that wolf couple can't survive, or any of the pups, is wheat." She waited for this information to sink in. The boy did not understand. Wheat had always been the pride of the family, ever since Earl Neff had been able to buy 40 acres and lease other lands for the production of wheat.

"There's just no place for a wolf," she said. "Sooner or later some farmer will lose a calf. Then the menfolk will come out with their rifles and shotguns." She got up, straightened her apron, and stroked back her hair, which was in a bun in any case. Mom looked quite old to Jim Bob. The boy figured she had aged quite a bit during recent months. Mom detested dust, and dust there was aplenty. She washed her hair all the time because she could not tolerate the film of dust. There had not been a duster for a couple of months, and yet everything seemed dusty.

Jim Bob wanted to reason with his mother. The wolf liked jackrabbits, he said. He offered this information not as a refutation but as an aside, because she clearly had made up her mind.

"Take my word," she said. "Your Rover dog will come back for table scraps, but her pups won't be welcomed. There's no habitat for them. Maybe that he wolf is smart enough not to rattle the farmers, but the young 'uns won't grow up. I want you to know this. Wheat owns us. It wrecked the soil, it wrecked our family. If we stay in this country, it'll wreck you." There was a note of bitterness in her voice. "Your Dad is a proud man. He's been a good husband and provider, but now he's beaten, beaten by wheat."

It was not until after 9 a.m. mass in town that neighbors and relatives arrived, as was the custom during good weather. The place had a hitching rail and plenty of parking space, and that was about all. The farmhouse looked more majestic than it had a right to, with its tall windows reaching for the extra high ceiling. It needed paint but was otherwise in good repair. The barn was not much to look at. It was really a shed with a 30 degree roof. Certainly it did not have the classic lines of the gambrel barn that Grandpa Xander Staab had. There was a stone chicken house that served as a storm cellar when twisters threatened. There was a smokehouse and an outhouse, a tool shed off to the east between the house and the bone dry pond, and a plum orchard, now dry as desert sage. In better times weeder geese had kept the orchard free of weeds and insects. Not a blade of grass grew in the yard between the house and barn. Dad Neff did not allow it. He swept the yard with a homemade broom the way his forebears did in Russia along the lower Volga. The first to arrive that Sunday was Xander Staab. He was at once a legend and an enigma. He arrived by horse drawn buggy. He had been baptized Jacob Alexander Staab in Katharinenstadt, a settlement not far from Saratov. That was almost a century ago. His father was known as Kirghiz Jake, and for nearly half a century the sobriquet hung on in spite of Xander's efforts to shake it. He did not like the name, yet he promised Jim Bob he would tell him the full story in time.

Xander Staab did not grow wheat. He had developed a fine herd of line bred, horned Herefords, 26 cows actually, give or take, all of them nurtured on grass. He pastured his animals on wheat grass belonging to neighbors some of the time, maintained his own pastures, and ran an irrigated alfalfa patch to carry his herd over droughts and inevitable food shortages.

At an estimated 98 years of age, Xander still had the posture of a soldier. He had been drafted into the army of the Tsar as a young man before he had enlarged a furlough into emigrant status the day a contingent of Volga Germans left for Baltimore, then western Kansas. His hair was as silver as a polished Morgan dollar. His mustache was just shy of being a handlebar, and his face had the wrinkles of a well worn baseball glove. He probably did not weigh over 120 pounds, yet the word was out that the old man was still pulling calves with the help of an Indian hired man.

A daughter who lived in the east came home each summer to make "this pig sty" fit to live in. Xander seemed to get by quite well. Each month he visited the grave of his wife in the Sacred Heart cemetery near the church in Ness City. Otherwise his social life consisted of visiting the Neffs, discussing literature with a teacher from the high school, and dealing with cattle buyers who came to his farm.

Xander was a unique breeder. He wanted bull calves, and he got bull calves. He sold sires, always guaranteeing potency, his bulls would settle over 80% of the cows during the 30 days of the first breeding season. The fact was, Xander knew cows the way some men know the sea. Xander always ended discussions on wheat with the most profound observations. "God seeded the prairie with grass," he would say, "and that's where it should stay."

Grandpa Staab gave Jim Bob a hug and a slap on the back as soon as he tied the buggy horse to the hitching rail. The old man loved the boy. Of late he had concluded that he would have to take a hand in the boy's education. "You're not likely to go to college," he told the boy, "so I guess you and I need to do some home educating." Xander was busy preparing a list of 100 works that Jim Bob was to read, some in German, most in English. The Wilder boys arrived a few minutes later. They would have had a gig on Saturday night with piano, fiddle, clarinet and slide trombone. The Wilders had decided to quit farming. They were moving to the St. Louis area. After all, they were the elite of the Volga Germans of the county and they expected to break into social circles. Finney played a Baldwin piano, Galen actually played two wind instruments, Andy played the violin, and Abner played the slide trombone. Only two had their instruments along, Abner and Andy. There was always time for a little music, yet no one realized what silence would follow once the relationship broke up.

Everyone knew that the talk today would be about moving out. It wasn't just that the high plains people were suffering from dust, or even the low price of wheat. These things were effects, not causes. Something devastating was happening. Grandpa Xander said it started with the World War, and it would not be long before the assembly got down to serious argument. There was robust talk about dogs and wolves and bull calves. During that afternoon, the Barlows, Wilders and Pfeifers unloaded the insight for which democratic people are famous. They talked over each other and afterwards failed to listen.

Only three seemed to bond, Mom and Dad Neff and Xander Staab. Xander was the scholar of the three. Mom came in second. Mom could read German text and deliver it in English without pausing to translate. She could also do the opposite, read English and deliver it in German. "A young dandy came to Socrates," she said, "fancied himself a statesman. Socrates asked him how much wheat it would take to feed Athens for a year." Her scholarly discourse ignited a debate that lasted much of the afternoon. The boy Jim Bob took it all in and tied it to the puzzlement his mom had proposed earlier that morning.

Grandpa Xander was as self educated as he was practical. He had had his fill of government and city life before he had come to the high plains in 1875. Kirghiz Jake, his dad, had sold hay to Fort Hays for Custer's horses and was paid for half as much hay as he had delivered. This incident stuck in Xander's craw like an undigested bone.

"Civilization starts with the city and its organization." Xander said. "Not so," Dad Neff said. "It starts with wheat."

"True. History begins with wheat," Mom said. "The Bible doesn't put it that way, but the soil between the Tigris and Euphrates was the birthplace of wheat. Wheat was an international crop before there were nations, even before farmers planted it. It's too bad wheat grows so well because all we ever have is overproduction."

That one statement, plucked from among many, set the tone for what became a heated discussion that afternoon. Yes, here was a crop that responded to the rhythm of the seasons. Immigrants from northern Europe had brought Red Fife to Canada and then to the United States. The Volga German immigrants had brought Turkey Red to Kansas and the high plains between Lubbock, Texas and Saskatchewan.

"Yes," said Xander. "I knew Bernhard Kenton. He was the Russkie who brought in Turkey Red. The wheat my dad brought in was a spring wheat. It was a failure."

Jacob Alexander Staab read at least a book a week. His extra bedroom became a library when his only son moved out to join the army. He subscribed to *Hereford Journal, Capper's Weekly, The New Yorker, National Geographic*, and farm magazines too numerous to mention. He understood what was happening and what was likely to happen to his adopted country. Even so, Xander was something of a recluse. He had not once left the county since 1918 when had journeyed to Beatrice, Nebraska to look at a bull.

Someone heard him speaking German to a man on the street. The local marshal and a magistrate subjected Xander to the humiliation of a fine and the final indignity of having a yellow stripe painted on his brand new broadcloth coat. He was told to leave town and never come back. Xander had stuck to grass and cows ever since. Ranchers interested in his bulls were required to come to his farm, a trip that knowledgeable cowmen took because the old man knew something about bulls that was not general knowledge. Outside the family, Xander had little to say about wheat. To do so would have caused him to reveal uncomfortable truths not even Henry Wallace would understand.

In the family circle where he was the resident patriarch, he could speak his piece with impunity. A coherent man of ample age was considered learned in a household where scholarship was hard to come by. Xander was saying, "That is why the mystery of our production is called supply and demand, and the mechanism is called low farm prices,

46

and the end result is called liquidation of the family farm." Xander took under advisement Sam Neff's audit figure that 1% of wheat imports, in terms of domestic production, was all it took to crash wheat to the world's level. "He's absolutely correct," the old man said.

An hour of argument did not really exhaust Xander, but he looked the part. "Earl, don't you have a little schnapps? Yes, with wheat at the world price level, the traders sell half the entire crop at world prices, half prices to Americans," Xander pointed out.

The syllogism constructed itself. Wheat was more than the staff of life. It was also the economic handle by which food surpluses were built above and beyond the need of the population. Therefore it became the mechanism for taking the food from the producer and giving him very little in return. The process, the patriarch said, has to start with wheat, because only with wheat can the copywriters of the fourth estate make a case for the scare talk of overproduction.

Some of the guests repaired to the kitchen where they found a Mason jar full of whiskey, which really was a slivovitz, since Earl Neff always introduced prunes into the mash. Earl Neff liked to distill the product even though he never drank the stuff. He did like to supply it at weddings and funerals, always volunteering his services as bartender. His devilish youth returned at such times, and he enjoyed his merry self getting attendees stoned out of their mind. Jim Bob, ever since he was six or seven, liked to sit atop one of the stone posts when Dad was distilling his wheat liquor. Once, when a black car looked like it was heading down the rutted section road, the boy gave the warning cry. The copper kettle was seized and its contents hustled to the then flowing creek. Unfortunately the contents were dumped a bit short of the water flow. The black car stopped, turned around, and departed. Crows came for the mash. Some became so staggering drunk they could not fly. There had been many distillations since then. A more recent one was handed Xander as schnapps.

"The problem," Xander noted, reopening the subject after his refreshment had been exhausted, "is that not one farmer in a hundred understands the problem. Everyone sets prices, but not the farmer. The farmer goes to the elevator, 'What'll you give me?' If you have the idea that those people in Congress know more than the dumbest of the dumb, then pardon me!" There were a few exchanges before Xander reclaimed the floor. "A literate housewife," he said, "knows more about wheat than the men in the field." Now the Neff household respectfully listened to Grandpa Xander Staab's soliloquy.

"The endosperm becomes white flour because it contains a protein called gluten. Gluten together with yeast makes dough rise, a paradoxical happenstance because the role of wheat essentially is to bring down farm prices. The international nature of wheat furnishes the key to how this is done. The fantastic adaptability of the plant provides a world of exploration. There are only two general groupings of wheat. These are spring wheat and winter wheat. The breeders were busy developing wheats with exotic names, but farmers who shook the dust off their overalls when they entered the house thought only of spring wheat and winter wheat. The Dakota farmers who drill in the spring are barely less than familiar with the wheat seeds sown further south. There are only fourteen species of wheat extant in the world, spelt being excused from the roster. Half are grown in the United States. Three figured among dust bowl farmers, Brown, Knight and Durham. Durham doesn't really work for farmers, it works for international traders. The college people should be helping American farmers work with the industry, but the fruit of research is sent off to Mexican soils, African high country, and the South American pampas."

After he had sipped a second glass of Earl Neff's slivovitz, he pointed out that some 30,000 varieties of wheat germinate, sprout, and ripen somewhere on planet Earth each year. "You think you're going to outsmart all those Department of Agriculture people? They've audited 15,000 of the world's varieties, it says in *Capper's Weekly*. Why? They want a favorable balance of trade. They want a working surplus."

The musicians, a splinter group composed of the Wilder boys, an uncle named Ott, and one lately hired hand from Ott's farm repaired to the parlor room, where they damned to hell Woodrow Wilson. The former president was called the evil Wilson. The conversation abated for want of information, for which reason old Xander was invited to provide added insight. Xander volunteered information from a recent issue of the *Weekly Kansas City Star*. "It says here," he said, "that wheat production is not keeping up with the growth of the population, now over 148 million. Then why the hell are there piles of wheat in every town and at every elevator?" He quoted that between 1900 and 1934 wheat production per capita dropped over a pound per capita per year.

Mom joined the fray. She announced that the kitchen was closed, that she was out of coffee, out of everything. "I don't think a trace of white bread remains."

"But store boughten tastes mighty good," Jim Bob interrupted.

"Maybe so," Mom said, "But you can't feed chicks on Wonder Bread. They would all die in a couple of weeks."

She turned and faced Xander, "Dad," she said, "the traders are stretching the supply like a rubber band. They're selling rice at the local grocery. They sell donuts and cupcakes that taste like cardboard. Talk about trash!" Xander added, "They always call inventory surplus. Surplus means low prices. Low prices means bigger farms, corporate farms, surplus farmers. When they get the prices low enough, all the farmers become poor managers, hayseeds, inefficient. Everybody overuses the soil."

"That's true," Earl Neff said. "The soil has sure as hell gone dead." The black blizzards that clouded the air seemed to say that the balance wheel had gone out of control. Even without production of bins and bushels, gang plows, big tractors, even with a down paced growth in population, there were other variables. Those variables served up one breathtaking fact: only 50% of the wheat produced in the United States was being used for domestic consumption. This one fact was nurtured into being and helped along by public policy and maintained by institutional arrangements against all odds. This caused the balance wheel to grind not just wheat farmers, but all farmers into the dust.

At the end of the day, Dad did not say much. He was a horse farmer and he did not take to seeing tractor lugs punching holes in roads. Farmers were quite capable of growing all the wheat required without super farms. An average well managed farm with horses could still perform. But the powers that be had declared otherwise, and this meant that at age fifty his life was over. He did not lose much money when Roosevelt closed the banks because he was broke.

Xander and the Wilder boys were always talking about *der schlecter* Wilson. Well, back in the 1900-1914 era, there was real prosperity on the farm.

Xander had always explained how the merchants of death ordered up a war in order to enlarge profits. The greatest production boom of all time came during the World War. The pressure to get big and efficient rolled in on the back of patriotism. Earl Neff was coerced into breaking virgin prairie and harnessing double teams to the task of breaking prairie sod. Wheat rolled in like a golden tide, clear out to the foothills of the Colorado Rockies and south to the Mexican border. As soon as land values had appreciated, the Federal Reserve knocked the props from under this profitable empire and sent farmers into bankruptcy. The planned great crash of 1921 either closed down farmers or put them hopelessly in debt. Earl Neff lost almost everything and barely recaptured a rundown farm operation in Ness County, Kansas. Egg money and a creamery check had sent Sam to seminary, but now there was not enough money to send even one child to high school, and Roy had not earned any off farm money in years. For the youngest member of the family there seemed to be no future at all.

Earl Neff did not even have a radio. He traded two pullets for a year's subscription to the *Weekly Kansas City Star*. He usually borrowed the *Capper's* paper from the barber shop. And Xander handed off one of his subscription copies to his daughter's family.

The papers were full of it. Bankruptcy filled pages of the newspapers. Once the imbalance of the 1920s and 1930s set in, farm poverty increased and consumption of commodities depended on broad spectrum buying power. The wheat bins at terminals were no longer empty, even with thousands of acres of drought. Investors behind the great commodities, market investors the world over, and other traders in other rooms saw to it that the bins were always overstuffed and under priced. All other commodities were yoked to a planned wheat surplus.

Earl Neff did not think the bins should be empty. He used to maintain an inventory, but he soon realized that the wheat in the bins, security for lean years, was a leg chain holding down the primary producer, with or without consideration of what was being exported. With export traffic came strange and subtle developments. It was all so puzzling. Xander had a handle on the machinery of exportation, and he told a close family circle that all he knew was what he read in the papers, "like Will Rogers."

The international cartels hedged and speculated, all to feed the world price into the primary producer's pocket. Yes, the evil Wilson saw to it that an income tax was added to the Constitution. With an income tax it was possible to reduce tariffs so that all farm products could be pressured down to world prices. Yes, the evil Wilson managed to get a Foundations Law passed so the super rich could preserve their wealth tax free in perpetuity. Yes, the evil Wilson destroyed the Senate so the members would no longer represent individual states and their interests, especially farm states. Since senators were no longer named by state legislatures, the contest for office was handed over to the super rich and their bags of money. Yes, the evil Wilson caused the Federal Reserve to take charge of the money supply so that every dollar in existence would pay interest to the holders of debt. Xander waxed eloquent when he got started.

"What does the catechism say? God created the heaven and the earth. He created both out of absolutely nothing. Now Mr. Evil Wilson has replaced God with the Federal Reserve. They create money also out of absolutely nothing." His case made, he paused, but then added, "He kept us out of war until he figured war was a better flywheel and balance wheel than agriculture."

Xander supplied his remarks at the drop of a hat. He had been an activist in Ness County during the McNary Haugen fights in the Coolidge administration. Then Calvin Coolidge, "that little wart," vetoed both bills. The price of wheat was not deep, dark, mysterious stuff to George Peek. He made this disarmingly clear even as he entered the Roosevelt administration. In those days it was protection for industry, free trade for agriculture. George Peek crossed and crisscrossed farm states during those battles, and Xander helped organize more than one rally. McNary was supposed to level the playing field. It passed.

Xander summarized without giving his source of information. "America raises about 800 million bushels of wheat even as we speak," the old man said. He was using data from the November, 1928 issue of *Current History,* and he figured it had not changed very much during the intervening years. "We use about 650 million bushels of this production, which means 150 million bushels have to be marketed abroad. If the world price is one dollar a bushel, the farmer gets not one dollar on 150 million bushels, but on 800 million bushels. McNary Haugen hoped to preserve the domestic market maintaining a stabilized American price."

Xander felt exhausted. He excused himself by saying, "Jimmy, come over to see me as soon as you can." Dad Neff accompanied him to his buggy. It was close to 6 p.m. when he arrived back at his home place. The Indian and his dog were changing pastures for the herd and feeding alfalfa to the herd bulls in a special paddock. The old man considered the fact that on grass his annual calf crop was making him a good living even in these depression times.

The propositions a few Kansas wheat farmers bandied about that afternoon may have been disarmingly simple to those who deigned to talk about it, but that did not disarm the manipulators. Cheap wheat was their key to profits. It was an infection that spread like germ warfare across the farm country. When wheat got too cheap, some farmers fed it to livestock instead of corn or grain sorghum. Low priced wheat sparked a surge of off pasture feeding. It ushered in price problems for hogs, poultry and dairy production. Cheap wheat never went very far before the farm came tumbling down. Backed to the wall, farmers plowed to the doorstep to grow ever more wheat. In trying to help themselves, farmers satisfied the goal of the absconders because surplus was perceived as an awesome Sword of Damocles over all the high plains.

The government experts sat and planned. It was always possible to empty the pipeline when farmers needed another jolt. *The Farm Journal* said there were too many farmers. California was providing the world with the wave of the future. Foolish people, deluded people, migrant workers migrated into the fields.

Late that evening the Neff family faced the reality of the situation. Leased land was not available to small farmers. The fourty acres Neff owned outright were heavily mortgaged, and there was no cash flow to satisfy the payments and taxes. Their assets were few, two work horses, two milk cows, two hogs, fifty chickens, a mule, and a dog. The machinery was not worth much even as scrap iron. A Graham plow, a two bottom moldboard plow, harnesses, a milk separator, and a harrow were not the kind of assets Earl Neff could take to the bank. The two Jersey dairy cows assured the family a milk supply, not much more. The boy Jim Bob fell asleep.

Then, next day, a duster to end all dusters struck without warning. Earl Neff could not make it to the barn without guide ropes. Schools held children through the night because travel was impossible. Even a mule would not venture into the teeth of the storm. It was darkness at noon, and nearly midnight for the high plains family farm.

It was a harbinger of storms to come. When it subsided, tales were traded of kids with dust pneumonia, cattle stuffed with soil until they suffocated, wells turned into muddy puddles, and trains derailed. The public prints reported 12 million tons falling on Chicago alone.

Jim Bob with his Dad and Mom hunkered down in the basement, damp kerchiefs over their faces, damp sheets over each window, and a damp tent over a table when hunger drove them to eat. The kerosene lamp flickered and went out. For the first time in his life, young Jim Bob was really frightened of the dark.

7

When May gave up the ghost with only a barely perceptible shower that little more than settled the dust, the men knew that June would vanish without rain. The great holders closed down their expectations early and set the big machines to work reorganizing the topsoil as if to erase the scars of nature's vengeance. The small holders waited and their women prayed. The dusters subsided in June as they always did, and if the cycle was broken there would be rain in time for winter planting. But the god of water held back the showers of June and July. Only weeds and grasses seemed to thrive during the ongoing drought. Not a cloud anointed the sky. Even a small puff of cloud merited a comment in the weekly paper that carried all the "For Sale" notices. The sun was hotter than anyone could remember. It caused temperatures to hover over 100 degrees for weeks on end. The buildings became so hot their occupants slept in the open at night, Jim sleeping on the slightly slanted roof of the barn, Mom and Dad finding comfort on the gangway that permitted entry to the basement kitchen.

A great silence spread across the land during late June and early July. Here and there a wind charger produced enough electricity for a light, but mostly kerosene lamps were brought out to conserve fuel. The sunflowers climbed fence lines and claimed the ditches as their own.

In low spots bull thistles claimed the kingdom for the year. Drifts of powdered soil remained undisturbed, pending the arrival of winds. Where once moisture had held the upper hand, the soil was cracked and open like the pieces of a puzzle. Water from a deep well could keep a garden alive, but the water was too cold, so the garden did not thrive. The sun bore down. By late July, a new tension gripped the farm families. The cost of fuel closed down the kerosene lamps that made the evening tolerable. Under the dried up plum trees, chooks could not keep up with the grasshoppers. By August, Dad Neff's time was being spent repairing and polishing harnesses. Then there came the day a rough looking man arrived with a trailer to take the riding pony away. He had been there before with a stallion in tow.

"What'll you have, Earl," the man asked, leaking tobacco juice through two days growth of whiskers, "a horse or a mare?" By horse he meant a male animal. The man paused to explain his procedures. He explained to Earl and to the boy Jim that there was an egg inside that pony. Conception would take place when the stallion fertilized the egg. If the point of conception was alkaline, the colt to be born would be female. If it was acid, progeny would be male. Dad Neff wanted a mare. This meant a slight bicarbonate of soda flush. A male animal would require a vinegar flush. That was a few months ago.

Now the pregnant pony was taken away, sold for the few dollars it would take to keep the family going. Every day the earth grew drier, the road ankle deep in a powder so fine it took wings with the slightest movement by insect, bird, animal, or vehicle. Hard clay soils were crushed by tractor lugs, iron wheels and tires, and the clays became powder.

Along bottomlands, grass survived until streams went dry, and farmers were reduced to hauling wagons loaded with horse tanks full of water for livestock and land use. Then, when the burden became too great, the animals were sold at auction or shipped, and the checks that came back were almost negative after fees had been subtracted. There were meetings, letters from J. Sam Neff, and postcards from Roy, who was on the bum again. Jim tried to assemble knowledge that was well beyond his years.

His parents talked of moving to Oregon, and they talked of California, but the boy did not want to go. He tripped over to see Grandpa Xander at least once a week during the summer. It came to him that he would stay behind and help Xander. He would do chores, he would cook. Those barefoot walks along the section road became uncomfortable when the dust absorbed the fire from the sun. He had always enjoyed the squeeze of dust between the toes as a pleasant sensation, but now he wished he had worn shoes.

Xander was to be found seated in the shade alongside his house on more than one memorable visit. When Grandpa Xander relaxed, it was almost always with a pipe going full steam. Jim came to Grandpa

Xander when he was troubled or when he needed wisdom beyond his years, and Grandpa did not beat around the bush. The boy was almost an adult, and he was treated like an adult. Xander always had the answers that his parents seemed reluctant to supply.

"Grandpa," Jim said, "why do they call us 'Rooshians' when I go to town?"

The old man took a couple of puffs on his pipe and blew a smoke ring. He spoke in German most comfortably, and Jim spoke German at least as well as he spoke English.

"The English," the old man said, "are very foolish. They don't realize that this is a very big and complicated world. So they look down on some of us." The boy waited for more, but a soft silence took over.

"Complicated, yet wonderful," Xander said. He resumed puffing his pipe until the smoke rings clouded his sun tanned face. When he spoke again, his voice seemed so much younger, as if his thoughts for the moment took him into the yesteryear of his youth, back to the stories his folks used to tell. "Your father was brought here in the great migration of 1876, but I came here in 1875. We weren't 'Rooskies.'" He spat out the word like a bad tasting grape or plum. Xander usually spoke softly in short sentences, usually with the verb at the end.

"If you weren't Rooskies, how did you come to be in Russia?" Jim wanted to know.

"It's a long story," Xander said. "Those were very bad times when my great grandparents lived in what is now Germany." With that opener, Xander Staab shifted in his seat and gave his grandson a lesson in history. "There was a Seven Year War. Armies would plunder the villages at least twice a year. They'd steal all the food, rape the women, take livestock and horses, and conscript all young boys. Most of them never came back. My grandparents lived at Isenburg, Hessen. At the end of the Seven Year War, my grandfather was a very young man. He and his sweetheart had planned to be married. Unfortunately the war impoverished everyone. There was no chance of setting up a household, no available land. The situation looked hopeless.

"Then Catherine the Great issued a proclamation inviting settlers to Russia. She was a German princess who married into Russia and became empress. Well, Ferdinand Staab and his wife Mathilda took the invitation. They joined the emigrants headed for the steppes along the lower Volga near Saratov. They left behind their parents, relatives, and friends. Ferdinand missed his 8 year old brother Otto most of all.

"The flatness of the land and the endless sea of grass frightened the immigrants. This was light and sandy land. Some of it was as rich as Western Kansas before the settlers came. It was not at all what the recruiters told people in the German states.

"Jimmy," Xander injected into his narrative, "if you read my old *National Geographic* journals, you'll see that the steppes covered a vast treeless plain, a zone situated at the center of the Eurasian land mass extending almost without interruption from Hungary to Mongolia in Northern China. Historians once called it 'the Steppe Corridor.'"

"Why?" Jim wanted to know.

"Because it was those great prairies and deserts that the great invaders used as their marching routes to Europe."

It was a wonderful story, and it held the boy's rapt attention. For the first time he learned about Marco Polo and the route he had taken to China. The great horde of Genghis Khan marched through this corridor into Europe. Attila the Hun used it as his avenue to the gates of Rome. They did not know it, but the young lovers of whom Xander spoke came to settle in the middle of a route followed by traders between the Mediterranean world and Asia. As traders and warriors marched back and forth, they brought about an interchange of genes, technologies, and religions. These same people were the foundation of several tribes, especially the Kirghiz. Much like the Cossacks, these tribes were under the nominal government of Russia, but not subjugated.

"My great grandfather and his bride found their free land. They built a house in Liebenthal. During the decade between their emigration in 1763 and 1774, they had two children. One was named Josef. The youngest was Johan, whom they called Hans.

"There was a bandit who plundered on the *bergseite,* or west side of the Volga. His confederates, the Kalmuks and Kirghiz, usually harassed the colonies on the *wiesenseite,* or prairie side of the Volga." Xander paused to order up a drink from his daughter, in residence for part of the summer. He offered Jim a drink of water while he repeated the inventory of information he had bestowed on the boy. He wanted Jimmy to remember these details, write them down, recite them to himself while walking the section road between his house and granddad's breeding farm. Second generation immigrants tried not to remember where they were from, and many even forgot their language. Of late, Grandpa Xander made it his business to guide the only grandson not destroyed by poverty, the English, or dust.

"Emelyne Pugachev was a Don River Cossack in open insurrection against the Crown. He passed himself off as the husband allegedly murdered by Catherine the Great. His intention was to march on St. Petersburg, arrest Catherine, and crown his son tsar.

"On August 5, 1774, Pugachev attacked Jagodnaja Poljana on his way from Petrobsk to Saratov. Here he whipped three men to death. The next day he sacked Saratov and executed officials. "One of the villages sacked was Liebenthal, the community in which Ferdinand and Mathilda had settled. He rode into town in a buggy to supervise hangings and murders of the people."

Xander paused to explain each fact, each digression, his pipe being puffed furiously as he continued. "Legend has it that my grandfather ran a grist mill on a stream near the town. Most of the record was lost when Emelyne Pugachev came to town. He was at the head of Kirghiz tribesmen, who raped women, impaled people on spears, threw babes in the air and harpooned them in mid air. Pugachev sat in his buggy while the Kirghiz hanged my grandfather from the tongue of a wagon that was propped up in the air. His wife was run through with a spear, and the oldest boy was whipped to death with a bull whip.

"The youngest child was four years old. He'd heard the thunder of hooves as the Kirghiz rode into town. He ran to the creek and hid in the bushes. When the Kirghiz were finished, one of the leaders saw the boy. Another tribesman wanted to kill him, but the first rider captured the boy by the arm and swung him into the saddle. Hans hung on for dear life. "It was on a day like today," Xander said, "August 14, 1774. They rode for days, crossed rivers one after the other."

For the next 16 years Xander's grandfather lived the life of a nomad. He almost became Kirghiz. The land to which he was taken was far to the east. As they crossed great rivers, he was required to take off his britches and swim behind a horse, hanging onto the tail. No one called him Hans. The language was strange. No one understood German.

The Kirghiz lived in tents and slept on floors. They lived in the open and prized horses more than humans. His first master was a horseman named Osar. He was a kind man. He taught Hans how to ride, tend sheep, hunt with a spear, and survive as a nomad. Osar measured his horses for conformation. The Kirghiz tribesman made himself a balanced triangle. A colt had to reach correct proportions by the time it was eight months old, or it was traded off.

He would view the horse from the side, then lay a triangle with its apex as high as the horse's head and midway between head and tail. From that high point, one line angled down at 45 degrees toward the shoulder. Another angled down at 45 degrees from the hip. The baseline ran horizontally through both fetlock and back. The objective was to find animals balanced with the apex exactly in the middle. The baseline was to exceed the length of an equilateral triangle. It was a lesson that young Hans refined as he grew older. Hans transferred his knowledge to the bull of the bovine species.

Hans lived with the great caravans that traded at Samarkand in Afghanistan and Siberia. He traveled with Osar to Uzbekistan, Kazakhstan and Turkistan. He mixed with people as remote as the handsome mountaineers from Hunza and the Kizibash from Persia. But Hans was not taken along on raids. He was required to spend weeks and months alone tending sheep. It took Hans almost three years to speak Kirghiz. By the time he was ten, he remembered no more of his German than the *Our Father* and the *Hail Mary*.

He was sold to satisfy gambling debts. His next owner was named Mustafa, also a kindly man. He took Hans to the Grand Rendezvous. Hans had to ride Mustafa's horses in tribal races, often winning the prize, usually a prize colt. Mustafa taught Hans about what the Kirghiz called *buzkashi*. He learned how to judge virility in a stallion.He was still an outsider, cut off from kin, family, and God. He did not know that his parents and older brother were all dead. He said the prayers he had learned at his mother's knee every night.

Then came the day Hans fell in love. The young woman loved him too much. In that society young people did not make love before they were married. When transgressors were caught, they were dragged to death behind a horse. The young girl's name was Fatima, and she was wise beyond her years. She knew that asking Hans to give up his Christianity would torment him for the rest of his days, even though her parents had agreed to the wedding.

She also knew that the young man wanted to escape. She offered to help him. When the master suspected that the youth wanted to run away, he sold Hans to a cruel tribesman who was rich in horses. Hans did not remember his name in later years because he escaped a day later. Fatima had taught him how to read the Pole Star, the Big Dipper, and other constellations for the purpose of navigation. By relying on the stars and light from the moon, he could find his way back to the German colonies.

"When I was a child," Xander said, "my father told me he had thought of only one thing, escape. "

One day all male members of the tribe got so drunk they could no longer stay on a horse.

It would take them at least a day to become sober enough to ride. That night Hans seized his opportunity. He stole the utterly fastest horse and headed west. The first great river was at least two days distant, and beyond it were other great streams before the Volga was reached. He rode all night and all the next day before he stopped for even an hour of rest. He rested the animal most of the next day and traveled all night again. Once, a patrol of Kirghiz spotted him, but his mount easily outran them and lost them for good when he swam a very sizable river.

Days later, out of food and energy, he entered Russian territory. Hans could no longer speak German, though he could still remember the Our Father. But he knew even less Russian. He did not even know the village from which he had been taken. The only city he could recall was Saratov. There, the officials who kept the archives put out the word.

When the answer came back that all the boy's people were dead, a letter went out to several colonies. The only relative officials knew about had been conscripted by the Landgrave in 1775 and sent to America to fight George Washington. He had not been heard from since then and was presumed dead.

Here Xander's story came to an end of sorts. He allowed that his father, Hans Staab, was almost sixty when he fathered his last child, Xander himself. His older brothers were conscripted into the tsar's army, terms of enlistment being twenty years.

Xander was born in 1836. He served a short career in the Russian Army before he emulated his father and walked away. In 1875 he was one of a few who migrated to Kansas a year before the great migration. He landed at Hays, Kansas and for a time became a participant in the development of the greatest breadbasket of the world.

"I saw no future in wheat, not for the farmer," Xander said. "The land was made for grass, the same as Kansas which nurtured the buffalo." Xander got up to stretch. He took a few steps, then motioned the boy to follow him. Xander's pastures were not the wide open plots Westerners like to consider cattle country. He liked to graze an area, then rest it according to the rainfall. Except when in service, his bulls were kept in special pens. The old man and his pupil walked down an aisle and paused in front of a bull Xander called Pericles.

"What do you see?" Xander asked.

"I see cattle."

"What kind of cattle?"

"Hereford."

"That's right," Xander said. "What sex?"

"Well, there's cattle and there's bulls. The close up bull is older, more mature."

"Would you say it's a good bull?"

The boy looked puzzled. He saw a bull. A bull was a *Hengster* in German, but he did not know what Grandpa was driving at. He was not sure what the correct English term was.

"I think he's a good bull."

"That's right," Xander said. "That bull has 30 to 40 sons and daughters a year. A stallion in the wild can have almost as many."

The Kirghiz horses that Xander's father learned to know as a boy caused Jim to make the connection now that they were discussing cows and herds. Xander Staab never entered his bulls in shows such as the National Western in Denver. He believed the show ring was destroying genetics. He would not support registered either.

"If you don't know how to read an animal, it's time to get out of the business," he counseled. Accordingly, he required prospective buyers to come to the farm to arrange their own transportation services. Nor did he bargain. Xander had his price and those who wanted genetically superior bulls were required to pay it.

Xander walked past Pericles to an equally virile looking bull. "This is Xanthippus. He's the father of Pericles. What do you see?"

"A fine looking animal," Jim said.

"Look at his eyes. They have life in them, not that sunken look you so often see. Look at the hair on his pate. That hair is like a clock spring. When you see a bull with fine silky hair on his face, you have a pansy. This bull can settle cows because he has the genes and virility. Now, son, when you go to an auction and you see that silk hair, that is a pansy, probably a homosexual. He's half queer. You get a bit of that if you have freemartins, twins. The cow isn't designed to carry or birth twins. Usually male freemartins are pansies." Jim wondered what all this had to do with Rooshians. Xander sensed the puzzlement. He did not pause. He pointed to the horns on Xanthippus. Xander told the boy that the pigmentation of a bull's horns changes during its lifetime. Those changes denote age, maturity, and fertility. During the first year, a bull's horns are white or creamy. Until that color changes, the bull calf is not sexually active. At puberty, sperm is produced. "When this happens," Xander said, "the color of the horns changes to ruby red from the base on out."

Xander paused to explain puberty to the boy. "Once the peak of performance has been reached, the ruby red proceeds to change to a gray to olive green. Why is this important? Well, if you see a mottled color, that bull is marginal. The dilettantes and greenhorns who have a few cattle," Xander said, "don't know this. At four to four and a half years of age the horn color becomes deep olive if the bull remains healthy. There are other signs, but for now that's enough."

He started back to the house. Xander and the boy talked most of the afternoon, and the boy returned time and again to the forebear his grandpa told him about.

"Grandpa, is that why some of the people call you Kirghiz Jake?"

"Yes, my name is Jacob Alexander, just like my father. So the English called me Kirghiz Jake, but they've given up on that. The English seem to prefer calling me *the Rooshian*."

"They say you have the finest bulls in western Kansas," Jim persisted. "Yes, that is true. I expect my bulls to settle 40 to 50 cows a season. This is during the first days of breeding season."

Xander ordered out a piece of pie for the boy. Between bites he told Jim that he and Dad Neff came out to Ness County in 1910. Wheat prices were high. "I tried to get your dad to go to cattle." He started to say, "Now I have a herd, and your dad is broke," but he stopped himself. He did not want to load down an eleven-year-old with the intelligence that hard times were driving the Neff family off the land, and he was too tactful to point out that with cows and bulls he himself was quite solvent.

He turned to the boy. "Son, there are things you should never say or even think." The long silence told Jim to be patient. Xander would get to the point in his own good time.

"I don't know what's going on. I do know that a bushel of wheat has as much energy at 17 cents a bushel as it does at $4 a bushel. It seems to come down to mind over circumstances. Jimmy, I hope you go to school and find out how it works."

He paused and re lit his pipe. "See those cows?" He did not wait for an answer. "Every time a cow drops a calf, that's new wealth. But it isn't new wealth at all if the calf has no economic value. When your dad had a good crop, it had value only as long as it had a price."

The red hot orb in the west was setting and revealing a dusty haze and gloom. Xander suddenly ordered his hired Indian to hitch a horse to the buggy so he could drive Jim home. It was a slow walking trip for the buggy horse. Xander made some of the trip evaporate the silence. Halfway to the Neff house, he spoke, "Jimmy, the problem with the farmer is this, he has the soul of a Russian serf."

The boy looked puzzled. The old man did not break the pace of his narration. "He has the food, and he has it first, but he ends up broke and starving because he has the soul of a serf."

"What do you mean?"

"God came to Ivan," Xander continued. "He said, 'Ivan, you're the salt of the earth. You feed the people. You convert sunshine into bread. You work dark to dark. I've decided to reward you. Do you want more land? I will give you more land, free and clear. I'll double your holdings. Or would you prefer money? I can make you a millionaire. Or would you prefer bigger crops? How about double the crops you've had in the past? I'll give you one choice, any choice of those I've mentioned, or any desire you have. But know this! Whatever happens to you happens double to your neighbor Vladimir.' Ivan was stunned. Certainly he'd like twice his holdings or double his crops or a truck full of rubles. But to see that scoundrel Vladimir end up with twice as much. Why, he'd be the laughing stock of the countryside. He couldn't stand that! So he went home. He couldn't sleep. That terrible neighbor Vladimir! And then a flash of brilliance came to him. He went back to God and said: 'God, put out one of my eyes!'"

James Robert Neff did not know whether to laugh or cry. Xander saw his dilemma. "Jimmy, do you see what I mean? When you study animals you come to understand people. Most people worry about the neighbor getting a dime more a bushel than they do. There's a saying: 'For two bits you can buy any farmer.'" The gate to the big wide yard was open to the buggy.

8

During the last part of the winter, a powdery snow barely covered the soil, and it stayed on the land only briefly. In places it did not cover the wind rippled dust, and when a brief shower rolled over the Kansas high plains, it made the wheat jump. The wheat had not been grazed, and there was some question as to whether the only killing frost had guaranteed the arrival of grain for late June harvest. Weeds seemed to thrive as a confirmation of this winter treatment. Sunflowers were making their stand along ditches, fences and waste areas. For a brief moment in the calendar of events, the dust seemed to stand aside as life presented itself.

Then, as March moved to the terminal position in the equinox, only a few whispers of clouds hung high, then slipped away. A lidless sun radiated its heat, and the heat sucked up moisture, first from the ambient air, then from the soil, finally from the plants. The weeds endured and the crops did not. The weeds closed their stomata and respiration ceased. Ponds dried up and cottonwood trees along streams ran out of moisture and died. In desperation, landowners tried to keep house plants and gardens alive, and when water became a burden to fetch, both bowed their heads and passed away. Before the month was over, small and great silvery orbs crossed the sky, and when they settled, farmers and townfolk alike were introduced to swarms of grasshoppers. Desperate farmers used gunny sacks to swat them off, and at times pastures were set aflame to goad the grasshoppers into leaving. When they found a target feeding ground, a promising field crop vanished in an hour. Gardeners who sought to salvage their vegetables by carrying water in buckets found the plants doomed as if they were succulents of every stripe.

During the 1880s, most of the high plains lands were taken, first by railroads, then by homesteaders with fences claiming boundaries. Cattle drives came to an end, and often great buildings and businesses ripped the natural nutrients from the soil. Immigrants settled the plains. Earl Matthew Neff's forebears arrived in 1876, and Neff became a wheat farmer when he came of age. Neff was a horse fancier, a competent farmer, and economically stable during the halcyon days called parity by Moline Machine Company executive, George Peek. It was the fall in prices shortly after the Great War and the administration of the evil Wilson that caused assets to be sacrificed to satisfy debts. A few good years in the 1920s were followed by five debilitating seasons crowned by dust.

Earl Neff sold off all but two cows to get survival cash. He barely rescued his 1928 Dodge from the mortgage holder. When wheat fell to 25, then 17 cents a bushel, the children could no longer attend high school. The two oldest girls took the veil, if not to serve God, then to escape the high lonesome prairie.

The weather menace was an excuse. "It was the farmers' own fault," Eastern people opined. Even before young Earl joined the CCC camp in Rocky Mountain National Park to build retaining walls along the Continental Divide, an additional menace was making itself felt. Jackrabbits exploded onto the half starved wheat fields. In 1935, in a last defiant act of desperation, Earl Neff and his eleven-year-old son joined one of the last Ness County rabbit drives. There was a duster the day after Joseph Samuel Neff departed for Wichita by way of Hutchinson almost a year ago, taking his brother Royal with him. Royal was too sick to work and on the verge of a nervous breakdown, a consequence of starvation. Roy could get medical attention in Wichita, possibly enroll in Wichita Business College and get a cash paying job.

Mom had not gone to the car when the boys left. She had packed an extra shirt and pants for Royal and given him a hug and a "Take care." This was all she could manage. Her hope for a tranquil old age was gone. The farm was gone. Now only an eleven-year-old boy remained. Dad was so deflated, she doubted he would ever turn a furrow again.

Jim Bob went about his chores always watching for the return of Rover. As soon as the current litter of pups was able to fend for itself, she would be back, he felt certain of that.

Chores were as defined as the swing of the stars. First, the two cows had to be milked. Jim Bob enjoyed milking most of all. He sat on a three legged stool, washed each of the four teats, massaging them gently one at a time to help ease the milk down. His thumb and forefinger rolled down from top to bottom of each teat to start a drop of milk. He felt the tug, then fell to the cadence of milking, rolling his grip from top to bottom until a milk stream fairly drummed a staccato tune in the bottom of the pail. Soon enough the sound lost its rain on tin quality and became a gurgle as the inch thick cover of milk developed foam. The cows liked his touch. They stood quietly when their turn came, rarely switching a tail while the delicate operation proceeded.

Next, the pigs received their hogwash, a combination of whey and bran and table scraps not demanded by Rover. Jim Bob watched for Rover, but she did not show up. However, two kittens made their appearance every time he sat down to milk. They stood in the doorless barn opening waiting for their treat. Jim Bob always gave a squirt in the right direction, and each kitten fielded the liquid fix with the skill of a baseball player. Last, before making the mile long hike to the Mount Zion country school, Jim Bob filled a bucket of water for his mother, placing it carefully on the reservoir of the iron range. He splashed a bit, causing a steamy sizzle to break the silence of the empty kitchen.

Dad arrived, wiping his feet on a burlap sack kept in the doorway.

"Jim Bob," he said quietly.

"Yes, Dad," the boy answered.

"Jim, there's no school tomorrow."

This was a wonderment. There was nothing to harvest yet, and probably would not be from the looks of things. Yes, wheat sprouts had emerged, and there had been a killing frost, which is a requirement for winter wheat, but drought and dust storms had been so severe that most people doubted there would be a harvestable crop. A funeral of a dignitary might cause school to be closed, but that had not happened in all the years of his short life. The boy asked, "What happened?"

His dad said, "The county has ordered up a rabbit drive. You're old enough, so you can go."

Wheat grass is most nutritious before it joints the first time. Over the years lawmakers, acting in their wisdom, offered bounties for the ears of predators until coyotes and wolves became an endangered species. Accordingly, jackrabbits recovered and multiplied. They fed their ravenous vegetarian appetites on wheat grass, not on the several species that painted the landscape green as prairie, but on the forage wheat crop itself, the farmer's reason for being. The jackrabbits had achieved status. The boy absorbed this information with enthusiasm. His dad handed him an axe handle. It had broken off while he was trimming an Osage orange stump down to ground level, but the handle would be quite serviceable for swatting jackrabbits. Dad continued to explain. "The entire town is coming out. There's gonna be folks from clear down to Ford County and Dodge."

Jim Bob had noted the construction of a red slat snow fence two sections north, just off the edge of Xander Staab's outlying pasture. Jim Bob knew that Xander did not approve of jackrabbit drives, that he considered the idea that the rabbits were eating too much wheat complete nonsense. "They're not going into Xander's property, are they?" Jim Bob had a vision of old Xander protecting his grass with a shotgun, not from the rabbits, but from the trampling horde of strangers who could destroy more pasture in a morning than jackrabbits could in a year.

The boy usually tripped to school using the country pace. This meant fifty steps walking briskly, then fifty steps running. Using this pace, he could cover the entire distance in less than half an hour. The excitement at Mount Zion was electric. The school would be closed, of course, since all pupils near twelve years of age would be involved.

Newspaper ads and posters had been announcing the event for two weeks, and there had been some speculation for longer than that, but Jim Bob had been unaware of the fact that the drive was to take place within walking distance of his family's farm. For his classmates, he pretended disinterest. He did not mind killing jackrabbits. He had killed plenty, cottontails too, but clubbing animals to death after they had been cornered against a snow fence by blood hungry people did not really appeal to him. Yet, he had to present a serenely acceptable front. It was a day for tragedy, and Jim Bob simply did not know how he would react.

Two eighth graders were very vocal in detailing how they would take the head off a jack as clean as a whistle, so blood from the beheaded creature would write their names in the dust the way boys pissed in the snow. These pupils were almost grownups. He had never heard grownups talk that way, not around the Neff home. Dad Neff was always matter of fact when dealing with animals. When a man came to the farm with a stallion, Dad allowed the boy to watch while the mare was being serviced.

Playing about with signatures in the snow was mild stuff compared to the rowdy clinical jokes he heard about cities, female anatomy and reproduction, but talk about rabbits squealing as organized slaughter unfolded had Jim Bob wishing there was some way to avoid this high plains ritual.

Instead of pacing off to school the next morning, Jim Bob and Dad Neff walked the two miles to the section line where an armada of hunters with bull horns, clanging noisemakers, and "all the people in the world," the boy told Mom later on, were assembled. They all had their clubs, axe handles, baseball bats, Osage orange sticks, and one fellow bragged that he had a cane made from a bull buffalo penis which could "slice a rabbit in two, it's that hard." The commander for the day's outing was Colonel Dorey Gasser, the title his own and the rank two notches higher than the rating he had been given in the World War in the Rainbow Division, he said. Actually Gasser served his time with a pack mule outfit that did not get its function worked out before the 150 day war was over. He assumed his command post in polished boots, a jacket festooned with dingle berries in the style of Buffalo Bill, khaki riding britches, a decorated shirt, and a cap with a visor. A riding crop was flapping back and forth in his left hand. He wore the ceremonial mustache of an officer, trimmed his sideburns like old General Burnside himself, and exhibited an impenetrable snarl. One old farmer observed that he had eyes like a fistful of fish hooks and that his mouth sliced across his face like the bite of an axe. "Gentlemen, ladies," came the boom of his voice over a megaphone. "Your attention, please! I'm Colonel Gasser, and I'll be your commander today."

A perceptible murmur followed, and a few comments became a matter of record in the notepads of a reporter, a member of the Humane Society, and a representative of the Kansas State Historical Society.

"Colonel, my ass!" said an ex dough boy who had been wounded at Chateau Thierry. "This asshole thinks we're going to march like soldiers!" Colonel Dorey Gasser had become a self proclaimed legend in western Kansas. He now had a dozen rabbit drives to his credit. His operation manual detailed the 1.5 to 2 square miles to be cleared of jacks. An underlying ring of baiters set hellfire in motion, usually by blowing horns and whistles, banging mallets or pliers in old pans, and otherwise breaking down the tranquility of the plains. Six to eight captains were assigned sectors, and each command was assigned the task of driving all the jacks in the operational area to their destiny. Colonel Gasser then named his "officers."

There was Jacques Hughes, a slack jawed tobacco chewing dwarf of a man who weighed about 120 pounds. He wore overalls with the sides unbuttoned and no undergarments. He had a club that equaled his four foot, nine inch height and was much too heavy for a lethal swing. "Captain Hughes will be in command of the east sector. When I give the word, he'll select his people. Any questions?"

There were plenty of questions, most of which were ignored. "Yes, you can volunteer under the captain of your choice. The sun is rising quickly, so let's get a move on!" he continued.

"Sir," a townsman said, "I saw that El Diablo wolf this morning. Can I take along a pistol in case he shows up again?"

"No! Absolutely not!" Colonel Gasser said.

"As close as we are, what if you hit somebody?" a young woman asked. "Well, keep your distance. I don't want any fights. Let's get the rabbits, not each other. Sector two, coming around from the east, will be under Captain Carl Amstutz."

Amstutz, a giant of a man carrying a short stick, held up his hand. "Form one line!" he shouted.

"On the other side of Captain Amstutz, linking in a half moon to the catch pen, will be Captain Jamie Stitz."

Stitz was a wheat farmer, who ran a cartage business on the side. He had taken this job to keep the mob from violating the farm of old Xander Staab. Stitz had been a carnival roustabout in his youth. He had married the daughter of a Ness County farmer and settled into wheat growing during the halcyon years surrounding the World War. Always chased by poverty, he never quite believed that prosperity was his forever, so he cleared his Ford, stayed out of debt, and hauled cattle for area farmers. When hard times came, he trapped jackrabbits. His wife could make a rabbit taste better than a Porterhouse steak. At sundown he would go home with as many as he could carry and skin. Stitz merely tolerated the colonel. He motioned those standing near him into a team, Earl Neff and his boy included.

The colonel had memorized a prepared speech, and now he recited it with gestures and vocal inflections reminiscent of William Jennings Bryan. Captain Andy Wilder was well out of earshot, taking a veritable platoon to the extreme side of the area, as he put it, "to get far away from Colonel Gasser." He had heard Gasser before. For all practical purposes the drive ran itself. Once the noise started and the rabbits started to run, no captain, no colonel, no leader really had much to do with management of the killing field. As the teams spread out, the master of tactics continued to assert himself. "We start precisely at 10 a.m. This is war, war on a pest," the colonel instructed, his voice low and sinister. "It is war for survival. The enemy is worse than the Hun, worse than the slimy snake in the grass. The reptile merely eats dirt, he doesn't taste and spit out your wheat grass. We annihilated the Hun on his own ground, now we're going to do the same to the jackrabbit on our own ground. You can't be soft hearted today and serve your sacred plains." He paused for effect as if expecting applause. "All right," the colonel said. "Here's what you do. Swing for the head when they come by. Hit them in the butt, and they'll urinate all over you and keep going. Hit them in the head. Drive them toward the corral. A team of clubbers will take it from there."

The colonel leader looked around, scanning the field and the dust laden horizon. As far as the eye could see sat parked cars, cars with their engines running: Fords, Chevies, Studebakers, Packards, Plymouths, Oldses, REOs, Erskines, even buggies and jolt wagons. Some people were in motorcars positioning themselves for runs down section lines, horns blaring. The colonel said, "I expected a chaplain and a prayer, but he's been detained, so we'll start. Synchronize your watches, 10 a.m."

Atop the bed of a truck, Gasser barked orders. Hardly anyone was paying attention. After the man in military garb paused to light a cigar, Jim Bob Neff heard Gasser say to himself, "Jeez, I love it!" Gasser loved the spectacle of hundreds taking positions around the perimeter. It was a day for dust, blood and record temperatures. Low prices and aerosoled topsoil goaded farmers and area residents into anger, anger at the coyotes they had killed for not eating the long ears that nibbled wheat into ruin. The papers became scientific, for they knew that *Lepus*

71

californicus melanotis, the black tailed jackrabbit with no predators, obeyed the Biblical injunction to multiply and increase. With the coyote more or less eliminated and the wolf off duty, the population threat came alive with a new litter every few months. In earlier times the jack had been a blessing. Meat could be canned in wide mouth Mason jars, or fed to hogs, or even sold into the market, usually at single digit prices. But as the prairie was turned under with the moldboard plow, habitat vanished, and the farmer's cash crop became a suitable food for this vegetarian. Colonel Dorey Gasser had made himself something of an expert on rabbit drives.

As farmers fled the high plains, those who remained grasped at straws. It was computed that there were 80 million rabbits in 30 western Kansas counties. The drives to contain these Hoover hogs were usually held in spring, but not always. Newspaper ads defined the areas to be served, and desperate farmers came to the anointed killing grounds. Someone usually assumed charge. People steeled themselves for command by tripping to rabbit drive sites with clubs in tow. Often county commissioners bought the rabbit or snow fences for the corral.

Participants were expected to have a club wielding rabbit slayer with a few years experience around a section or two. Some drives were several miles square. The largest drive was near Dayton, Kansas. It involved 10,000 people who sought to flush out rabbits from eight square miles. The kill came to 35,000 rabbits. Colonel Gasser claimed bragging rights for many drives, even for some he had merely read about.

There had been an even bigger attempt at Kalvesta, 15,000 clubbers hammering down rabbits over ten miles square, 64,000 acres, but it was aborted by a sudden dust storm. The drive had to be terminated when clubbers could not see each other or the rabbits. Dust also closed down a drive at Oakley where 108 sections were to be cleared of jacks. The two section drive in Ness County was of no particular interest to Earl Neff, but he wanted his boy to have the experience, and also he wanted to make some contacts for selling off forty acres of mortgaged land and his collapsing pieces of equipment.

Earl Neff and Jim Bob joined the team with Mexicans in manning the south border of the area to be made rabbit free. At first the clubbers were eight or ten feet apart. On signal all the rabbit slayers started walking or driving vehicles, sounding horns, and slamming sticks against homemade cymbals. Guns were prohibited. "This ain't no Polish firing squad," the colonel admonished, laughing heartily at his ethnic humor. Jim Bob stepped up with his axe handle. A big jack came his way. He swung and missed, and the jack escaped from the designated killing field. "The head is a baseball," John Stitz advised. "Come on! Let's hit a home run!"

The next rabbit tried to hide behind a Russian thistle. Someone threw a clod of earth at the animal, and it came straight for Jim Bob. The boy saw the rabbit halt, defiant with red glaring eyes. Suddenly it jumped to the left of Jim Bob's right hand swing. Whap! The axe handle connected, literally tearing off the animal's head. Blood from the jugular raked Jim Bob across the knees. The boy paused for a moment, then ran to catch up with his dad and his uncles. As the cordon closed, two lines formed, the hecklers in front, slower clubbers a few yards behind.

By now the rabbits literally rose out of the ground. Those that had sought shelter under Russian thistles along fence lines, alarmed by the cacophony of sound, tried to run the gauntlet. The line moved like a ragtag military formation, women and children lagging behind, a cadre in front. In less than an hour, the snow fence troop came into view, and jacks entered, some wounded, some screaming out a death agony, some so bewildered they did not know what was happening. The trap enclosure was an oval shape about a hundred feet long.

Tenders closed the snow fence gate, and now the clubbing proceeded in earnest. Jim Bob reached the fence after it was closed. He stood there watching the carnage. One mother was in the throes of giving birth to her litter before a club caught her on the head. The man who delivered the blow stepped on the newborn with hobnailed boots. Jim Bob turned away from the scene and vomited. He did not stay on for the final ritual. The victors brought five gallon cans from their vehicles and started soaking the squirming mounds of flesh, making the smells of death wet with kerosene and gasoline.

Those who wanted rabbits could gather all they wanted from the fields outside the fence. Once the mounds of carcasses had been soaked with flammable liquid, a trail of fire exploded over the last of the squirming life. A match was dropped, and the flame raced back to the kill of the day. The fear thundered into the sky, then settled down to serious incineration. Before Jim Bob and his dad started for home, Jamie Stitz came over.

"Jimmy," he said. "Come here." They walked about 100 yards to a small ditch. Two year old wolf Rover pups lay clubbed to death. "They look like Rover," Stitz said. Jim Bob bent over to take the half breeds. They were already getting cold.

"Can I bury them, Dad?"

Jamie Stitz volunteered, "I have a gunny sack. You can take them home."

Dad Neff agreed. "You can bury them down by the cottonwood tree." As Earl Neff and his son walked away from the scene, past Xander Staab's place, back to the farm, Jim Bob asked his dad, "Why can't they just shoot them?"

"Bullets cost too much," the weary farmer answered. They did not talk for some time as they left the fields and walked down the section road. "Jim," the elder Neff said. The boy looked up at him. His dad's face was lined with dirt caked wrinkles. Tears must have carved guilt in the dirt. He had never seen his dad cry. No, his eyes must have watered, that's all.

"Jim, there are things you shouldn't tell people about, and there are things you should never say."

Jim Bob's dad had seldom called him Jim. He had never seen his dad flinch when wringing the neck of a chicken or cutting the throat of a hog. Jim Bob had studied the skulls of swine and cows so that he knew exactly where the brain was. Slaughter of food animals did not bother either of them. But this business was not humane. "The people back east will think we're doing this for sport," said Earl Neff. "The sad part is that there are those who see this as fun. That Gasser fellow, for instance. You'll run into fellows like that."

"I guess I should have brought home a few rabbits," said Jim Bob.

"No, not this time," the boy's dad said. "I don't think I could eat one." As Dad Neff and Jim Bob came down the last half mile of the trail, Rover came out to meet them. The dog could not make up her mind. Did she want to run in the wild with her new husband and their litter of pups, or would the lure of table scraps win out and claim the loyalty of the half breed? Mother was reading when father and son entered the basement kitchen. Mother looked up from her *St. Josephs-Blatt.* "Good God," she exclaimed. "Get those bloody clothes off."

Then to her husband, "Did you let that boy club rabbits to death?" Earl Neff admitted that he had.

Jim Bob took off his shirt and pants, and stood there in his underwear. "Go get the wash tub. There's water in the reservoir. Get that blood off you," she ordered.

Mom did not order Dad to change clothes, not with words. But her look said it all, "Earl, get out of those bloody clothes." After a while, after calm had descended again, she told her husband, "We've got mail."

She had heard from Joe Sam that afternoon and his message bore much promise. The wind had died down, and dust storms had ceased to be news. There was hope, a resurrection of sorts. It would have sustained a man and his family, except for the drought. Next year would be a better year if you could only hang on.

Jim Bob listened carefully to all the exchanges between family elders. He gathered in and sorted out their arguments, and he vowed to himself that he had to stay, if only he could. The leaves on trees and row crop plants would survive, but if his parents went through with the crazy idea of leaving the high plains, he would not be there to see it. The storms, the grasshoppers, the winds had not wrecked lives. A life elsewhere would be no life at all. He would survive as Rover and her friends survived, on the high plains. Each day, the earth absorbed and yielded. A powder finer than flour filled the ruts in prairie roads. When the old Dodge came down the section line road, a billow of dust three times higher than the car marked its progress, taking the better part of an hour to settle.

Jim Bob never ceased being able to deal with developments in his young life. Dad and Mom were both exhausted and the boy, too, needed his sleep. In a day or two, come July, he would find an afternoon he could spend with Jacob Alexander Staab.

The blind man dances,
The cripple sings,
The sot a hero,
The lunatic king.
Hope springs eternal
In the human breast,
Man never is,
But always to be blessed.

The high plainsman who could not recite Alexander Pope's poem remembered one line just the same. "Hope springs eternal." Hope was riding high when fall came and nature's snow offered another chance to grow a crop. As crispness came to the air, the drills seeded wheat, and everyone prayed for rain.

A shower came in time, and little shoots of wheat crawled out of a cover of dust. These plants would not run out of moisture for two weeks or more, and if the gods of weather did not hold them back, there would be more, and the cycle of dust would be broken.

But it did not break. For the first time ever, dusters anointed every month of the year, even in the dead of winter. Some rolled over in hours, some stayed on for half a day. By January, one knew that the world would end, for another wave of defeated February was mean and ugly, and April delivered the *coup de grâce* to Earl and Eloise Neff and family. On April 14, 1935, the black blizzard set new records. It roiled and boiled until chickens died in their coops and humans died in their hospitals, lungs clogged with what had once been climax achievement, the grass sustaining soils of the high plains.

The only epitaph for the day appeared in every newspaper from Amarillo to North Dakota: Black Sunday. Jim Bob's diary said it all when he wrote, "Here it comes!"

9

On the bulletin boards, in the weekly papers, on telephone poles and auction house walls, the message is always the same: "Having decided to quit farming." On the last empty lot in the field at the edge of town the barbed wire fences come down. Soil is shoveled over a ditch for a makeshift driveway, and the scrap iron called machinery is offered in the local news. Farmers abandon their tractors, and drills, and harrows, and farm tools that in reality have antique status. "Come on Ed, snake that tractor down to the end. I want the one that runs up front by the office." The office is an old beet worker's shed trucked in from Colorado. There's a desk and a candlestick telephone.

"Damn it, Joe, I want a light in here. Where the hell is that power and light company when I need it? For crying out loud, get a chair in here. Keep that ink well full. No, hell no, I'm not writing any checks. Nobody'd cash them. Silver is approved, but good crisp feeling money will do." A risqué calendar hangs on the door. This week's newspaper sits on the end of the desk. "The stuff they're bringing in is scrap iron. We'll take that iron off their hands, well, hell, it's got scrap iron value. Tractors up front! Jeez, where in blazes he get that dog? By gawd, it actually runs. Scrape off the dust so we can see the name. That's a 1918 Massey Harris. Bad lug. Put a little sawdust in the pan, Joe. I think that sucker'll sell. That's right, keep the good names up front. Park it by that International Cannon, and leave enough space to walk."

As farms close down, the tractors are sold or discarded, kicked out like unwanted dogs, driven early or late into the sale lot.

"What the devil is that? A Keck Gonnerman 12-24. That one's a Heart Parr."

"Does it run?"

"Hell no, it won't run, but it must have been a dandy in its day." The tractors have names: Case 918 Minneapolis, Gray, Illinois Farquahar, 130 Farmhorse.

"Come on, Ed. Are you in the collector business? That's a Russell Smythe Cylinder Steamer. Hell, you've had it six months. Let's get a torch and cut some of this stuff up. Nobody's gonna buy that two ton Caterpillar. Let's move some of this stuff. For gawd's sake, you can't even see that John Deere in those Jimson weeds. I want those tumbleweeds cleaned out of there. Nobody's buyin'. We gotta get 'em otta here. I'm no charity."

"You all buyin', a penny a pound?"

"Oh yeah, we're buying. Well, sir, there's not much market for a Nicoles Sheperd 20-42 that won't even fire. Hell, I never knew they made that many tractors. Who ever heard of a Wallis? No, no, cut it up. Clean up that McCormick Deering Farmall, now there's one that'll sell."

The farmers drive them in. Lugs chop up macadam, and the County Commissioner arrives.

"You're gonna have to pay for that road."

"Well now, you possess the farm we got it from. I'm not their guardian."

"Boy oh boy, that last one was a creepo. All he had was a few plots. I wouldn't mind cutting up the rug with his old lady. Here, Ed, take a little folding money. Tell them they're freeloaders if they want more. Make 'em de-dust themselves on the gunny sacks before they come in the front office."

He says "front office" as if the sales shed was more than an outsized outhouse. "Don't fool around. Go straight to hell, Mister. I ain't got time to screw around. Did you come in to do business or to yack? 'Tweren't me that put your ass in a sling. Blame that asshole in the White House, or that fool Hoover. Them Hoovervilles are going from hell to worse. The sales offices are gonna make their killin' while the sun shines."

"Ain't this the only sale you got, this and auctioneering?" They have a language all their own, these denizens of the dust. A junk dealer loads up the scrap iron, loads up the aluminum.

"Watch 'em, they're trying to nab something. Holler at 'im, and he'll leave in a tizzy. It ain't in the cards to make a buck out of iron and junk. Take the iron out. They'll probably ship it to Japan and send our sympathies to China. It's just one of those things. The office gets steel and pulls the oil out of a crankcase. What the devil is this country coming to anyway? There's too many farmers, Joe. They're not all piss poor managers. They're the guys who get snookered. This country will really improve when they get the land in a few strong hands. For crying out loud, make a new pot of coffee. Look at this, a genuine Whiting Hammerville!"

Joe comes back to the office deflated. "Nutty as a fruitcake, that one," he says. "I'd say he's got the IQ of a toadstool, if it had half its marbles. They're listening to Huey Long or Father Coughlin."

"Get used to it, Joe. People that have been shared out gravitate to communism. This is a fact, Joe. You can't start from scratch nohow. Besides, it ain't my problem. Sure ain't no shortage of losers."

They talk politics. They curse Roosevelt. They seem out in left field with their shoes off when examining AAA [Agricultural Adjustment Act] and other federal agencies. "The CCC's [Civilian Conservation Corps] not a bad idea, gets a bunch of loser bums off the street."

"That don't hurt," says Joe. "If somebody don't. Well hell, I better not say it. He'll get creamed the next election. If he don't, there'll be literal hell in this country. That's life. This sorry world is up for grabs. Here comes another one."

"Did you read Darwin's Survival of the Fittest? If you haven't got it, you're off to hell in a handbasket." One piece at a time the horse drawn stuff is discarded. "You won't see a vehicle with a steel rim, no sir. Just lugs and iron wheels."

Earl Neff unloaded a wagon filled with junk, then bargained away the jolt wagon itself, but he would not even discuss selling the horses. "No, sir, they're going with me. My son has land way out in eastern Kansas." He continued to mumble his quasi-fiction to the used equipment hustler who was not listening. "I can buy a wagon back there." and his voice trailed off.

The usual supper period passed before Jim Bob discovered that a great deal of late night talking was taking place. Roy came home now and then, usually riding the rails. He had bummed his way to California during one of his trips. He was no longer frightened about hopping a boxcar in motion or outrunning the bulls. He encountered a Ph.D.

during the early hours of a trip and bummed with him for over two months. A professor of English, the man had not been employed for over three and a half years. Once he got on the Santa Fe's Raton Pass, he slid through Gallup, New Mexico, and on north to Kingman, Arizona and Las Vegas. The yard bulls were quite rare and, though the hours between trains were interminable, the professor was always in rare form during the long waits.

The trains were filled with boxcar hobos. They got off when the trains slowed and begged for food, rarely bought a meal at a Harvey House, met the people who populated Hoovervilles, then awaited the next available train. There was an art to hiding in the brush near a parked train until one short whistle followed by two short whistles announced that the engineer was ready to roll. Roy and the professor found one stop well into California where they picked fruit with the migrant workers. When the harvest was completed, the workers were required to move on. Deputies and sheriffs usually did not want to "court" the migrants as they were not good for a fine, and usually too ill to do much work. So, in the main, they were told to move on. Still, the threats of a vagrancy charge were real enough, but often the order was "move out, we don't allow no vagrancy here."

"There just ain't no work there," Roy reported. "And the people I traveled with said there ain't no work in Oregon or Washington either." There seemed to be no work anywhere. The whole country was in stagnation. The professor said the Farm Bureau was organized to keep the farmers from organizing. Support for that outfit came from industry, especially the grain trade. The professor said all the world's grain farmers are really serfs to five grain cartels. The businessmen want their raw products cheap. They have tariffs fixed that way. When income for basic commodities goes down, so does buying power. Depressions are farm led and farm fed. Roy allowed that all this was difficult to understand. "Not more difficult than people starving in the midst of plenty," the professor had said.

"He's right," said Earl Neff. "You don't often have a horse so stupid that it will starve when it's standing up to its knees in oats." "They have their big lie," the professor had said. "They say supply and demand. When the demand is great the price is supposed to go up."

"That guy in Idaho who's storing his inventory is supposed to drive up the price of a pullet," Dad Neff said. "A pullet should be worth its weight in gold when a man is starving."

"Not if he doesn't get any money," Roy said. "And you don't have much money if you're paid a penny an hour."

"The farming months can turn anyone into an owner, but the fact remains, they're not going to allow the commodity producer to make a living. If there is anything left over, the bank sells it off. I don't know anything but farming. I figure if I had a few acres outside the dust bowl, we could last it out."

The sessions went that way, night after night. Mom would clear the table and read the latest letter from J. Samuel. He had found a small town in eastern Kansas where there was a surplus of housing and cheap land. The prospects for moving the family became the topic of discussion via letters well after Jim Bob went to bed.

"Maybe you can find some way for the journey," J. Samuel wrote in one of his missives which also contained a ten dollar bill. "Jim's about twelve, he should be able to help. The rest of us will have to pitch in until you get on your feet." When Jim Bob was asleep, Rover asked for the door and a night out on the prowl.

Morning came too soon, announced by the blowing of the kettle on the stove and the smell of pancakes and eggs frying. In time for the 11 a.m. service, the family went to town piled into the old Dodge: Dad, Mom, Roy and Jim Bob. On the steps of the church they ran into old man Buehler and his wife. Amos Buehler had made a success of life on the high plains running an icehouse. During the winter he sent teams of men with horses to ponds and streams where ice could be harvested. After logging and sawing walls of ice he insulated well enough to make the ice last until the following fall. Well past the age of retirement, Buehler now wanted to return to his native village on the lower Volga.

"For God's sake," Earl Neff said. "The Reds have taken over. You can't go there."

"I have plenty of money," Buhler said in broken English. The sermon that morning was built around the story of Jonah. The Lord told Jonah to go forth and preach to the people of Nineveh. Jonah did not believe that he was equal to the task. "Now, Jonah knew the people of Nineveh for what they were," said the priest. "They were blasphemers,

81

sodomites, reprobates, fornicators, people with no redeeming qualities whatsoever. Jonah decided to run away. He boarded a ship for the ends of the planet Earth. It was headed for a port now called Cadiz. This was out in seas where no one had ventured. Surely it was outside the jurisdiction of God." The sermon proceeded in pin drop silence. "Jonah was furtive. He paid for his passage in cash. He boarded after dark and hid below deck. He emerged only at night when no one could see him. It was on a calm night that the ocean stood on end. Jonah was swept off the ship. A giant fish took him into his mouth. Oh, my friends, there are great whales in the sea. The Right Whale can accommodate a card table, a few players, and all their chips and close its mouth during the game. We don't know whether Jonah was taken down into the belly of that whale. But we do know that he was spewed out onto the shore. As the Good Book says, we know he returned to Nineveh. He converted the sinful. Jonah is our neighbor for these trying times. His story tells us to trust in God. It tells us that when God beckons, we have to answer. God has given us a guide to behavior. God's commandments are over all the earth. We cannot escape them." The voice from the pulpit thundered, eye contact going to Amos Buehler like a dead on arrow. The arrow also went to Eloise and Earl Neff. They felt it but it did not dull their reserve.

"You cannot go just anywhere with impunity. Your immortal soul is in jeopardy. Some of you wish to flee what easterners call the dust bowl. Think before you seek the advice of Sodom and Gomorrah. We pray for rain and there will be rain if we endure our trial. Don't sell your community for a mess of pottage. Don't abandon your own for an unknown Gommorah. Do as Jonah did. Pick yourself up off the beach and do the right thing." It was quite a sermon.

Jim Bob wrote down as much as he could remember when he got home. He could not understand why everything, every city outside Ness County was sinful. Nor could he understand what Dad, Mom and Roy often talked about, supply and demand, world market, economic forces, and farmers organizing themselves the way William Lemke and the Non Partisan League suggested. Farmers always discussed these things at funerals and weddings and at auctions, rarely in public except for funerals. They dressed in their Sunday best and did most of their Christian duty all the months of the year. Xander and Jim's big brother,

J. Samuel, were probably right. The country should have been kept in grass.

While he wrote, people were making plans to leave the high plains. Jim Bob found refuge in books in the attic during schoolhouse days. He was puzzled when he read the account about Kit Carson. Kit Carson was an army scout when the Navajo Indians were ordered to march some 400 miles from their homes to Fort Sumner, New Mexico. Old men and pregnant women who could not keep up were taken behind wagons and shot while the tribe moved on. Kit Carson stayed behind to see to the execution of the old, the infirm, and pregnant women, at least according to a handwritten note someone had pasted into a chapter. "Lies, lies," he wrote in his diary. Jim Bob could not understand why someone would want to slander Kit Carson.

On day trips to Ness City and Bazine he often heard disparaging remarks about the subsidized farmers. "How in gawd's name do they live that way?" And, "Christ, don't they ever quit having kids?" In the bank, he heard a giant man in a big cowboy hat wearing fancy cowboy boots tell a vice president, "There's too many farmers. When we get the land into a few strong hands, why hell, then there'll be a price rise."

"Sorry, Mr. Neff. I can't roll over your account," the bank man told Earl. "When Roosevelt closed the banks, we lost all discretion. It's a shame, but all my friends are dead." The banker fidgeted with the cigar in the ashtray on his rolltop desk. His signal for Earl Neff to get up and leave was to pretend to be upbeat. "Maybe after the elections next November, things will change." He didn't say it, but there was a chance that Mr. Roosevelt would be swept from office.

Jim Bob, now age twelve, saw that Mom and Dad were worn out, defeated. For all practical purposes their family had disintegrated. The boy realized he would be an adult soon enough. He would have to stand on his own two feet. Jim Bob now realized how lucky he had been all his life. He barely knew J. Samuel, and Roy was too weak to do heavy farm work. He seemed to spend a lot of time going here and there with no purpose in mind. Mom kept saying that Xander, her father, would not be here very much longer, yet at age ninety-nine he seemed healthier than either Mom or Dad. Then one day Jim Bob's world fell apart. The breeder came to take his pony, Brenny.

All summer long, Jim Bob had spent hours reading books and writing. He often seized a book, disappeared into the barn or a spot near the water tank, and read. He had promised Xander that he would read a hundred books by the time he graduated from school, yet they both knew there would be no school if the situation did not improve. Jim Bob took to writing between trips to Xander's house and while waiting to receive instructions. He filled his tablet with notes on agriculture, cows and bulls.

Xander had a radio. Every Sunday late afternoon the boy sat with the pipe smoking old man while they listened to a famed radio priest who spent much time denouncing the poobahs of privilege. He was not exactly interested in what the priest was saying until he suggested that the World War started with a fountain pen rather than with a pistol like Jesse James. "The fountain pen was drained of its ink at Versailles and now young boys would have to die on the world's killing fields to make good the promises of senile old men," Xander once told him. He wrote this down in his tablet, and then he added something he had heard in a conversation at church. Mr. Buehler and his wife had reached Russia after a week long trip. At the border, officials had taken their passports and their money. The letter did not say very much. Relatives steamed off the most recent postage stamp for a one word message. The message was clear: *Mir* (hunger). Folks who had emigrated only one generation earlier could not understand how starvation had come to the rich farmland of the lower Volga, nor could they understand what had gone wrong on their beloved high plains.

10

The *Farm Journal* said there were too many farmers. California was providing the world with the wave of the future. Foolish people, deluded people were staying on only if they wanted to be peons for factories in the field. There was no future at all for a boy like Jim Bob on the farm. Sam came home after the rabbit drive. The Neff family, he pointed out, had to face the reality of the situation. First, leased land had disappeared, and Dad Neff's planting for the year had been cut in half. He owned forty acres outright, but the mortgage payments were long overdue. There was a balance at the end of the month that could not be paid. The assets were: two horses, a pony, two hogs, a few chickens, furniture, a wheat drill, and an obsolete gang plow. A two bottom moldboard plow was rusting, on its way to oblivion. The harnesses were in fair repair, and the 1928 Dodge still ran. Most other chattels had been sold, and the rest of what the Neffs owned was not worth listing.

Sam got out his Phillips 66 road map. He pointed to an industrial town that once housed 40,000 people. Now there were only about 6,000 people there.

"I've been all over this state," Sam said. "Iola, Kansas has a lot of cheap housing. No jobs. But you can get several acres for ten dollars a month. You can raise your own meat and milk, no wheat."

Sam had a salary, but it was meager. He could barely defray the expense of moving. Since he was in the transportation business, he knew about back hauls, cheap empty railroad cars. He could book a car to haul the horses, chickens, livestock and machinery.

"Sam, you don't need to do this. I'll pay you back," Dad Neff said. Sam went on as if to divert Dad's attention. "Take the machinery. Take the chickens, if possible."

"What about Rover?" asked Jim Bob.

"You can take Rover," Dad said, adding, "if she'll come."

Mom turned to Dad as the ins and outs of the move were discussed. "You mean it, Earl? Are we getting out of the dust bowl?" Earl Neff cracked a smile, the first smile to come over his face in years.

"Yes," he said. "We've got a couple of months and a lot to do." He did not say it, but the price of wheat had beaten him. Other crops; peas, beans, potatoes, sweet corn are perishable. But industry has found ways of canning and preserving them. Wheat is only semi-perishable. Industry has found ways of making it perishable as flour, pasta and pastries. Both wheat production and flour milling demand exact results, and exact results have been translated into low prices for farmers, the primary producers, and new power for secondary suppliers. Wheat is no longer simply wheat, and flour is no longer simply flour. This was what was so disturbing, and Earl Neff could not understand it. His wheat always tested at 19% protein. Hard winter wheat was what the flour mills wanted, and the bread bakeries required it. When the wheat flour did not have the right amount of hardness, the miller rejected it.

Earl Neff knew that the dust storms would end one day, and combines would be featured in newspapers, always starting in Texas, then heading north, always leaving great piles of wheat on small town streets, but he would not be there to see any of it.

In farm country, the fastest growing occupation in rural America, auctioneering, shattered a moody silence. The cry was as stylized as any western Kansas cafe meeting; informal, oral, personal. The best of the machinery was reclaimed by the mortgage holders, the small stuff that cluttered the household was tabled in the front yard, all of it to go to the highest bidder. The sales were advertised wherever they could be posted. The message supported gossip, finally the only real departure from weather, wheat and politics.

Unsold milk separators, butter churns, washtubs, harnesses, wire stretchers, post hole diggers, wheelbarrows, carts, buggies, wagons, even row crop equipment went to the highway junk pile.

Stationary engines, pumps, hammers, carpenter tools, ancient one way plows, all were prospective junk. Buyers were prepared to bid a penny, stop the auction, and face down the well paid deputy with a hogleg on his hip. Saturday was the best auction day, and all the weekdays served as word of mouth bulletin boards. It was the entertainment of the neighbors' week. The pulp paper flyer served up the rules. Everything to the highest bidder. The tables always came first.

"What'll you bid?" the auctioneer mumbles to his audience. "This stuff is too cheap. Push it together. Maybe I can get an opening bid. All right, folks, we'll start with a dollar. Hey, one, one, one. Start with ninety cents. My gawd, this is a treasure, looks like pure crystal, ninety cents, seventy-five cents, probably worth twice the money. Now, folks, I'm going to drop it to the floor. If it don't break, the price'll bounce right up shoulder high. Twenty-five cents, now thirty, thirty, I got a bid, now thirty-five, now forty." The chant goes on.

The sales go on week after week, and the same non-bidders patrol the scene like vultures at a desert feast. The people who have had their lives hammered down stay out of sight. This is a real embarrassment, a shame that can be extinguished only by moving far away, to California, to Iowa, Illinois, even Florida, wherever there is family or kin, or to some godforsaken place where no one's ever heard of the dust bowl. The signs are nailed to telephone poles, elevator doors. There is no wheat for sale. The only presence readily recognized is the victim. Wheat not devastated by jackrabbits closed its stomata to conserve moisture and hung on. Then plants dried up until the tragedy constituted a disaster.

Depending on who was present at cafes and restaurants, men stated what was eating at their entrails, forgetting their manners and humanity, and satisfying their Russian peasant's joy over someone else's hardship. "That Neff has lost his place," a farmer in bib overalls said as tobacco juice escaped his sunburned jaw.

"Yah, he's rented a boxcar to haul his ass out of here," a buyer added. No one knew what he ever bought, but he was a buyer just the same. "Vulture" someone said *sotto voce*.

"Where the hell did he get the money?" a truck driver asked.

A farmer with a German accent speaks up from the far end of the counter. "You sound like a bunch of psychologists and spiritual advisors, not bookkeepers." A few in the place laugh.

"Hell," the one with the big mouth says, "he's mortgaged to his eyeballs. I don't think he's got a pot to piss in or a window to throw it out of."

Most of the men are subdued. They know they are all in the same boat. They know they are being liquidated by bankers one at a time.

87

Neff was not the only one being hunted down, proscribed, destroyed by a system not one in a thousand understood.

The year 1935 started with a duster that covered all the counties of the dust bowl. The insanity seemed magnified by longevity. The needles on the few evergreens carefully planted and nurtured fell to the ground. As if to acknowledge defeat, weeds and pulverized soil rode the wings of the wind upward 10,000 feet, 20,000 feet according to flyers who had strayed into forbidden storms. An aviator landed just south of Xander Staab's place, and he could not take off for a day and a half.

The Amarillo newspaper reported dust storms as early as 1931, but no one up north paid much attention. Down there the storms would blow north, west and east. A year later there were reports of dust in St. Louis and New York, and Walter Winchell reported low visibility from ships at sea. March became April each year, and the sales notices went up on telephone poles, sides of buildings, and free spaces everywhere. The print shops kept the type quoined in the chase. Each new job had only to follow the format of the one that was carried a week earlier.

"That bastard Neff owes," a wizened man with a few days growth of beard said.

"Does he owe you?" a voice said.

"Well, no."

"Then shut yer trap!"

A silence ensues. "He's a good farmer. It's the dern dust," the one who announced "Shut up!" said.

Maybe so, but that was not the way the newspapers saw it. The lead editorials said this is good country, probably the garden spot of America. We have had bad luck, but bad luck always evaporates. Wheat will again become king, just like King Cotton in the Deep South.

"Bullshit!" a coffee drinker said, slamming his newspaper on the counter. Hot grease sizzles from the coal black grill where a hamburger is frying. Someone opens the screen door permitting a swarm of fat flies to enter. "Don't just stand there! Come in or get out!"

The coffee drinker has his audience. He does not have a soapbox, but he is a soapbox orator just the same. "The Board of Trade in Chicago . . ." His sentence dangles. He takes a swig of the hot java and continues, "Here we grow the wheat and some son of a bitch in Chicago gambles with our product. He can move the price up or down, usually down. If he needs more wheat, he'll give us two bits. For two bits you can buy any farmer. We have the wheat, and we have it first. We're a hazard to the American market first. If Henry Wallace had any balls, he wouldn't allow one bushel of wheat to be imported until our crops are sold." The soapbox orator silences everyone with his spate of words. "That's what they do!" he says. "They import just enough wheat to break the market, then they can buy the rest of the American crop at world prices."

The men talked, and the customers opened the screen door. The dusters usually came only two weeks or thereabouts well into June, and then they slowed. But this year was different. They seemed to come earlier and faster now, and they stayed longer. The air became indescribably hot. Dust devils formed at the ground and raced across the fields and pastures.

In late June, Earl Neff, Royal Lee Neff, Grandpa Staab's Indian hired hand, and a friendly neighbor loaded the freight car between 4 p.m. and midnight. Barrels of water were hoisted aboard, then furniture was strapped to side slats. A few pieces of machinery were draped with padding and blankets next to the water barrels. Household effects in paper boxes took up less room than anyone had thought. Earl Neff sold some harnesses by private treaty, but he decided he would be damned if he would have strangers pawing their way through the family's possessions.

Joseph Samuel Neff arranged and paid for the trip out. The tab was not that high. The town he had selected was down at the mouth, but there was plenty of cheap housing, and lots of pasture available for a song. Roy had been bumming around the country, but he arrived on time. He would drive the family Dodge while Dad rode in the boxcar with the horses. Mother cried as the rooms were emptied. She cried most of the time these days. As she folded sheets, towels and blankets, she prayed a lot. She almost stopped eating. The smiles so prominently evident in the wedding photos she kept on the bedroom dresser were gone. She wanted to stick it out, and yet she wanted to leave. Logic told her that farming was no longer possible. They would get out now just ahead of a sheriff's sale, or suffer even more humiliating consequences. During the past several weeks, Earl had spent hours in the barn repairing and polishing his harnesses. He did not take the shotgun to the barn as several others had done, but he no longer went to work early.

Hunting became Jim Bob's personal chore. The boy brought in plenty of rabbits because there was a shortage of food and the hunt was easy. Always, Rover was at his heels. Rover seemed to know that something was amiss. The dog followed the boy to the storm cellar for a jar of pickles. There was not much left in the storm cellar any more, just some tomatoes from two years ago, some canned beef, and three jars of garden peas.

The dog followed Jim Bob to the milking stall and waited patiently while the boy stripped the last few squirts of milk from the teats. The ritual of tagging along was observed while the thirty remaining chickens were fed. The only available feed was three year old wheat. The dog seemed to shun the cluttered house as moving day approached.

When the day came, it all seemed over in a matter of hours. Tools that cost a fortune a few years ago were trundled off to town, the railroad siding and the boxcar, or abandoned. Jim Bob made one trip to town with the dray man, who transported horses and equipment to the rail car. He helped stack household goods while Dad and the neighbor rolled two barrels of water on their rims into the car. Later Dad Neff gave the boy a hug. "I'll see you, son," he said, as he settled down to wait for the switch engine.

"You riding with the car?" a friendly yardman asked. "You got it!" Earl Neff said.

"If you want off, just ask the caboose conductor how long the stop for water." Jim Bob, Royal Lee, and their mother slept on the floor in an empty house that night. In the car they had a breakfast of eggs and bread, coffee, a few remaining biscuits. They pulled out at 6 a.m.

The dust of a few weeks earlier had settled down, but the grasshoppers were out in force. There had been a few calm days with good weather. Mom was no longer afraid of the storms that had haunted her since 1933. Now the calm, the silence, almost frightened her. She could hardly wait as Royal Lee tied a burlap wrapped gallon jug of water to the front bumper. The burlap was sopping wet, and evaporation would cool the water. It was over 80 degrees as the sun climbed the sky.

Jim Bob was half asleep, but anger kept him awake. He did not express this to Roy or their mother, but he curled his lips in hatred. Why were they doing this to his parents? He did not know who "they" were, but he had heard things from his elders. He wondered in silence who was this Cordell Hull who, as a Congressman, had ordered up a drive to unregulated free trade that debilitated the price of wheat. The men had been talking about *der schlecter* Wilson for months. Dad had moved out and went on borrowed money because of Wilson. Unseen men in unseen offices had caused the price of wheat to fall, and other unseen men in banks had decreed that outstanding loans were to be collected while the price of wheat was down. Dad survived the post war depression, but then came confiscation of wheat in the Volga Republic, and Dad Neff was forced to sell his wheat at seventeen cents a bushel. "Sacrament!" Grandpa Xander had exclaimed. It was an expression the English did not use or understand. "How can a man survive bad years with prices like that?"

Jim Bob heard these things, but he did not understand any of them. Xander once said that Mr. Roosevelt had usurped the law. He almost always spoke in German. Jim Bob had a Chief tablet for a journal which he kept in English. He puzzled over translations, but it seemed that Mr. Roosevelt had unveiled an Executive Order. He also got strange new laws passed. He took over the farms. Xander used the term command economy. During the winter, snuggled behind the big cook stove in the basement, Jim had heard it all, not once or twice, but a dozen times.

The government took over agriculture via the mechanism of regulating basic storable commodities. The government would regulate production, price, supply and demand. The government would regulate export and import traffic.

"You've become a public utility," Grandpa thundered. "This means the government has taken it upon itself to see to it that you make a profit. But that's not what they're using those powers for. They're using every power to solve the farm problem by extinguishing the farmer!"

When Jim Bob asked Roy about any part of this, Roy said, "Don't start talking like a Red." Since Jim Bob had no idea what a Red was, he bottled up the joy in his life. He stopped smiling as the family moved out. He had not spoken two words since he got up.

They drove out through Ness City. The streets were as empty as a stockyard pen on Friday night. They drove down the main drag. Jim Bob started counting the little mounds that were wet with dust and oil under previously shoulder parked cars. The buildings had the look of a ghost town. Only one neon sign still remained lit. It was said to be the most common sign in America, Roy said. The sign said "EAT."

Royal drove across the railroad track. He noted that Dad's boxcar was long gone. Roy dropped into high as he scanned the map for a road to U.S. 54. Mom rode in the front seat. Her eyes were closed as her fingers quietly moved through the mantra of her rosary. Rover was jumpy when the boy put her in the back seat. She refused to lie down, and whined in a low, throaty way.

Automobiles operating in dust storms soon become oil thirsty. The fine particles seem to penetrate engine, cylinders, even oil pans and sealed engine parts. The dust turns into an abrasive that attacks metal with a vengeance. It wears away piston rings. As a consequence oil burns up near as fast as it can be replaced.

At the first filling station stop some 40 miles down the sunburned road, an attendant came to the open window on the driver's side. "At your service," he said rather formally.

"Check the oil," Royal said. The man opened the hood, wiped off the dip stick, reinserted it, then presented it to Royal. "Put in a quart."

Jim Bob told Mom he had to go to the restroom. He opened the door. Rover jumped out, and in a second or two she was across the road and headed south. The boy whistled and called her name. The dog stopped, looked back, then ran another ten yards. Jim Bob whistled again and called the dog's name. Rover looked back, hesitated a moment, then took off. She was out of sight before Roy had paid for the gas and oil. "What got into her?" Roy asked.

"I guess I don't know," answered Jim Bob. He waited for a moment as if to admit that he had just spoken a lie. "Maybe I do know," he said. "Rover has a family out there. I think she made a choice between us and her family." After a while Mom stopped praying. She turned to Roy. "Royal Lee!"

"Yah, Mom"

"I keep thinking of your brother Earl."

Roy kept his silence. If Mom wanted to talk, he would give her plenty of room. "When he finally comes home, nobody will be there. He won't know how to find us."

"I suppose anyone would go over and see Grandpa."

"My dad is ninety-nine. He looks perfectly healthy, but it's not reasonable to expect him to live very long."

Roy said to himself, she can handle the truth. It will not get any easier to tell her. He waited barely a minute to speak. "Mom," he said. "Earl isn't coming back."

He thought she would start interrogating him, dragging out details the way women were wont to do, demanding more information than he had. He waited in vain. Mom seemed to relax. She tucked her rosary into a small purse and adjusted her sitting position in the old Dodge. "Roy, do you want to tell me something?" She waited. "I think I know what you're going to say."

"Mom, you might as well know." With that, Roy told of the hobo ride that had landed him in a Colorado county jail. He told her about the Mexican trustee who thought he saw a ghost because Roy and a previous inmate had looked so much alike.

"He probably had money," Roy said. "If he did, they took it. This meant they had to get rid of his identification. They're used to tumbling hobos into unmarked county graves. Mom, you'd have to be as rich as Rockefeller to get court orders, writs, and all that stuff, and you still couldn't identify a body that old. I'd bet a thousand dollars that's what happened." Roy half expected his mother to cry. She did not. His message gave her closure. She had already suspected that young Earl had met with foul play, but she always believed it had happened among the hobos.

"Not so," Roy told her. "A hobo wouldn't bother to dispose of the body. The deputies have a Potter's Field available, even a cheap coffin. Ma," Roy said, "he isn't coming back.

The car had passed through Bazine on State 96, then Alexander, as the sun climbed above the morning haze. At Rush Center, Roy swung into a filling station. Oil was available in bottles with a pouring funnel for a cap. "How much for oil?" Roy wanted to know.

"That's fifteen cents a quart."

"Let's check it."

The gas station man lifted the hood, wiped the dip stick on his pants, put it in again, then held it up for Roy to see.

"Put in a quart," Roy said.

After they paid the man, Mom counted the funds remaining for the trip. She and Roy computed the quarts still needed and the gasoline at fourteen cents a gallon.

"It'll be close," Mom said. "But I think we'll make it."

The towns came and went: Timken, Shaffer, Albert, Heizer, then the road dipped south, with Great Bend coming up. The soil was dry, but it was no longer the dust bowl.

Every 30 miles or so, the scene was the same. "Check the oil!" And after the exhibit of a pan getting low, the response, "Put in a quart!" Mom opened up a bit and started talking. She did not talk about Earl and his likely death. She remembered her days at Hays, Kansas and life during the first few halcyon years on the Ness County farm. The crops were so bountiful and the people so lively. Joseph Samuel was born before the Wilson debacle, and the rest of the family came along at regular intervals. Jim Bob was the caboose child trailing the rest, unexpected but not unwanted. Roy drove carefully, never faster than at a "Burma Shave" speed, about forty-five miles an hour. At forty-five per, he could read and enjoy the series of six signs that carried their commercial message.

Hinky Dinky
Par Ley Voo
Cheer up Face
The War is Through
Burma Shave

Jim Bob emerged from his taciturn mood. He asked for help writing down the messages, usually one between each town.

The first message past Great Bend counseled:

Take a Tip
For your Trip
No Wet Brush
To Soak your Grip
Burma Shave

Jim Bob made notes. "Dartmouth, Ellinwood, Silica, Raymond."

You'll Love your Wife
You'll Love your Paw
You'll even Love
Your Mother in law
If You Use Burma Shave

"Lyons, Mitchell, Windom. Check the oil. Put in a quart. Not a jackrabbit in sight. Not a dust drift anywhere."

Out of the car, Roy said, "Mom, there's going to be a war. There's already a war in China. Sooner or later we'll go to war. I've heard them talking. They all remember the good times in Wilson's war, and I believe they'll get us shooting people and make a bundle."

"I hope not," Mom said. "Joe Sam might escape, but you're a dangerous age."

"Makes no never mind," Roy said. "As soon as you get settled, I intend to enlist."

Mom turned for a sharp look at Roy. Their eyes met. "You wouldn't do that," she said.

"Ma, it's better than starving. There's no jobs. I haven't earned a dime in years. I have no idea how you'll live if some of us don't send home some money."

The Bearded Lady
Tried a Jar
She's now a
Famous Movie Star
Burma Shave

Just west of Conway, Old Baldy, the right rear wheel, gave up the ghost. The blowout was slow but just as lethal as any big flat. Roy broke out the tire iron, tube patching material, and a hand pump. It took him the best part of an hour to fix the flat.

Jim Bob tried to entertain Mother by reading his notes on the trip: "Kansas, flatter than a pancake, temperature 102 degrees, town markers give the population, and road signs supply the entertainment." Jim Bob missed a few because he could not write fast enough.

"Mom, did you see the last one?"

Keep Well to the Right
Of the Oncoming Car
Cut your Close Shave
From the Half Panel Jar
Burma Shave

Roy limped into McPherson, where he bought a used tire for two dollars. Then they headed south on State 81, Moundridge, Hesston, and Newton just north of Wichita. A park like clump of cottonwood trees invited the migrants to stop for a sandwich and possibly a new jug of water. The encampment was not a Hooverville, but it might have rated as a hobo camp. Some of the guests had been made permanent by the fact of an irreparable breakdown. The deputies had been by the night before with a command to move on. "But how the hell do you move on when it won't run?" a worn out man with a gaunt face asked.

He had been a school teacher in Springfield, Illinois before he was fired from his job. He was heading for California, but now the jalopy would not make it.

"If I didn't have three kids, I'd hop a freight train."

Roy, Mom and Jim Bob passed them by on their way to the food stand, then they moved on. Federal 81 turned south, then east, and the next town was Whitewater, then Potwin, then El Dorado, still on 196. U.S. 54. It was still a two lane road, but the U.S. designation implied less potholes, less broken concrete, albeit not less road construction. Mom watched the dimes and nickels disappear each time the red tinted gasoline left the gravity station pump. The glass cylinder always contained ten gallons when pumped up, and the old Dodge seemed to drink ten gallons at a gulp. Ten times fourteen cents put $1.40 on the other side of the equals sign, and the twenty dollar bill budgeted for the rest of the trip was all but consumed. That litany "Check the oil, put in a quart" made Roy resolve to do a ring job as soon as possible. He would have to drop the pan, remove the pistons and rods, re-ring each, and reassemble. Without a ring job, the car would be worthless to Dad.

There were no Russian thistles long before the Dodge crawled through Rosalia and Sally Yards, and Eureka.

"Was that a town, Mom?" Jim Bob asked.

"Yes, it was once, just a wide spot in the road now."

The big highway sign said: "Yates Center — The Hay Capital of the World."

"Grandpa would like that," Jim Bob said.

"It's only a couple dozen miles from Iola," Roy added.

The sun was setting, but it was still not dark enough for headlights. "We'll just stay on U.S. 54 until we hit Batesville, another wide spot in the road, then Iola, another wide spot."

"Piqua," Jim Bob said. "Does that count?"

"Well, it has a church, so it must be a town," Mom said.

The destination J. Samuel Neff had found for his family was Iola. J. Samuel knew his geography. East of the Isohyet line at approximately the Topeka meridian, mean annual rainfall increased one inch for each fifteen miles. This meant that Iola would get over thirty inches of rainfall per annum. During a dry year, all bets were off, but even a dry year did not create a dust bowl. "Never again," Mom said half to herself.

Roy navigated his way through town to a small acreage J. Sam had ordered set aside, sight unseen. "Never again wheat," Roy added. "Never again is this family going to get in debt. Those bankers, they sit down at the table and eat with you three times a day, seven days a week, always taking the first helping."

"How can you stay out of debt if you can't earn any money?" Jim Bob asked. "That's why we're going to get a war. It'll make those damn fools in Washington get off their swivel chairs and put some money into the economy." Roy did not know how this would be done, but he was certain of his war prophecy.

The Dodge crawled around the town square, caught West Street going opposite the East Street just traversed, made the correct turn, left town, and entered, via a cattle crossing, a yard with a dilapidated farm house. Western Kansas, the open road. Now this! Roy figured he had meant it when he said he would join the army. It was frustration building in the soul of a young man who had no place to go.

At the end of the road, Ma knew that life would go on. She knew that. Even though the house had no electricity, no water, no indoor plumbing. She had not had those things out there on the high plains either, but here there was clean air. That was enough. It would be all right now. Here, the youngest could go back to school. Dad might be waiting. Maybe he had everything unloaded. Maybe he had work. He could do custom work with his horses. Maybe a self sufficient farm could be started.

Jim Bob had his plan. He would get a quality calf somehow. He would start breeding a herd just like Grandpa. He did not know how any of this would happen. There was hardly a dollar in the family.

The rental on the small house was $10 a month, and Dad did not have much more than that. Maybe Dad should have sold some equipment to the vultures. Dad called the sale barn people vultures. Some of the people called Dad a failure. But no! That was not the way it was going to be. "I'll show them!" Jim Bob wrote in his Chief tablet. "If anyone makes fun of my dad, I'll get even."

He fantasized better times. He no longer believed he was a child when he nailed a skunk and then a pheasant with a single shot .22. At Mount Zion he had been the best shot in class. During the last hundred miles of this trip, Jim Bob, the boy, grew up. He would make his mark. He would earn and save. He would erase shame and defeat from the faces of his parents.

The door was unlocked. Obviously, Earl Neff had not yet arrived. Mom, Roy and Jim Bob sat in the car for a few minutes. Before they got out, a man in a Ford pickup drove up.

"You the Neffs?"

"Right here," Roy said.

"Well, you've got yourself a place. That'll be fifteen dollars up front."

"We thought it was ten dollars," Mom said.

"Ten dollars plus a five dollar deposit against damage."

She did not see how the place could be damaged beyond its present state. But she said quietly, "Dad will be here tonight or tomorrow."

Roy said, "He'll pay."

The man squinted. "Highly irregular," he said. "OK, tomorrow." He added, "Ma'am, you've got a good deal, four acres! If times wasn't so hard, this place could go for forty dollars."

"We'll clean it up good, Mister," Mom said.

11

They left reluctantly, those farmers who ate up their capitalization while traders managed corn down to ten cents a bushel. The dust bowl was getting empty because of crop failure. The fantasy of corporations crowding out small farms prevailed because they exercised a sort of eminent domain over families. Farmers who had not applied the knack of creating money out of thin air missed out on the greatest invention since God created the blade of grass. The old art of capitalizing on savings and expanding on earnings disappeared into the folklore of yesteryear when captains of finance began creating money, as with the God of the Catechism, out of thin air. So the farmers left to scramble for cash money jobs selling shoes, digging ditches, performing day labor for the great land holders. Selling cream and eggs no longer lifted the mortgage. The mysteries of college lured those who were able and could endure the poverty of the student without resources.

Those who emptied the countryside hungered for the best job of all: government work. Those with a passion for the land and the miracle of crop rebirth hung on longer than most, usually until grasshoppers or poverty made them face a moment of truth.

J. Samuel Neff was considered a man of the world by his family. He traveled constantly, observed the poverty that held most of the nation in thrall, and concluded that self help with low out of pocket costs could be best calculated to rescue his family. He found a county seat town in Allen County, Kansas in the last stages of decline from industrial town status. It had a history of escaping pillage in the Civil War and an industrial buildup based on zinc smelters, then declined back into a pleasant atmosphere with plenty of cheap housing. There were no jobs, but each house seemed to have ample land for a garden. The rivers and creeks were full of fish, and the countryside was a veritable Serengeti full of small game.

Iola, Kansas became a county seat after a first try community with the unpronounceable name of Cofachique discovered that it had no readily available water supply. Iola grew the way most towns grew in those days, a mainstay being the carriage works that promised to make the town a rival for any in the state, if not the nation.

In 1872 an enterprising young man named Acres drilled a well on his four acre plot on State Street. He had been prospecting for coal, but took to hunting for natural gas. He found gas all right, but more importantly he found a geyser of mineral water, an ancient deposit with all the minerals of the ocean in tow. As often happens with a serendipitous discovery, plans changed. Mr. N.C. Acres built a hotel and cabins for a spa on the now six acres he called Acres Park.

Acres thought in terms of ownership and large quantities of mineral water to sell. He started bottling and barreling his product. He reasoned that it had to be good because it tasted so bad. With baths and lodging, Acres Park was in business.

By the hundreds, people came to recapture their health. Gas from the well was used to heat the water. Leaflets advertised this "mineral park" with copy proclaiming to the effect that the water cured almost everything. Small kegs of mineral water were shipped to Europe, South America, Canada, and all over the country. The gas that Acres discovered was considered a waste product, but not for long.

Area industry discovered gas in abundance. There was so much of it that the experts figured it would last for at least two centuries. Accordingly, the wells went down and the smelter plants went up. Smelter plants were constructed on the basis of the fact that free gas was inexhaustible. There were no less than three cement plants during the boom time and as many zinc smelters.

The town grew to over 20,000. It featured a light rail system that ran from Bassett in the south to Gas City and La Harpe in the east. The king of the hill was the Banyon smelter, the collapse of which left east Iola looking like a moon landscape, its cinders now used to absorb the refuse that goes into any city dump. When massive unemployment came, out migration began. All at once, there was surplus housing, cheap housing.

The two smelters of free gas evaporated in little more than two years. As more wells were drilled, gas pressure died. One at a time, the plants pulled out. By 1918 they all were gone.

For reasons left unexplained, or for no reason at all, Mom and Dad no longer called Jim Bob by that double name. It seemed to disappear even while crossing Kansas, and now it was James or more often Jim. So when the boy James Neff first walked to town he found the courthouse square full of farmers who spent their Saturdays holding their own court, making and annihilating candidates, cursing the administration, sometimes praising it, wondering whether native son Alf Landon really had a chance against the suave easterner, Franklin D. Roosevelt. Iola had a majestic courthouse situated in the middle of four square blocks. At one time a perforated pipe had ringed the square. Jets of gas lit up the night sky with one of the most picturesque displays ever to highlight a 4th of July celebration.

Iola was a wonderment to the boy from western Kansas. He walked the town and hunted rabbits and squirrels around the edge of town, especially along Rock Creek and Elm Creek clear down to the confluence of the Neosho River. He found a Hooverville, really more of a hobo jungle, on the south side of Elm Creek near the Santa Fe track. The men were always polite, always hungry looking with that hollow look of defeat in their eyes. Young James hunted in and around the shale mounds, often bringing the hobos a rabbit or two for the stew pot. Once, when deputies arrived with the usual fanfare, he quickly hunted a hiding place in the bush. The deputies were as polite as possible.

"You fellas can't stay here. You'll have to move on."

"Tomorrow?"

"Well, yes, early in the morning. I don't want to see you here tomorrow." It was a perfunctory try. The deputies would not be back in a week, and they probably would not be able to recognize any of the jungle's residents, anyway.

The first automobiles had arrived in Iola at approximately the same time as the big gas discovery. Soon the carriage works was gone. That was the way of things. Jim Neff absorbed some facts at the Carnegie public library, and for the first time he encountered the intelligence that no art of man could sustain a buggy whip factory once the Ford Model T made the scene. Agriculture was the same thing, one of James's teachers told him. "Now that we have machinery, there's no need for family farmers."

"But where do people go?" the boy asked.

"Makes no never mind, they have to leave," was the laconic reply. Old Doc Mark Podolinsky drove his frontier buggy around the square now and then. His buggy whip was much in evidence even though he rarely used it. When the good doctor stopped near Reynold's Drug Store, Jim Neff spoke to him.

"Sir, your buggy reminds me of one we used to have."

The doctor smiled. "Really? But don't you have it anymore?"

"No, sir, Dad had to sell it."

The doctor looked at the boy. His clothes were well worn but clean. He had a perpetual smile when adults addressed him.

"Do you want to ride around the square?"

"Yes, sir." Jim scrambled aboard as elated as a prince.

By the time the two arrived in front of Shannon & Shannon Hardware, the doctor had elicited a well rounded impression from the boy. He learned that there was no employment in the family, that food was largely small game and fish that the boy supplied.

The doctor slipped the boy a dollar. "No, sir, I can't take that!"

The doctor insisted. "It's an advance. Maybe you can come around on Saturday and help my groom curry and comb the horse." Jim shook hands with the doctor. "I'll be there," he said. On the place that Dad Neff rented, a few chickens provided eggs. The cows provided butter and milk. Jim brought home as much small game as the family could use. One problem remained, how to pay for gasoline and rent.

During the first eight months in Iola, the Neff family moved no less than four times. At each, Dad Neff owed ten dollars per month for rent, but he simply had not the money to pay. The economics involved caused young Jim to steel himself to a new discipline. First, he wanted to know why a product such as the tomatoes he grew by the barrel were nearly worthless. A half bushel sold for fifty cents. People still needed food, but food was all but worthless unless it came from Bert Fryer's grocery store. New inventions, a teacher told him, closed out the existing order. The farm was not exempt from this iron law of economics.

The editorials in the *Iola Daily Register* and the *Kansas City Star* iterated and reiterated this point. "You see," the teacher said, "you have to get bigger or get out. The policy of this great nation is to put the land in a few strong hands."

James had a hard time believing what he was told. "Who's going to stay up with a sick calf?" he wondered. "Who's going to bring in five hundred acres of wheat when nature allows only a small window of time?" At age thirteen, Jim started handling ideas that few grownups even thought about. There was this mystery about farming. The farmer produced his crops at cost. He sold his production to vultures at wholesale or less. He took all the risks, yet gamblers in the Chicago pit set prices. Everyone gets taken care of except the grower.

Before coming to Iola, James Neff had never been out of the county in his life. Now he was hustling to make money badly needed at home. He still milked the cows most of the time. He turned up a sizeable garden, but each time the garden got started, the family had to move. Most of the housing units were unoccupied, so they were barely livable. Only one had running water.

Most of the boy's earnings went to pay the rent. Once he squandered fifteen cents to see his first movie: *Stand Up and Fight,* with Robert Taylor and Wallace Beery. He concluded that that was what he had to do during what everyone called hard times. In a text at school he read that one of the railroad builders made more money collapsing a railroad than running it. He was scavenging in the city dump when it came to him that during the halcyon zinc smelting days, there was real wealth in that ground. It was still there as scrap iron. He gathered it up and trundled it over to a scrap iron dealer in a wagon. Copper brought in more money than iron. Jim Neff became an expert at finding copper. When a local garage burned down, he negotiated for the radiators that had been destroyed.

The old city dump was a treasure pit in more ways than one to anyone who saw what he looked at. There was a bootlegger not six rods from the dump. He was always in the market for pint bottles as long as they did not feature the raised lettering "FEDERAL LAW PROHIBITS THE SALE AND REUSE OF THIS BOTTLE." The old fellow believed that by avoiding this condemning language his activity was less a crime. He offered five cents for every bottle without the offending language. James found a bed of clear bottles, but when he made delivery he was told that the Feds had been around. They did not want to send the old man to jail, so would he please agree not to distill or sell illegal whiskey. With that confrontation went the market for pint bottles.

If you wanted work in Iola, you had to create your own job. Dad did this with custom plowing, but when the horses ran out of feed and started exhibiting their ribs to passing traffic, Dad Neff concluded that he would have to sell the animals. He was a horse lover and that was why he spent some time finding Amish buyers a couple of counties away. The proceeds picked up delinquent rent, and then Dad Neff was really broke. One of the two cows was slaughtered, and the meat canned in Mason jars. Both Dad and Jim hoed corn at ten cents an hour.

Somehow most of 1936 and 1937 rolled by without incident until that September day when James came home from school at his usual country pace, fifty steps walking, fifty steps running. The deputies had been there with a court order. There were workmen with the deputies who had carried the stove and furniture to the ditch at the edge of the gravel road. Mom was in tears. The deputies had left. Dad had a short term job in Bronson and could not be reached. J. Samuel was on the road somewhere "quite unavailable," an unsympathetic clerk at the post office reported in response to a telegram.

Jim tried to comfort his mother. "Go to the neighbors. I'll take care of this," he said. He knew the people with trucks parked across the street from Bert Fryer's grocery. They displayed a sign "DRAY." At first he did not know what "dray" meant, but during the summer months his father had employed a fellow named Olson for the short term moves from one hovel to the next. Jim decided to see Doc Podolinsky first, then Olson.

Doc Podolinsky owned the old Banyon mansion with twenty acres. He had picked it up in settlement for some bills when the previous owner and occupant had pulled out of town. The property had not been occupied or sold for five years.

Jim presented himself at the doctor's office.

"Are you a patient?" the nurse receptionist asked.

"No, ma'am," James said. "This is business."

"Well, I don't know, the doctor is with a patient."

From an examining room came Dr. Podolinsky's voice. "In here;" it said.

There followed a muffled conversation, a subdued argument from the nurse, and a moment later both walked out to confront the boy. Most young people quivered in their boots when Dr. Podolinsky raised his voice or displayed annoyance. He was a mountain of a man, a champion wrestler during medical school, and justly famous in Iola for having faced down five or six Ku Klux Klanners who fired a cross on Doc's front lawn because he was a "Polack".

As legend had it, Doc suddenly appeared on the front porch.

"You looking for me, boys?"

His large physical structure atop a porch overlooking the burning cross and sheeted pranksters must have frightened the Klanners, all of whom ran for their lives. That was in the 1920s. Doc had been living off his reputation ever since.

Doc came out to meet James in his unbuttoned white coat and wearing a stethoscope, a bit irritated.

"OK, son, what goes?"

"I want to talk."

"I have patients, so out with it!"

"We don't have a place to live."

The doctor knew what was coming. He already knew that Earl Neff was being evicted for non payment of rent. He turned to dismiss his office employee, then said, "How old are you, son?"

"I'm going on fourteen." This sounded better than thirteen. The boy continued, "I have an idea. Vandals are tearing up the Banyon place. Would you allow Dad and Mom to move in as caretakers? And we'll pay you rent as soon as we can!"

"How would you get the money?"

"Can I take over grooming your buggy horse?"

The doctor was not facing cowards such as the Ku Klux Klanners. He tried to look stern and then broke into a smile. He reached into a drawer and produced a key.

"I think I can earn the rent," young Jim said.

"Do your parents know you are here? Let's go into my office."

The place smelled of medicine, probably iodine and alcohol. "Sit on the examination table." The chest high table was covered with leather.

"Thanks, but I don't want to dirty up your table."

"You can tell your parents they can have the place as caretakers, no rent. I have not been able to sell it for six years. It has no electricity, but it has natural gas and a good well and running water if the pump is still working." Dr. Podolinsky seemed to be making calculations. There was absolutely no market for the property. The pasture was worth a little, but not enough to cover ad valorem taxes. "Tell your folks we'll work out the details later. I've got to get back to work."

Jim left the physician's office as if walking three feet off the ground. He ran straight to the courthouse square to find Mr. Olson. Mr. Olson's truck was a high bed, all purpose dray with side stakes. It was big enough to haul all the family's possessions, probably in one haul.

Jim approached Olson. "Busy?"

"Naw, Say, why aren't you home milking?"

Jim let the dray man have the full story. The word spread to others parked on the east side of the square.

"You mean you've been dispossessed?"

"They carried our stuff out to the ditch."

"Who are 'they?'" Olson asked.

"The deputies." Jim paused while the men chewed this over. "I've rented a place from Dr. Podolinsky. If I can get our stuff hauled over to the old Banyon place, I'll get you paid, I promise, in two months." Mr. Olson bit his lips. "Holy Mackerel!" he said.

Jim added, "Mom always said, if you need help, don't ask the idle."

"Well, I ain't rich, so I guess I'm nominated," Olson said. This was the absolute low point for the family. Mom was in bed for a week as a result of the shock. James swore that his family would never be humiliated again.

Letters were coming at regular two or three week intervals from Grandpa Xander. They told the boy to read, to set goals, to learn from the mistakes of others. One of the novels on Xander's list of one hundred works that James was to read before he graduated from high school was *Great Expectations* by Charles Dickens, and Xander hinted that a young man with great expectations was bound to reach a turning point in life quite soon.

12

The old Banyon Place stood like a monument over the rim of yesterday's promise. It had been built in 1901 and featured all the trappings of a gilded era. Well ahead of its time, it had gas, plumbing for the kitchen, and well water from a spigot that did not even leak. Bathroom facilities were not greatly improved over what the Neffs had encountered in the three or four previous moves, mainly an outhouse, a sink with a tub, and a gas heater for hot water. The kitchen needed a cleaning and paint. In fact, the entire two story structure needed paint. Four windows had been broken by vandals and needed glass replacement. A widow's walk on the roof suggested an overview of the countryside and Iola city in the far distance. The place was entirely too big for a small family, but Eloise Neff figured that for once in her married life she would have enough room for domestic tranquility. The place had a carriage house, a tool shed, and enough blessed land for a garden and chicken coop.

Jim Neff started acquiring knowledge and insight, first by haunting the local library and next by soaking up the practical knowledge from older men, unemployed men who had been shared out of the workplace. An unemployed mechanical drawing instructor taught him how to set up a septic tank using galvanized pipe, replete with laterals big enough to service a stadium. He plumbed water only in, effluent going out to the digestion tank and lateral distribution to a nearby field. Electricity was a bit makeshift. Natural gas served the place from its own deep well. With the counsel of a friendly unemployed man, Jim outlined a channel for wire to run from meter and distribution box, basement to attic, and replaced the knob and tube service with cable. It took the boy months to learn and do, but by winter he had installed state of the art wiring to at least the first floor. By the winter of 1937 he was receiving regular correspondence from Grandpa Xander, "Jimmy, be sure you keep a journal. Keep a check list of the books you read." Only once did he hint that time was running out. Then in late December came a letter with Xander's home address in the hand writing of Mom's sister, the daughter from Vermont. At supper that night Mom and Dad discussed Grandpa in hushed tones. The decision was made for Mom to take a bus back to Ness City.

"He's a very old man, about 103," Mom told Jim. "I'm about sixty." Jim wanted to go with his mother, but one ticket was all the family could afford, even more than they could afford. Mom was back two weeks later. Grandpa Xander had passed away in his sleep. All that was left of the family, the daughter Eloise, the daughter from Vermont, Mathilda, and a son from Colorado, stayed for funeral rites at Sacred Heart Catholic Church in Ness City. The priest said a few comforting words to the effect that the tolerance, wisdom and fortitude of one generation cannot be transferred to those who are left behind, and how this was one of nature's wisest provisions.

Xander was well atop his affairs. His will was completed with the guidance of an attorney. Xander sent Jim a packet of books, assembled and annotated months before his last illness. Mom said that this was the end of an era. The bundle of books that Xander transferred to Jim before he died dealt with Kansas history and ephemera. There were volumes on Wild Bill Hickock, Jesse James, Billy the Kid, the Dalton brothers, Wyatt Earp, and Bat Masterson. One short volume caught Jim's attention immediately. It was *Frontier Doctor* by Forest Crumrine, M.D. In it the doctor told how on one cold night he had seen giant circles on the prairie. Finally it occurred to him that the circles marked the path where bull buffalo had circled the milling herd at night, which they did to deflect and ward off predators.

A Department of Agriculture bulletin on grass included a speech by John J. Ingalls, an old time Kansas senator. It was a paean entitled *In Praise of Blue Grass*. Jim read the passages over and over, savoring the poetry of the politician and the beauty of the English language:

"It was blue grass, unknown in Eden, the final triumph of nature, reserved to compensate her favorite offspring in the new Paradise of Kansas for the loss of the old upon the banks of the Tigris Euphrates. Next in importance to the divine profusion of water, light, and air, those three great physical facts which render existence possible, may be reckoned the universal beneficence of grass. Exaggerated by tropical heats and vapors to the gigantic cane congested with its saccharine secretion, or dwarfed by polar rigors to the fibrous hair of northern solitudes, embracing between these extremes the maize with its resolute pennons, the rice plant or southern swamps, the wheat, rye, barley, oats, and other cereals, no less than the humbler verdure of hillside, pasture, and prairie in the temperate zone, grass is the most widely distributed of all vegetable beings, and is at once the type of our life and the emblem of our mortality."

Ten acres of green grass was a bit more than Jim had hoped for. Just how much grass did a man require? Jim asked friends at the courthouse square. "Well, it depends on the terrain," came the laconic reply.

Actually, it depends on a great deal more, Jim soon found out. Grass grows just about anyplace. It will grow on sand and it will grow among rocks. It will grow on poverty soil with barely a trace of nutrition. Yes, it depends on the terrain. That is why cows can feed on short grass in western Kansas and grow fat, and starve on really high grass in Mississippi. One wise old farmer told Jim that "to grow crops you have to rotate."

By the time Jim reached age fourteen, his journal was chock full of diagrams illustrating how the land available to him could be cut up into paddocks. He computed that forty acres could be worked from paddock to paddock, how pathways could be set up so no animal had to walk very far for clean water. His designs for gardening were exciting in spite of the hard times. His parents worried a great deal. They worried that Dr. Podolinsky might actually find a buyer for the old Banyon place, that Dad might lose his job at the cement plant. Just the same, Jim plowed into high school work and athletics with great determination. He got A's in classes that graded on a curve. He wanted to be on the winning side in school athletics and he was usually disappointed because he often won as an individual but lost when part of a group.

He was a quick study, fast on his feet. Under the expert teaching of Luke Palmer, he mastered the fundamentals of pugilism. He even scored well in his team for varsity, he made the difference. He learned how to dance and dazzle. While opponents were still thinking about their next move, Palmer advised, "confuse the opponents, get set for the knockout punch." The Roosevelt administration set up commodity programs. Surplus fruits and vegetables were given to the unemployed. A person in the countryside had little trouble feeding his family because there was plenty of food, and light subsistence farming was possible.

Jim went hunting at least once or twice a week according to the weather. He sharpened his skills at hunting and seeking game. The county was full of rabbits. Jim found out he could crawl under an abandoned farmhouse and wait. As soon as his eyes became accustomed to the dark of the crawl space he saw the resting place of many a cottontail and brought them into focus. Using a .22 short single shot rifle bullet, he fired away. The noise of the shots did not seem to disturb the rabbits in waiting. In short order he shot up to a dozen rabbits, too many to carry. He put them in a burlap bag and dragged them home. Mom had a good recipe for rabbits. She made them taste better than steak.

The Rock Island Railroad ran one, two, or three trains a day near the Banyon house that was the Neff home. Hobos soon placed their sign on a stone fencepost. It meant that "Banyon" was occupied. A steady run of unemployed men came after learning about the Neff kitchen, and mother Neff fed them all. Her specialty was chicken and biscuits. She still yearned for a farm and security. Dad seemed to have come to terms with reality. Dad Neff explained to Jim that the days of free capitalization were over for a homestead, that a bank would not touch you with a ten foot pole. Soon Jim Neff was repairing the automobile. He had helped Roy and Sam before he moved to Banyon Place. He even helped them re-ring the old Dodge engine. Jim and his dad enjoyed the windmill most of all, not because it was an efficient way to lift water from a deep well, but because it reminded them of a place near Ness City. An electric pump did more work with greater reliability. Earl Neff did not like subsistence farming. Competent operators accomplished many tasks others referred to service people, but subsistence merely implied being paid for less than farmers produced. The way Earl Neff saw the farmer was that he was not being paid.

In his first year of high school, Jim had a teacher who seemed to enjoy leading the boy in his studies. One day Mr. Miller promised his students a piece of pie if they could recite all the names of the presidents. True to form, the students tried. Almost every one could rattle off Washington, Adams, Jefferson, Madison and Monroe. Two students got as far as Lincoln, naming the second Adams, Andrew Jackson, Martin van Buren, Harrison, Tyler, Taylor, Fillmore, Pierce and Buchanan. For some reason no one could get past Lincoln. Jim Neff was the exception to the rule. He left Lincoln in the dust, naming Andrew Johnson, U.S. Grant, Rutherford B. Hayes, James Garfield, Chester Arthur, Grover Cleveland, Benjamin Harrison, again, second term, Grover Cleveland, William McKinley, Theodore Roosevelt, William Taft, Woodrow Wilson, Warren Harding, Calvin Coolidge, Herbert Hoover and Franklin D. Roosevelt. The classroom broke into applause.

When the class was over, Mr. Miller caught Jim by the arm. "About that piece of pie." Jim flashed a smile.

"Oh, that's OK. I know you were just kidding."

"No, I wasn't," Mr. Miller said. "Right after the last class, you come back here. We're going down to Hart's Lunch to have that piece of pie." The diner was almost empty when the teacher and his student took a window booth. The waitress slid two glasses of water into place. Before the waitress could ask for an order, Mr. Miller asked, "Apple pie OK?" It was fine with Jim. Mr. Miller ordered a cup of coffee. Jim refused a soda. He did not want to impose on Mr. Miller, so he said, "Just water." There was small talk, the usual questions about Banyon Place. Finally, Mr. Miller got to talking seriously. "Jim, you're a young man with a lot of promise. I don't want you to squander it."

Jim did not answer. He was almost straight A. He had taken a Weschler Bellevue Intelligence Test and scored a neat 147. He knew that Mr. Miller knew this.

"Jim, I know you know more about farming than I do. I've seen your garden plots and I've seen produce for fifty cents a half bushel. My point, fifty cents is a crime. Jim, you need to understand more about farming. You need to understand agriculture."

Jim looked puzzled. His usual smile dropped to somewhere below his chin.

Mr. Miller went on. "The flywheel for all of agriculture is basic storable commodities: wheat, corn, grain sorghum, soybeans, rice; cotton and tobacco included. Don't look to major international operators for commodities prices. A handful of traders own every producer in the world. They own every peasant."

"Aren't farmers free to produce what they want?"

"Not really, not here. What they produce is taken to an auction. It doesn't matter what it costs to produce, the international grain cartel decides what the traders will pay. There's five big ones: Bunge and Born, Continental, Dreyfus, Andre, Tradex. There's also ADM and Cargill. What happens to them happens to dairy and a few hundred lesser crops.

"Mr. Miller, isn't that your place about a mile down the road from Banyon Place?" Jim asked.

"Yes, I have eighty acres. I'm sixty now. I'm still teaching, but I'd rather be operating a farm. I couldn't make it so I went back to school to get teaching credentials. That's why I'm teaching."

Jim Neff, usually a very talkative boy, was quite speechless. "When the founding fathers set up the U.S. of A. as a going concern, they empowered corporations. They usually certified them for ten or twenty years. By the time the frontier was closed, those limits had been erased. The operators became so powerful they came to control the press and to see how little they could pay the farmers."

"The press?" Jim said.

"That's where the funny stuff about too many farmers comes from. I'm going to discuss H.L. Mencken tomorrow. In the 1920s he wrote many pieces, most of them negative to country folks. But there was one writer who hit the nail squarely on the head."

Jim listened in silence. He started to ask, "Who is that?" but before he could speak, Mr. Miller destroyed the silence. He told of a USDA bulletin that explained the detail, a concept he dubbed "parity."

"That bulletin was written by Professor George Warren. It was published in 1921. Warren had been going over the presentation, a varicolored chart stating the price of twenty farm commodities, the weighted averages for thirty-one farm commodities, and the average of all commodities compiled by the Bureau of Farm Statistics."

Mr. Miller paused to express the rest of the equation, how the level of wages and profits in all the sectors furnish the prices that basic storable commodities have to be if depression is to be avoided. When he believed the boy was on track, Mr. Miller continued.

"Warren was summoned to Washington to explain this to the United States Department of Agriculture. This was in 1921, a little before you were born. The USDA published the price index series in March

1922 under the title *Water, Crops, and Minerals.* There was one thing that stuck out like a sore thumb. There was a disparity between the commodities figures and what the farmers were actually getting. There was a George Peek of the Moline Plow Company. He took to the road exploring Professor Warren's fifteen computations. In effect he started a political movement. All he wanted was parity, a fair exchange of values. Mr. Miller wanted Jim to come back to his classroom. "And what can we do?" said Jim.

"Well, the president did manage to get a Triple A bill, an Agricultural Adjustment Act, passed. The Supreme Court found a part of it unconstitutional. The upshot was scuttled commodity prices. They then cut the price of wheat to fifty-five cents a bushel. At this time, prices for wheat, corn, and soybean commodities had been lifted to 75% of parity."

"What is parity?" asked Jim.

"I was afraid you'd ask that. It's a measuring device that tells whether a farm is worth as much as someone pushing a broom in an office building. I used to operate my farm. My Dad raised six kinds of product on that farm and was quite prosperous. After the great war I had to work terribly hard just to stay even. We weren't getting parity."

"Parity," Jim repeated in a quizzical way, as if to seek a reason for it. "I want you to go to the library tonight, see if they have the USDA Bulletin 999, *Prices of Farm Products in the United States.* If they don't have it, we'll write to the Department of Agriculture for a copy." Mr. Miller asked the waitress for a refill of his coffee. Jim again refused a Coke. Mr. Miller decided that his pupil wanted one. He had never had use for the body of knowledge he had assembled in the classroom and not one farmer in a thousand understood the gravity of the subject. But here was a boy who wanted to learn. He proceeded to show the boy how to compute parity, how to select a base period, how to compute exactly what the price of a bushel of wheat needs to be. It was to have an exchange value equal to labor, retail sales, or the value of a postage stamp.

"For now I have to tell you to look up the Fordney-McCumber Tariff Bill and the McNary-Haugen Measure of the 1920s. The dust bowl wasn't the only thing that put us in our present predicament. It wasn't the only thing that caused the farmers to flee the high plains. Jim, farm prices are a political problem and they admit only to a political solution. We're now up to 70% parity."

"Why 70%?" Jim asked.

"I don't think there are too many people in government who understand parity. Government, in effect, takes over commodity agriculture under the rubric of basic storable commodities."

"How did they do this?"

"Under 7 USC 601 and 602, Congress proceeded to rule the basic storable commodities by regulating the trades, monopolies, plantings and international exchange. Farmers think they are free, but they are really in a command economy, and the powers that be have decided that most of them are to go broke."

All this was a bit heady for a boy in his first year of high school. "Mr. Miller, where do you think we are going?" Jim asked.

"I'm not an oracle, but I think we are going to have a war. If I were you, I'd buy some land. As it is, I have eighty acres and I'm too old to make a go of it."

"War!" Jim said. "Are you sure?"

"No, I'm not sure of very much. I do know that the Second World War has started for the Chinese. It is likely to start for Europe pretty soon. The date for the U.S., that's still open. Charles Lindbergh wants the U.S. to keep its agents within its own boundaries. But we're not likely to do that. In fact, another seventy-five years of time will tell you exactly what really happened. Right now you're in the same shape as Will Rogers. You only know what you read in the papers."

Writing in his journal that night, Jim noted, "Mr. Miller said that history is inflationary. Hard times will end when government appropriates enough money to employ every man, woman and child in the U.S. War can cause government to set up that kind of an operation."

A few days later Jim was milking the one surviving cow in residence at Banyon Place. A hobo sidled his way into the milking shed. His eyes were sunken. He had a three day growth of beard. He was thin as a rail. His cap looked like a garage rag, and his overalls and denim suit matched his cap. "Mister," he said, "I'm starving, can I have a cup of that milk?" Jim soon had the cup filled with foaming milk. "Mind if I rest a while and watch you?" Jim did not mind. The hobo rested himself on his hams.

"I've been to California and more. All you see is bindle stiffs and hobos. No employment from sea to sea." The hobo spoke in lengthy sentences and words.

"The only jobs are on WPA and I can't get up the steam to do them. I'm afraid to ride the rails. The railroad detectives are mean as hell." He elaborated while Jim milked. "I used to walk the box cars." The hobo took a stool as if by habit. Jim said, "When did you eat last?"

"Day before yesterday."

"Come with me," Jim said. "I think I can get my mom to give you some eats." The scene was played out again and again as the passage of days became months and 1938 arrived. Small farmers survived as subsistence farmers, government projects employed people, and free traffic on the rails declined.

"There are too many farms," editorialized the public prints, even in the areas where farming was free and important to the communities served by the papers. "Where are the people to go? Out, that's it. When those hinds punch time clocks," wrote H.L. Menken, "we'll all be better off." A peacetime draft was on the drawing boards. It would take quite a few men off the streets and out of the unemployment lines.

13

The letter from H. Dudley Thomas, Esquire came addressed to James
Robert Neff. An identical letter to Eloise Staab Neff was tucked inside
Capper's Weekly and other miscellaneous advertisements and first class
mail. The letter told of the will of Jacob Alexander Staab, the father
of Eloise Staab and grandfather of James Robert Neff. The recipient
was referred to as a young man of great expectations. Enclosed was the
obituary of Xander Staab who passed away at age 103, and disposed of
his earthly assets under Kansas law with H. Dudley Thomas, attorney
of record, and Mathilda Staab, spinster, executrix. The newspaper told
of that legend of a man who had survived service in the tsar's army
and Kansas dusters, whose life mercifully seemed to be over, who at the
time of his death was recognized as a successful line breeding operator,
whose bulls named Xanthippus and Pericles had been written up in
Hereford Journal, and who was also recognized as a successful seed
stock operator.

The point of the letter was the will. Xander gave most of his assets
to his daughter in Vermont. He left $10,000 to Eloise Neff, cash money.
Next, he thanked Jimmy Neff for his companionship, a worthy student
of history, geography, literature and line breeding. The will required
the executrix and the attorney of record to cooperate with fellow beef
cattle producer, Jamie Xavier Stitz, for the purpose of shipping four
cows, settled for spring delivery, and a son of the Xanthippus blood line
to James Robert Neff. The will directed that the shipment be handled
by the Jamie Stitz Cartage Company, an overnight stop to be made at
the Carter Hereford ranch, near Cunningham, Kansas for resting, feed
and water. Xander further provided that James Robert Neff receive
the assistance of rancher Art Cobb of Chanute, Kansas, so that in
the fullness of time James Robert Neff would be able to proceed with
the expansion of his line breeding development and comply with the

great expectations that diligence and heritage would account for. Jim started the countdown on when he could expect his calves. Dinner table conversation became heated. Eloise Neff asserted herself as never before. The legacy was hers, she said, calves excluded. She was tired of being homeless, always at loose ends, always being required to move at a moment's notice. With $10,000 she could buy a "home of her own," even a bit of land! Earl Mathew Neff did not argue. He had an income, around $2,000 a year, but this was never enough to buy property, even a goat farm. He did not like working at the cement plant, but jobs were so rare he dared not hope for anything else.

When disposition of the Xander Staab estate was finally made, Eloise learned that Mathilda had received almost twice as much as her own legacy. Xander's son was left with a dollar. Eloise never quite learned why Xander and her brother Aden had become estranged. Local rumor had it that son Aden Staab kept animals in inhumane pens, fed them high carbohydrate feeds, required the animals to consume great doses of bicarbonate of soda to battle acidity, and ridiculed the line breeding that Xander championed. Two days after Eloise received her check, a well polished Olds with two side mounts pulled into the Banyon house drive. It was Dr. Podolinsky, arriving late on a Saturday. Jim met the doctor, opened his door, and took his offered hand.

"Hello, Jimmy. Your parents home?"

They were, and Jim ushered the physician into the big dining room. The doctor surveyed the room. It needed paint. Otherwise the place was in good shape for a thirty-nine year old house. Some damage from vandals was still evident. The doctor wanted to walk through the house. Eloise led the way. Caretakers Neff had a modest amount of furniture. They had painted the part of the house being used and scrubbed the rest squeaky clean. The doctor calculated the costs required to make such a place saleable in a county where little had been sold in ten years. As far as he knew, only one new unit had been built during that same period. When the touring group returned to the kitchen, Dr. Podolinsky said, "There are ten acres. If you buy the house, I'll sell the land for $15 an acre."

Eloise did her calculation. $150 for ten contiguous acres was not bad. A lot of land was selling for $12 an acre, but $15 was not that far out of line. The doctor continued. "I offer you the rest of the property for $4,000."

"It would take quite a bit more to fix it up," Eloise said. "I suppose you're right. If you hadn't put in that septic system." The doctor stopped talking. He did not want to undo the only sales prospect he had had in five years. As city sanitation engineer, he had decreed the closing down of outhouses some time back. This property was in the county. If it was located inside the city, he was not sure he would not order it torn down. Vandals had raised hell with the upper floor. Yet the structure was sound. Its slate roof would shed rain until the next ice age.

"All right," he said, "$3,500 for land and buildings. Cash deal. No mortgage. I'll furnish the abstract and quit claim deed." Jim noticed that his mom could hardly restrain herself. She looked at Dad and gave him a perceptible nod.

"I'll have a banker's check as soon as you have the papers. All taxes have to be paid."

The doctor agreed. He was relieved that this white elephant was off his hands. It was really found money, he reasoned, because he figured he would never be able to sell a place so out of touch with the community. Mom lost little time writing the boys. Roy's postcards came from Needles, California, where the army was training soldiers and testing equipment. J. Samuel wrote home from Los Angeles. She sent regular letters to them, but their responses told her that they had become distant from the family. The visits that had punctuated the weeks and months since the exodus from the dust bowl would be no more.

Jim also read the situation. He realized that he was on his own, seeing to it that his animals had plenty of grass. He knew he would not overgraze his ten acres. He calculated that for two months, grazing might be impossible. This meant he had to consider storing alfalfa hay and figure out proper placement of water tanks. He did not want his animals drinking muddy creek and pond water.

Jim carried the news of his good fortune to Mr. Miller, his history teacher, who promptly offered Jim the use of his eighty acres for grazing, at very cheap rent, of course. Mr. Miller did not do much with it except mow it anyway. He was nearing mandatory retirement age and was looking to sell off his acres, in any case. All he really wanted was peace and the right to live in the parklike atmosphere that his small farm afforded.

Jim became obsessed with pastures, native grasses, virgin grasses, seeded grasses, and grass recovered by nature herself.

Tucked into a book on soils, Xander left behind a writing that was not a letter and it was not an essay. If anything, it was a bit of homely advice by which, tongue in cheek, he hoped to get Jim to see what he looked at. "Too many farmers pick up very bad advice at coffee houses. If you look carefully, you'll see and hear how they lose money quite independently of what public policy does to them."

"Jimmy, you'll see how men plan their breeding so that calves arrive well before the arrival of new spring grass. They want the calves half grown by the time forage arrives.

"I once wrote a poem:

Grass all a blight.

A man is a fool if he don't see the light.

Here's my take on this, dear brother,

A fool on one end, an ass on the other."

"As you go around Allen County, you'll see pastures burned out. If the rains come, they may have a crop of weeds. All this because the fools figure they can't carry grass over till next year. What they do is end up buying inputs, nostrums that are supposed to fatten cattle on Jimson weed and tree bark. The trade magazines are full of ads for nostrums whispered by a dying monk to a titled traveler. Phooey!"

"What do you see when a rancher feeds in the same place all the time? Ruined soil, pollution in the drainage landscape."

"Some of your neighbors will want to plant grass every year, like a wheat farmer. This ensures that input costs will go up."

Xander went on for ten pages in his classic cursive. At the end of the missive, Jim realized that the old man was only half finished. It was his last testament. Jim read and re read Xander's admonitions not to go heavy in equipment, not to impress the neighbors or squander his birthright buying expensive pickers or alligator boots.

As Jim examined the library brought by Stitz Cartage when his pregnant animals were delivered, he found other papers that were a distillation of Xander's wisdom. Jim realized that it would take dozens of readings to enable absorption.

Jim graduated from high school in the spring of 1941. By then he had become a farmer entrepreneur. He bought five calves at an auction using borrowed money from Mom and a small amount of credit from the Iola State Bank. He enlarged his pasture resources at twelve dollars an acre, always hunting acres with some forty species of grass, forbs, and legumes. He found forty acres contiguous to Banyon Place on which row crops had failed. Fencing was cheap. Using electric wire, he allowed animals into the field for grazing. A handful of classmates went off to college. Most did not. Jim enrolled in junior college with a schedule of morning classes. Home at noon, he tended to pasture changes and chores that required half an hour before working his day job at S.H. Kress Company, which hired him in the stock room. Few of his classmates found work, and this frustration piled up like cord wood. It was during late summer of 1941 that Jim exhibited a measure of raw courage. There was a bandstand in the northwest corner of the town square. Young people assembled there to enjoy band music and to dance on a makeshift wooden platform east of the stand. On warm summer evenings, it was all clean fun. Only rarely was there as much as a hip flask in evidence. Most years and months came and went without any rumble or incident.

Lately, a hulk of a boy from near Fort Scott had made his presence felt. Jim heard about one Whitey Smith who made very inappropriate remarks in the presence of young men escorting their dates. Whitey was as snow white as Mount Kilimanjaro, round faced, and at least thirty pounds heavier than his height called for. He was muscular, "strong as an ox" was the usual description. "Hey sweetheart, why don't you drop that pansy and come with a real man?" Those who did not cower and retreat were mauled badly by this street fighter.

Jim did not have much time for friend making, but one such was a lad named Bill Earp. Bill was five foot five, weighed 130 pounds, and knew that he had no chance at all tangling with Whitey the hulk. Bill could out walk and outrun Whitey, and probably outperform him in most tests of endurance, but he could not deal with him as a brawler.

"I'll go with you," Jim Neff said. "I don't think he'll bother us." Jim had in mind the last boxing tournament at Pittsburg. He remembered the character named Whitey, and he knew of his reputation. He also knew that Whitey did not have the sand to get into the squared circle.

The boys discussed Jim's calf project half the night, and the young lady did not mind dancing with each of them during alternate numbers. The purpose of the double outing with one girl was almost forgotten when Whitey turned to muscle in on young Earp.

"Get out of the way!" he commanded. "Let a real man have the floor." Earp objected and received a smashing blow to the temple. With this, Jim was on his feet. He took the arm of the young lady and helped Bill Earp to his feet.

Jim had always been slow to anger. Some teachers detected in him an indifference, definitely a lack of outrage in a world that asked for, indeed demanded, outrage. Some said, "Still water runs deep." If so, it came to the surface when Jim looked in the face of the bully.

"I'm offended," he said. "I'm as offended as I would be if you did that to me."

"Mind your own business," Whitey ordered, adding emphasis by delivering a round house punch to Jim Neff's ribs. It was the only blow Whitey was allowed to land.

Jim did not like to fight without gloves, but he had no option. He assumed the stance that had made him the high school champion for southeast Kansas. "Stand still, damn you!" shouted Whitey. As he spoke, he took a left jab to the mouth and two stiff rights to the left side of his head. Blood gushed from his cut lips. A left to the jaw followed and two quick jabs landed flat on Whitey's face. Whitey staggered. Jim Neff danced, side stepping wild uppercuts, each time answering with three, four, five powerful jabs above the shoulders. Whitey could not see. He stumbled like an ox, then went down. He vomited.

"You damn dust bowl papist you and your dad think you know . . ." He did not finish. With that, Jim came back and gave him a soft kick in the butt. "Don't you ever make fun of my dad," he said in a voice only the nearest could hear, "or the next time I won't be merciful."

"Sometimes you have to fight," Jim said apologetically, and with that the conversation returned to Jim's theory about pastures. He explained about a 1938 movie he had seen called *Honky Tonk at the Pic Theater*, starring Clark Gable. In it, a character named Candy Johnson (Gable) was shaking down the local businessmen. Some of Candy's henchmen told their boss that the natives were getting restless. If care was not taken, some of them might go to the state capital, and this would bring out the gendarmes. Clark (Candy) responded, "Don't worry! Tell them to add it to the price of the beans."

"I think that's what Mr. Miller meant about the difference between farming and agriculture."

"That guy was a real economist," said Bill. "Say, Jim, why don't you go down to the carnival next week? You could take any of those bozos. You know they promised $50 if you win"

"Yeah," Jim cut in, "and nothing but shame and abuse if you lose. No, thanks, I have no intention of spending my life fighting. If I hit anyone, there'll be a doggone good reason."

A Stitz Cartage truck drove onto the Neff place in mid-September that year. The four pregnant cows provided by Xander Staab's will were unloaded and placed in their own paddock with grass eight inches high. Jim remembered Xander's several buffalo. Ruminant animals do not get sick if they're kept on grass. Corn silage, alfalfa hay, forbs, manufactured feeds, dirty drinking water, and running out of the green stuff all caused immunity to decrease and harmful organisms to increase. Fabricated feeds are a crutch, he remembered hearing.

Jim plotted grazing areas with the dedication of a chess player moving rooks, castles, and queens. He went over the program with his dad. "Dad, I don't have the expenses that go along with raising row crops. Except for fencing, I don't expect many expenses. If I do have any, well, they'll just have to be added to the price of the beans."

The older man looked at the youth quizzically. Jim went on, "Those calves are special. I'm not going to spend money for fancy supplements. I want four calves next spring and double that a year later, maybe! If they're female, the line will double by 1943. If I get a bull, he'll be a son of Pericles. In the meantime, I'll hustle the sales and keep going. Dad, you'll see, I'm going to have the finest seed stock outfit in Kansas."

Jim had one more trick up his sleeve. A little bulldozer time would enable the construction of a pond for the type of alfalfa irrigation Xander had recommended. Town lawns were sprinkled, but no one had ever seen any pasture irrigated before. By late October, he expected to have square bales of alfalfa hay. If snow lasted very long, his animals would have to have feed. It was the key to maintaining health and reproduction and warding off a long list of diseases that support veterinarians and starve farmers. Shortly after escorting his mother to mass on Sunday, December 7, 1941, Jim turned on the radio. The Japanese had bombed Pearl Harbor. Dad caught up with Jim just as he was stripping the last of the milk from the old Guernsey.

"How's she holding up, Jim?"

"Well, for a thirteen year old cow with eleven calves to her credit, first rate!"

"Yes, I guess we're at the end of an era. We sure as hell don't need both beef and dairy cows. With just mother and me and one boy ready to be drafted, I don't know."

Jim said, "I guess not, but those two beef cows from Xander's will are still coming."

"I want to talk to you about that."

"Dad, I know I'll be drafted."

"Don't worry, son. I'll maintain them until you get back."

"How about serviced?"

"That's arranged, thanks to Xander. There'll be calves and we'll keep them all."

"I've got the map inside. There's enough grass to feed fifty head."

"What about the land?" asked Dad. "Some of it is virgin pasture, some tame prairie. You get overworked, you'll have to hire help." It was true. People were off to jobs at the Sunflower Ordnance Depot, and whole families abandoned the land for work in Kansas City and Wichita and Parsons.

"Jim, I'm not worried about feeding the cattle. The problem is that wheat and corn are getting a price, and I'm out of it. We're going to get pretty cash strapped feeding cows with no sales planned."

Jim countered. "I've worked it out." He had. He had instruments for deferred payout and leases deferred for as long as he was in the service. Fallow land could be had for a pittance as long as he did not grow row crops, and payments for land he had purchased were suspended for as long as he was serving in the military. He had picked up some of this insight from his dad, even more from other men around town, one a shop owner. "Son, don't come around a dump like this," the only Jew in town told him.

Jim did not listen. He liked the man because he told stories about old timers who could not discipline themselves, who acted like farmers by begging for someone to take their product off their hands at less than rock bottom wholesale prices. It was exactly the way Clark Gable put it in *Honky Tonk*. Everything has to be added to the price of the beans. "Jim, this isn't what I wanted to talk to you about," Dad said. "Son, what do you really think of me?"

Jim hesitated. Actually, Dad had not been much of a provider, but dust storms and bad luck had gotten in the way. He had never been violent or drunk, and as far as he could see, Dad was a wonderful man. Jim simply said, "I love you, Dad."

"That's the problem. You're so much an altar boy, I worry about you in the army. You worship your brothers and sisters, and your mother. What do you really know about Mother?"

In all his eighteen years Jim had never expected such a question. He remained silent.

"I'll tell you about your mother. We grew up together, and she fell in love with me. She really did. She told just about everyone who would listen that if she couldn't marry Earl Neff, she'd never marry, she'd go into a convent."

"Do you believe that?"

"No. I love her. Oh, maybe not in terms of bells and whistles, but I told her, now don't go getting any ideas about marrying me. She just smiled. Don't get me wrong. She's been the best wife a man could have. If I had one criticism, I'd have to say that she was hit in the belt with a prayer book."

"She does pray a lot."

"Good God, she wears out rosaries. She stayed on Joe Sam's case so long he went off to a seminary. I knew it wouldn't wash, and after he got his belly full, he stepped out, and he's kept his distance ever since." Jim started to say something. He had finished milking by now, so he set the pail down. He knew Dad was on a roll, a talking roll. Usually it took a cable and winch to pull a few words out of him. Jim said to himself, "I want to hear this out."

"So, Joe Sam keeps his distance. Oh, he'll help the family. He paid for that boxcar to move us out of the dust bowl. I said I'd pay him back, but he knows and I know it will never happen. Jim, I don't think you even know your older sisters, Amanda and Catherine. Your mother hustled them out to a convent when they were young girls, younger than you are. They've turned distant, and there isn't a darn thing they can do about it. They write letters that say nothing, I suppose some all seeing eye oversees what they write."

"Do you blame Mother?"

"No, she's a good wife. She sews, cleans, keeps house, sees to the education of the children. No, I have no complaint. She's too good to be denied my deepest respect and love."

Jim furrowed his brow with genuine puzzlement. Just as he started to make some minor comment, Dad lapsed into German. *"Di haldes uns fer Nara!"* he said.

Jim fished for the words. *They're making fools of us!* "Who do you mean?"

Earl let that pass. "Look, son, I'm not super holy, you know that. You're going to be thrown in with all sorts, WASPs, greasers, wops, spics." Then he hesitated, realizing that Jim probably did not know what even one of those words meant. Earl changed the subject. "If you play cards, three out of five will be cheating."

"I don't play cards."

"You will."

Jim did not know how his dad could be so certain. "Always look everyone in the eye. If you run into a player with an off colored eye, he's probably wearing a ruby."

"What's a ruby?"

"An infrared contact lens. That fellow can read the invisible ink on the back of cards."

There was a whole roster of do's and don'ts. "Don't expect others to be educated. Don't expect too much of your buddies. They have their own problems. The only absolute friend you have is the dollar in your pocket."

Had Dad been drinking? No, Dad never drank. There was something else about Earl Neff. He was a good man, but there was also a streak of mischief. Yes, even cynical mischief in him. He had always kept these impulses in check and never spoke of them. Besides, he knew there was no use at all telling anyone anything. You might as well tell it to a fencepost, he often observed. Jim was different. He asked for information and he listened, and he liked to soak in the wisdom of his elders. You can not let a boy like that go off into the military with illusions of grandeur and the idea that there is glory in ritual death.

God, how he hated war, this dust bowl farmer. He had hated it ever since he had caught a lungful of chlorine gas from a rail car spill. His forefathers had left the lower Volga because of militarism. Before that, they had left Germany in 1763 because of the culture of death. On the killing fields the chore was messy, but when the bodies came home, oh, they came home, alright! They were nested and encased in a jewelry box called a coffin, flags were flown, very clean rifles in the hands of very clean boys firing volleys over very green grass, the raw soil of which was hidden by a very green artificial carpet. And the mother of that boy could hang a very clean gold star in her window that announced to neighbors and the world alike that her boy had given his life for freedom.

Dad Neff did not say all this, but he felt it, and Jim, ever the listener, listened.

"Have you ever gone to a war?" Dad asked.

Jim knew what he meant. He was embarrassed. "No," he said, "not that way. You know most of the duties I've had."

"Well, you probably know I never extract promises. But I want one now."

"What promise?"

"I don't give a damn if you obey officers. Use your common sense. But that's not the promise I want." After a long pause, the boy's father continued, "Don't go into whorehouses. If you have to, hang your thing in a bowl of cold water, but don't pollute yourself." He paused again.

"They'll teach you to kill people and destroy property. Imagine that! The most honored profession! Compared to the military, the farmer is just a clod." There was a tone of bitterness in that statement. It seemed to say to Jim that all does not turn out well just because you wish it. You have to factor some of the devil's darkness into the equation of life and death. Jim had never heard his dad talk so much or so openly. He had never heard him express his knowledge of agriculture as opposed to farming. "My father and mother purchased an eighty acre farm in 1912. They raised a big family on those eighty acres. Pa sent all but one of us off to school. Nowadays, you can't make a living on 500 acres, not row cropping. I don't understand why. So here comes along the war. I could make out with the prices you get nowadays, but I can't put in a crop. You don't want to destroy your grass, and I'm not going to argue with you."

"Dad, I'm going to create a seed stock operation. I hope to raise and sell prize bulls. Everybody is going to sell their beef cows. I don't want to do that. I want as many calves as the cows can drop. I'll be getting herd calves. With grass, the costs will be low. We won't need farming machinery. Grass and water and some alfalfa hay!"

Jim went on with the insight he had assembled from old Xander and now from a local Hereford breeder.

"This war won't last forever," he concluded.

A few months later, in mid 1942, Jim concluded that the war would indeed last forever.

14

High school graduate James Robert Neff and his dad did not know that agriculture was no longer free. They did not understand that free enterprise had passed from the scene with the passage of 7 USC 601 and 602, the "taking" statutes that presumed to regulate agriculture as a public utility. Men wise beyond their years and reputations reasoned that railroads and industry and traders and bankers had assembled so much clout that they routinely busted farmers by overcharging for services and underpaying for products. In the halls of Congress they voted to make the farm a public utility. They did this in a manner not one farmer in a thousand understood. By regulating the basic storable commodities; wheat, corn, grain sorghum, oats, rye, barley, soybeans, cotton and tobacco grown on about 80% of the harvested acres, the public utility would create the economic ocean on which all of farming sailed. If the storable commodity trade rose, so did the little riverboats called specialty crops, vegetables, nuts, fruits, meat protein production, and dairy. Caught up in the miracle of production, James Robert Neff and his dad did not know and, not knowing, did not care. This regulation of the agricultural public utility was to rely on acreage and crop controls, on subsidy payments when necessary, on control of monopolies, and on management of international trade that often adversely affected agriculture.

The wise men of Washington desperately wanted to stay the exodus from the farms during the war, and men who perceived themselves to be even wiser crafted a medium that merely regulated the flow, so that it did not proceed too fast or too slow to bring on open revolt. The dust bowlers thought it was dusters that drove them out of farming. The Iowa victim of drought thought it was lack of rain. Elsewhere it was said to be overproduction.

By the time young Jim graduated from high school, he had read all of Willa Cather and Mark Twain, Will Durant's book, *Our Oriental Heritage,* and American novels too numerous to catalog. He had not encountered the post Civil War Grange, or the Alliance for Progress that hung horse thieves, or any of the four hundred or more farm organizations characterized as national that had already passed from the mind and memory of men. Because of this, he missed out on the Populist movement that once upon a time installed a third party governor in Kansas and put enough hell raisers into Congress to bring on Cheney-Stokes palpitations in the chests of the establishment. Neither Jim nor his dad nor his mom understood that, once out of farming, the dismissed were not to go back except as time clock punchers. We would all be better off, wrote the smart aleck H.L. Mencken, if the hinds drew a paycheck and the industrialists operated the hog and cattle pens, in such words, or words to that effect. The really bright people decided that since there were too many farmers, efficiency would decide who stays. The utility program of the 1930s computed parity in terms of an average.

Those above the average could actually make a profit if they invoked the best technology, the best machinery, the best fertilizer. Those who fell below the average consumed their capital until they finally joined others on the road or disappeared as stoop labor on the plantations of great land holders, who were known as strong hands.

For ten years the unemployed and underemployed filled the boxcars and soup lines. They could only dream of a plot for a garden, and they knew to the depth of their souls that they would not go back. Jim did not know this, nor could he have a real appreciation of how Napoleon had solved his unemployment problem by putting the unemployed and underemployed into uniforms and sending them off to the killing fields to keep them from starving.

Now the killing fields were beckoning again. Mr. Miller, Jim's old history teacher, reminded him that "in about seventy-five years we'll know what really happened." In the meantime, "The hand that held the dagger stuck it into its neighbor's back." It was the duty of every patriotic American to do his or her damndest for the country.

"Why aren't you in the army?" was the snide greeting young men encountered within hours after the radio brought news of Pearl Harbor.

This was especially true for any boy who had graduated from high school.

Jim registered for the draft exactly as required by law, and the draft board, usually a seventy-year-old man and a seventeen-year-old girl, filled quotas with an efficiency unknown to settled rural communities. "Settled" meaning that the social order was well established, that certain elements had best be extended the opportunity of deferment before less essential persons were called to duty. Men in the upper age bracket considered draftable were tapped first, before they reached the safety of the age cutoff.

Jim Neff kept an excited eye on two deadlines: one the arrival of the mail, and the second an expected cartage delivery with Xander Staab's prize bull aboard. The cows had already dropped their calves in the spring. The arrival of his legacy cows had served up an inventory of registration forms for young Neff. He was already thinking in terms of ownership. He had paced off the paddocks needed for the pregnant cows and the son of Pericles the bull. He was, indeed, a young man with great expectations. He did not hang around the pool halls. He was all business, and now his future was being shelved. He fantasized leaving a homestead well beyond the reach of the army, but he realized there was no such place. He could not run or dodge the draft. That was beneath his dignity.

Grandpa Xander had taught him well, but Xander's limited vision did not appreciate the resolve of wise men and extra wise men. His lessons were about conformation of horse flesh as taught by his grandfather and as observed by Kirghiz tribesmen, about breeder suppliers of herd bulls, about soil management. Xander did not appreciate the sheer political genius behind the utility status of all of agriculture, nor could he have told Jim anything about what a major war would do. The puzzlement was ever greater because war for a time set aside the industrial model that had reigned so adroitly during a solid decade of defeat.

A day before December 7, 1941, the U.S. and its rural component was the most peaceful nation on earth. A day after December 7, 1941, the U.S. and its rural component had become the most warlike nation on earth. The President asked Congress for an appropriation of $200 billion to fight the first year of the war. That was enough money to hire every man, woman and child in the United States at then prevailing wages. The Great Depression was officially declared over.

The wise men of Washington had crafted a program to achieve 70% of parity for basic storable commodities. Within a month or two after Pearl Harbor, that goal was raised to one 100% of parity. It was correctly reasoned that the political game of transferring all of agriculture into a few strong hands had to be put on hold for the duration. A faltering food supply or a faltering economy might bring on bankruptcy in the middle of the war and cause the great democracy to lose the war.

Mr. Miller came by while Jim was moving his cows into a fresh paddock. He had computed the growth of grass and the amount needed by each animal for maintenance of mother and calf.

"They've passed a Stabilization Bill," Mr. Miller said. "This means that basic storable commodities from 80 to 82% of the harvested acres will get 100% of parity at the market."

"How are they going to do that?" Jim asked.

"Well, as the commodities go into trade channels, they'll have to be paid for at parity at the tailgate or elevator."

"What if they won't pay it?"

"Then the wheat or corn or whatever goes into storage. Don't worry!

They'll have to pay!"

"What about red meat?"

"It'll adjust to the reality of the situation," Mr. Miller said. "I think a lot of people will be eating meat instead of beans. Also, there's an army that has to be fed."

Jim and his dad surveyed the situation. They had more land in pasture than even two dozen cattle would require. Some of it ought to be planted in corn or oats, but how do you plant without machinery? The few pieces of machinery freighted east from Ness County had been sold for scrap iron during the bad years. Even with Mom's legacy, there was not enough money to buy a plow or harrow. The Neffs had not even installed a telephone, money was that tight.

"No," Jim said. "I think we'll just keep the grass. Maybe have a custom man put up the hay."

It has been said that the most intense human pleasure is the orgasm. Not so! For a young man it is achieved when he realizes a dream on

131

target, swinging a bat, sailing on the ocean, being allowed to run the throttle of a locomotive.

He had experienced that sensation when the Stitz Cartage truck arrived with four pregnant cows. Stitz had complied with Xander's orders, regularly watering and resting the animals in transit. Jim relived that day at least several times a week, each step of the procedure etched into his memory with a recall so detailed that he could dwell on it during the day and dream about it at night.

"The old man must have liked that kid," Stitz told the estate lawyer. "I've never seen five finer animals."

"I never cease to be surprised," answered the lawyer. The registration papers had been signed. To Jim they were like gilt edged bonds.

Even while the animals were being unloaded, young men were being drafted for a peacetime army. The day after Pearl Harbor a military career was a certainty. Jim and Dad and Mom worked out the details; water, feed and observation. With Dad working at the cement plant, Mom knew it would fall to her to nurse the animals and deliver calves.

It was the arrival of the bull, son of Pericles, that attracted most attention. Xander had created this genetically superior bull via his program of line breeding. "Fat is energy," old Xander once said. "Energy causes cows to get pregnant. The same goes for bulls."

Xander explained as much and as often as he believed the boy could assimilate the information. "In the seed stock business, low maintenance and high fertility go hand in hand."

Jim translated this knowledge into a report he made in one of his classes. "Reproduction is more important than price. A one percent move in the reproduction rate is twice as important as an increase in price."

That was Xander's conclusion. The reproduction rate was 50% of the cow-calf operation.

Jim spent hours observing his animals. He no longer worked for Doc Podolinsky, even occasionally, because the buggy pony had been retired to pasture, but he talked the physician into coming around for a look at the animals and pastures.

"That's a pretty big house for two people," observed the doctor.

"We've closed off the top floor," Jim told the doctor. "It's a sound structure, lots of vandal damage. One day I'll refurbish it."

132

"It'll take a lot of money." The doctor, now in his seventies, stood erect, no extra fat on him, all muscle, and discipline evident in his Polish countenance. Jim asked the doctor about the significance of a navel cord. Old Xander said if there was no navel cord on a new calf, it signaled health problems. Jim also had questions about pinkeye and retained placentas. After a while, Dr. Podolinsky said, "Jim, I'm out of my element. I don't know the significance of long hair on cattle. I don't know what it means in human health."

As soon as he graduated, Jim volunteered for the army, preempting the draft. The spirit of the time took hold of him quite early when news filtered in about Bataan and Corregidor. Here were Americans fighting for peace and high ideals, and the crafty Nip was committing all sorts of atrocities. If he had any fears, they were set aside. He was in excellent physical condition. He now stood at five feet, eight inches, weighed 140 pounds, and exhibited not one pound of fat. His light colored hair still danced like a choreographed troop of fairies atop his amply populated head. He read about soldiers standing in formation for an hour, and practiced to see if he could take it. It was a cup of tea. Jim tried push ups, chin ups, mile running. There was nothing the army could dish out that he could not take.

It had to be. The Nip and the Kraut had to be put down. Jim promised to send home some of his pay for maintenance of the animals. A new glow of life came to Mom and Dad.

The usual penny postcards arrived from Roy. He wrote, "For God's sake, delay going into the service as long as possible!" He was now in Louisiana on training maneuvers. The whole outfit, it was believed, was headed for the European theater. Roy drove a truck, then a tank. The military life seemed to agree with him. For the first time in his life he had friends, buddies, men who would risk their lives for him, as he would risk his for them. Before the peacetime draft, he had never found employment, and the farm could not support him with any dignity. This left a hidden scar. Still, his postcards tried to protect his younger brother. "You silly kid, this is no picnic! Stay home!" On the day that Jim signed up, Mom and Dad realized that the family was gone. J. Samuel chided Jim in long letters for trying to get back into farming. By degrees, J. Samuel had lost his interest in agriculture. Where once he had computed the shortage of income for Kansas because farmers were not getting paid for as much as they produced, he now dismissed farming as work for down and outers. He might get Jim on in the hotel management program after the war, so why attempt this fool business of starting a cow herd?

The fact was that Earl Neff now had a better grasp of what was guiding J. Samuel with all his education.

The basic storable commodities from 80% to 82% of the harvested acres would draw a full parity price for the duration of the war plus two years. The mechanism for this management of the great utility was simple in the extreme. If the traders did not pay the mandated price, the product would go into storage and the farmer would get paid. The cost for this program was projected to be, and turned out to be, absolute zero. With the flywheel and balance wheel of America's largest industry paid at least as well as common labor, production would keep coming and national security was certain, leaving the nation free to fight the war.

The parity floor, Earl Neff understood, was created by what was happening in transportation, factory, and service occupations. All the Stabilization Act did was to enable agriculture to recover cost, just like the power plant on the Neosho River.

Storage did not become necessary. The war effort required all the grain, all the red meat, all the fruits and vegetables that the great agricultural industry was capable of producing. Import invasion was no longer capable of scuttling farm prices because German submarines inhibited the debilitating traffic that usually undercut the wheat, corn, oats, rye, all commodities producers.

"Ruthless culling, Dad. Cull and sell the sale barn cattle and their offspring. Don't sell the dams Grandpa gave me," Jim counseled his dad. "Don't sell the calves from the four. Don't sell bull calves. I have a hunch we'll have prize bulls. If you have to sell any of them, get a premium as sires. I think Son of Pericles is going to be our star performer." Jim made the rounds in town before he departed for Leavenworth. He had never partied, had not even followed sports. Except for boxing, he had never been much interested in sports. Some called him a loner. "Not so," said Mom. "He's just a little shy." Before he boarded the bus to leave, Mom gave him her blessing. She added, "Remember, keep your agreements and stay out of other people's business."

15

As he approached the protected gate at Fort Leavenworth, it came to the youth how provincial he really was. He had never been out of the state of Kansas in his life. Except for the move out of the Ness County house, he had not been out of Allen County. He had watched the war on the silver screen, worked harder than ever before setting fence posts, exercised by sparring in the ring at school, and consecrated himself for the rigors of army life. He knew nothing about the army, about the reception he would get "in cold nakedness," he wrote in his notebook diary, where shots were delivered, people issued shoes and clothes, where a barracks chief screamed everyone into each new day at 5 a.m., or "0500" military time.

James Robert Neff met more new people in a few days than he had met in all his life, and a few he got to know more than superficially, like The Oracle. The Oracle had a name, Spangler Arlington Drew, but he answered only to The Oracle or Oracle. He bunked next to Jim, now Jimbo, and took the upper bunk on the Pullman that took the new recruits to "Somewhere." "I specialize in information," The Oracle told Jim. "Jimbo, if it's going to happen, I know." The Oracle knew. When others were predicting a destination in Texas, Oracle answered to all who would listen that they were going to California, two days journey, so be prepared. Before lunch was served Oracle named the contents of the lunch box. When the mess sergeant ordered a collection for the cooks, Oracle blew the sergeant out of the water. "It's quite illegal," he pointed out. He was a sleuth, this pseudo clairvoyant. In fact, he had no ESP, he just knew how to read documents upside down, pull a card from a deck, and how to cozy up to orderly personnel, trading know how for information. The Oracle recruited the second, third and fourth players for euchre and poker. Number two was a lad named Michael Foy, ostensibly a shirttail relative of the vaudeville actor, Eddie Foy. Number three was a boy from the Ozarks who liked to play the role of a rebel, but was really quite erudite, a genius when it came to handling a deck of cards. His name was Yancy, Belton Yancy. In poker he always asked what beat out what. "He's cool as a snake. He'd swindle a Jap out of his sake ration." Number four to orbit The Oracle was Allen Smithcors, a six footer who towered over Foy the way the Eiffel Tower loomed over Paris.

It became Jim's role to sit in if one of the foursome needed rest. They traveled for days on the railroad cars arriving at Camp Roberts, and they ended up on the second floor of the barracks filled with basic trainees. Up front, Jim decided not to write a dairy. He wrote letters instead and told Mom to save them.

The days were hot and the nights were cold and morning came so fast that the day's training prompted Jim to hit the sack two hours before "lights out."

"Day after tomorrow," noted The Oracle, "the weather will call for only boots with sox and raincoats."

"You're kidding," Jim said.

"Nope. It's short arm inspection."

"What's that?" came the refrain from Foy and Smithcors in unison. "The medics will require you to prepare your penis for inspection. If you have a chancre, you're out of here. If you're not circumcised, you'll have an operation. Right, Jimbo?"

At first, Jim bought into the tricks played on him, but in less than a week he discovered that often The Oracle was lying. The Oracle had a slight twitch of his mouth when a practical joke or a whopper was coming. Basic training was full of excitement and agony, depending on the recruit.

Jim's score on the AGCT, Army General Classification Test, was some 20 points above the average, according to the orderly room sergeant. This information went into his record. After a day of basic training, Jim asked The Oracle, "What have they got scheduled, and how long?" The information man was ready. He had searched the orderly room and struck up conversations with men about to complete the course.

"Jimbo, it ain't pretty. Say goodbye to sleeping late. My friend, you're about to become acquainted with Highway 101 halfway between Los Angeles and San Francisco. You're destined to walk these barren hills."

"I don't mind walking," Jim said. "But I hate to throw a horse out of work."

"Oh, my dear child," The Oracle said. "Dismiss Paso Robles and San Miguel from your dreams. Think of the fifty-eight square miles of cactus plants you'll get to know. Think of all the glorious perils we'll face, my boy, in the next fourteen weeks of life. Jimbo, you're about to cross the grand elusive nothing. Almost before breakfast, we'll work out. Unfortunately, my friend, we're the infantry and we'll parade the roads, the hills, the beaches, the obstacle courses. God, that's what bothers me. We'll survive for an all expense paid trip to the South Pacific and Mr. Japanese."

There was not much time for cards. But Sundays permitted a round or two, leaving at least a half a day to play cards. Private Yancy was the first to go broke. By the time basic training was over, Private Foy was also broke. By the time Jim and the survivors of training boarded a boat at Fort Ord, a new cast of characters became associates of The Oracle. Jim dropped out. He preferred to stand at the rail most of the day and sleep on the deck most of the night. As the ship pulled into Brisbane, Australia, the beauty of the beach beckoned.

Jim was glad to leave the stench of the sleeping quarters once they had landed.

Disappointment presented itself when The Oracle delivered word that the replacement recruits would bunk in a horse racetrack, possibly a week or more. The sheer boredom of daily dry fire, closed order drills, standing still in parade was trumped by restriction to a horse track. When the order came to board a narrow gauge train for Rockhampton, a new level of discomfort reared its ugly head. Seats on the train were planks. Uncomfortable nights of plank travel allowed so little sleep the recruits went numb. Jim endured the ordeal in silence.

Rockhampton, Australia was a gigantic, staggering combination of troops kept busy with more drills, more classes, more of everything the military could conjure up as it led to official troop deployment for the Pacific Theatre of war in New Guinea, especially Hollandia.

The name of the game seemed to be, tear down new recruits, then build them up again. On night marches, Jim told himself he had been there before. If he could learn to track a wolf, to hunt and fake out prey, he would not get iced by a Jap. Exercises in the Australian Outback surely illustrated the ability of the Army to organize anything. Here and there he encountered an officer or non-com that had good sense. The best response was to stay out of the way. One Thursday, Jim was nabbed to stand guard duty in a hospital tent. All the soldier patients were flat on their backs. Hardly anyone even moved. About midnight a Light Colonel with a Sergeant in tow presented themselves. "Soldier," the officer said. "Where is Private Yanello?" Jim consulted the roster. He led the officer to bunk 18.

"On your feet, soldier," the Colonel said. Yanello was a private, and he had terror written all over his face.

"On your feet," repeated the Sergeant.

"Sir," Jim said. "He's not able."

"Stand aside," Jim was told.

The Sergeant took Yanello's arm in a vice like grip. Jim stood back as they led the private away. When the shift ended, Jim returned to his tent. An hour later, The Oracle shook him awake. As a reward for the Thursday night guard duty, Private James Robert Neff was free for the day. He would have leave until Saturday morning. The Oracle said, "The place is buzzing. You let a prisoner leave the hospital unit. They're looking for you."

Jim observed The Oracle. His mouth was not twitching. The Oracle did not pause for an explanation. "I heard them in the orderly tent. They're talking court martial. Hell," said Oracle, "they're talking Leavenworth."

"The pen," Jim mumbled.

"Can I help you?" The Oracle asked.

"What the hell can I do?" Jim asked.

The Oracle supplied, "Make yourself scarce."

"How do you get scarce in a place surrounded by desert?"

"Go on soldier's leave. Hell on Wheels Beeler is doing the court martial this week. Then he goes back to Brisbane."

"Who follows Beeler?" Jim asked.

"Major Connors. You might stand a chance with him. With Hell on Wheels you'll get in a jam."

"I've had all the horse shit I'm going to take," Jim said. "I'm out of here in a minute." Jim had assembled his own version of a toiletry kit. It consisted of a safety razor, a collapsible toothbrush, a strong slice of soap for washing, comb and fingernail clipper. The entire package was no bigger than a pack of cigarettes. He borrowed a ten spot from The Oracle, then quietly walked between tents toward the railroad station. Toward dusk the train made the noise of an engine ready to pull out.

His brother Roy had schooled him in the fine art of free railroad travel. "You wait until the train is in motion. Don't fall down or you're a goner." He cautioned Jim to slip aboard the train a little after dark if possible. He told him to enter a freight car, cover himself with some material, and hunker down for the trip.

As the shadows lengthened and the travel signs turned favorable, Jim stepped aboard a flat car and snuggled down under a weapons carrier. The train arrived in the early part of the morning, and Jim sauntered down to the beach. It was a Saturday. He was exhausted. He found a spot with shade far from the water and went to sleep. About 10 a.m. he awoke with a start. The shade had slipped away from his resting place and the warmth was pleasant. A young lady was casting her shadow over him. "Hello, Yank," the lady said. "You have good judgment. That's the spot I usually take."

Jim started to get up. "Oh, no, don't," she said. "Did you sleep well last night?"

"A little bit."

"Well, Yank, two blocks away are Military Police. I hope you have papers."

"I'll just get moving," Jim said.

"Don't do that. They'll spot you for certain," she said. "Have you eaten?" Jim shook his head.

She promptly prepared a sandwich and offered it to him. She had a fine tan. To the boy from Kansas she looked very handsome. Handsome? In fact, she was a stunning beauty in her two piece bathing suit. She was exactly the same height as Jim, and hair the most beautiful shade of red with a face that blended perfectly with nature's scheme of things. Her upswept breasts were perfectly proportioned for a slim body that must have seen exercise every day.

"You're not on leave?"

"Not exactly." One item at a time, she got the information she wanted. He was a lonesome boy who had gotten the bloody shaft. He was going back, even if he did not realize it. She was a receptionist. That was her job at MacArthur Headquarters, to greet VIPs coming and going. Hell on Wheels Beeler was an old classmate of the general. She did not think the general liked him, nor did he like the general. Now and then the general ordered Hell on Wheels back to headquarters. Hell on Wheels court martialed errant GIs and sentenced them without mercy.

"Do I call you Cassandra?" Jim said.

"Don't you call me that!"

"Alright," Jim said. "I guess I already have a prophet in my life."

"The Oracle?" she asked. "I hope he's right. Cassandra was a prophetess of ancient Troy. She could foretell the future, but her ability had one drawback. No one would believe her."

The Military Police patrol was coming into view. Sandy paused with what she was saying, threw Jim to the sand and started smothering him with kisses. They were not false kisses. The MPs passed. Sandy said, "I had to make it look real."

"It was real enough," Jim stated.

"You know, Yank, You can't sleep on the beach."

She bent over and gave him a very soft peck on the cheek. She continued to talk but he was only half listening. He was eighteen years old, a deserter from the Army because he had listened to The Oracle, and now a redheaded beauty was offering him a meal in her apartment. Did he really think she wanted no more than to help a wayward Yank? He knew all about sex, about animals coming into season, and yet he knew absolutely nothing about human relations.

This long legged girl with the tan of a goddess and the legs of Betty Grable liked Yanks and saw the patrolling MPs as a menace. He was tired. His time on the beach had drained him of more reserves than the ride on the train.

"Be careful," she warned him. "The landlord hates Yanks. However, he goes out for a constitutional precisely at 9 p.m." That is when he could walk nonchalantly up the walk and into her flat very quietly. This he did. As he raised his hand to knock, the door slowly opened. She motioned him inside. He was ordered out of his uniform and she handed him soap and a towel. "Yank, you should take a shower while I fix you something to eat. Be very quiet. No singing in the shower."

He did not sing. He scrubbed and scrubbed, and felt the comfort of clear water take the salt and grime down the drain. He had his safety razor and toilet kit in his possession, and after shaving, his beard too went down the drain. It was then he realized that he had no clothes. The goddess was laundering them, but in the Australian weather, they would only take a short time to dry. He sheepishly opened the door, "Sandy," he said in a stage whisper, "my clothes."

"Sorry, Yank, they're wet. You'll have to make do with a towel for now." She handed him a beach towel, taking a moment to enjoy the sight of the freshly scrubbed Yank. She knew he had no experience. She could tell he had probably never been away from home before. A little conversation had assured her that she was right. That is ok. She decided to do her Christian duty for the war effort, save this boy from jail, and give him some really good food.

As James stepped into the living room, kitchen combination flat with hair shampooed and scrubbed skin, darkness engulfed the apartment. A card table was now set up in the middle of the living room with a candle in a wine bottle.

"You don't mind dining in a makeshift uniform, do you?" she asked. "I'm afraid you'll have to."

He said he did not mind.

She applied some Sun Glow ointment to his sunburn, saying, "We better heal that sunburn. Well, that should get better," she said. He afterwards applied it all over his red skin.

Sandy was busy putting food on the table, pouring a little red wine that MacArthur had given his staff at Brisbane. "Your outfit is moving to New Guinea starting Monday morning," she informed Jim. Then she brought some kind of baked fish to the table with two glasses of wine. She picked up his hands and offered a sort of prayer addressed to the deity of the prairie that the Godhead was surely supporting the Allies against the Japs. James did not need encouragement to eat. He dispatched a helping and asked for another.

"No, no," she said. "You have to drink a little wine between helpings." He had never tasted real wine before. "So this is what they talked about all those years," he said to himself. He sipped some to find it was not nearly as bad as whiskey, and continued sipping. He set the wine glass to one side and continued eating.

"That's correct," she said. "Just sip it. It's really a very nice wine even if it's from New South Wales. Yank, you married?"

Jim felt a tinge of embarrassment, but he had the presence of mind to reply, "Well, I dated a little bit, but I had a lot of work and study and it all ended there."

Actually, he had had one date in his whole life. He had always been attracted to girls, but he had been too tired to ask them out, and no one had set up a date for him again. His life and work picked up the rhythm of things, and just like that he returned to normal.

She spoke. "Yank, there's no place to go, no place to hide, not in Australia nor anywhere. If your clothes don't give you away, your language does."

"I talk Kansas that much, huh?"

"You do." Her eyes met his with a fixed gaze. "Yank, we've got to face reality. In a day or two they'll mark you down as a deserter." He had thought of that, but the anger that caused him to hop a train had not abated. It was not like James Neff to lose his cool. "He didn't know how to cope with the absurdity of the military mind," he said to himself.

Now, however, the moment of truth had come.

Sandy was still talking as she removed the dishes. "They shoot deserters," she said blandly. "I couldn't stand that."

She sat down across from him and gently interrogated James. Talking to the boy from Kansas was like pulling teeth at first, then he opened up. She had bred horses as an adolescent. She and her parents had two racehorses that were still to find their way into the winner's circle. His forte was cows. They talked well into the night, past midnight, and into the morning. She walked him through his life experiences, she walked with him on hikes at Camp Roberts, went on leave with him when there was nothing to do. She came to know that he was motivated and driven. God, what a soldier the boy will make. He has to look on Japs as so many jackrabbits. He has to let go of some of the anger and sentiment of Kansas and his mother with her rosary. After an hour, Jim stopped talking.

Wasn't she supposed to tell him about herself? She worked in the office at MacArthur's headquarters. She was single, age 29. She had family in Melbourne. She had joined the civil service at Brisbane because it was the next best thing to joining the Army.

Suddenly, she said, "There's a train loading up in the morning for Rockhampton. I'm going to show you where there is a tough grade and the train slows. James, you have to go back."

"I know," he said. He forgot that he was staying in a lady's apartment with a towel wrapped around him, his clothes trying to dry in the stuffy apartment of an Australian stunner.

"Come. I'll show you where you sleep." As they entered her bedroom she sat on the edge of the bed. "Slide between the sheets. You can slip that beach towel off and lay it on the end of the bed."

Jim complied by pulling the towel and tossing it across the foot of the bed.

"I'll be up early to press your uniform."

Jim thanked her.

"No problem," she said. "It is worth the effort." She went on after a pause. "About 0900 we'll catch a train to Walla Walla Crossing Knoll. The train comes to a crawl there. It is a real easy jump."

Unexpectedly, she dropped her robe and jumped into bed. In a second she was all over the boy virgin soldier. Soon he responded. The exercise exhausted the youth and he dropped off to sleep.

She was as good as her word. She presented him with a freshly pressed uniform and a cup of tea with toast. The radio that had played soft music and newscasts ever since he had entered the door broke into a report. Australians were preparing for an invasion.

Sandy interrupted, "That's why MacArthur is going to New Guinea, to keep the Japs from taking Australia."

She took him to Walla Walla Crossing Knoll.

"I'll write," he said.

"No, don't do that. I'm too naughty for you."

He started to speak.

"Don't," she said, holding a finger over his lips.

Jim caught the train and endured the rocky ride to within 40 miles of Rockhampton. The MPs who picked him up off the flat car gave him a drink of water.

"What outfit, soldier?" was the perfunctory query.

"41st Infantry."

"I'll give you a ride," he said, matter of factly.

When they arrived at the staging camp, the MP said, "Go find your outfit."

It took Jim an hour to find his company. "Jesus H. Christ," the morning report clerk said when Jim walked in.

"Neff is back." That brought the First Sergeant to attention.

"Private Neff, front and center."

Jim came to attention. "We have a little problem, soldier."

Jim noticed all the stripes and his rank. He was a Sergeant Major, six feet tall, 200 plus pounds, but he seemed as gentle as Grandpa Xander. "OK, Hot Shot," the Sergeant Major said. "Stay right there. An MP will take you to the guardhouse. He'll bring you back for your court martial." Jim said softly, "Thank you."

You'll be taken to the front tent with the flag under order of the Presiding General at 0900 in a day or so. You'll be charged with assisting a prisoner to escape. We'll have to add "absent without official leave" to that. When this is all over, you'll have a week of KP coming." By the time the MPs arrived, guardhouse lawyers had descended on James Robert Neff.

"Shut up, be quiet, and say nothing," advised Private Foy.

"They may offer you a lawyer. Don't take him," advised Private Young.

"Place yourself at the mercy of the court."

The Oracle merely smiled. "I checked. Hell on Wheels is in Brisbane. Your primary officer is First Lieutenant Fischer Ames. He was a defense lawyer in civilian life able to find every defendant innocent. He hates convictions."

It turned out that the Oracle's surveillance and espionage were right.

"Soldier," came the query, "what's your story?"

It was the First Lieutenant speaking. The four other members of the court barely listened. "I didn't do anything," Jim said.

The judge of the court came to the point. "Did you receive instructions on how to plead?"

"No, sir."

"Why did you let the prisoner go?" the court asked.

"A Light Colonel ordered me to point out this prisoner, Yanello. I was taught to obey orders."

The court had a short whispering session.

"We find you guilty as charged and order one month pay to be forfeited.

You can return to your outfit," the First Lieutenant said. A downy faced Second Lieutenant spoke up, "What about the AWOL charge?"

"We've ruled on this case. Bring in the next one. Private Jensen, AWOL trouble."

16

It seemed to James Robert Neff that the only emotion left to him was anger. He had languished under guard with little food for three days and he was angry. Right now he wanted to see his mother and only his mother could comfort him. He had always felt close to his dad while working on the farm, digging post holes and doing chores, but it was his mother who gave him solace. He had obeyed her rule, "Keep your promises and stay out of other people's business." There was only one rule in the Army, "obey your superiors." He had disobeyed the rules and his punishment was forfeiture of a month's pay, $21.00, and not one, but two, weeks of KP. Fanning his anger was the orientation message decreed by the rule of political officers. It was hard not to believe the stories of torture, decapitation and savage brutality by the Japanese because unfortunately most of them were true. The boys who fought at Hollandia, New Guinea heard firsthand from a German missionary how the Japanese had mutilated nuns and put their breasts in glass jars. As the war ground on, American soldiers would respond with a savagery of their own, wearing necklaces of Japanese ears and the like, but they could never hope to match the Imperial Army for pure unshuttered horror.

Now, abetted by an official racism which he only recognized years later, James Robert Neff was fed a steady diet of fact and fiction that was believed and worked by the authorities. Where there was no burden of racism among the soldiers, it was soon instilled. On ocean ships and in base camps Jim wrote V mail letters, but what could he say? The sky and ocean were blue. He could not tell his mother and dad about the soldiers mangled in the fields, or body parts being cut off and put into a dead GI's mouth. More than anger was left out of the letters home. Only the real socially acceptable news in the South Pacific was communicated. There were no POWs at Hollandia when he arrived.

When the Americans came, the Japanese departed. They left their food uneaten, they abandoned supplies and vanished into the jungles, approximately 10,000 of them. Only a handful survived. Jim's unit slept in foxholes.

"You've had it if you're captured," Captain Arnold told them. "If you see a Jap, do not capture him, just shoot him. If he takes you, you'll be tortured to death."

The captain was firm about finding safety in a dugout or behind any rock. "A good clean kill is a cleansing experience. Clean out the Nips, the lice, monkeys, Japs, vermin, the little yellow bastards."

How could Jim write home about anything but horrors? How could he obey the Ten Commandments under such circumstances?

Jim arrived at the staging area. With a few terse words in a stuffy tent with a First Lieutenant in command, he became the equivalent of a felon for something he did not do, and the anger boiled. He remembered his dad's advice, he did not care if Jim obeyed his officers as long as he used his own judgment.

The first battle assignment was a non-protected hill. At the top of the hill the men fell out. The goal of the excursion, ambush forty Japanese. At dawn four hundred Tiger Marines arrived. All were well over six feet tall. Jim was in an infantry unit. Three of the few friends he had made in the Army were there. The Imperial troopers came on in waves. They screamed. They shouted *Banzai* and offered their bodies as targets to the entrenched Americans. Their useless bayonets bit the dust when they hit the bullet curtain rising like a leaden fog out of the half moon trench. Jim counted seventy-two dead Japs in his line of fire. The total killed was over four hundred. Arlington Spangler Drew, The Oracle, was shot between the eyes. Foy, the card shark, died with half his face blown away. There was another casualty among the seventeen, a Finlander from Minnesota named Oris. Out of ammunition, the private had clobbered a Jap with the butt of his rifle before he had met his end. Bullets, shots, rifles, grenades, and gunfire lasted about twenty minutes. It was a baptism of fire that dissolved much of the anger and hate that had filled the boy from Kansas for the past month or more. The great General ordered bombardments and bombs and shells from the great ships, none of which seemed to humble the Japanese soldiers.

After each rain of death they seemed to emerge from their caves or trenches or fox holes able to fight again.

It was the pistol and the machine gun that best suited Jim. His talent for tracking humans and animals was put to use when he trailed a seven man patrol by some fifty feet. After the main patrol had passed, a Jap emerged from a spider hole. The Jap saw Jim, but Jim saw him first. The Thompson spoke and then the patrol came running back. All had passed within a few feet of the sniper without seeing him.

That very evening Jim was promoted to scout for the lead patrol. He was no longer angry. He'd been as calm as Wyatt Earp at the OK Corral. Jim cleaned his weapon and kept to himself.

With his basic training buddies gone, he seemed reluctant to make new friends because he knew they would get blown away. He stopped attending mass or religious services. Two days after a firefight that cost four lives, the chaplain motioned Jim into his tent near the back. "Son, you're from Kansas?"

"Yes, sir," Jim said.

"I nodded to you at mass some time ago, but you didn't respond."

Jim did not answer at first, then he said, "I'm usually on patrol." He, at twenty, had never missed mass except in the Army.

"Yes, I understand you volunteer a lot. Why don't you let the others take their turn?"

Again Jim paused before answering, "I don't want to see them picked up by Graves Registration." It was true. Few wanted to risk patrol without the expertise of Jim Neff.

"Jim," the chaplain said, "all the men have problems. I know you have yours. I'm here for you."

Jim offered a "thank you," but he did not go on. He preferred silence to expressing any words.

"They tell me you got quite angry when they fined you for allowing a prisoner to escape," the chaplain said.

"I didn't do anything except obey orders. They taught me to obey orders, so a Light Colonel ordered me to let him go and I did. That's an injustice, I'd say."

"You did go AWOL."

"Yes, sir."

"What happened?"

"I caught a train to Brisbane. I was only gone a few days."

"Where did you stay?"

"I slept on the beach."

"By yourself? You stayed on the beach by yourself?"

"I met a girl." Jim did not elaborate.

"Did it end there?"

"No. I stayed at her apartment." There was nothing more from Jim.

"Look son, I don't want any details, only one, was she married?"

"No, she was a career lady with a low level job with the government."

"Well," the chaplain said, "how do you feel about that?"

Jim merely shuffled his feet.

"I don't think you feel very good about that. It's not you, Jim. It is not how you were brought up." The officer laid back. "I know what you hear, a lot of loose bragging by men who fear what we all fear. We can't allow ourselves to feel the absurdity of the situation we're in individually. So many of the men slip their moorings and their ethical ballast, but that's not you, Jim. Now, having said that, I want you to put all this behind you. You'll learn that in the scheme of things it's not that important."

The chaplain waited for this to sink in, and then he added, "Is that the only thing you're not telling me?"

"Partly."

"What else?"

"Sir, it's this killing. How are we going to square with Commandment number five?"

The chaplain said, "I wish I was wise enough to answer you. I see war has to do with the betrayal of the young by the old, started by the Philistines and the savagery addicts. We didn't start the war but we are obliged to finish it. When you're an old man you'll have a perspective you do not now enjoy." He did not add, "if you survive."

"We just slaughter people and they slaughter us," the Kansas boy said. The conversation ran on for a few more minutes. Jim told of the six Japs who were almost starving at cave six. "I shot four of them. Private Denton cut down the other two. We just shot them down. They had Private Murdock strung up and were cutting meat off his body.

Poor devils, we just shot them down. I don't think any of them had a weapon within reach."

"James, you're a good soldier. You're well within your mother's guidelines. Your main job is to stay alive."

There was a silence Jim found hard to endure. At the terminal point of that silence, the chaplain made eye contact that caught and held the soldier in its grip.

"Jim," the chaplain said.

"Yes, Padre," came the acknowledgment.

"You're a student. I don't see you playing cards with the others. You read everything loose in this camp."

Jim warmed to that statement. He smiled a bit as the chaplain continued, "Sooner or later you'll encounter Greek civilization."

"I already have," the soldier said halfway interrupting the officer most of the men called Padre.

"The Greeks have two words for love. One is eros. It means the physical love between a man and a woman, best a husband and a wife. It is often abused because it is God's sacred gift. The Greeks have a second word for love, agape. Agape is the spiritual love that holds man and wife together. It is pure, unconditional. No one finds it in a bordello or in casual sex." The eye contact was still there as the padre picked up Jim's hand. "Son, go home when this is over. Find that love with a wife, treat her with respect. Don't let this sorry experience color your life to your detriment." Then he added, "What else? Now, do you want to make any of this official in the eyes of the church?" He waited a few seconds and when Jim nodded the chaplain produced a stole of office. The ritual proceeded.

"Bless me, Father, for I have sinned." Jim recited everything *sans* details. The priest spoke the Latin words of confession as prescribed by ancient ritual.

"*Indulgéntiam, absolutionem, et remissionem peccatorum tuorum* . . .*" Jim found himself experiencing a measure of well being, "whose sins you shall forgive, they are forgiven," ran through his mind. He thought of his religious mother and his sometimes skeptical but straight arrow dad.

"... *tríbuat tibi omnípotens, et miséricors Dominus. Amen.*" concluded the priest. He had said only the prescribed Latin. He looked at Jim, "Son, avoid the occasion for transgression. Go and sin no more."

With New Guinea more or less secure, the guards ordered an invasion of Biak, a small postage stamp of an island in the Pacific on an imaginary line called the equator. The several landings were more or less perfunctory, sometimes meeting hostile fire, sometimes not. MacArthur expected the state fortress to fall in three days. It took approximately six months and nineteen days for General Fuller and his associates to defeat the enemy's fifty units. The objective was an air drome facility called Mokmer, a big petroleum and supplies depot. Overrun Japanese facilities had revealed the intelligence that an American ambush was to be ahead. This information was involved in a propaganda ploy by Japanese field operatives. They sent Jim Neff ahead to reconnoiter, to see if the threat was for real.

Jim was working solo in the Biak jungle that day, tracking a wild boar. It was as tough as tracking El Diablo on the high plains. At the crossroads of two paths he was stopped by a dead body. The dog tags said Stan Wittier. His head was missing. He followed the pig to a spring and a cave so cleverly camouflaged only a person with gifted eyesight could detect it. The cave was full of equipment, ammunition, and uniforms. Incredibly, the cave was unguarded. When he reported back to field headquarters, a patrol was sent back to inventory the place.

Three months after troops landed at Biak, General Fuller regrouped. During this time, some men had sickened and died, some were wounded, some victims of diseases, especially malaria, which was easily identified by its effect on skin and eyes. Many left the island never having seen the enemy. Jim stayed on.

"Neff, front and center," went the routine.

"Sir, I was on patrol already. Why me?"

"Jimbo, I want to stay alive."

They all wanted to stay alive. They walked the jungle trails, into and out of Japanese held territory. They encountered artillery shells. Jim walked the 40 miles into that territory, always conscious of the threat of bombs. Often, Jim volunteered for patrol because he preferred it to being idle. Waiting bothered him more than danger.

It was a senseless war. It was senseless for the Japs to enter and play victor in the jungle, but they did. Jim had only to step into the foliage and let them pass, but he did not do that. He fired the Thompson and four Nips returned fire, but when the bullets caught up with him, he left their bodies, skirting a wide perimeter around them in the jungle. It was that kind of war. Europe was a different war. The latest soldiers to arrive still had the bitter taste of Europe in their mouths. They drank Bacardi rum and other soothing beverages. Some tried jungle juice. On maps in faraway places men in pressed uniforms informed world presidents and defined battle lines. On Biak it was a matter of addition and subtraction.

"Did we kill more than the Nips replaced last night?" No one gave a definitive answer while the Japanese stayed close.

"I was in the same building with Riley Grant," Jim wrote home. Jim kept a sort of diary on a notepad he carried. He dated it July 15, 1944. Most of Jim's diary came home a year later, but he was writing it here and now.

"We came across a Johnny Luke. He was a boy from New Orleans. The Nips had eaten his arm. When we caught them, we shot them. They were starving."

When the general fighting came to a close and only patrols went out, Jim found time to keep more than a short diary.

"It's pleasant work, really, I carry only a Thompson. The others carry the ammunition. I certainly have the safest job." To Jim it was safety plus. He admitted to his parents that he did not think the enemy could get him. "Jim," the chaplain said, "you're getting reckless."

"Not with these eyes." He was right about that. In training he had blown away all the tests with perfect ease. He could spot and see at night. Hunkering down in a foxhole or walking the lush green patches of the jungle, the infantrymen knew everything about the grand strategies of military planners. Still, the intelligence surfaced that the only reason for taking Biak was Mokmer air drome. To take this prize, infantrymen had to take and control the hills, jungles and acres surrounding the airfield. Days of land fighting came and went. Many a GI never saw an enemy soldier. Still, the very air was dangerous with flying shrapnel and the steady drum of machine gun bullets.

When General Fuller failed to meet MacArthur's expectations, General Eichenburger was sent in to salvage the great general's reputation. Eichenburger called for a halt in operations. He ordered new uniforms and rations. He opened new operations and installed safety measures for soldiers who after two months up front needed shoes and supplies. Once the airfields were secured, the soldiers wrote home, but they said little about the battles, the kamikaze counterattacks, or the death of comrades.

The mop up involved no battle lines. Flamethrowers produced casualties in the jungle and artillery tore away at the enemy. The Japanese held on, undaunted, tenacious, refusing to surrender.

"No prisoners so far," read one of Jim Neff's diary entries. "The Japs issue hand grenades to enlisted men, and if they are cornered, they kill themselves. An officer, a major, I think, carved up his stomach committing hara-kiri."

The west and the east sides of the island fell by the Fourth of July. The last pockets fell on July 22, 1944. Jim wrote, "The gods must be laughing their heads off at mortal men. The Nips have tried to drive us into the sea at each of the six landings I've made. We shot them down like dogs and they shot us on the beach. I often wonder what led the Nips to attack Pearl Harbor. Babe Ruth found them to be gentle, loving people and now we see them as ogres." The best possible entry by James Neff was that the 41st had lost more than 400 men at Biak. Some 2,000 were wounded. Off the record, 7,000 non battle and disease casualties had been experienced. Jim himself experienced jungle rot and dengue fever. If a combatant survived, he ran the risk of drinking water polluted with parasites that delivered fevers and malaria. Spots and scales covered his own yellowed skin. Now, new raw recruits started arriving. By August, the last of his card playing friends from basic training were gone. For these newly arrived soldiers, Jim filled in details not recognizable on the trails described in their handbook's training maps. When the enemy bombs led to death, he read his pocket sized Bible.

After attending midnight mass at Christmas, Jim ventured over to the tent of the parson. The parson was a laconic thirty year old from Tennessee named Homer Smythe. The parson quoted the Bible as rapid fire as Joe E. Brown told jokes. The boy from Kansas arrived in the doorway of the tent. The usual small talk was fired with speculation about a move to Luzon in the Philippines. The lanky Tennessean offered Jim a cot to sit on and a shot of jungle juice. His furrowed brow looked like a Kansas wheat field with no history of rain. He had a mixture of Mona Lisa's smile and crucifixion sorrow. "What brings you here?" was the inevitable question.

"Parson, I've noticed in all our fire fights you never seem to shoot." The silence was one of a tomb in a ghost town. The parson produced a small pocket-sized Bible, King James version. The parson paged his Bible with the dexterity of a shark handling a deck of cards. He did not need to see the pages because he had committed most of them to memory years ago. He had been drafted away from his calling by the Allied Operations. At first he had thought of registering as a conscientious objector. The family's tradition had made him a Phineas priest.

"What do you mean, Phineas priest?"

The parson simply said, "Numbers 25, the chapter is eighteen verses long." Jim asked for an explanation. "Numbers 25 refers to a member of the royal house of Israel having an unsanctified relationship. Phineas drove his spear through the both of them."

Jim started to object. He was only really interested in the stories and metaphors of the Bible, and what did this have to do with not firing a rifle against the Japanese?

"Stay a moment. Let me explain that our concept of marriage first comes from the Babylonian cuneiform writing code. The words wife, husband, and marriage are commented on in the Roman law. Under God's law, the first act of communion is the marriage. When the minister is reading the words, 'Do you take this woman as your wife to be your lawfully wedded spouse until death do you part?' he is reading laws that existed in the book."

"Whereabouts?" Jim started to excuse himself. He was not getting an answer and he expected no answer.

"Stay," said the parson. "The Ten Commandments deal mostly with sex, stealing and killing, correct?" Jim gave the obligatory nod. "Thou shalt not covet, you know nine and ten. Thou shalt not kill."

"Is it a just war?" asked Jim.

"For you, yes. For me, no. I am restrained by my office. If ever I am called to kill, I will kill. But I believe that my weapon will not be spear or gun, but something more devastating, the pen, perhaps." He waited for this to sink in. "Sleeping with the neighbor's wife is a property crime under God's law."

"Parson, I've got to get back to my unit."

"Certainly." He then quoted verbatim Leviticus 20 in the King James version: "Yahweh spoke unto Moses saying, 'Again God will say to the children of Israel, whoever of the children of Israel or the strangers that sojourn in Israel that giveth any of his seed unto the Moloch he shall surely be put to death. The people of the Lord shall stone him with stones and I will set my face against that man and I will cut him off from his people because he has given of his seed to the Moloch.'"

For some reason Jim did not readily identify with the problems narrated, though he enjoyed access to the strange man's mind. When he proceeded, Jim asked him for some more jungle juice.

"A great plague fell upon Israel. That's when Phineas the son of Eleazar, took a javelin in his hand and ran it through the offending couple. The plague was lifted. Phineas achieved a new level of priesthood. Some 24,000 people died in that place. Yahweh said to Moses, 'Phineas, son of Eleazar, son of Aaron the priest, has turned my wrath away from Israel.' Yahweh said, 'I give him the covenant of my peace and he shall have it and his seed after him and a covenant of everlasting priesthood because he was zealous for his God and made amends for the children of Israel.'

"Was the story a metaphor or an allegory?" Jim still wanted to know the point, and the parson supplied it.

"The tradition in my family is that of the perpetual Phineas priesthood. The Muslims and Jews have the Phineas priesthood, as does the Smythe family. In every generation there's a Phineas priest. A Phineas priest is immune. These seventeen-year-old Japanese boys are not the real guilty. In terms of the literal explanation of the metaphor, when Israel became involved in a just war they never lost."

"Isn't this a just war?" asked Jim.

"For you, yes, for me, no! Jim, my father was a prophet. He could foresee. I do not have the gift. But I have intuition. I can foresee to an extent close-up questions."

"What do you see close up?" Jim asked. The parson shared a little jungle juice. He smacked his lips and continued.

"Close up, we're going to the Sulu Archipelego, not Luzon the way everyone thinks. You should not be going. If you go, you'll be hit." Jim did not believe the parson. He had convinced himself that no Japanese bullet would ever hit him. He smiled at the parson. "Far out," he said. "We will have a great celebration to commemorate winning the war, but in fact we will have lost more than a war; we will have lost the American tradition. For the next century it will be personal wars and expanding debt. Just wars are not in the preview I see. Take care, son, the vibes do not parallel the luck you've had so far. We all should be running scared from the financiers. They organized the war, didn't they?"

Shortly after New Year's Day, 1945, MacArthur assigned the 41st a role in the invasion of the Philippines. The point for assault was Zamboanga. The city, its surroundings, and the nearby watered plain fell rather promptly. Outnumbered Japanese troops retreated to mountains ascending to a peak that offered fortress possibilities. The 41st fought its way to the top, and it was hard, bloody work. Jim hung onto his Thompson and accepted extra clips of ammunition for support. Before Biak, everyone had been given gas masks and bayonets. No one thought they would get to use them. The assault on Jolo Island lasted two and a half days for Jim Neff. The landing was uneventful, except for the naval troops that kept wading into the surf, then returning to the shore under the direction of the producers developing "adventure" footage for the army's public relations department. The drive up "Shalbo Hill," Jim's term, was something else. The war was now bigger than a stroll through Biak's jungle pathways and an occasional firefight with two, three, or a dozen Japanese soldiers. The squint-eyed Major recently installed as commanding officer knew he had a few veterans and mostly raw recruits. In the refurbished 41st, replacements were to deliver an organization as defined by the movies to glorify and sanitize history. The losses on the first day in the Sulu Archipelago were frightful. The assault on "the hill" was small scale in terms of Pickett at Gettysburg or the landing at Normandy, but the Major drove the men without mercy. The second day they came on with grenades and machine gun fire denying all but the most exhausted even an hour's sleep. By mid-morning of the third day, the survivors of charge after charge were the walking wounded and comatose.

156

Jim thanked God that there was no real shrapnel gun on Jolo Island. That weapon had first been used in the Great War of 1918. It was really an overgrown shotgun shell that sent BBs the size of a ball bearing into the enemy, always taking away bits of clothing and causing infection.

Correspondents did not understand this. As a consequence, they called every steel splinter shrapnel, after the British officer who invented the shell that had his name.

"They won't get me," Jim told himself, "not with a mustard gas bullet or a piece of shrapnel." Still, the fighting was lethal. Corporal Homer Smythe, known to God as Phineas priest, caught a bullet along the edge of his helmet, and still he believed he was immune since the dent in his helmet left no damage.

As troops wended their way up the mountain, they set up perimeters each night. It took days to push the Japs into the steel death trap, like rabbits against a snow fence. The Japanese loved to dig tunnels. Each step of the way up the mountain meant a new group of tunnels. Jungle growth made old tunnels a veritable trap.

On the day the parson warned about, Major Oren gave the troops their orders. "I want you men to take that hill." The men thought they heard him say under his breath, "or don't come back alive."

Jim had a reputation for leading an exercise called run and shoot. There was a time when the order to run and shoot met with outright refusal, not from Jim Neff, but from those disinclined to obey the order. All except Jim had been court martialed. This afternoon the Major seemed to have a special plan. His uniform was clean and pressed. Jim thought he had little pig eyes squinting from under his gold wire glasses.

"Major," Jim saluted. "We haven't eaten in two days. There's only us. We're too tired. We have to have some food and water."

"I want you to go now."

"He's right," Lieutenant Callahan interrupted. "The men are exhausted.They haven't got the energy." His words became inaudible. "No dice, Major."

"Who said that?"

"I did," Jim Neff said.

The Lieutenant stepped up to the Major. "Sir, there's food coming up from the base camp. It'll be here in half an hour."

"We're going now! You hear? Now!"

No one moved.

"Move it!"

Lieutenant Callahan did not move. Jim just stood there, his Thompson more or less ready.

"You'll be court martialed for this," the Major growled. "Doesn't matter," Jim said. "We'll all be dead, but damn, we're going to have some pancakes before we die."

The men waited, and they ate. Then they strode up the hill. Jim climbed and carved a trail. The rest of the assault party had the vantage point from which to spray the enemy who were setting up all the fire. Now Jim drew fire. He was surrounded with bullets flying over, under, and around him. "I'm coming down," the Lieutenant shouted. He came running down hill broken field style, jumping over logs. He got to within five yards of Jim when he took a bullet in the armpit. Jim came to his aid, but he could not stop the blood, which was shooting out like a stream from a broken hose. The Lieutenant's face turned white as a sheet as his life drained away. While the officer died, Jim shoved the second clip into the Thompson. He was standing near an entrance to a cave in the side of the mountain. With the skill of an opossum egg thief, with the Thompson at the ready, he stepped into the mouth of the cave. The Thompson spoke, and the place lit up like a pinball machine. First, he raked the right wall, then the left, his curtain of bullets expressing surprise to what appeared to be a cave full of people. He felt confident as he stepped back into the sunlight, then he glimpsed a Jap disappearing into what appeared to be a stone wall. He strained to see. Got to get closer, he said to himself. He crawled into an old trench and inched his way toward the spot where the image of the Jap had appeared. Prob'ly the Nip who got Cal, he told himself. Then a cleverly camouflaged cave came into view. As he cautiously took a step, a bright light blinded him. Was it the sun? No, body fluid was blinding him, then the pain set in. It came to him that a grenade out of nowhere had found him, labeled Neff. But he was still alive, wounded from head to toe, but still alive and on his feet. Not too far from the cave was a path made by a tank through the razor grass. Two wounded soldiers were moving cautiously in the deep tracks. "The wrong way, you're headed the wrong way," Jim shouted. The light was beginning to fade. "Follow the tank tracks to the aid station," he ordered. By then, the shooting had moved on up the hill, so the three walked together down the hill to the aid station a mile away. Jim collapsed on a stretcher. "Let me take the gun," the medic said.

"Nobody takes my gun," Jim said.

A needle was put in his arm and the medic repeated, "Give me the gun, soldier."As the morphine took over, James Neff agreed, "Yeah, I guess I don't need this anymore."

17

When Private First Class James Robert Neff awoke, he asked, "Where am I?"

"You're on a transport plane to Luzon," a medic said. The plane was full of wounded men, some bandaged and sedated, others in stretchers on the floor. South Pacific danger zone personnel wore no insignia. A stripe or a bar or a Red Cross was simply an invitation for the Japanese to take this target in preference to any other GI.

One of the medics who had picked up wounded on Biak and was now at the Jolo Battle Facility picked up the news: "Neff's been hit!" He rushed to the hospital and was directed to the bed of the fallen comrade. The mangled form on the stretcher could not speak. He had a terrible body wound, a kidney shattered beyond repair, multiple shrapnel wounds all over his body, especially on his left foot and leg. The attending physician doubted that he would ever see again.

"There's pressure on the optic nerve," the doctor said. He wore a miniature pin that designated him as a Captain.

The medic carried back the news, "Jimbo is dying."

The men of the 41st assault team did something they rarely did. They prayed. They also petitioned their officers to give James Robert Neff the Congressional Medal of Honor. His daring assault on the Nip's cave had probably saved the group from heavy casualties. His one man assault on the cave resulted in the deaths of eighteen Nips. Later, Smythe counted them one by one, even though his rifle was still unfired.

The Zamboanga hospital did what it could, then sent the wounded men on to Luzon. There they remained in escrow, often for a month or more before being hand carried to a hospital ship in the bay. From there, they were to board a ship for transfer to San Francisco by way of Hawaii. The usual military efficiency prevailed. Seriously wounded men remained stretcher bound in the tropical sun while healthy replacement troops refused to carry them aboard. By evening, some sailors had carried Jim Neff aboard and down into a stinking ward with beds stacked up six high. A Second Lieutenant went from patient to patient. His stethoscope raced over Jim's Body. "Medic," he shouted. "This man has pneumonia. Get him to the hospital ward." Jim made the trip that way, always enjoying fresh sheets and individual attention.

At the veteran's hospital in San Francisco, Jim started improving very rapidly. The physicians managed to take pressure off the optic nerve, and Jim started seeing shadows. He was in residence fully two weeks before he was pronounced fit to travel, which meant a three day train trip to Springfield, Missouri, the nearest available hospital to his hometown. A minder traveled with each patient in a Pullman car.

The boy from Kansas, in his own words, was "treated fine." The physicians gave him back his vision, fixed up his face, and rolled his gurney to the operating room no less than fifteen times to remove shrapnel. Three months into an eight month stay at O'Reilly General Hospital, Jim started having nightmares. He was a lead scout on the Wewak Trail in New Guinea. Some of the 10,000 Japanese soldiers that ran into the jungle at Hollandia announced their presence with talk, talk, talk. The Sergeant in charge placed his men in a half moon line and the men dug their foxholes. Here they came making the sound of jackrabbits on the run from their hiding places in the wheat fields. They came in waves, thousands of them, shouting *banzai*. As they approached the half moon line, they morphed into Japanese soldiers with great jackrabbit ears, thick caricature glasses, and Japanese faces much like those cartooned into consciousness by wartime propaganda, and overran the infantry position. One great jackrabbit of a Jap leaped into the trench and bit Jim in the neck. His bed was shaking with the staccato vibration of a submachine gun being fired, sweat pouring from his face. A nurse was standing over him, gently slapping his face. "Wake up, soldier, wake up." The scent of the woman was overpowering. She quickly took his hand, and dried his tears with Kleenex. "James," she said gently. "James, it's all right." She held on to him and finally settled him onto his pillow.

The 10,000 Nips who ran into the jungle had hoped to walk 125 miles to Watki. There was a massacre en route. The 41st had caught up with the survivors and killed them en masse. The power of Jim's will would not let the episode fade into limbo. The forty Nips, turning into four hundred, became a battle fought again and again, and with each tortured dream came that handsome nurse with the scent of a woman, a tranquilizer to the subconscious.

"My name is Nora," she said softly. She offered him a drink and a slight peck on the cheek. "Where are you from, soldier?"

"Kansas," he said. "My name is James, and I don't answer to soldier any longer."

"Well, James," she said, and for the first time her eyes met his. He saw a slender beauty as in a fog. He could make out her dark hair, that classic form of her slender body, and he blushed when she picked up his hand. "You'll probably have these disturbing dreams for some time. One of the doctors will want to talk to you about them. You might want to write down what you remember."

Nora wore the obligatory white with a headpiece that caused his pulse to increase. During the two weeks that followed, she seemed to hover around him when he was asleep.

"You know, I'm from Humboldt," she told him one day. "James, we're practically neighbors."

When he told her about his cattle operation, she beamed with interest.

"I'd love to see that house, your Banyon Place," she said.

"It needs a lot. I plan to refurbish it top to bottom when I have the money." He told her it had a widow's walk. She told him she could use one as a window "among the stars."

The next time she came to his bedside, he handed her a message written on a napkin. "This is a standing ticket for a Humboldt nurse to visit Banyon Place for the purpose of enjoying the widow's walk and such other interests as may reveal themselves."

After four months in the hospital, Nurse Nora brought a letter to Jim.

"James," she said. "This is from your father."

Jim seized what he believed was an opportunity. "Can you read it to me? I still can't make out writing very well."

She opened the letter, unfolded it carefully, and read.

"Dear Son,

I don't have a good way of telling you that your mother passed away. The funeral was at Highland Cemetery last Saturday. I tried to reach you by telephone and maybe by now you're better. I went down to the Southwest Bell office. The woman there tried to get a call through to you, but no one at the hospital would allow it. They said you were not able to receive a call." Nora turned to Jim. "James, I'm so sorry. If you want, I'll write your father and tell him you couldn't travel anyway."

"Go ahead," he said. She continued:

"I will tell you this. Your mother heard from Royal. He was in Patton's Third Army.

Now that the war is over, he decided to stay in Germany. He's landed a job with an artificial insemination institute and he's married a local girl. He gave up on American agriculture when he joined the army. This made your mother very sad. Then came the news that you were seriously wounded. She prayed a great deal for the both of you, but neither of the above caused her to give up on life."

It was a long letter. Nora pulled a chair near the head of the bed so that others would not overhear. "Shall I continue?" she asked. "Please," he said.

"Kansas got a Highway Patrol just before the war. They didn't have many troopers at first, but several months ago I managed to have coffee with the Sheriff and Trooper Pat Martin. I told them about what we figured happened to Earl Mathew, Jr. The trooper took notes. He said he'd follow up. Well, he found the Mexican and interrogated him. The fellow led officers of the Colorado Highway Patrol (they cooperated) to where that crooked sheriff buried indigent people and victims, I guess. They dug up the coffin. The experts matched everything to the dental work Earl Jr. had and identified him. They shipped the bones back here some months ago. Your mother took it hard. She seemed to give up on life. I couldn't get her to eat. Doc Podolinsky couldn't help. So she passed quietly in her sleep. For the first time in years she had a smile on her face."

The letter went on about the ranch and the perfect line of heifers and bulls born since Jim had volunteered for service. Nora read it all, and with a few words of condolence she laid the missive on the little stand by his bed. Jim wanted the piece of steel the physicians took out of his foot.

163

"Can't do that, it has to go to Washington," the doctor said.

Six months after arriving at O'Reilly, Jim was wheeled into an examination room without the usual examining table. The man in a white coat over his starched shirt and necktie wanted to evaluate the long term effect of stress on combat soldiers.

"My God, a shrink," Jim said to himself. Jim did not remember his dreams very well. The recurrent one with jackrabbits turning into Nips horrified him to even think about. There was a dream in which he and two buddies rescued a downhearted soldier with sake and scotch. The higher ups knew about the cache and the boys stealing two cases. In real life, there was this big cache of potables on skids down at the beach. Guards circled the rum, vodka, scotch and sake the way guards must circle the gold at Fort Knox. It took Jim and two soldiers from Company E to find it and organize a team to transport it to the troops. The officers wanted to take it over.

"Not so," a hulk of a Sergeant had said. "We'll smash every bottle before we get cut out." The officers exhibited good sense and everyone shared. In the dream, Jim and two buddies approached the cache and offered to smash the entire mountain of liquor for the price of a case each of scotch and sake. "If you don't give it to us, we'll turn the whole business into shards of glass and alcohol."

The guards did the sensible thing. They surrendered a case each of scotch and sake which the three of them took to their down hearted friend. That was the end of his dream. When Jim awoke it came to him that it was really quite a satisfactory dream. Jim told Nora about it. The dream was based on an actual incident because Jim had helped one of the sergeants liberate the treasured booze. It was Jim's happiest dream. The only dissenting voice was Corporal Homer Smythe, the Phineas priest.

In his dreams he scouted for N Company, calmed the men, and settled his own nerves. The medics were his favorites. During long hours on his hospital cot, he found time to tell the medics why he had elected to be a scout: because a machine gun barrel weighs 45 pounds, the tripod weighs 45 pounds, a base weighs another 45 pounds, a casing for a mortar shell weighs 58 pounds.

When all the ammo bearers got killed, Jim volunteered as a scout because he did not consider himself a candidate to throw a horse out of work. For eight months, Jim re-fought the war, all of it. While the shrink was probing, Jim was recovering most of his eyesight. The army psychiatrist had questions. Had he dreamed of flying like Captain Marvel? Going over a cliff? Falling victim to unbeatable foes? The shrink mumbled jargon about prefrontal cortex and deep REM sleep. Often shrapnel in the brain deprives one of REM sleep, but this was not the case with James Neff. In sleep, REM, heats up the brain and instills post-traumatic shock.

Body language tells all who wish to see that the patient is dreaming of firing a machine gun and warning his buddies and medical personnel. The dreams are a byproduct of life, the shrink explained. James cooperated. He dreamed of dust storms, tracking El Diablo, clubbing rabbits, assisting and following his father, but most often he dreamed of Japs on the Wewak trail, Japs in the jungle, Japs in the trees, and Japs overrunning a highly defended position.

"Get him away from me," Jim asked Nurse Nora Braun. "Tell him my headaches are gone."

"Are they?"

"Yes," he said. He didn't admit that a new person had become a fixture in his REM sleep. It was Nora, and the dreams were mostly pleasant. After about five months of bed rest, operations, counseling sessions, and answering questionnaires, it came to Jim that he was in love. He did not dare declare himself because he was still as shy as he had been in high school. Still, each day became an ordeal of anticipation, and the weekends when Nora was not on duty challenged his stoic endurance.

Was she just being a good ward nurse? Did she have an interest in him beyond that of a professional, and what kind? In spite of his military exploits, he was still a provincial boy from Kansas who three years ago had not been out of the state.

Nora brought reading material to Jim, magazines, then books. "A little gift," she said, handing him a volume of *Thucydides*. There was a bookmarked passage she wanted to call to his attention. "He calls for moderation. James, please accept this from all of us on the staff." He accepted the handsome volume. He knew it was not a gift from the hospital, and so he treasured it. The books kept coming, some of them from the library. During the last few months of his stay at O'Reilly,

Jim read at least two books a week, some novels, some history, a lot on cattle. His brother Roy wrote postcards, a habit he had adopted during the Great Depression. "I am working for *Neustadt Aisch,* the *Besammungs Verein* Genetic Program," one of Roy's cards said.

In November, Jim received his honorable discharge from the U.S. Army. "You'll have to be content with a lot of bed rest in the next six months," a physician told him. "No lifting, no work, lots of bed rest. I don't want to see you back here."

He was scheduled to be released at noon the next day. He meandered back to his bed and packed the few belongings he had assembled since being medically evacuated from the Philippines. At 4 p.m. he walked to chapel for a scheduled Mass. While the candles were being lit, Nora came in and took a seat beside him. He was not entirely with the service. As the few in attendance rose and knelt, and the server responded in Latin, Jim almost missed the offertory and the consecration. He was jolted out of his reverie when everyone got up to receive communion.

The two lingered in the chapel after everyone left.

"Are you okay?" Nora asked.

Jim took his time answering. "I haven't talked much about what happened when I got hit."

"Only in your dreams," she said.

"Everyone thinks I played Jack Armstrong and cleaned them out. The fact is that I was so scared I could barely hold the Thompson." She started to say something.

"No," he said. "Let me finish. I shook like a leaf." He took her hand. "Nora, I'm at least as scared now as I was then."

"Let's sit down," she said. She guided him to a pew.

"I'm leaving tomorrow. I wanted to ask you to step out with me tonight. I'd like to take you to dinner."

"That's sweet of you," she said, planting an intense kiss on his cheek. He pulled her to him. The kiss was now full on the mouth, sustained, passionate. Finally she pulled away. "We're in a chapel," she reminded him. Jim took her by the shoulders and pulled her to within half an arm's length.

Their eyes locked onto each other and their mirroring smiles did likewise. "Tonight?" he asked.

She nodded. "Tonight!"

18

As Jim packed the books he had accumulated over the many months, he reflected on the lessons he had learned. The agriculture he would find when he got back to Banyon Place would be quite different from the one he had left shortly after the war broke out.

There were some six million family farmers in the United States at the end of World War II. Debts had been lowered or erased during the war years. Land purchased in the late 1930s was paid for by 1945. Yet there was a permanent, haunting fear that the depression of the 1930s would return with a vengeance. The farm leadership was afraid. The drought cycle had been broken, still there was this awesome fear that there would be no rain. The soldiers came home on the whole to resume their upward mobile lives, the wounded to be tucked away, saluted but almost forgotten in dank hospitals or in odorized recovery rooms at home. James Robert Neff could look out on his growing herd of Herefords: fourteen animals. For nearly a year he rarely left his bedroom, and then his health came back. He read a great deal: Balzac, Erle Stanley Gardner, Raymond Chandler, *The Shepherd of the Hills*, histories of the presidents whose names he had memorized. He followed *Time* magazine. By the second year after the end of the war, his old history teacher saw Jim as a self educated young man.

In 1946 Congress passed the Employment Act. "My God, they're going to give farming a fair shake!"

The Act called for a Council of Economic Advisors that would issue the annual Economic Report of the President, and see to it that a structural balance would prevail, which meant that the basic storable commodities from 80 to 82% of the harvested acres would continue to receive parity, that is, if the full parity goal of the War Stabilization Act was extended when it expired in 1948.

Figures do not lie, but liars figured. They had names for their distorted accounting principles. These became styled as agribusiness, vertical integration, and factory in the field. They bandied slogans such as "the family farmer is as obsolete as the horse and buggy." There were speeches to the effect that if farmers did not straighten up and fly right, fifty million people would starve. Anyone who questioned hydrocarbon rings in the food chain was consigned to intellectual underworld status. Chemical fertilizers, pesticides, hormones and antibiotics were the wave of the future. It came to pass that full parity for the basic storable commodities lifted almost all farm products to a prosperity level undreamed of since 1910-1914. Farmers seldom had to borrow to put in crops or buy replacement calves. Banks became alarmed when they were unable to find borrowers for the loans the fractional reserve allowed them to make.

When the next calf crop came due, Jim Neff would have at least a twenty-eight cow herd. He would have at least a bull or two to sell, even his own meat, all from a line bred herd started with a few calves from an old Western Kansas patriarch, the late Xander Staab.

Why could not a man make a living off eighty acres? The more Jim dug into the whys and wherefores, the more he visited with now retired Mr. Miller, the more Jim Neff became a philosopher farmer and a farmer entrepreneur. Real wealth came from grass, a gift of rain and sunshine. It was the price mechanism that conferred value, that in effect monetized grass and turned it into the gold that the old alchemists had forever sought. "Civilization is what happens in cities," the great professor had said, "and the city is dependent on there being a surplus from the food producer and some existing organization that can take it away from him. With this food surplus the political organization feeds kings, priests, armies, architects and builders, and the city comes into being. Political science in its earliest form is the knowledge of how to take the food surplus away from the food producer without giving him too much in return."

Another great professor had put it just as bluntly, "Exploitation of the weak by the powerful, organized for the purpose of economic gain, buttressed by imposing systems of law, and by decorous draperies of virtuous sentiment and resounding rhetoric, have become a permanent feature in the life of most communities the world has yet seen." So wrote

R.H. Tawney in *Religion and the Rise of Capitalism in 1926*, an era that saw raw materials producers the world over exploited mercilessly as a prelude to world depression.

Classic models, Ricardo's iron law of wages, and Manchester formulas notwithstanding, economists came to know that the economic equation started with raw materials taken from the earth, chiefly the raw materials called food. In any working equation, raw material production prices had to reflect the cost of production plus a profit in ratio to all cost factors. To the price structure had to be added the cost of handling in terms of transportation, processing, and capital costs so that in the end the consumer price level reflected parity, with all cost factors in balance, and a market sufficient for the production. If this statement comes terribly close to rephrasing Say's *Law of Markets*, then it is only because J.B. Say could reason better than he could write. Yet Say was right. Production creates its own demand in a complete economy, if properly priced at every level of exchange. America, as Ralph Waldo Emerson clearly taught, has one of the world's only complete systems. That is to say, America has all the raw materials required to operate a complete economy. Unless the system dynamic collapses, business profits come fastest through exploitation. Much the same is true in farming. Farm profits come fastest when virgin soil is exploited, even when half-life soil is exploited, until finally, Nature revolts and diminished returns set in. Taking the surplus from the country to maintain armies and services depends on farmers wanting to produce, and therefore it has never been wise for the Crown to take everything.

Exploitation procedures become more complicated when business is involved. The businessman is not interested in consuming the production, but in profiting from the traffic therefrom. He knows it takes imbalance, an oversupply in one commodity in one place, and an under supply in that same commodity in another place, to create a differential advantage. Only an exchange equation out of balance delivers fantastic wealth to a few and poverty to many. There is a subtle difference between creation of wealth and the manipulation thereof.

"These jobbers, loan issuers, banks and insurance companies," wrote Vincent Vickers, former Deputy Lieutenant of the City of London, a director of Vickers, Ltd., and former Governor of the Bank of England,

169

"create nothing at all. They are the parasites of the national good and life and are dependent upon the money that others collect. Like the unemployed, they are supported at the cost of the nation."

So what about the bankers? They grow rich with the ups and downs of trade, whereas, "production industry grows rich upon stable markets, a constant price level, and the absence of economic fluctuation." Thus the name of the international trade game, playing off one nation against the other, involves each nation in an economic gamble none can win. First to feel the shock waves have always been the farmers. By the time manufactured goods become involved, it is already late in the game. Farm leaders have not understood this point entirely.

"There is something radically wrong in our industrial system, there is a screw loose," said Colonel L.L. Polk of the Farmer's Alliance in 1890. "The wheels have dropped out of balance. The railroads have never been so prosperous, and yet agriculture languishes. The banks have never done a more profitable or better business, and yet agriculture languishes. Towns and cities boom and grow, and yet agriculture languishes. Salaries and fees were never so temptingly high, and yet agriculture languishes." Agriculture languished, in Bernard Baruch's words, because of the business posture and lack of organization. It was an industry with high fixed costs and low variable or out of pocket expenses, just the opposite of most commercial enterprises. Moreover, most of the fixed costs are imputed. The farmer owes himself a wage. He owes himself a return on his investment. He owes it to himself to build up a depreciation reserve.

But if he fails to meet these imputed costs, even if he consumes his capital, he will continue to produce. He will not be carried into bankruptcy as fast as, say, a shoe factory with a union payroll. As a result, the farmer's minimum supply price has the earmark of being low. With the world of business forever barking at his heels, the farmer's low minimum supply price is taken out of nature's hide.

"I've worn out two farms," was an old frontier saying. "I'm still young enough to wear out another."

Dangle money or bankruptcy in front of the farmer and he'll plow to the doorstep. The dust storms of the 1930s became an illustration of what nature can do when in revolt. The minimal supply price became the focal point of Baruch's report to the Kansas State Board of Agriculture in the 1920s. He said farming was uneconomical and inefficient because the farmer could not adjust his production to meet market conditions the way the factory could, and that the farmer was always at the mercy of nature. His final point was that agriculture's trouble was compounded by its lack of market organization. Each sale was a forced sale. This precisely was what made it possible for institutional business and government to keep a commissary for the nation and at the same time pursue policies geared to exploiting the farmer, his land, and his production labor. In the meantime, industrial business had come into its own. The point must be made that veritable pirates learned how to rig the exchange equation.

While farmers, labor, and investors languished, the money game overtook the production of wealth, harnessed real wealth, and ushered most of the body politic into a bondage few could manage to understand. This bondage all but canceled out the rules set down by the Founding Fathers. Robert L. Heilbroner, writing in *The Worldly Philosophers,* belatedly provided an illustration. The sequence he told about would be rejected as fiction except for the quoted exposure it now enjoys. He tells how William Rogers and William Rockefeller bought Anaconda without spending a single dollar of their own. Here's how: Rogers and Rockefeller gave a check for $39 million to Marcus Daly for the Anaconda property on the condition that he would deposit it at the National City Bank and leave it untouched for a specified period. They then created a paper organization known as Amalgamated Copper Company with their clerks as dummy directors and an agreement to buy Anaconda not for cash, but for $75 million in Amalgamated stock, which was newly printed for the purpose.

From the National City Bank Rogers and Rockefeller now borrowed $39 million to cover their check. As collateral they used the $75 million in stock they had created out of thin air. Now the Amalgamated stock hit the market, having been touted through their brokers. They repaid the original $39 million loan from National City Bank and pocketed $36 million as their own profit on the deal.

The existence of real wealth in the form of Anaconda made flim-flam wealth manipulation possible. That this represented breathtaking dishonesty could be understood by all except academic economists. Somehow, sleight of hand became thrift and accumulation. Robber baron fraud became enterprise. Lavish display of wealth became conspicuous consumption. In the classroom, one never learned about rigged markets, exploited farmers, or legislators who were bought and sold like popcorn. The world needed a de Tocqueville. It got John Bates Clark, S.H. Taussig and Alfred Marshal. When a Henry George came along to live and die, his soul went to heaven, but his economics went to hell.

More important than all this was the fact that business and industry homesteaded in the government quite early in the nation's history. In fact, Woodrow Wilson complained that "The masters of the government of the United States are the capitalists and manufacturers, the big masters of commerce, and the heads of railroad corporations and steamship corporations."

Against this spectacular foe stood the independent farmer and the farm organizations staffed by self made leaders who were in love with the status quo. Instead of analysis, they turned to agitation. As a South American aphorism had it, "agitation is beautiful, organization difficult." Oliver Hudson Kelley's Patrons of Husbandry, or National Grange, grew rapidly after the Civil War. It finally became a powerful group during the panic of 1893. The Grange became powerful not as a business organization, but as a farm bloc, and for one bright shining moment in history it looked as if farmers and their leaders were making their case as to how the exchange equation should work, but did not. They did not arrive, but they came to realize that the farm problem was not to be solved with "go it alone individualism." Agitation was beautiful, but as political hoopla lost its clout, so did the Grange.

Belatedly, the group went into buying and selling, and setting up cooperatives, creameries, wool houses, produce barns, elevators and the like. Unfortunately, do it yourself business could not compete with business structures that siphoned the ablest people from the farm front, salaried them, and set them to work undoing their own. Business success and ballyhooed success made the political arena balance sheet. Anti-monopolists, reformers, farmer's parties, populists, on and on, fought battles in state assemblies, finally spilling over into Congress to set up the Interstate Commerce Commission. As for the wool houses and co-ops, the disciplined business of record keeping and traffic management soon took its toll. By 1895 the Grange fell to a low of about 100,000 members.

Biting into the backbone of the Grange was the Farmer's Alliance. Founded in Texas in 1875, the Alliance hoped to fight horse thieves and land sharks and keep Negroes in their place, unsophisticated aims, all of them. A Colored Farmers' Alliance had come to Texas in 1866, ultimately claiming a substantial membership. It seems useless to catalog all the farm groups that have passed from the mind and memory of man. Almost all have been forgotten.

Not so with the Farmer's Union, also chartered in Texas. The Farmer's Union sensed from the start that the political arena was bought and paid for stuff, and that to deliver parity for farmers they would have to out captain the captains of industry. The Farmer's Union warehouses and elevators soon dotted the landscape from Texas to Minnesota. Again, the agrarian myth worked its damage. The best leadership was excited because they did not look like farmers. Newt Gresham, the founder of the group, was expelled from the organization because he was a newspaperman, not a farmer, although he farmed on the side. By the time the Farmer's Union made Charles Garrett of Georgia president of the group, the glow of the business approach had dimmed.

"The ballot is the deadliest weapon known to modern history. Handled in the proper way, we can shoot down the hypocrites and shysters," he said. History records that wartime prosperity, poor organization, and poor leadership caused Union co-ops to dwindle in Texas by 1920. The dollar had been dangled in front of the farmer and it bore the imprimatur of high patriotism. World War I saw some fifty million acres of agricultural lands in Europe go out of cultivation. Some forty million grassland acres in the U.S. were plowed and cultivated for the first time. It was estimated that more food production land was lost by erosion during the twenty years between 1914 and 1934 than in the whole of history.

Still, the political power of farmers remained at high tide. During the years immediately following World War I, the Farmer's Union led the drive for the Capper-Volstead Act in 1922, and almost all of the general farm groups figured mightily in hammering home the great farm legislation of that era. If the farm leaders did not understand the cunning nitty gritty of trade ethics, or lack thereof, at least they understood that the exchange equation required full parity. During the first and second decades of the twentieth century, farm leaders knew enough about parity and how they could get it. They marched into Congress and got the Fordney McCumber Tariff Bill. They sent men to Congress who delivered McNary Haugen, interstate commerce laws, and co-op laws. They understood quite well that independent farmers could enjoy a proper exchange equation only with the proper game plan, and only with an economy dominated by something less than monopolies. Although the 1920s saw the greatest farm statesmanship in the memory of living man, countervailing forces had been put in motion. The first came in 1911. At that time the Grange was kicking the devil out of the railroads.

At Binghamton, New York, the Lackawanna Railroad and the Chamber of Commerce combined to form a farm organization with a unique role. This group was organized to keep farmers from organizing and created conditions that permitted rural exploitation. The Chicago Board of Trade agreed to help and backed its agreement with drafts for $1,000 per county. As Farm Bureau chapters came into being, the $1,000 checks kept coming until $100,000 worth had been dispersed. The Board of Trade president later said, "The Board of Trade was sort of a godfather to the Farm Bureau movement." He did not say, "Because we had to organize farmers to keep them from organizing," but it was a fact just the same. The Farm Bureau could boast by the late 1930s, "Two years is the time required to sell all of rural America thoroughly." This was sheer braggadocio. It took longer. It took from 1911 until the late 1920s for the Farm Bureau to put into motion the forces unleashed by the early Grange, the Alliance for Progress, the Farmer's Union, and the other great movements. First, money, lots of it, had to seize control of the intellectual advisors to the community; journalists, teachers, ministers. So they would serve the needs of the great industrial combines and, not least, the emerging agribusiness giants. This feeling of a bond between Bureau leaders and the powerful classes could not be allowed to reach a level of full consciousness. Indeed, great pains had to be taken so that no county, state or national Farm Bureau official would come to feel subservient to the ultimate authority. Such a recognized consciousness might bring on revolt by honest teachers, publishers, writers, speakers and farm leaders. Crude forms of intimidation might work on some few individuals, but the new body of farmers had to be influenced by more subtle techniques. Other men with other voices had already seen to it that a Foundation law had arrived. Tax sheltered foundations could drain tax money from a parent corporation, feed it into the educational machine, and make certain the discovery of the right laws and perpetuation of the right ideas. Technology that was not selling could be sold if the intellectual advisors to the community became a subtle selling force. Still other men had seen to it that a central banking structure had come into being. Such a structure could create debt when farm prices fell. Capitalize on savings and expand on earnings went out the window. Under a fractional reserve, a mere $100 on deposit would be multiplied to over $10,000 in debt, and debt became the mechanism for transfer of the wealth of the nation into the hands of a few. What farm leaders of the 1920s did not understand was their position on the curve of history. They did not realize that they had neutralized the exploitative capacity of domestic business, or that a new power play was in the making. "I'm not worried about agriculture as long as the crops keep coming," said Calvin Coolidge when someone asked him about agriculture. So Silent Cal vetoed both McNary-Haugen bills.

In the wake of those vetoes was born a great infatuation with foreign markets. The troubles that were to arrive did not spring so much from the evils of individual businessmen and bankers, who were as sailors on a battleship designed by geniuses to be run by common men, but from a total lack of understanding of the way in which the mechanism of free trade would ultimately work. The simple-minded idea of Richard Cobden, a mere business equation, was enlarged into world economy. This, without either a world government or a world currency.

The industry of free international trade soon prescribed exploitation of the land. Poison Control Centers were soon to be established so that farmers could farm with poisons.

Private First Class James Robert Neff, now discharged from both the hospital and the army, added his notebooks to the box of volumes an orderly had promised to ship home for him. He carried only a duffle bag with clothes, his discharge papers, and a bus ticket the army had supplied as he left the medical building to make his way home.

He had studied history enough to know that he was being discharged into a vacuum. Brother Joe Sam had said it was damn foolishness to figure on a cowman's career. Was he right? Right or wrong, Jim had a passion for what he wanted to do, and, like Homer's heroes, he would rely on mind over circumstance to win out.

19

Jim Neff could barely walk when he got off the bus from O'Reilly General Hospital in Springfield, Missouri. He still had eighteen shrapnel wounds and iron splinters which would take years to remove. His stay at the hospital had been two days shy of eight months. He still read slowly because of pressure on his optic nerve. Much iron had been removed and the prognosis was guarded, though good. From the first, he listened to the radio a great deal, and he cried openly the day President Truman ordered the atomic devices dropped on Japan. The military had estimated it would cost one million lives should it become necessary to invade Japan's home island. He knew the survivors of the 41st infantry would be coming home instead of being slaughtered on Japan's killing fields.

For months he suffered, first at the hospital, now in lonely Banyon Place, a leftover from an earlier era. The nurses and doctors had been kind to him, all of them, but his thoughts went back to the dark haired nurse who had calmed his shattered nerves set into motion by a dream. Nora Braun, Nora Braun, he repeated to himself because he could not get her out of his mind. He told himself, "For all your gutsy forays, the fact is you're a coward." It was a harsh assessment. Yes, he followed orders like an automaton during almost all of his months in service. Only anger seemed to crank a decision out of him. Now, no longer a teenager, he questioned his path through life multiple times.

He did not look the part, but he was really a student. He had aced all his courses at the junior college before he was given a free, all expense paid trip to the South Pacific. He had already mastered much of the material college sophomores get. If Dad could hang on with the farm, he would like to get a degree, probably in animal husbandry. Long before his bus connections returned him to U.S. 54, he recalled select scenes from the bedrest life he had just concluded.

"Hello, James. I'm Nora Braun."

Jim was wide awake."You can sit on the edge of the bed," he said.

"No, I'll pull up a chair," she said.

Jim had heard her voice often while fog still obscured everything that fell within his limited view. She was always carrying a clipboard, always adding to a record that must be miles high in some archives. She had dark hair, green eyes, and a figure worthy of a model's runway. Even with fog in his eyes, he could tell that much. He felt a rush of adrenalin when she first removed bandages from his head. Some of those wounds exuded serum for weeks and months.

The first time he really took note of her presence was when she found a *Reader's Digest* article that had to do with agriculture. She called him James, not because she wanted to be formal, but because she loved to roll the syllable off her tongue. She sat down and read the article that day. He noted that some of the vocabulary was beyond her understanding. He knew the grammar of the subject much better than the *Reader's Digest* writer. As a matter of fact, Jim Neff was self educated well beyond the level achieved by most of his army contemporaries. He was quite literate in history thanks to the guidance of his high school history teacher, Mr. Miller.

Jim dreamed his way through Fort Scott, La Harpe, Gas City, and into the bus station at The Kelly Hotel. As the driver announced "Iola," he was concluding a delightful inventory of the many times Nora visited him after hours at his ward bed, culminating with a secret tryst in the chapel and a clandestine dinner in Springfield. He had wanted to give her his phone number, but then he remembered that Banyon Place had no phone. He did not have the nerve to ask her for her address because it was clearly against regulations to supply such information to patients.

The terminal worker asked Jim if he wanted a ride home.

"Why, yes. Is there a taxi?"

"No, but the police come and give service people a ride home when they come in."

"Where do you live?" a cop barely out of his teens asked when he picked him up.

"Do you know Banyon Place?"

"Yes, about three miles out with those registered Herefords."

He hoisted Jim's duffle bag into the back seat.

"Glad you made it home."

At Banyon Place, Jim thanked the young man.

"My pleasure."

Jim surveyed the homestead. It looked beautiful like a monument, majestic yet run down, an artifact from yesteryear, yet a bright and shining castle on a hill. The hill was only a knoll, but to the young ex-soldier's eyes it was the promise of the life he and his buddies had fought for. The shutters needed paint, as did the structure itself, all except the slate roof and the widow's walk that skirted the roof and invited a calming breeze on a summer evening.

He paused only briefly before shouldering his duffle and limping into the kitchen. He did not say a word. He put his arms around his father and gave him the embrace he would have given Mom were she still alive. "Jim," his father said, and then fought back the tears. "Jim, Royal isn't coming back." And with that, the exchanges were off and running. Earl Mathew Neff put a pot of coffee on the stove, pushed aside the clutter on the kitchen table, and asked Jim to fill in the details. That request lasted for only a moment, then it died. Jim was not very talkative.

Those lapses into silence caused Dad to bring to the fore the happy news of prosperity at Banyon Place. The mother cows Grandpa Xander had given Jim had increased and multiplied, courtesy of Pericles the bull. Jim now had nearly thirty-six animals ready for reproduction. Sales of calves dropped by sale barn cattle had earned well during the war years, so well in fact, that Dad had discontinued outside employment.

A helper had moved into the old tack room of the stable. He was an otherwise unemployable man known locally as Dummy Ortman. Dummy moved cattle from paddock to paddock as ordered and helped with chores. He had lost his hearing as a consequence of a childhood disease and rarely spoke, but he was a faithful worker, except! Except Dummy announced his take-off every few months. He would simply disappear. Some say there was a bordello in Sapulpa, Oklahoma, where he enjoyed his savings. Around Tuesday morning a week after disappearing, he would show up, contrite, eager to go to work, happy in his improvised apartment.

"I offered him a room in the house," Dad said, "but he wanted his *privacy.*"

"What about Roy?" Jim asked.

Roy Lee Neff became a Sergeant in the 10th Armored of Patton's Third Army. Always fluent in German, he had graduated from tank driver to interpreter during the drive toward Berlin. At one point, an entire platoon surrendered to Roy because he knew how to talk to them. Instead of becoming a prisoner himself, he escorted the entire unit back into American lines, Roy being the sole guard. By the time the war ended, Roy had made contacts.

First, he married a young lady whose uncle was associated with a post-war program designed to improve herd health. Roy's letters home told of the devastation brought on by war. The entire animal population was ravished by disease. People had tuberculosis, and so did the cattle. Hoof and mouth disease was only one of the numerous problems with no end in sight. Most of the animal population had been annihilated by the starving population and by invading troops. Very few farm livestock even survived. Under the direction of Jan Bonsma, the agricultural doctor from Pretoria, South Africa, a breeding program based on artificial insemination was developed. Only tested and quality animals were allowed for reproduction. Apparently, Roy managed to get a laboratory job under the auspices of a scientist. They figured they could eliminate all disease by eliminating unregulated copulation between disease bearing animals. "I'm afraid we're not going to see much of Roy," Dad said. "He's decided to stay in Germany. He wrote that one Jan Bonsma is a consultant. He expects to visit the U.S. one day and Roy tells me he's to look in on you." Dad and Jim discussed the prospects for artificial insemination. The use of processed semen from proven bulls made the German development something to watch.

Jim was exhausted after the long bus ride. "I want to talk about Mom," he told Dad, and then added "tomorrow."

He reopened the letter Dad had written, and reread it in his mind. "She gave up on life," Dad had said.

When he arose at 10 a.m. the next morning, he asked Dad about her retreat from life.

"She lost it when they brought Earl Jr.'s body back from Colorado," Dad said. "She could no longer read, cook or garden. Then we got news that Roy was a prisoner, and after that we received a War Department telegram that you were critical."

179

Dad spun his coffee cup in its saucer. "Well, the war ended and we heard Roy was OK, but that telegram about you laid her low. Your mother was never very robust after we left Ness. That day the sheriff and deputies put her out in the street. I think that broke her spirit. When we got that followup telegram that you weren't on the critical list anymore, she went to bed. She seemed quite well that night. When I went into her bedroom with breakfast, well," He paused for a moment, his voice breaking. "she was gone." Jim and his father went back and forth for days, reliving everything from the high plains to Banyon Place, especially Banyon Place, and the start of the closed Hereford line. One of the bulls born at Banyon Place would not track and could not mount properly. Dad Neff had sold him off. There was no breeding between animals over 50% related. Dad Neff kept ledger records noting the eligibility for service. Last year he had ordered in artificial insemination service for one group, that service having become available from what appeared to be a prize bull. Withal, it was the prospect of a solvent agriculture that intrigued the soldier boy come home. Dad was happy to explain.

"About the time you enlisted, the government passed the Stabilization Act of 1942." This act made it possible for producers of grains from 82% of the harvested acres to receive full parity at the market. If the traders did not want to pay that price, the farmers had the option of putting the crop in storage.

"With the Stabilization Act and the Steagall Amendment, basic storable commodities and semi-storable farm products, including milk and meat, become equally profitable. Jim, if this stabilization thing holds, you're in the money not merely running a beef operation."

Dad looked out the window longingly at the north two 80s. "If I had those 160 in corn, I could really make out. Boy, oh, boy, what parity prices do for the farmer!"

"Let's not get into grain," Jim said. "We don't have the heavy farm machinery. We don't have a tractor. Grandpa told me not to let the trade vultures get on top."

"You still think grass?"

"Yes. With grass, costs stay near zero. Machinery and interest will break anyone, even with the parity we'll likely get."

"We'll see," Dad said. "The Stabilization Act is up in 1948." Jim did not figure he would be paid for much until then, a year and a half down track. While he was building back his strength, he made mechanical drawings that concerned Banyon Place. The place looked used, but was clean as a pin. Its oak floors needed sanding and varnishing. The woodwork was in excellent shape, even if weathered. The roof was good enough to last until the next ice age.

Jim's diagrams showed the channel route for wiring and new plumbing to the second floor. A special conduit was proposed to handle water and inside toilets to two bathrooms on the first floor plus kitchen, and similar facilities for the second floor.

"It'll take a mint," Dad said.

"Not if I can do most of the work," countered Jim. "It won't take a mint to get new kitchen cabinets, but it'll sure take a mint to paint the whole place and the barn and the carriage house," he admitted.

There was more, the bathrooms would need tile, the living room would need carpet. Most importantly, a storage tank connected to the well would have to provide gravity flow to the entire place as well as to the field water tanks for the livestock.

"We'll start small," Jim said, and with that, he ordered in a telephone service.

"First off, we'll have some of that Western Kansas steppe." Using letters from Germany, Jim learned all that Roy had to offer, which included the measuring lessons that consultant Jan Bonsma taught the German breeders. Testicles had to achieve a certain girth and length. The bulls capable of settling most of a fifty-cow herd during the first thirty days of the breeding season were required to measure out with an exactness once detailed by an old Kirghiz tribesman to Xander's father. The intelligence that Roy's letters delivered was that when a bull calf reached six months of age, the rancher should be able to tell whether it would become a useful sire. On that basis, three of the sons of Pericles, sons called Son I, Son II, and Son III, measured up.

Grandpa Xander taught Jim one lesson that became etched into his memory. "If you go into debt, remember: the banker will sit down to eat with you three times a day seven days a week and always take the first helping." He said, "Those banks can counterfeit money, you can't! Don't even try to play their game!"

Against his better judgment at the time, Dad Neff had conducted the business according to the rules of Xander while Jim was away. The sales of bulls and cows, always at a premium, landed profit on the Neff household, while Jim regained his health.

Jim was ordering in college catalogs from Kansas University and Kansas State when suddenly his dad passed away. The doctor said it was gray lung, a syndrome not unlike the black lung that cut down so many coal miners. Cement dust brought on lung congestion.

He died peacefully exactly one year after Jim returned home. He smiled before he closed his eyes. His last words to Jim were, "You're in the running!" He found it unnecessary to say the obvious: "Don't expand too fast. Don't get greedy."

Jim really did not mind being alone, but Banyon Place was a big house and a lonely one. Dummy Ortman still lived in the tack room and did not have anything to say that did not concern the cows. Jim hired a Mexican woman to come in and tidy up the place once a week. His visitors were few, one being old Doc Podolinsky.

"Jim, I have a proposition for you," said the physician on one of his visits. Jim waited, finally he acknowledged the gesture. "And what would that be?"

"I have a bad heart. I may not be here very long."

Jim started to fidget.

"No, let me finish," the doctor said. "My buggy horse, can you put him to pasture for me as long as he lives?"

"Well, of course, Doc," said Jim.

"If you do that, you can take the eighty acres adjoining your Banyon Place." Doc gave him a price.

"I can't afford that," Jim said. "I don't have enough cashflow to handle that."

"It's not a question of cash," Doc Podolinsky replied. "I'll pay you enough for keeping my horse to make the payments. If he dies, I'll reduce the price enough so you can keep the land. If you have to put him down, do it humanely. You'll be paid."

Doc Podolinsky finished, "I'm having my attorney draw up the papers as soon as possible." Jim was happy to take Doc's horse as a permanent resident in his own pasture. He found time to visit the horse each day, to proffer a lump of sugar, to deliver a human voice to the equally lonely pony. Since his discharge from the service, Jim had been too busy for much social life. A coffee at local restaurants once or twice a week kept him in touch with the community, but not much more.

One day, not long after his dad's funeral, a simple looking station wagon pulled into his gravel driveway. He did not recognize the car or its Missouri plates. He walked to the driver's side.

"Well, hello, total stranger," he said, imitating Amos 'n Andy. "For God's sake, it's Nora!"

"James," she said. She had always called him James. The name rolled off her tongue in what he took to be a sensual sound, and he liked it. "How's my soldier boy?"

"Out!" Jim was beside himself. "Out of that car, and into the house! I'll make us some coffee."

She opened the door, got out, and gave the ex-soldier a hug, a real bear hug, a hug such as he had never received in his life. She was over at Fort Scott where she had read of his dad's death in an old *Iola Daily Register.* She could not resist driving over to check on her patient. She was out of uniform now, trim as a goddess with the face of an angel. She had on pedal pushers and a short-sleeved blouse. Her sweater curved thrillingly, revealing the maturity he forgot he had noticed under the starched nurse's uniform. No mistaking it! Here was that scent of a woman, that clean scent that made his heart pump like a swing drummer. He held her at arm's length, then he pulled her to him for one real hug and a mouth to mouth kiss with an exchange always forbidden before. Her tongue darted between his teeth as if to say, "I mean business!"

Dummy would see to the feed and water and changing of pastures. They talked through supper time and well into the night before it came to them that they needed something to eat. After invading the refrigerator and pantry, she rustled up a sandwich with eggs and toast. Bacon and beans followed. It did not matter. She was as hungry for love and companionship as he was, and readily accepted the offer of Mom's bed.

He started to ask, "Shall I wake you or nudge you?" but he thought better of it. He knew she was for real. She had booked, then cancelled, a room at the Kelly Hotel.

"Yes, I would love to sleep in this palace," she said.

183

"One day I'll have it looking like a palace," he assured her. He disappeared to her station wagon for her luggage, and set it in her room.

"Do you have to run in the morning, or can we have a late breakfast?" She was a visiting nurse. She could disappear for a day. "And this," she said to herself, "is the day!"

20

Nora woke up when she smelled the bacon frying. The place was a bit untidy but comfortable. In her mind she did some redecorating, moving furniture, hanging out carpets. It was a grand place, rich in expensive woods and the opulence of a gilded age. There were six bedrooms, closets galore, and a yawning living room she instantly perceived as a library.

They ate their breakfast and talked, not about the war at all, but about the cow-calf and seed stock operation her soldier boy was running. She had to run for now, but she promised to be back.

"Please!" he said pleasantly.

Nora returned a half dozen times over the next several months. When calving time drew near, she came for an extended stay, put on boots, and joined Jim in the calving chores. She had not done any farm work since she had went off to nursing school in Wichita. She enjoyed the work and marveled at the beauty of the calves being born, struggling to their feet and taking their first meal of colostrum. By the time the last heifer had dropped her calf, both Nora and Jim wanted to celebrate. They talked it over on the widow's walk with a spring breeze sweeping the slate roof of Banyon Place. Her kisses had become more than platonic. They spread a blanket on the widow's walk and picnicked together and opened two beers.

"When I was a very little girl my Uncle Bryant, he brought back a potted banyan tree from Florida. I kept it in the kitchen until it was too big to remove from the house in Humboldt. I cried for days when my uncle cut it up." Jim listened intently. The way she delivered the story was sad. "Don't you see, James? God saw to it that you had your banyan tree with room for it to grow. Don't let memories of Biak destroy you, us!" He started to say something but he thought better of the impulse and continued to listen.

Nora continued, "I see the symbol of the old banyan tree reborn as Banyon Place. It's here, James, ready to grow without limit, without boundaries. That tree to me is a symbol of perpetual love and it's yours, James, all of it. Oh, how I love this place! I know you love this house and land and I want to be a part of it, James."

Her eyes fastened on his with a peculiar energy.

"James," she said, picking up his hand and bringing it to her breast, "you know what these are for, oh, you're blushing." He squeezed the mammary very slightly. She said, "They're for nursing babies. And for husbands to kiss."

He still did not speak.

"James, I want a family. I've never had a family." She had not, true enough. Her parents both died in a common tragedy: a car wreck. This one had taken place under the overpass north of Humboldt. A childless uncle had raised her. "I've never had a brother or sister."

Jim kissed her gently. "I think that's a capital idea. I'll help you have those babies."

"I take it we're engaged?"

"I think so," he said.

The banns of marriage were read on the next three Sundays, and the words of the prescribed ritual were exchanged a week later on Saturday. The children arrived, all at three-year intervals. First, a dark haired, eight-pound boy, then a seven-pound blonde haired girl, and finally a handsome boy, eight-and-a-half pounds on June 18, 1955. During this period, the house at Banyon Place got a renewal. Under Nora's direction, Jim worked from the top down. First the attic was fitted with lights and plank flooring, this so that storage space was forever available, replete with space for storage boxes. Nora proved to be a methodical wife. She had a place for everything and usually kept everything in its place.

The upstairs rooms and baths were next. New plumbing was installed, new wallpaper, and throw rugs. "You can't bury gorgeous oak flooring under a carpet," she said.

Only half of the bottom floor was finished by the time Nora became pregnant with number two son. The living room had been turned into a library and office, with shelves from the floor to the extra high ceilings. The year 1955 made Nora a true believer in the philosophy Jim had picked up from Grandpa Xander. Corn prices fell to depression levels, and hogs were selling at ten cents a pound. In every direction, farmers were going belly up.

In the journal Jim kept, he noted the birth of a son and the price of corn. When the mail arrived that day, the dire warnings of Xander and Dad came back to him.

From Ness County came word about Jamie Stitz, the man who ran a cartage business and a farm, and who had hunted next to Jim in the big rabbit drive. Stitz had excused himself from the dinner table and headed through the back door toward the barn. It was his routine after dinner so no one paid much attention. Most men use a shotgun when they have given up on life. Not Jamie Stitz. He tied a hangman's knot replete with thirteen coils around the pilot slip, one end of the rope was fastened over a barn rafter, the noose around his neck. He climbed to the bed of his Omaha Standard and stepped off into space. His neck was broken instantly and his body described an arc partly reminiscent of the pendulum of an eight-day clock. When they cut him down, they found a note. "I'm sorry."

Jim had seen plenty of deaths on the battlefield, but this economic fatality caused him to retreat into nightmares.

In every direction, the "Having decided to quit farming" notices were going up once again. As far as Jim could see, it was out of one depression into another in less than a lifetime. Here and there farmers were forming up into correspondence committees. Some signed petitions. All wanted to know what was going on.

What happened was that public policy changed within days after the war ended. The stabilization measure had been written to expire two years after the end of the war, which could be considered officially over either by treaty or by Presidential Proclamation. President Truman took the appropriate step on the last day of 1946.

Jim's neighbor, Mr. Miller, now retired as a high school history teacher, was more astute than most farmers. He went through newspapers like a vacuum sweeper. "The issue," he said, "is parity. The grain traders don't want it, and they own Congress." He was talking about the parity formula developed by Professor George Warren and sold to FDR by George Peek. Fully implemented during the war years and up to 1948, it had brought prosperity to farmers.

Mr. Miller explained to Jim, "The day before the Democratic Convention that nominated Harry S Truman, the conferees fired the chairman and installed a new conferee for bills just passed by both houses. They decided to offer Mr. Truman a bill that extended parity for a year. They also gave him a bill that put parity on a collision course with solvency. Well, Truman signed them both. During the rest of his administration, your farmers received parity, usually with piecemeal legislation."

"What happened then?"

"Dwight D. Eisenhower became President. He made Ezra Taft Benson Secretary of Agriculture. Benson's first words were that he was not going to mollycoddle the farmers."

"What did he mean?"

"The producers of commodity grains from 80% to 82% the harvested acres would henceforth receive somewhere between 60% and 90% of parity."

"With subsidies?"

"Yes, with subsidies. The idea is to have American products sell at world prices. American farmers are to receive relief checks in order to keep the natives from becoming too restless."

Little Jacob Alexander Neff was now old enough to check water, patrol fences, and help move cattle from paddock to paddock. Nora had her program. She would do a room, then take off two months. She figured that in one more year Banyon Place would be completely rehabilitated.

During his forays into surrounding counties, Jim picked up farm rumblings. A machinery dealer from Independence, Kansas called a meeting together, inviting an ex-governor to speak. It was a hell raising talk during which the politician relived the days of the Populists and Mary Elizabeth Lease, the fiery lady from Osawatomie, whose contralto voice told farmers to raise less corn and more hell.

"By gory!" one white headed farmer shouted. "We ought to hang the bastards!" There were other shouts. The ex-governor figured he had better cool them down a bit. "Sit down, Jason," he said. "You don't know which bastards to hang!" Tension was broken that way, but it would not last.

Thus was born the idea, "Petition your government!" They signed petitions in Independence, Parsons, Chanute, Fort Scott, Pittsburg, Bronson, and Iola. Everyone threw a dollar into a hat — membership dues! — and an organization of sorts was off and running. Jim heard about the meetings. He even signed one of the petitions addressed to Congress. Newsmen picked up on the story, usually with no real concept of the issues or of the character of rural revolt. Farmers who tried to explain might as well have talked to fence posts. Jim was in a cluster of sociologists and newsmen when the row-crop farmers explained, "Everything is related to everything else. The price of commodities from 80% of the harvested acres determines the level of profit not only for farmers, beef producers included, but for the entire workforce."

At the Chanute meeting there was a fellow everyone called Professor Talbot. He was not a professor any more than an auctioneer is a Colonel. Still, he used the appellation because from a practical point of view he had earned his title. He tracked what happened in Washington the way a vice cop tracks drug dealers.

"We had ten years of parity," he said. "This meant that bankers didn't have much of a market for all the money they were entitled to create." A few "god dammits" rose above the crowd's murmuring.

Professor Talbot continued, "You guys got parity because of Fred Stover and Roosevelt. Fred was with the Farmer's Union. He had FDR's ear. He made the point that a farmer ought to be paid at least as well as a schoolhouse janitor." Talbot explained anew the mechanism. "If the grain companies wanted the grain, they had to pay. If they didn't pay, the government would take the grain in storage."

"What if they refused?" came a voice from the audience.

"They couldn't."

"So that's what they meant by the War Stabilization Act of 1942?"

"That's right. The traders needed the grain."

"What did this cost the government?" came another voice. "Not a dime, not a brass farthing," Professor Talbot said. "The government actually made money in the few instances when it had to take over grain."

The discussion went on well into the night. Clearly, there was confusion about the concept of parity. It was simply a measuring tool. It was at such a meeting that a newspaper reporter recalled an Act passed in 1922, the Capper-Volstead Act. Someone had a copy of the law, and the text was read aloud even though it came to glaze over many an eye. Briefly, farmers were entitled to join together for the purpose of marketing as long as they did not unduly enhance prices.

"Hah! But what does 'unduly enhance prices' mean?" Almost everyone asked that question, either silently or aloud.

A farmer from Nevada, Missouri had the answer and he stood up to speak. When he got the floor, he said, "That was decided by the farm legislation of the early 1930s. The answer, gentlemen, is parity. You can enhance prices to parity without running up against anti-trust. We have the right to stay on par with wages, gas for the tank, and the price of a hundred items we need every day."

These were heady meetings. They sent Jim Neff back to the books he had neglected, and they instilled in his mind truisms he accepted as Holy Writ. Yes, he agreed that U.S. farmers were entitled to first crack at the U.S. market.

He saw coming up a test of wills. He read Louis Brandeis, and accepted the declaration that a man must involve himself in the tests of his time. These farmers were not talking seed stock or cattle ranching, and he wasn't sure how many were interested in herd improvement, but he saw the connection between what was happening to fellow farmers and new pressures on seed stock producers like himself. He realized that an agriculture based on depression prices lacked only drought to bring the country to its dust bowl knees.

Jim caught up with the little professor named Talbot at a Chanute, Kansas meeting. The professor liked Scotch, a flask of which materialized soon enough. The nectar brought new life to the wary scholar and seemed to erase a few wrinkles from his face. Now he spoke with authority. "In 1948 the traders made their move for free trade. You can take it from me that a lot of campaign money changed hands that year. So they got their world level trade and made farmers the goat by having them take subsidies. The bright boys figured it out after the stock market crash in 1929. They invested in refrigeration ships so there was cheap beef from parts of the world where they pay cowboys a dollar a day. All these Capper-Volstead people have to remember is that unless you control imports, you'll always be taking the short stick."

Jim talked it out with Nora. They wondered what kind of a world would little Jake, age seven, and his sister, and the infant boy find as they grew up. Jim surveyed the area visible from the kitchen. "Sweetheart," he said, "when we wind up the last of this building, let's go to the Ozarks for a week or two, just the two of us."

"No way," she said. "Jake and Heidi and the baby come along." She came over to him and gave him an obligatory kiss on the cheek. "We've got a lot more to worry about besides prices," she said.

"What's that? We have no debts."

"No, but we now have Poison Control Centers. We're getting poisons in our food, hormones in store milk, hormones in beef. James, if you teach me history, I'll teach you nutrition."

She changed the subject. "James, I love this place. I'd live with you in a tent if that's what we had to do. I don't want debt hanging over us, not for a vacation or even for more cattle."

"I know," he said. "The bank is always after us to borrow. Sweetheart, I think we ought to join the Capper-Volstead Alliance."

"What is it?"

"There's talk. A lot of farmers think they can move government. They think they're entitled to first crack at the American market. We can't let imports, the grain trade, and a few fat cat cattlemen sell us down the river."

"James, let's do what we have to do." She paused a long time. "But no new debt. Let's allow our banyan tree to grow without battling that kind of fungus."

191

21

On a gray October morning ever afterward known as "that day," Nora watched the children walk the quarter mile to the gravel secondary road where the yellow school bus stopped. They boarded, and Rover II duly returned to Banyon Place. There was a touch of frost in the grass that crackled to the tread of his boots when Jim crossed the yard.

Even if the sun failed to penetrate the mist, it started out as a good day. Nora's prize rooster had announced the new day on time, her "rooster clock," she called her chanticleer. It gave her the opening thrill of the day because she loved the farm, her family, and her husband, not necessarily in that order of importance.

"Hurry," she called to Jim. "There's a telephone call."

A few seconds later, she heard her husband say, "Well, yes, I do believe I'll be there. I'll call St. Joe and get a reservation."

Nora waited. After ten years of marriage, she'd attained a radiant beauty even without makeup. There was a glow to her face and a sparkle of joy in her eyes. Yet those eyes became misted whenever anything telegraphed or even posed a threat. She wanted to ask Jim, "What about St. Joe?" but she did not. She merely set breakfast on the table and waited. "Honey," he said, "sit with me a few minutes." Nora complied. She poured two cups of coffee and offered cream to her husband.

"It's that group that's been meeting, the ones I've spoken to in Chanute. That was Leon Taylor from Chanute. The boys have set up an organizational meeting in St. Joseph, Missouri. They want to formalize the organization and think I ought to go."

Nora waited a second or two before she responded. "Yes, I think you need to be there." Just the same, some of her morning radiance disappeared. "How long will you be gone?"

"Two days at most."

"I know you need to go. I know you feel it deeply every time one of our neighbors quits."

They counted the neighbors they had lost over the last half decade, good farmers with well managed farms, in the main. Their neighbor to the north was just hanging on. Jim never saw such good looking corn and soybeans, and yet Ralph Spear was in trouble.

"I'm going to ask Ralph to ride with me. We can share a hotel room." Ralph, too, was a veteran of the South Pacific war. He had lived through the Okinawa campaign without a scratch, but the war had taken its toll, just the same. He and his patrol had sought shelter in a tomb after throwing out all the bodies. The experience had left him with battle fatigue, "shell shocked," as WWI vets would have it. When he had gone off to war, the 300-acre farm was deeply in debt. Parity prices during the war enabled his dad to remove the mortgage cloud free and clear. Since about 1950 the financial picture had changed. Corn and soybean prices crashed. Ralph's dad had become injured when a tractor rolled over, pinning him to the ground for hours. On top of that, Ralph had bought a new line of equipment when he took over. Jim had cautioned him about going into debt, but the Svengali types at Extension explained that we had to install modern efficiency if we were going to feed the world. Now this debt was drowning him.

One time Jim had accompanied Ralph to see the loan officer at the Federal Land Bank and another at the Farmer's Home Administration. These loan officers made Jim uncomfortable. One and all, they talked down to the farmer. They scanned them over with their eyes as if examining a new species of vermin emerging from the woodwork. They parked their feet atop their desks while issuing their putdowns. They liked to smoke cigarettes or big cigars, clouding the smoke into the faces of the people they were supposed to serve. They told Ralph that he had to get efficient or get out. Jim had counseled, "Stay away from those guys, they're not your friends. Before they're done, they'll set a trap for you."

It had been several months since Jim had joined Ralph for the office visits. He was not sure what the situation was, but he knew that it had deteriorated. Later on, Ralph's wife told Jim that her husband often sat in the darkened den, staring at a TV set that was turned off. She said he seldom talked to her. He cried a lot. His only solace seemed to come from working the land. He loved that land, life without it simply was not worth living.

Jim drove into their yard. He asked for Ralph at the house and was told, "Dad went to the barn. He said he had to get some rodents," the youngest daughter said. "He took the shotgun."

Just then Jim heard the explosion of a twelve-gauge shotgun shell. He ran to the barn. He saw a tablet page tacked to a hay bale with a pitchfork. It said, "I did this to myself." It was signed with Ralph's clear cursive signature. Between two bales of alfalfa kept for the children's pony was the lifeless form of the farmer. Jim could not get himself to tell Nora the real details. The distraught farmer had inserted the gun barrel into his mouth. He'd used a short ruler to push the trigger.

When the sheriff was finished with him, Jim came home. He had not been this sick since some starving Japanese had carved Murdock up on Biak Island during WWII. The children came home to a silent house that afternoon. "Do your homework," they were told.

Jim did not say much until well after Jacob, Heidi, and little Xander had gone to bed. Late in the evening Jim and Nora started to talk. They talked until well into the morning.

"You've said it a hundred times, James," she said. "Your parents lost their farm because of debt, admired you when you refused to go into debt." She had seen the agents of lenders forever trying to lure her husband into debt. "Doesn't this herd need expanding? Forget this business of working off the farm while the Xanthippus line reproduces and reproduces. Your wife does not need to take on nursing work."

Nora and Jim had seen the syrupy talk of lenders become as harsh as a sadist's instructions. "Well, whose responsibility is it to pay this debt? You took the risk. We have no alternative but due process."

"You said it, James. Debt is death. Ralph is dead because of debt. We have this place free and clear and a good seed stock herd because we lived with garage sale furniture, a kitchen garden, and the love we have in this family."

Nora needed to explain, "James, you have no idea how I longed for this life. I grew up without parents. My uncle raised me. I had no playmates, no brothers, no sisters. I have no treasured childhood moments. The minute I graduated from high school, I entered nurse's training at St. Francis in Wichita. It was made worse because of the war."

They sipped hot chocolate. She saw that Jim was starting to relax. She spoke softly as if in a dream, "Then I met this boy on a hospital bed. I came to suffer his wounds with him. I suffered most because I didn't know how he felt. I wanted to smother him with kisses, but he was too shy and too sick to respond."

She saw that Jim's eyes were misting over. She reached across the table and took his hand. "James, let me say this, I need to say it. I knew you required a year or more to get your health back. You were a patient for eight months. I knew you had your reasons. You did not even ask me for my address. The night before your discharge, I saw you go into the chapel. Remember, I came in and sat beside you? When mass was over, we stayed behind. Remember, we had that kiss in the chapel? I tremble to this day when I think of it."

Now she reached over the table and took both of his hands. "I want you to know why I risked making a nuisance of myself, stopping in after your father passed away, helping you pull calves, helping you put this place in order. Do you really want to know why I admired and loved you?" Jim remained as silent as stone. Her honesty was relaxing him. He had always appreciated this strangely handsome woman and her natural beauty, but never as now.

"Of all the men I've known, you're the only one who didn't come on like gangbusters. I know you're a man, but you behaved. Remember the night I lured you up to the widow's walk? I would have sinned with you, James, I was pretty brazen. Remember, I asked you if we were engaged, and you said, 'I think so?'" For the first time Jim smiled.

"Oh, James, I love our family. Jacob is already becoming a man. If there's a calf out there without a naval cord, he'll tell me. He observes everything, and how he adores you! And Heidi, she's already a competent cook. And God couldn't have made a more perfect creature than little Xander. James, those children need you the way I need you."

By 2 a.m. Nora and Jim had agreed that efficiency was merely a metaphor for a farmer making a business loan and going into debt. Public policy too obscure to contemplate was leaving a jagged scar on the countryside. Farms, once considered the pride of the country, were suddenly gone, and a great sorrow filled the void. The auction flyers went out with their declaration to quit farming. With each thump of the gavel, a nail was driven into the coffin of a heritage.

During the decade of the 1960s America lost an average of 2,400 farms a week, sometimes via the shotgun, more often by foreclosure. "That's farmers gone each day," said Jim, "as surely as Ralph is gone." In the years of their marriage, Jim had assembled a library of well over a thousand volumes, and except for the German volumes inherited from Grandpa Xander, he had read and studied them all. He saw no clearcut economic mandate for the death of those farms, but public policy had made the result inevitable.

Starting in the mid 1900s, farm parity was ever scaled downward. Always it was kept low enough or high enough to pace the rate of bankruptcy, to provide for liquidation of the family farm without embarrassment to the several administrations. This policy not only paced the rate of farm bankruptcy, it did it in a subtle manner. To survive, many did what Jim did. They temporarily worked off the farm.

Jim himself computed that it would cost about one half as much to provide a living for a cow, feeding them forage only, than it would cost taking the advice of Extension and the university.

The survivors held on, and the losers departed, often quietly, sometimes dramatically, seldom with much embarrassment to the powers that be. "I suppose Ralph's wife will hold an auction. The vultures will buy the equipment," Jim said. "They'll even auction off the canned fruit she has in the storm cellar. I suppose she'll go back to live with her people."

"James," Nora said, "I know you have to go to that meeting. You're too well known to be ignored. So I suppose you'll be offered a post of some sort, perhaps an office."

"I suppose that's likely," he conceded.

"Can I ask you to consider one thing I have to say?" Jim nodded.

"There will be those who demand your services as the leader. James, your family has first claim. Honey, you're as solid as they come, I know that. But you're vulnerable. If we have this discussion now, what we decide will suffice when decision time comes. I think it boils down to this. The farm needs you. Your children need you. I need you, not once a month, but each day. I've seen people caught up in the politics

196

of constitutions, bylaws, minutes, endless meetings, you know, busy nonsense."

"I've thought of that," Jim said.

"When I married a very silent man, I didn't expect him to become a spellbinder. James, your talks really inspire. Speak, talk, give them hell." The hour was getting late.

"It's time to go to bed," Nora said. She knew that the tragedy of the morning had faded a bit, that her husband was back on track. From that small Kansas farm, he had developed a knack for taking facts and figures by the nape of the neck and the seat of the pants, shaking out real results. James, she told herself, was a self educated giant. Perhaps he could help the new populist movement identify the unseen forces operating in the background that put shotguns into the hands of defeated farmers. James had will power to offer, not participation in the wrangling of organization. Real judgment had to be free. Most importantly, the first order of business was to keep the mundane aspects of work from debilitating progress. James had a right to live and benefit from the organization without sacrificing himself to unreal expectations and irrational objectives.

Nora did not burden Jim with what she was really thinking. In her mind's eye she saw the economy and its assault on agriculture as a cannibal society. It was existing by devouring its suppliers, and was destined to collapse like a cancer infested organism. She did not think a few farmers could alter what was happening. The larger body would implode in the fullness of time, but cells would live. The farm was such a cell. Jim was the most reasonable man she had ever known. He was no longer the immature boy his government had turned into a soldier on the killing fields. In war, the irrational trumped the rational, the fate of most societies. Between the death of Ralph and the St. Joseph meeting, Nora offered inspired conversation that caused ideas to swim in the ambient air of reasonability. "This business of not paying farmers for as much wealth as they produce," she said, "means that some have the right to make property out of others. The competent have nothing to gain from the incompetent. This prompted the incompetent to own producers and use them as lackey slaves. What was it the philosopher Spencer said?" she asked before answering her own question. "The attempt to excuse man for his follies can only result in a world full of fools, or something to that effect. It's folly to think a farmer can best the money creators. They are hard where we are soft, and soft where we are hard. Our arena is the management of the farm. They can't compete with us. But when we stick our noses into debt, well, the shotgun becomes a solution, or more likely, the sales notice becomes a substitute. James, we're survivors. You're a survivor." She paused. She knew it was not so much what was said, but what was really heard.

Jim straightened up with what he heard. They were not Nora's words, but his own. Perhaps 75% of the family farms with staying power were without debt. The great grain farmers, the cotton planters, the sugar cane growers, most of them were losing their capital at 2% and 3% per year. The biggest of all were technically bankrupt. Some beat the average this year and perhaps will do so the next. But they were doomed by debt, doomed for buying into the fiction that they were to feed the world, doomed from here to eternity because greed overruled common sense, and fear cut their legs from under them.

Clearly, industrial arrangements created the playing field. For months he had been speech-making, teaching cattlemen and grain producers to capitalize on savings and expand on earnings. In open debate he cited the factors that caused family farms to go broke. He was a survivor. More than that, he sought to prevail. If the silent revolution, about to become organized, had answers, he expected to learn about them at St. Joseph. Nora left her chair and came to Jim's side of the table. Her eyes sparkled as she engaged her husband in an exchange of penetrating looks. "We're in the same boat," she said, "I have had no family and you have no family. You told me yourself that you haven't seen your oldest brother a half dozen times in your entire life. You get a Christmas card, no signature, no message, just a printed name. First, it's from Missouri, then from Boston. Once you heard from Belgium where he was negotiating the purchase of a bus."

Jim had to nod agreement. The move off the Ness County farm had effectively demolished the family. It was all part of the program that now scarred rural America.

"Your brother Royal, he's gone for good. We know he has a German wife and a little boy, and not much more. In ten years we've had a few letters. That's not family. Family is right here in this house with Jacob,

Heidi, and little Xander. Family isn't an assembly of farmers. What's that story your grandpa told you about crazy Ivan asking God to put out one eye rather than suffer Vladimir having more land, crops, or money?"

"I know, Sweetheart," Jim said, "but I also know that you never know who'll walk with you, and I would like to see how this movement plays out."

22

No one really knew Billy Jon Poole. Some of the wire services traveled back into his career and found a young farm boy in overalls who had made a name for himself as a second runnerup in a 4-H steer contest. He had gained an upper hand on the competitors by pressure cooking the feed rations for better digestion. Billy Jon was out to win. He was a portly boy in his teens with chicken legs and a pencil mustache he trimmed once a week. He did not care much for sports and only occasionally played softball, always at first base because he was left handed and that position did not require heavy running. His face was almost oval shaped and his eyebrows linked together as they traversed the sea of Orion.

It was that calf that got Billy Jon on the map. He kept the required records backed by receipts, many of them manufactured for the purpose. He clipped and combed and before showtime he used hypodermic needles and a small compressor to pump air under the hide of his animal wherever an unwanted concave area was detected.

Second runner up carried a cash prize and opened a career as a calf jockey. This profession required scouting out calves for county fair presentation, the feed ration being trucked along in the back of his pickup. When Billy Jon graduated from high school, he took over the family farm. His dad was "plain wore out," the press said, and he looked forward to working, say, half time. The farm was average for Iowa, well managed, always a bit short on labor, but a model of rural efficiency, once the REA delivered electrical power. The farm was diversified, a few dairy cows, chickens, hogs, corn and edible beans.

"Billy Jon," the elder Poole had said, "you take over."

That was at the approximate end of the Depression, after the last of the banks was reopened. A few days after December 7, 1941, Billy Jon felt a call. He joined the Greater Harvest of Blessings Full Gospel

Tabernacle Mission Church, and quickly volunteered for foreign service in Peru. Billy Jon received his revelation after a church official explained that mission workers would be required to register for the draft at the American Embassy in the country where they were performing the Lord's service. Since registrants at embassies were never called, Billy Jon was not able to enter military service. Billy Jon did what is done at mission stations. Using skills developed on the farm, he engineered a fresh water supply for a village near Aquitos. Press notices suggested a star role for Billy Jon Poole because the founding fathers of the new organization were all from Iowa. All had been fanning the prairie fire ever since commodity prices crashed in 1955. When Jim Neff entered the big sprawling auditorium, he calculated that there would be four hundred people in attendance. The place was full of homemade signs flaunting states, crops and slogans. One said, "Welcome, Fred Carlson!"

Carlson had been a governor somewhere, but no one seemed certain of just where or when. One wizened old farmer said it was during the depression, "not this one." Carlson had been recruited to keynote the affair. Jim detected a surprising amount of organization. Proposed by-laws were being circulated, and the name Capper-Volstead Alliance was being displayed prominently. There was to be a board of directors with twenty-one members, and there were to be two delegates, two per organized state. The way the instruments of organization were written, real power was to be seated in the presidency. However, there were provisions for "direction." Under Article 5, Section 8, ten delegates could draw up a special meeting by telephone. Such a meeting could vote to "direct" an action or reaction. It read like a constitution to Jim, a mechanism too cumbersome to be used. Since Billy Jon knew something about *Robert's Rules of Order,* and since he had installed a half dozen screamers in the audience, and since his uncle had instructed him on the finer points of union voting, he was easily named temporary chairman. In this role he was to introduce the governor and later on to preside over the selection of a permanent chairman. Billy Jon took twenty minutes to introduce the Honorable Fred Carlson. During those twenty minutes the sizeable crowd became acquainted with the hog farmer who had endured ten cent corn and ten cent hogs. He referred to himself eighteen times by name, using the third person.

"Who ordered corn to drop to ten cents a bushel?" he asked. "Not Billy Jon Poole! Who caused hogs to have no economic value? Not Billy Jon Poole!" He reminded the farmers that they had paid for their land with the years of parity prices, and now that framework was gone.

The crowd started getting restless. Billy Jon caught the signal from one of the screamers, and so he morphed his message into the much delayed introduction. The words were not fast enough. A thunderous applause rolled over the place like an avalanche. The friend of farmers stepped to the microphone.

The Honorable Fred Carlson was a small man, only five feet tall. During his political days, he was known as the "Little Giant." He was close to eighty, but spry as a grasshopper. He grabbed the microphone, and without saying a word took off his coat, then his tie. He rolled up his sleeves. "By gawd," he said, "we're going to win this thing." He waited for and got a thunderous response. Then Fred Carlson did the unimaginable. "Folks, we can hoot and stomp, or we can listen. If Mr. Roosevelt could deliver a state of the union message from the oval office without everyone stomping and jumping to their feet like popinjays, then by gawd, I can sure as hell talk to you better if we change the rules. I ask you to hold your applause for the rest of my talk. Then I want to tell you we're going to stop farming the farmers and start processing the processors."

The crowd could not restrain itself. It started to applaud, but Governor Fred Carlson held up his hand like Casey at the Bat. When things quieted down, he recited every episode that the Great Depression and the Miles Reno Populist movement had accounted for. "Yes, Woodrow Wilson was evil. He used the Great War to demolish the Non Partisan League. Yes, Warren G. Harding stuck it to the farmer. Boy, oh boy, did those fellows know how to write laws. They wrote the Fordney-McCumber Tariff Bill to protect industry and put it to farmers. Silent Cal followed suit. Twice, the Congress passed the McNary-Haugen Act and twice, that little wart, Silent Cal, twice he vetoed that worthy attempt to protect the farmer. Those evil spirits are still hovering over us. They demolished the Ten Commandments. They strafed the Sermon on the Mount."

Carlson half expected applause, and then he remembered that he had forbidden such display during this serious presentation. He knew

202

Senator Arthur Capper of Kansas, he said. He knew Andrew Volstead. "They wrote the Capper-Volstead Act in 1922 because the monopolies were looting the country. The Capper-Volstead Act allows you to join yourself together to market your products without offending the anti trust laws. My friends, the only prohibition in the law is that you not "unduly enhance prices." Hold it! Hold it a minute! What does the law mean by *unduly*?" He spat out the word straight into the microphone. "The legal eagles have had a good time with that word, and I confess that it troubled me in the 1920s. But we need be troubled no longer. Mr. Roosevelt has come to the rescue." The mild mannered voice of a few minutes earlier was now quite audible, even without a microphone. "In the early 1930s, 7 USC 601-602 became law. It mandated parity prices, not 60 to 90%, not some rigged figure, but full parity. We ask that the law be enforced. So let the word go out from this assembly that we want American law, not Cargill law or ADM law or shyster law initiated by university parasites."

Carlson rushed into his next sentence. "Senator Capper told me that the right to collectively bargain and market is your legal right, your birth right. He had no doubt that the trades would fight you tooth and nail. He said that if industry can violate anti trust, why hell! He'd make it legal for farmers!" A choreographed chant went up, "Capper-Volstead, Capper-Volstead, Capper-Volstead" The chant could not be silenced for several minutes. The governor thanked the crowd for its enthusiasm, "Now let's listen." And with that he embarked on a 15 minute explanation of the law that was giving the organization its name. The crowd was taken with emotion. They were on their feet. One giant of a farmer with a baritone voice shouted, "By gory, let's do something about it! I'll get my gun!"

The governor chewed his lower lip until it felt like hamburger. For the first time in 40 years of politics, he was scared. The last thing he wanted was a riot. He could almost see his listeners scurrying out of the auditorium, setting cars on fire, breaking grocery store windows, even attacking *Farm and Home* offices. He had to instill calm, for which reason the term "scoundrels" was dropped, as was "running dog lackeys." He cited John Adams, Thomas Jefferson, and Abraham Lincoln, and mixed in the rule of law. He brought the discourse back to present officials of the Land Bank, then he said, "So sit down! You don't know who these fools are yet!"

Then he paved the way to peace. "You have a right to organize," he said, and he asked the chairman to hand out instruments to be considered. "These people are your servants," he said, meaning Washington. Laughter swept through the audience. The governor figured that he had miscued on that one, but he continued. "You have a right to state your case in a manner the Creator gave you the intelligence to use. Organize, organize, organize!"

With that and without an additional word, the politician sat down. The screamers, not needed before now, forgot their role. Finally, one started the applause.

Billy Jon resumed command. The affair exhibited a reasonable amount of organization. Some ad hoc committees, self appointed, had met before the great event. Now various groups gravitated to assigned posts where introductions and conversations continued.

Billy Jon talked his way through it all. Three of his neighbors became temporary officials, and a pilot board of directors was suggested. "We'll get into heavy organizing tomorrow," Billy Jon announced as he closed down the meeting for the night.

The Kansans assembled around the chair in which Jim Neff remained seated. He told a man from Ness County, "An awful lot is being steamrolled, don't you think?"

"I suppose," the Ness County wheat grower said, introducing himself. "I understand you hail from the High Plains."

"That's true," Jim said.

"Well, you wouldn't recognize the county today. Half the farms are sections in size."

"What about debt?"

"After your grandpa Xander Staab died, a lot of farmers followed his example. They went to pasture, bred from bulls, and tapped the Ogallala aquifer. With irrigation, the dust died down. I suppose the cycles changed." The rest fit the wheat pattern. Some of the High Plains farmers were among the 2,400 going broke each week, or they got big, carried a backbreaking load of debt, and reversed their baseball caps so they could peer into the mailbox looking for a government check. The check went straight to the bank and the farms failed on schedule when their time came. The star of the day was Billy Jon. Everyone spoke of him that way. He was never Mr. Poole or William Poole. His whispers were stage whispers to be heard by all. Even now, with a cluster of admirers around him, he spoke of himself in the third person. He was well known in Iowa for his two hour speeches. A reporter came once to where Jim Neff was holding forth. "Any comment, Mr. Neff?"

"No. But I support collective bargaining in Billy Jon's message. You can fill in the substance." That was the point. There was little or no substance. You could not drive a ten penny nail through what he said. It worried Jim. After the fifth or sixth "in conclusion," this same reporter had thrown his pencil in the air. The reporter said, "I worry about feedback."

"No comment here. I'm just an attendee."

"I hear they'll squirm when we strike!"

"No comment."

In his mind, Jim transported himself to the next session. It would be Billy Jon, Billy Jon all day. Many farmers were seeing the Iowan as a prophet on par with Elijah, or at the bare minimum a Messiah. Would the new organization come to grips with the real farm problem? The old ex-governor had at least hinted in the right direction.

The Ness County man stayed on until the last of the hand shakers moved off. "That man, Billy Jon, has the crowd walking two feet off the ground," he said. "Is he really making true believers out of everyone?"

"Well, I believe a show of solidarity is essential," Jim said. "In the military we'd call it *resolve*." There was something in Jim's voice that sounded like a question mark.

He knew his wife was home with the children. Likely, she was having supper, and a strong pot of coffee would be on the table. "She ought to be here. I need her," he said to himself. "This is not my ticket. At home, she would ask, 'Jim, are you going to get involved?'" He knew how he would have to answer. "Nora, I am involved. I don't think many people can see it, but we're up to our neck with this farm problem."

"With cattle?" she was bound to ask.

"That's right," he said, half to himself.

The Ness County man asked, "Did you say something?"

"To myself, yes. I think I was drilling myself on what I would tell my wife, and what I would tell people the next time I spoke."

"Can you tell me?" The farmer removed his hat, revealing a lily white forehead.

"It starts with the fact that the farmer has no control over the market. Prices are always set by public auction or speculators. Face it, an auction is a distress sale. I admit that we can always sell at a distress price. That's why, nationwide, we're losing 2,400 farms a week."

"Out our way the farmers are little more than concessionaires for the government. Without the subsidy, very few can put in a crop."

"Yes," Jim said, "and the grain is sold at a world price. The subsidy is a relief check. But the cheap grain is a subsidy to the feedlot. You've heard of feedlots?"

"Not really."

"Well, they're coming on strong." Jim fished a clipping out of his pocket. He offered it to the conversational farmer. It told of cattle trains moving out of Wyoming and Montana to Minatare, Nebraska. Range fed cattle were to be fattened in the lots, cutting the production time of forage fed cattle in half. The clipping read as follows: "It was in fact a brilliant fall day at Walden, that the university spawned idea came to fruition. Starting early that day and working through an October week, cow waddies loaded nearly ninety rail cars with feeder cattle for what was to become the largest cattle shipment in forty years.

"After some 3,000 critters had been gated aboard, the train rolled east to a 40,000 head feedlot. The cattle had been sold from the A-Bar-A property and State Line Ranches operated by Gates Rubber Company. A week earlier some seventy carloads had left Encampment, Wyoming and another twenty-five carloads had moved out from Northgate. There were other transfers from the cow-calf end of the business to the feedlots. All this complied with the new factory in the field idea being touted by academia, provisioned by politicians, and embraced by consumers, all without a perceptible thought of the implications."

The implications had been around for a long time. They did not have to wait for the Kern County Land Company, with holdings two times larger than the state of Rhode Island, nor did they have to wait for the international holdings to punch up imports. The trade, a few favored packers and chains, knew all about Gates and Kern County and the rest.

Kern County had moved into Arizona in 1948, the year post-war parity met its Waterloo with the Aiken Bill. Basically speaking, the firm's out of state ranches were cow-calf operations. On the California side, Kern County maintained stocker ranches and, of course, the great Gosford feedlot. The sprawling giant operated in more than a dozen states and in France, England, Brazil, Austraila, Canada, Ireland and British Honduras. Discovery of oil on Kern County acres in 1936 gave the industrial model for cattle growing and feeding a shot in the arm, sending it on its way. By the time those trains rolled into Nebraska, the aspiration of all European operators was to make the iron railed spreads bigger, stuff the cows with high carbohydrate feeds faster, and time the harvest of carcasses with the likely drop-dead rate of cattle in the pens.

These several developments confirmed to the public the idea that cow-calf operations were gigantic novice-type ranches and that it took lots of corn to make beef fit to eat. In fact, perhaps 80% of the cow-calf operations in the U.S. have no more than twenty-five head of mother cows in any year. Animals were transferred to sale barns, food producers, truckers, finally to the feedlot and intensive feeding with hormones, coccidostats, antibiotics and fabricated feeds. Punctuated with shots a plenty, animals ended up as a commodity grade product, mule meat in short.

Cows on pasture and the infrastructure that sees them spend the last few months of their lives in a dust or mud manure choked pen are a few country miles removed from the glory arena of show biz.

"The whole industry is being destroyed. In ten years you won't find fat cattle on the farm."

"What will they do?"

"The pressure is to send them to feedlots. They'll stuff them full of carbohydrates, shoot them up with five-way or seven-way vaccines, load their feed with antibiotics, and hit them with hormones. It's all being worked out by the land grant college, university system. They want to feed the cows chicken shit! They'll feed them cattle cake and protein bypass, in effect turning herbivores into ruminant hogs."

"Good God!" was all the wheat farmer could say.

"And that's not all. I know that you can't feed cattle that way, but they will! The bigger the relief checks, the cheaper the corn and the bigger the subsidy to the cow pen operators. That's what the Washington charade is all about. Keep corn and wheat cheap, keep some few farmers from starving so that Wall Street can get into the cattle business."

"In other words, an underhanded subsidy?"

"Yes, you have it."

"What kind of meat is that going to put on a steer?"

"Well, the animals will go acidic. So they'll haul in Arm and Hammer bicarbonate of soda in eighteen-wheelers. If they make it to slaughter before they drop dead, you'll have a meat with omega 3 fatty acids on a one to twenty ratio with omega 6. It should be one to one. That cow needs six cubic feet of clean air a minute. It'll get nothing but fecal dust and pesticides. I wonder why the animal cruelty people don't raise a tizzy over this? If this is science, I give you voodoo."

"Not to be facetious, but other than that?"

"Other than that, you have the *E. coli* problem. Under acidic conditions, *E. coli* migrates from the cow intestine to cellular structure elsewhere in the carcass. So the meat simply becomes contaminated. So FDA recalls hamburger by the thousands of tons. That's malarkey. Recall does not mean recovery. Most is not recovered. It is consumed. No wonder the word goes out to cook the living bee Jesus out of the junk food hamburger before serving."

"What kind of operation do you have?" the Ness county man wanted to know.

"It's a seed stock operation. I sell quality bulls. I line breed a closed herd. I'm here because my customers are being annihilated. Hopefully, the Alliance can help."

The man shook Jim's hand. The place was almost empty. As Jim left, a tall shaggy looking man in horn-rimmed glasses fell into stride behind him. "Multitudes, multitudes in the valley of decision" he intoned in a portentous burr.

23

"Multitudes, multitudes in the valley of decision: for the day of the Lord is near in the valley of decision." James Robert Neff spun around in his tracks. He knew that voice from yesteryear, and as the cadaverous image of the speaker came into view he recognized Phineas priest, the deacon, formerly Corporal Homer Smythe, late of Biak Island and the Sulu Archipelago.

"Jimbo, it is I," said the lanky man in faded corduroy pants and hat to match. He wore no tie and the shirt must have required laundering a while back.

"Phineas priest!" Jim said. "What the devil are you doing here?"

"My boy, I am now a school man, a credentialed and tenured professor, Ph.D., specialty: populist movements. My God, Jimbo, they told me you were hit and they said you wouldn't recover."

"I suppose it's a case of that legendary exaggeration," Jim said.

"Jimbo, I need to talk to you. I want you to meet a treasonous Colonel.

Can we repair to yonder eating sty, three blocks, I think?" The long legged Phineas priest set the pace and direction, walking a bit faster than Jim could travel with a leg still compromised by old war wounds. The cafe to which Deacon referred was styled Oink Smith's Eatery. It specialized in pork sandwiches, pork chops and sausage types too numerous to mention. Oink himself waited on tables, carved meat, provided commentary if asked, and communicated with the kitchen by shouting at the top of his lungs. Just the same, the place was relatively quiet even with all six booths filled and the counter occupied.

The two slid into the rear booth, received glasses of water, and placed orders for coffee and sandwiches.

"He is fond of his food," Jim remarked.

"No more than most," Deacon said. "The beauty of this place is that it isn't too crowded or noisy."

Oink came over and deposited two monstrous sandwiches on the table. He scribbled a number on a piece of butcher paper and said, "Leave the money on the table."

"He doesn't write tickets," the Deacon said. "He doesn't accept checks or make change."

"An innovator," Jim said, smiling. "I have a hunch his accountant is also his spiritual advisor." Both of the men took their sandwich bites simultaneously.

"What do you make of Billy Jon Poole?" Jim asked.

"Oh, he has many of the mannerisms of a *schickel gruber,* very low on information, high on bullshit. You're going to get lots of slogans from that boy, but little information."

"What do you know about populist movements?"

"My dear child, I am a walking catalog of trivia. On a well financed quiz show, I'd be an instant millionaire. But it's you ought to be telling me, Jimbo.

"After all, you Kansans once elected a Populist governor. And you had Mary Elizabeth Lease, you know, 'raise less corn and more hell.' And the Grange, they knew how to blow up railroad tracks in those days! Now, those boys knew how to raise hell! I wrote a book about the Non-Partisan League called, *Your Old Men Shall Dream Dreams, Your Young Men Shall See Visions.* I always like Biblical titles."

"This business about Phineas priest, is that a belief sincerely held, as the lawyers say?"

"It's the culture I grew up with." My family has traced its genealogy back to King David and beyond.

"And you're eating pork?"

"That prohibition had to do with scavenger animals, according to my great, great something or other. I have accepted that revised tradition." The deacon paused to take a bite once in a while and to sip coffee. "It's the culture I pass on to my son. Are we speaking of a metaphor? I suppose I'd run a spear through the absconders in order to court Yahweh's favor. The problem is that the economic prostitutes are like a Hydra with a thousand heads. There is no one head on which you can

210

deliver a lethal blow." He paused, bit into the pork, took another sip, and repeated the pattern as he got on a professorial roll.

"Let me digress," the schoolman said. "Why am I talking to you? Jimbo, you emerged from under the radar when you spoke at Independence, Kansas. Someone gave me a tape of your talk, one of my students did. You came on like a genuine Will Rogers, aw shucks, and all that. You're a fraud, you know that? I know genuine erudition when I hear it."

"How's that?"

"Jimbo, you told those hungry farmers that when you produce, you have to balance it with credits on the other side of the equals sign. If you don't, it comes out of someone's hide. That's wisdom. Then you suggested that the sabotage of income to agriculture would likely be equal to the buildup of the public and private debt. I don't recall a single populist organization coming up with a single new idea such as that one. Did you listen to the governor damning the middleman? Why the devil won't even one farm organization get a handle on the real problem?"

"Do you think the university has the answer?"

"Oh, hell no! I confess to you as you might confess to a Catholic priest that I am involved in the biggest scam in America: higher education. We loot every family in the country and pass out worthless degrees that won't let a student make a living. Oh, we graduate doctors and engineers, but in the main, 80% of the courses are bullshit. I say this privately and deny what I've said publicly. Don't look to the university or extension for an understanding." The professor changed the subject. "We lost a lot of good men at Biak. Have you ever wondered for what? Now, remembering your own equation, have you wondered why all these wars? When the Japanese bombed Pearl Harbor, Mr. Roosevelt was able to ask Congress for enough money to hire every man, woman and child in America at then prevailing wages, all without a hearing or debate. The decision to take down the family farmer was made in 1948 by the 80th Congress and signed by Mr. Truman. Jimbo, there has to be a balance. As agriculture is deprived of its earnings, balance is annihilated by cumulative debt, and war is the credit engine."

"Do the observed facts support this?" Jim asked.

"Well, let me put it this way. Mr. Truman handed North Korea to the Russkies at the end of WWII. He had a couple of colonels draw a line across the peninsula, and he handed the North to the Russians. It was an insurance policy for war in five years."

"That sounds a bit incredible!"

"It is, for which reason the farm population won't believe it! They go on producing until relieved of their property by the bank. Add this, the French collapsed during the war, and for all practical purposes exited Vietnam. Mr. Truman gave them merchant ships to haul in the French Foreign Legion. This ended at Dien Bien Phu. Exit the French. Enter the Americans. That's why we're in Vietnam even as we speak."

The man who came to the booth had ordered a sandwich from Oink Smith. He left his money on the counter, squeezed into the booth, extended his hand to Jim Neff. "I'm Colonel Wargo, U.S. Marines, retired, resident gadfly."

"Tell the truth!" the professor said. "You got court-martialed for making an indecent overture to the wife of a diplomat from Norway."

"Doc, we haven't used that one for years. You have to forgive the professor. I invented that story ten years ago when I needed stature. I'm not using it anymore."

"Colonel, will you tell our friend how the hogs ate the chickens economically?"

"Where do I start?"

"At the beginning," said the professor.

"Bingo," the old marine colonel opened. "I'm not a farmer. I'm just an old soldier who, like St. Ignatius, has come to his senses. I'm interested in your movement because it may be the last chance to save the country from the empire builders."

Jim and the Phineas priest nursed their coffee while they waited for Oink Smith to bring another round of coffee.

"I'm ninety-two years old. I worked for General Smedley Butler for most of my military career."

"Who was Butler?" Jim wanted to know.

"He was the commandant who led the Marines into Nicaragua a bit before the Russian rebellion of 1917. In other words, I've been around the horn." The colonel did not expect to be interrupted. He was anxious to tell his message to someone, anyone with the intelligence to understand it. "I helped the general expose a fascist plot to stage a coup against F.D.R. I sat in the hot seat when a Congressional Committee was investigating the plot. Like most committees, it trapped the small fry and allowed the bigs to escape. I sat in the general's corner while he unmasked the warmongers and phony patriots and war profiteers and military martinets.

"It took me a few years to suspect that war was a racket. When I retired, it came to me that wars were ordered up by industry. I had spent over three decades in the service. During those years I spent most of my time as an inside man for big business, Wall Street and the moneylenders. In short, you can consider me a hit man for the absconders. I worked diligently to make Mexico safe for the likes of Preston Walker Bush. I helped win over Cuba and Haiti for the National City Bank people. I helped the same crowd rape half of Central America, this for Wall Street. Nicaragua? Hell, I helped sanitize it for the administration. I opened the Dominican Republic for the sugar interests, this in 1916. I delivered Honduras to American Fruit and humbled the Chinese in 1927 so that Standard Oil could go in unmolested. I spoke Butler's words, and he spoke mine, so what I'm telling you goes for both of us, and my 'I' is really a 'we.'

"Son, I'm an ex-racketeer, so they gave me medals and certificates suitable for framing, and they gave me promotions. Al Capone was a piker compared to the honorable Marines. Al only milked three city districts. We Marines did our work on that many continents.

"I want you to know this so you know where I'm coming from. Today the experts move into a country. They sell the natives on big projects to be built by big construction firms with borrowed money. The poor suckers can't feed the interest mill, so the shysters move in. First, they seize control of the UN vote. They take control of the raw materials and assets and of the leadership, yes, by intimidation, often by murder and bribes deposited in Swiss banks. I want you to know this! In order to keep the war racket going, they have to demolish the individually owned farms. They have to engineer unemployment so young people have no place to go except to be cannon fodder."

The Phineas priest spoke up. "Jim, I wanted to have you hear this so you'll understand the absolute necessity for structural balance between production and services and manufacturing if the war game isn't going to run rampant."

The proprietor presented himself at the booth occupied by the three in dialogue. "You people have been here for two hours. You need to eat." Jim handed the proprietor a five dollar bill.

"No thanks."

The trio got up.

"I have a room at the Rhubi Dioux," said the professor. "It's early."

Without a word, the three walked the short distance to the hostelry. Once the Phineas priest had ordered up soft drinks, a knock on the door served to admit the three attendees to an organizational meeting.

"Steve Tyler, California," one man said, extending a callused hand with the grip of a vice. He was a rice producer. His flooded fields were going under at the rate of 2% a year, not in water, but in red ink. He could not understand why.

His associate was an Oregon nut grower, short of stature, sun tanned, and a smile under his wrinkled face. His grip was solid, yet moderate. "The name is Isaac Carter," he said. He turned to the third visitor. "This here is Steve Peter Lynch, Quincy, Washington."

Lynch stood five feet six. He carried a look of puzzlement, the look Jim Neff had come to expect of wheat growers. Small talk faltered after a while, and the colonel slowly yet surely took command. He had a story to tell, one that did not brook much interruption, yet one that focused on the purpose of the organization that would be formalized tomorrow.

"I spent my life as a pimp," he said.

California and Oregon got up to go. "No, hang on. I won't bore you with my story. But I can explain to you how the debauchery of agriculture proceeds and what it has to do with our policy of perpetual war for perpetual peace."

"OK," said California, "we'll listen."

Jim Neff did more than listen. He started taking notes. The colonel was in rare form, much as had been the case when he lectured at the War College. He chain smoked as he talked. "For reasons that troubled the international money lenders no end, American manufacturers remained sublimely indifferent to foreign markets between 1813 and 1914, an entire century. At the end of that era, a market basket of goods cost approximately the same as it had one hundred years earlier. Generally speaking, this era saw the act of production create the credits for the consumption of that production. The basic result, even with wars and depressions involved, being structural balance for the American economy, meaning no rupture of price structures via import invasion. "During the era in question, Henry Ford took the lead in raising the American wage level to fifty cents an hour. With other industrialists following suit, the common worker could buy a Model T car. Moreover, broad spectrum distribution of land meant broad spectrum distribution of basic farm income, agriculture being then, and now still, the largest sector of the economy. Later, in the 1930s, statistical workers selected 1910-1914 as base period 100 for computations. This meant that base period 100 designated an era that had relatively full employment with a stable price structure. Using this platform, protection for the economy was indicated by every reasoned approach to national security. It pushed almost all manufacturing to new heights. Indeed, the act of production created the money for consumption of that production under equitable pricing conditions.

"This situation stuck like a sharp bone in the throats of international lenders. Free international trade required price dislocation between nations. Thus, the policy of the international lenders to so reduce the purchasing power of the American people that they could no longer even approximately consume their own production. Gentlemen, I refer you to *The Breakdown of Money* by Christopher Hollis. Hollis was a British historian on loan to Notre Dame University during the 1930s. He wrote that as long as U.S. purchasing power was adequate, the American manufacturer was sublimely indifferent to foreign markets, but with domestic purchasing power reduced, foreign markets became essential. The more the manufacturer could be persuaded to look abroad for markets, the easier it became to dismiss wages as a balance to production. With high tariffs and high wages, he looked on the worker as a constant, but when he was forced to look abroad for a market, then wages became merely an item of cost, and it became his interest to reduce them as low as possible. With lower costs, manufacturing became more profitable for the financiers. Are you still with me?"

Jim Neff nodded, "yes!" The professor smiled like a movie star. Gawd, did the ex-soldier know how to lay it out!

Oregon asked, "What has this to do with farming?"

"Just this," the non-uniformed soldier said. "When foreign goods can flow into free trade America, then debt enables continuation of purchasing power. That's the why and wherefore for breaking the purchasing power of the money. The business of breaking the family farmer started in 1873 via the mechanism of the silver exchange, at that time an international money. From that date up to 1896, the price of silver broke from $1.32 an ounce to sixty-five cents an ounce. The commodity exchanges did it with raw manipulation, much the way the Chicago Board of Trade breaks soybean prices today. For every cent that silver went down, the price of wheat on the High Plains went down a penny a bushel also. These probes continued well into the Wilson administration, at which time the international traders struck pay dirt. Target? The family farm structure!

"During that administration we got the income tax. It did away with the requirement that tariffs provide the funds for government operation. Wilson got a foundations law to protect the fortunes of the super rich. The Wilson assault on the Constitution targeted the Senate. Because of a Constitutional amendment, the control of the Senate by state legislatures was left behind. The Senate now became just another House of Representatives. Sentence by sentence, paragraph by paragraph, with laws, bureaucratic rules and regulations, and judicial decrees, the Constitution was annihilated until little more than a shell now remains. Then came the Federal Reserve. Don't even get me started on that one!"

Oregon nudged California. "I wish he'd get to the point." The colonel overheard the stage whisper. He had given this lecture countless times before. He knew every comma, every syllable, and his syllogism delivered the stunning blow that said that the debauchery of agriculture was simply public policy.

"The target of breaking the purchasing power of the American dollar via lower prices on basic storable crops was achieved by import invasion. The Great Depression followed. Here's something you farmers need to understand. There was a short period after 1942, when national security actually prevailed for America. We had to fight a war, and it called for a stabilization measure together with the Steagall Amendment. Raw material prices were raised to a parity level. This was all swept aside the minute Eisenhower took office."

"How?" came a question from the nut farmer.

"In homage to free international trade, the farmers' grain commodities, those which are grown on 80% to 82% of the harvested acres were sent into an abyss. How? Here's how it happened. The 80th Congress gave Mr. Truman the Aiken Bill to sign the night before the 1948 Philadelphia Democratic Convention. It opened American ports to traffic from abroad at world prices. To keep farmers from going broke too fast for comfort, it set up subsidies. The international flim flam men won the day. The Council on Foreign Relations suckered USDA Secretary Charlie Brannan into accepting principles that made the last years of the Truman administration look like an assembly of internationalists. "As long as American agriculture had parity, traders of every stripe went hungry. At the end of the war, the banks were full of money. Applicants for loans were few. In fact, there was only a market for 16% of the available loan funds. The minute Secretary of Agriculture Ezra Taft Benson took office, he struck down parity. Farm operators started the painful process of consuming their own capital. Loan applications soared. That's when new lending agencies were started, in order to take risky customers off the back of banks. As prices continued to sink, Extension and newspaper pundits hit farmers with the efficiency routine. The Committee for Economic Development did its black work on a continuing basis. Starting immediately after the war, policy papers discovered a surplus agriculture. They had names: *Toward a Realistic Farm Program,* and *Economic Policy for American Agriculture,* and *An Adaptive Program for Agriculture.* They all explained why the farmers had to get bigger, more efficient, or get out!

"Your kids in college read the Bible-style texts of Don Paarlberg and Dale Hathaway. They explain how the job of liquidating agriculture could proceed without bringing on open revolt. By the time those two volumes had been thumbed to death, Johns Hopkins published *Policy Directions for U.S. Agriculture,* which was issued under the auspices of Resources for the Future, Inc., a non-profit organization based in Washington for the altruistic purpose of serving the powers that be. The writer, one Marion Clawson, came to Resources via the customary route out of USDA and the Department of the Interior. His message came from the mature fortunes of the nation by way of tax-supported instrumentalities that no longer knew who did the feeding. Instead of support programs, Clawson sold the idea of a relief check for technically bankrupt producers of the political crops: wheat, corn, soybeans, cotton, grain sorghum and so on. It was the Brannan idea: institutionalized poverty for the producers of food. Gentlemen, there is a trade network that has your crop in tow. They trade at world prices."

The professor, sociologist, Phineas priest, ordered up sandwiches and coffee, and the discussions continued until 3 a.m. The two gadflies in effect summarized much of what Jim had learned from a thousand books, and they had enlarged the scope of the reason for being of the new organization. Could this be communicated to the rank and file, a rank and file that saw the farm problem in terms of middlemen, processors, and skinflints at the livestock sale?

Jim asked for the floor. "Go ahead," the colonel said.

"What is the bottom line that you've been seeing?"

"The bottom line is that you boys have about twelve, maybe fifteen years to get your act together. If you haven't done so by that time, the country goes into bankruptcy."

"What does that mean?" Jim asked.

"It means the knuckleheads finally bankrupted the country. Oh, we'll be able to operate, people won't even be aware of it for a long time. Probably we'll close down the gold window and destroy the money to save the banks. *Vox populi* will glory in the first round of inflation and believe they are prosperous. Then inflation will cut their legs out from under them. They'll probably continue to be fed on junk food and most will lose their mental acuity. To keep the thing going the military will furnish new wars to stoke the engine of credit."

It all seemed mysterious to the attending farmers and to Jim Neff.

"Can you explain?"

The colonel spoke with the authority of a man used to being obeyed. "When you turn that sunshine and grass into corn or cattle, both become earned income. When you create debt you create money. But, it is owed money, it compounds itself exponentially."

Three of the six in the room were baffled. The professor and Jim understood. It was getting late and the convention would pick up early in the morning.

"I'm going to my room down the hall. Don't follow me, but remember, you have a dozen years or so to save not only your farms, but the country itself. If the farmers fail to stand up and be counted the way the blacks stood up in Montgomery, then it's goodbye to American freedom and hello to a military dictatorship, subtle at first, but closing its tentacles on a free society an inch at a time. Big business will sleep soundly with a copy of Ayn Rand's *Atlas Shrugged* under their pillows."

24

Seated in the big auditorium listening to a parade of amateur speakers and Billy Jon's endless ramblings, Jim Neff reflected on the steps that had carried him here. As a barefoot boy on wind rippled fields of dust, life was free and delightful. He did not come to feel his parents' poverty or their humiliation until the farm failed and life failed. He came to town as a shy boy. He did not date girls. He had volunteered as a scout on Biak Island because he felt a measure of comfort dodging Japanese patrols or annihilating them with a Thompson, a weapon he handled with lethal skill. The barefoot boy was wearing combat boots by that time. When he was dismissed from the hospital, he made application for a pair of street shoes. The wound in his left foot had not healed properly, and army boots were uncomfortable. The drone at the ration office said "No!" emphatically. The medal he had won, he told himself, and a nickel would not get him a cup of coffee.

He owned nothing except a few bred cows and a bull. At a time when traditional farmers were losing their farms, he took over Banyon Place and a few acres by common consent.

Joseph Samuel Neff signed over his share of the estate when his parents died. It was not worth very much, and besides, he was not interested in farming. He was now an executive in a hotel chain and ensconced in an expensive home in Miami.

Royal Lee Neff wrote from West Germany once a year or less. He had become a German citizen by the mid 1950s, the father of a boy, and a laboratory worker in the famous West German breeding program. The farm revolt was three years old before it came to those with a passionate state of mind that a new organization should take form. So this is the organization, he told himself. He had participated in beating the drum by making speeches in southeastern Kansas, but he did not figure he had come to the notice of the ad hoc promoters of the conference now

220

underway. He was mistaken. Jim Neff was looked upon as a leader even though he shunned leadership. He had not been to college, but he had egghead status because he was constantly enlarging his knowledge of agriculture, economics and public policy. He wore comfortable boots these days. He stood tall in them and commanded for himself the authority that travels with knowledge. When the time came, he refused the role of delegate from Kansas, a state still to be organized. In fact, there were only seven states with enough members to the conference that merited the term "organized." They were Missouri, Iowa, Wisconsin, Minnesota, Michigan, Illinois and Indiana. A farmer from New Jersey asked for inclusion. He claimed that he was 30% of the dairy production in his state.

Jim said no to the delegate post. He had no intention of enduring endless meetings, tiring speeches, self-puffing politicos and headline huggers. He offered to provide critical study and evaluations. Before the day was over, he picked up the assignment to provide a report on poultry and red meat. He ran into the Phineas priest again.

"Have you baffled everyone?" Jim asked.

"Just about. You know something? This is an excellent laboratory for a sociologist. I have a hunch the movement will get put down like a cur dog. This is pretty evident. But I believe you will have a lasting educational effect, probably the only residue after the new populism has spent itself."

"I know where you're coming from," was Jim's response. "You think we're only dreamy headed true believers."

"Ah! A philosopher!"

"No, just a farmer who thinks the Creator has given us one last chance. If we fail, the next step for the country is banana republic status." The pecan tree was heavy with nuts the year the Capper-Volstead Alliance was formed. Heidi was nine the day Jim returned from the organizational meeting. He had refused the role of delegate, but he had agreed to present a study of at least one part of agriculture: poultry. This at the first possible opportunity. Heidi and Xander had birthdays barely a week apart. Wisely, Nora combined the two into a whopper of a party, and Dad being present made the celebration a red letter day every year. Banyon Place became a near showplace farm. Nora personally supervised upscale redecoration. All the old garage sale furniture had been discarded long ago. The kitchen garden east of the old mansion was birthday perfect, courtesy of Heidi and Xander constantly weeding the place. Heidi breezed through the house like a miniature whirlwind, usually followed by Xander. Everyone called Alexander "Xander." His dad had started the practice, usually by telling the boy that he was named after Kirghiz Jacob Xander and that he was the namesake.

"Why didn't you name me Jake, instead of Xander?"

"Because we'd already used that name for your brother." That seemed to satisfy the boy. The subject was never brought up again, possibly because a new bombshell fell on the homestead. Jake was baby sitting while Nora made a quick trip to town. When she came back, the children had a small ball of fur in a cardboard box. "Momma, Momma, can we keep it? Can we keep it?" Xander asked this as fast as he could speak.

"We found it on the road," Heidi supplied. Nora got them to slow down, assigning the floor to Jake. "OK, Jake, what happened?"

"There was a big maroon colored car. It came tooling down the section road, then it stopped at our driveway and put this pup out. I tried to get the license plate, but it drove away too fast."

"They just put it out," Xander said. "Can we keep it?"

Jake went to the library to find a book on training dogs. In a few weeks Banyon Place had a doghouse replete with carpet and a name above the door: Rover II. Exposure was to the south, this for sun in the winter and shade in the summer. When the children tried to bring the dog into the house, Nora put her foot down.

"Not in our house," she said. "Animals belong outside." She waited for that to sink in. "A farm dog needs to assume its duties outside." It was a mongrel, but Jim detected the markings of wolf blood somewhere in the ancestry. He thought of the Rover he had had as a boy. No, it could not be. Jake taught Rover II to fetch a stick. After a time, it joined the boy in moving cattle from paddock to paddock.

Jim had concluded that each animal requires 3% of its body weight in feed each day. By measuring the height of the grass, he computed the carrying capacity of a paddock in terms of single-day grazing. The calculations were simple enough. Jake measured the height of the stand.

Simple observation told him how closely grazing animals cropped the grass. His dad taught him how to factor the forage available into the animals to be fed. If a four hundred pound cow needed twelve pounds of forage per day and failed to get it, any shortfall meant debilitation, possibly disease. Cows need clean water and grass. Shelter from the wind in winter is also to be considered. The dog took Jim back to western Kansas, back into the calm of the Osage orange shelter, back to the sandpit where the wolf and a different mongrel Rover had reared their pups. It was such a good life until it came crashing down as it was now doing again for some 2,400 family farms each week of the year.

He had fought for that life, had rebuilt that life, but now it was again being threatened, and the threats were bringing open revolt in the countryside. Dust and drought, it turned out, were only spot causes. Few farmers understood the real cause.

Within a few months of that organizational meeting, there were probably a hundred farmers on the road telling the story. They were not trained speakers, but they spoke from the heart. Usually volunteered to their feet, they shuffled and stammered.

"Tell us your story."

Now the words started to flow. Shy farm boys became spellbinders. Jim Neff attended several meetings in the southeast Kansas area. One day he got the expected phone call.

"We need your report," Glass Splinter roared into the phone, his baritone voice faintly reminiscent of a rat tail file on a sore tooth. Glass was a roly-poly hog producer, now a PR man. Everyone joked about his family name, even more so about his first name. He claimed that he was named after Carter Glass, one of the actors during the Federal Reserve debates a generation earlier. Glass was a veritable sponge for information. He soaked up news clippings, reports and, last but not least, government bulletins. His duplicating machine cranked out copies until the cylinders wore out. "We need the skinny on poultry and red meat. The board meets starting Monday. Can you make it?"

Jim was well prepared. The big library at Banyon Place was an orderly fort of knowledge and published resources.

The provisional headquarters of the Capper-Volstead Alliance was functioning from a storefront in St. Joseph, Missouri, about one block off the main drag. There were no carpets on the floor. Desks looked like war surplus. Temporary partitions cut up the ample space into cubicles, a public relations room, and an office for Billy Jon Poole, who had made the transition from temporary chairman to president with hardly a dissenting vote.

Jim met the vice-president for the first time. He was an Arkansas cowman who grazed rough country and had accepted the idea of rotational grazing.

"Frank Vincent," the veep said, extending a hand. "I'll probably serve as long as Billy Jon is in charge." He was a flyer. His nondescript airplane was fabric covered and could do about sixty mph. He used it to patrol cattle in the county, but his overview gave him a glimpse of poultry houses that had been stuck into the hill country. Frank Vincent looked like he did not bother with eating. He had a Lincolnesque face with large eyebrows. He came on with a style so low key that it was easy to mistake him for a hired hand. Vincent was anything but flat. He had once taught mathematics at Fayetteville. No one could take the country out of him, and at age forty he had taken over the family farm. He was more solvent than most of the Capper-Volstead officials, but he was slow to tell his associates very much about his affairs. The hand shakes came on in waves. Secretary Bill Hallo raised corn and beans, soybeans. He was a small man with a loose grip. Without machinery to turn work into merchandise, he probably could not have handled hard work farming.

Glass led Jim Neff down the aisle, into and out of cubicles designated "Meat Department," "Grain Department," "Dairy Department," "Specialties." The names were hard to remember. The one he remembered best of all was "Wood Splinter," the brother of Glass. Wood had a telephone propped to his ear like an added appendage. He now had a dozen paid organizers in motion, and assured Jim that the day was not far off when the Alliance would swing into action. Wood and Glass administered a speaker's bureau jointly. The boardroom was on the second floor of the old store front with twelve states considered organized. More introductions were in order. Glass did the honors. "This here is Laughing Wolf, Salina, Kansas." Jim shook hands. There was even time to say, "Glad to meet you." "Meet Stonewall Jackson, Missouri."

"No relation," Jackson supplied, and another hand reached out.

"Ted Reno," Glass said, "Iowa."

The drill went on until Jim Neff had met about half the board. They represented the middle rung in agriculture. Fully half exhibited creeping front porches. Work on the farm had changed that much since the war. Jim doubted that any of these farmers ever handled a bale of hay without the aid of a machine. Introductions were terminated the minute Billy Jon Poole entered. About half the group stood up.

The Secretary called the meeting to order and handed it over to Billy Jon Poole. "Well, boys," Billy Jon came on, "we're getting ready to swing into action." For the past couple of months, he said, he had been in consultation with trade experts, government officials, and professors. "Frankly, boys, I've never heard so much bullshit in my life. They've got us figured for a bunch of rubes. They think we're too damn dumb to add or subtract. I swear these people at USDA believe they can do anything they want with impunity, that we'll go right on producing, that we'll continue feeding the nation." Billy Jon abandoned that thought in order to tell a long story about Uncle John and a bull with one testicle cut off by barbed wire. The point of the story seemed to be that people who would not join Capper-Volstead had not one ball, but no balls at all.

"What do you think would happen if we didn't market for two weeks or a month? I'll tell you what. You'd start having food riots." He paused to take a drink of milk. Billy Jon always drank milk, not water, when thirst caused him to pause.

"I'll tell you what I'm thinking, and Mr. Neff has been studying the situation. We intend to find the weak spots, the solar plexus. There's no point in staging a hold back on peas and asparagus. Gentlemen, we'll have to test our strength. We may have to test a dozen times before we're ready for a big move."

An hour into the session, Jim got the floor, courtesy of the president. He had had the floor before in restaurants, sales barns and credit unions. He had fielded just about every question afloat in the countryside. "If you guys get what you're asking for, people would go hungry," was a common refrain. Jim had his answers. "Economists show that the American people could buy more with an hour of work during the 1946-1950 parity era than they could when that system was discontinued. They earned that much more buying power."

Jim's reputation had preceded him. He had picked up a measure of polish. Billy Jon liked to work his audience into his presentations. For a half hour he posed questions, always ending with "Isn't that right, Sam?" (Sam Cook of Wisconsin). Jim kept track. "It's a good question," he would say. It was always good form to thank the questioner even if it was exquisitely stupid. Often the questions did not seem stupid, but they needed answering. At times he lectured. "The function of science," he said, "is to foresee that when we put together enough evidence we can join our observations together into working relationships called laws. We can then use these laws to predict or design outcome. Outcome has to be understood."

At this particular board meeting, Jim opened as he usually did, without preamble or the usual flim-flam about being glad to be here, thanks for the great introduction, or other honorific asides.

"I have here a thirty-two page report on poultry. You can read it when you have time," he said. "I'll give you a synopsis."

Jim dropped a copy of the report on the table. Glass and Wood Splinter had duplicated the report, and by now had passed copies to each of the board members in the chamber, twenty-three present, the member from North Dakota, Howard Espy, being absent.

"In these pages you'll find data on how intensive animal raising hopes to add the greatest weight gain in the shortest time frame. I said 'weight gain,' not 'nutrient gain' or 'quality gain.' The trade has concluded that weight gain is best advanced by putting on fat, not protein. This holds for chickens, ducks, turkeys, veal calves, and even beef cattle. I have data and charts dealing with trout, salmon, and catfish, as well."

Jim saw that only half the board was listening. He cut in half what he intended to say. Poultry used to be a mortgage lifter. Unfortunately, the land grant colleges saw to it that capital took over poultry. How? "Broilers are raised in 20,000 to 40,000 batches. This means that the hatchery brings out that many birds eight times a year. Each crop is grown for forty-two days. Feeds used are best calculated to put on fat. So carcasses of previous generations of birds, cats, dogs, harvested off the streets, laced with fish meal, antibiotics, hormones, vaccines and coccidostats serve as nutrition. "These birds are different from their free living counterparts. The big difference is the fat content.

The fat to protein ratio is often a hundred times greater in animals in concentration camps, so to speak, compared to free ranging animals. In the case of poultry, the fat ratio has risen about 1,000% compared to when chickens were raised on every farm. In my report you will read about saturated fats and unsaturated fats. Polyunsaturated fats are essential fatty acids. In a word, they are essential for brain development and healthy cellular growth. The best fats replete with hormone like substances once presided over sexual development. Saturated fats are indicted for causing heart disease. Unfortunately, gentlemen, poultry is barely organized. Any questions?"

The questions came for about fifteen minutes. "Did this fat information affect hogs and cattle?"

"Yes." Jim followed with data on free ranging pigs. He paused to hint at the difficult comparison to feedlot finishing. The modern pig, Jim said, has five times more saturated fat than polyunsaturated fat. The transformation, he said, is caused by feeding in the wrong way.

"What about disease?"

"The limited space for living facilitates and enhances the transmission of microbes."

Jim noticed Vice-President Frank Vincent looking at his watch. "Thank you," he said as he sat down.

During a brief strategy session, Jim was told about Billy Jon's hold back idea. As clusters of organized strength developed, holdbacks would be called for in Omaha, Kansas City, Des Moines, and perhaps in Denver and St. Joseph, Missouri.

There was energy in those Capper-Volstead halls, and that excitement was fueled by seminars. Gadfly professors came to test the waters, and newsmen pretended to report the depth of the subject. Usually, they were unequal to the task. Mostly, they failed to comprehend the nature of raw wealth extracted via photosynthesis from nature, and what that had to do with general income for the community. Clearly, they could not make the connection between earned income and income based on debt enlargement pretending to be earnings.

Many of the Capper-Volstead members were on the receiving end of government handouts, called subsidies. No one blamed the grain growers for accepting these deficiency payments, and fully half the members did not grow grain or cotton or sugar or tobacco, and they wondered aloud about the inherent fight for parity.

There was a professor named Joe Watkins from a small college in Illinois who came to St. Joseph now and then.

"The last president who believed in a balanced budget was Eisenhower," he said. "Unfortunately, Ike did not understand that by allowing farm parity to drop, he made debt enlargement necessary to avoid suffering another 1930s-type depression. Debt engines led to inflation," he concluded. Confused farmers who heard such words often posed themselves as devil's advocates.

"I'm not a favorite at the university. I've accused Extension of trying to annihilate its clientele. I added that to my credo, crop income serves the farmer for income. But it serves everyone else even more. Sir, if people really understood this, they'd be out there with shotguns to prevent farmers from selling at less than parity at the tail gate."

Jim picked up literature from Glass Splinter. He sat in on a seminar. He left St. Joseph certain that he was one of the few who understood the problem, the problem of staging a hold and the consequences.

He asked Professor Watkins, "What do you tell people when they say 'you worry about debt.' But don't we owe it to ourselves? All farmers admit they'd like better prices, but they don't want people to go hungry. They all want the right to make a profit, but they also want the right to go broke." The little professor laughed. It was a deep, baritone laugh. He almost said, "My dear child," but he thought better of it. "I'm here to tell you that they do have that last right." He didn't bother to point out that the U.S. was selling itself out at fire sale prices, all because the farmer wasn't getting paid. Jim asked, "How do you explain the statement that debt transfers the wealth of the nation into the hands of the few?"

"You can't, if people can't handle abstraction!"

Maybe Billy Jon Poole was right. There's only one story. You have to be able to tell it on a fast elevator moving between the fourteenth and the first floor, going down. This, Billy Jon said, could best be done by beating up on professors and handlers. The business for now was "Sign up more members." Then a holdback on production would succeed. When everyone got hungry, they would come around. All this highfalutin' stuff about national income and how under the laws of physics it starts with raw materials, isn't saleable, not to people who get theirs via campaign contributions passed along over rubber chickens and hard pea dinners.

Billy Jon dominated with his simple equation. Professor Watkins looked back to when Capper-Volstead farmers threw a dollar bill in a hat in 1955. "As an economy move, Ike struck down parity in 1955. The nation had only $300 billion income that year. On the basis of that, he allowed $72 billion debt expansion, twice as much as profits and savings should have allowed. If farm income had been maintained, that toe in the door debt expansion would not have been necessary. That debt expansion is destined to double and redouble until we'll be talking trillions. Get the picture?"

The picture remained illusive. The intellectuals were too intellectual for the rank and file, but sweet, syrupy sayings sold, especially when Billy Jon spoke them.

"We've got the production, and we've got it first," he said. "To the devil with supply and demand. That one is a fiction straight from hell." The Meat Department exhibited a publication know as a yellow sheet. It calmly told buyers what a packer would pay. So much for supply and demand. They bragged, those buyers did, that a nickel or a quarter higher than the yellow sheet would tone down any withholding action. Non-member farmers would swamp the stockyard pens. Billy Jon caught Jim Neff as he left the crude but serviceable headquarters of the Capper-Volstead Alliance.

"I read your poultry report. Excellent! Can you do one on red meat?"

25

The phone rang at 11 p.m. It was the St. Joseph, Missouri headquarters of the Capper-Volstead Alliance. Glass Splinter was on the line. In compliance with Article 6, Section 2, the president was calling a special meeting to evaluate the holdback effort at 8 a.m. Monday. All board members would be there, and they wanted to hear Jim's paper on red meat, especially cattle. Further, James Robert Neff had been named to fill the vacancy created by the departure of Carlos Lopez, who had died after suffering a heart attack. Jim was being recognized by fellow Kansans because of his in depth studies now circulating through Capper-Volstead territory, and they honored his loyalty and dedication to the cause.

Jim said, "Thank you," and hung up.

"Who was it, dear?" asked Nora. The children had not heard the phone ringing.

"St. Joseph," he said.

She waited for more. Finally she said, "Can you tell me what it was?" Jim went to her, gave her an intense kiss and hug, and said, "Let's sit down." He told her about the phone call. He had not refused the board member post, but he had not accepted it either.

Board member Lopez had run a small cattle ranch in the Flint Hills. He had farmed the land his Mexican father and Irish mother had settled at the beginning of the century. His postage-stamp-sized operation had not expanded because Flint Hills land was in the hands of absentee owners. Just the same, Lopez had kept the farm solvent by driving a school bus and earning off farm income. He traded off the bus driving chore with his wife whenever Capper-Volstead meetings caused a conflict. He was the smallest farmer on the board. Most of the Board members operated comparatively average sized farms. Fully 55% staved off insolvency by taking employment with the Alliance even while serving as board members. This was proving troublesome to Jim. He had a vision of board meetings becoming rubber stamp operations, Billy Jon proposing, the board disposing. However, Jim had no inclination toward taking either a paid position or a board post. The Alliance would cover his mileage and expenses,that was all. Nora mused. "I think I see what the New Testament meant when it said Christ took upon himself the sins of the world. Jim, let's not take on the sins of agriculture."

"No, I won't do that, I promise." He reached over to take her hand. "I know what the shortfalls of organization are. You can tell farmers to organize, to bargain collectively. Experience tells me that only about 20% will ever join. Farmers will stop what they're doing and sell if they can get an extra dime."

He went on. Not many had on-farm storage. The grain farmers were little more than supplier peasants.

"Sweetheart," he said. "I've told you Grandpa Xander's Crazy Ivan story. It's true. They'll put out their own eyes if it will stress their neighbors."

"Then why not operate our own farm and let the rest of the world wag?"

"Sweetheart, this has to run its course. It's like that useless killing field exercise called World War II. It had to run its course. This revolt has to run its course, too."

The observation became self evident a half hour after the gavel fell. If nothing else, Billy Jon was a patient man. He had his votes lined up, but he insisted on hearing the whole enchilada, not just a short summary. He hoped to cool tempers that way.

Jim took his place at the podium. He had asked Glass Splinter for an overhead projector. Now he positioned his transparency on the projector. When the high-powered tube came on, the front wall of the chamber was turned into an illustration the size of a highway billboard. It was a blowup of a flash card all buyers carried with them when grading cattle. They ran one finger on a horizontal plane, the other vertically, Bingo!, the exact price. The board members could not help staring at the numbers. They had a mesmerizing effect that stunned and produced inertia.

Jim covered the buying structure, the import factor, the total disregard of the Justice Department in the matter of the Packer's and

Stockyard's Act enforcement, and then he gave the board a lesson in history. In 1827 a man named Archibald Clybourne set up a mini-slaughtering operation on the Chicago River. He had ready markets, the small garrison at Fort Dearborn and a small insignificant outpost called Chicago. During Clybourne's first year, some 150 cattle were killed and dressed. That year, and for a few years still to come, every community in America grew, slaughtered, and consumed local beef only.

A few years later, in 1846, a man named H.R. Smith decided to obey the businessman's calling by buying cheap and selling dear, buying 225 head of cattle cheap and selling them at eight dollars a head profit in New York after a thousand mile trail drive. After that, the production of red meat was destined never to be the same again.

By 1849 locomotive whistles were shattering the quiet prairie air near Chicago, and a year later Chicago slaughtering operations were rivaling their counterparts in Cincinnati. As an economic fact, the timeless West had come into being. From that day forward, red meat was destined to feed an entire nation. Cowboys would come to reap glamour and poor pay. Packers would reap denunciation and incalculable riches. Abilene, Newton and Dodge City would become household words.

In 1867 Joseph G. McCoy shipped 35,000 Longhorns from Abilene, Kansas. A year later, 300,000 head made the kidney wrecking trip from Kansas railheads to Chicago. Two years later, the figure came close to 750,000. In 1881 General James Brisbin, a regular U.S. Army officer told the world *How to Get Rich on the Plains,* thus codifying what had been informed financial talk for several years. As a report on free land and free grass, it told New York, Boston, Philadelphia, and European readers with money something about the beef business. The High Plains abounded with succulent grasses, the report said. The country was almost featureless, rather, it was filled with features that ran in set patterns for miles on end. There were natural cuts and canyons for winter protection of vast herds. Millions of acres belonged to the government and could be controlled by filing on a few critical waterholes. To a crowded agriculturalist in Scotland, it sounded too good to be true. Within a decade, even more Scotch, English, Dutch and Eastern capital arrived. As early as 1880, the U.S. Commissioner of Agriculture told Congress that western ranchers "practically use and control millions of acres of land belonging to the government, for which they pay neither rent nor tax." With this added "oomph" to the "free" in free enterprise, cattle ranching became a major industry. A speculative fever caused boom to compound boom. There were lots of opportunities. For instance, one single year saw twenty corporations with over $12,000,000 capitalization organized under Wyoming law. Between 1870 and 1900 some thirty-six British companies had poured $40,000,000 into cow-calf operations scattered across a dozen western states. For instance, Chicago capitalists arrived in Texas in 1879 with a real deal. They built Austin for the state, and finally ended up with the XIT Ranch some three million acres and 160,000 head of cattle.

There were others. Free or cheap land and even cheaper taxes became the byword for efficiency, and the homesteaders even then endured the cry of "get bigger."

By the mid 1880s, the King Ranch in south Texas had 614,000 acres and 40,000 head of cattle. Wyoming's Carey Cattle Company reported 32,287 head as early and as late as 1884, and was worth well over $1.2 million. The $1 million class did not stop there, nor did the take home pay, not until overgrazing and the cattle killing blizzards of 1885 and 1886 put an end to 10 and 20% dividends.

The expansion of the cattle trade can be detailed with a few figures. Between 1870 and 1890, Montana's cattle population jumped from 36,738 head to 1,442,517. Wyoming rolled up a similar rangeland change, 11,130 in 1870 and 934,000 in 1890. The pattern held clear across the western cow states.

Some of the great farm corporations formed before the turn of the century passed out of existence in the fullness of time, their investors losing great sums of money. Others, such as California's Kern County Land Company, stayed on to grow and consolidate, and then to grow some more. Kern County was started in the 1870s by one Ben Ali Haggin and one Lloyd Tevis, but it was not incorporated until 1890. In 1899 the same two men incorporated the Victoria Land and Cattle Company, headquartered in New Mexico. The objective: produce cattle.

Great Plains and Corn Belt production from farmers and ranchers, large and small, poured into Chicago during those years. At the Windy City terminals a reception committee awaited the arrival. When producers brought their animals to the stockyards, Big 4 buyers would take turns bidding, and after "buying" the animals, all four firms would share equally in processing the killed animals. It worked. After that, red meat farmers became the sport of the century, second only to the exploitation of the laboring man. Near the turn of the century, Philip Danforth Armour and G.F. Swift had become darlings for the pages of *Scribner's* and *Harper's*. Only a lone, dissenting voice spoke for the laborers they exploited. It mattered little. By the time Upton Sinclair's *The Jungle* appeared, McCoy's 35,000 red meat animals of 1867 had mushroomed into ten million cattle and as many hogs for Chicago each year. The Big 4 had become more powerful than public opinion. Farmers who had endured exploitation organized: first the Grange, and then the Alliance for Progress, the Farmers Union, and all the rest. A consent decree against packers, antitrust legislation, court rulings, even new administrations in Washington changed the tempo of farm exploitation now and then, but never quite erased it. As a result of the consent decree of 1920, Armour, Swift, Wilson, Cudahy and Morris (the latter eventually gobbled up by Armour) were told to stay out of grocery retailing, to quit dominating the terminal yards and market publications, and to avoid the various forms of vertical integration, forward or backward. As late as the beginning of the twenty-first century, packers have sought to have this decree lifted. The decree did its work then, and is doing it now. But nothing, absolutely nothing, has prevented the chain store corporations from accomplishing what packers set out to accomplish during an earlier era.

Jim turned off the overhead projector. It seemed to attract the board's attention and was a fitting move because the operator was getting to the point that mattered. He was about to cover the delicate balance required by a sound economy, and he was not sure that the attendees could handle the abstractions involved. It was the role of red meat in maintaining a high standard of living that needed explanation.

By the early 1960s, red meat meant the equivalent of 200 million head of hogs and cattle. These animals made up the biggest manufacturing industry in the United States. This industry worked twenty-four hours a day, seven days a week, without a wage or a strike, or without an expense other than the capital invested by farm operators. This workforce turned grass and foodstuffs into meat. It increased the consumption of grains over six times, grains subsidized by the government and hauled to feedlots at world prices. Jim paused to fish a news clipping out of his briefcase.

"Gentlemen, I now want to discuss an economic trend, and I suggest the hour is getting late for dealing with it before it closes down most of the farms in the U.S. This is coming on because red meat producers are demanding a price."

Jim read, paused to insert comments, then read some more. It was the message that had become a drill, and was being memorized by nearly every red meat producer in Capper-Volstead.

Then came the flip side of the presentation. "The perception most people have of cow-calf, roundup operations is a Hollywood perception. Actually, fully 80% of the animals are from herds between twenty-five and thirty in size. There are large ranches, but they are only a drop in the bucket. Stuff the cows and time the slaughter with the likely drop dead rate in the pens. That's the formula.

These several developments have planted in the public the idea that cow-calf operations are as big as John Wayne. With that perception goes the idea that it takes lots of corn to make red meat fit to eat. The rest you know, sales barns, traders, backgrounders, intensive feeding with hormones, on and on." Jim had been asked not to editorialize. He was to present the facts and allow the board to come to the appropriate conclusion, but he supplied his opinion that for the family farmer the danger of corporate agriculture loomed large. The arrival of corporate agriculture represented a new style of collective farming. It would see to the liquidation of most independent farms unless the voice of Capper-Volstead prevailed.

During the two or three years before the founding of the Alliance, beef cattle accounted for 19% of farm income; dairy 14%, hogs 11%. When the collapse came in 1955, USDA issued its disclaimers. Cheap imports cut the legs out from under producers, and the frustration economists of USDA dusted off still more theories. Always, USDA action meant too little, too late. The process was wrecking red meat. Red meat was wrecking corn and feed grains, and grain prices were wrecking agriculture.

Now agriculture stood ready to wreck the stability of prices. The role of red meat in holding together the exchange economy, the standard of living, and the income equation itself indicated that the pragmatic observations made by one seed stock breeder had been correct, and that former Kansas State Senator John James Ingalls was also correct: "meat eaters were the kings of men." Jim told the board that the silent revolution amounted to war, and he quoted Senator Hiram Johnson of California in saying that the first casualty of war was the truth.

Missouri board member Ted Huenfeld made a motion that the Capper-Volstead Alliance stage a test withholding action on the faltering Kansas City Stockyards market. Wisconsin Board member Sam Cook seconded it. The voice vote was unanimous. The press was told the full story, in effect: "until public policy meets our just demands." No one questioned Billy Jon, even though the Alliance did not have the clout to make good its threat.

After Jim had presented his written forty page report on red meat, the next order of business was to work up similar reports on corn, wheat, soybeans, small grains, cotton, rice, and finally, on milk. The months went by in their packages of twelve, one test holdback after another, testing Omaha, Des Moines, St. Louis and Wichita.

The stockyards were failing. Buyers now made their purchase treaties in the countryside, and feedlots with their yawning pens gobbled up half finished cattle much like an ocean tsunami.

The words and data flowed down on Jim's yellow legal pad, and Nora transmitted both to paper. During calving season, Jim made no meetings, heard no speakers. He talked to St. Joseph every other day. When legislators were in session, he tripped to various state capitols to testify. It took only two or three sessions to record the fact that no one was listening. "The place is full of people who can't balance a checkbook, but there they are pretending, when they don't even understand the grammar of the subject," Jim told Nora.

In the mid 1960s, after even more test withholding actions, a nuance of frustration came to haunt the soldier turned cowman. He surveyed the life he had created for himself and his family.

Jake was becoming a solid cowman. He spotted signs and symptoms before problems developed. "Dad, bull calf doesn't track. He'll never be able to mount a heifer. His hind feet won't hit the tracks of his front feet." Ruthless culling had become a practice on the Neff farm. Genetic misfits had to be removed. Bulls that could not settle 90% of the cows during the first thirty days of the breeding season had to go. Jim had developed a unique evaluation procedure for determining pre-potency while a calf was little more than six months old. Seed stock that left Banyon Place had to perform, otherwise the reputation of Banyon Place would suffer. Reputation was everything. Once extinguished, sires would drop in price and even be shunned.

It came to this young cowman that there were some things he could do something about, some he could not. Saving fellow farmers who failed to position themselves properly for survival in the insane world of debt and war belonged to the latter.

Still the question remained, "Couldn't the average well managed farm be allowed to survive?" Or was there a mandate for industrial agriculture to rape the soil and present ever worsening products to the population? Finally, when would the pecking order of debilitation reach Banyon Place? The boards and committees and executive enclaves of Capper-Volstead met and studied and planned, and now a decade had gone by since the first dollar day when members had rallied and protested.

Organization squads penetrated the Texas Panhandle, California, Oregon and Washington State. They picked up members in New Jersey, Vermont, Maine, Pennsylvania and New York. They brought the High Plains itself under organization. Glass Splinter's PR department planted stories in newspapers and magazines clear across the country. Broadcasters even toned down their criticisms of the militants.

The old billingsgate, "Sure, there's a farm problem, but this is not the way to solve it" became a bit subdued. Jim often talked about the free market, an unillusioned self-sufficiency attempting to beat it. At times Jim debated with university spokesmen. He said to himself, "One and all, they would go broke in less than a year taking their own advice."

The year the Chinese were embracing their tragic Great Leap Forward, Billy Jon Poole zeroed in on the single commodity that the board identified as the vulnerable head of the market Hydra. It was milk.

237

26

The milk withholding action came on during the spring calving season. It filled the TV screens and front pages with lurid accounts of farmers dumping milk coast to coast, albeit chiefly in the Midwest, in Wisconsin, Minnesota, Michigan, and in the Corn Belt. Back to back, organized farmers were dumping milk rather than send it into trade channels at prices that caused them to consume their capital. The turmoil penetrated Congress and the White House. The President knew how to count votes, and the God forsaken truth was that rural votes no longer counted. The pressure of an inflationary age told the Chief Executive that farmers did not count and that food needed to be kept cheap. Alliance people chanted, "Cheap food ultimately means hungry people," but lawmakers could not handle this seeming contradiction. The 1948 Farm Act and its faltering parity provision was ancient stuff to the press. Hardly any of the reporters were old enough to remember or understand it.

Milk, even more than cattle or hogs, was a mystery to reporters no less than nuclear science. It took fantastic faith for Alliance members to continue dumping milk. From every quarter they were told of a world faced with malnutrition, as though the pangs of hunger would disappear if family farmers simply agreed to go on milking until courts and sheriffs took their farms away. There were no Hoovervilles in the 1960s, but there were plenty of clients for institutionalized poverty. There were whole populations shorn of self sufficiency as a consequence of the biggest, greatest expropriation in the nation's history. The families slid away, not *en masse* as did the dust bowl Okies during the Thirties who joined California's stoop labor force, but one at a time. They took only a few of their meager possessions and hit the road like dust bowlers running from black clouds. They just vanished. In the best case scenarios, they displaced city folks and handed to others the role of being unemployed. As milk slid quietly into drains, Washington fielded more depressionary measures than the New Deal uncorked during the 1930s.

The great minds did not trouble themselves with the data and proofs that Jim Neff prepared for his Capper-Volstead Alliance colleagues. The future did not exist for the legislators who could not balance a checkbook. For the milk producer, the future was here, and that is why it took the faith of Job to continue dumping. The industry had its pecking order. Jim Neff laid it out in his Report #10.

The first market in fact was telescoped into three-layer marketing groups. Marketing orders were steadily certifying territories, and co-ops were forming negotiation teams. These associations were forming dairy geographic regions. One encompassed the eastern end of the nation along the seaboard. A second was formed in Ohio, Kentucky and Tennessee. A third included everything between Ohio and the Rockies.

Massive confinement dairies were aping the beef feedlot system, possibly with hormone added to the product. Confined dairy cows are prone to Para-T, or Johne's Disease, a precursor to irritable bowel syndrome and Crone's disease, problems averted on small farms, family farms. There was Class 1 milk and Class 2 milk, the last reserved for cheese making and processed foods. Class 2 could become Class 1 on an as needed basis. The trade liked to talk about unregulated milk and regulated. "What do you mean, *unregulated?*" a laconic dairy farmer in Wisconsin would say. He had as many as five inspectors hit the farm once a month from as far away as Chicago. Milk that started out as Class 2 and became Class 1 still commanded only a Class 2 price.

Jim's Report #10 about the cheese monopolies identified the imports, pointed out the presence of estrogen- and phytate-laden soy milk, and the real connection between soy estrogen and the misdirected sexual development of young boys and girls. "You wouldn't feed soy to a bull," was one of his offhand remarks.

The milk strike came on during calving season, which is why Jim Neff found himself on the outside looking in. Even so, he spent a lot of time on the phone. He made short holdback meetings and he subscribed to a clipping service so that he could know what the press was saying. A scrapbook received headlines such as the following:

"31,000 Pounds of Milk Dumped in Genoa Area"
The Lincoln Star, Lincoln Nebraska.

"6,500 Gallons of Milk Dumped on Ground North of Sibley"
Gazette Journal, Sibley, Iowa.

"1,390,000 Pounds Milk Dumped Daily"
"Family Of Milk Strike Leader Goes Into Hiding"
Chicago News, Chicago, Illinois

"Dump Tons of Milk"
Detroit Daily, Detroit, Michigan

"$16 Million Suit Filed Against Milk Group"
Philadelphia Times, Philadelphia, Pennsylvania.

"Over 29,000 Gallons of Milk Dumped Here,
    Capper-Volstead Members Report"
Hamilton Tribune, Hamilton, Ohio

"Farmers Demonstrate White Power"
Glascow Examiner, Glascow, Kentucky

"Farmers Feeding Hogs Milk Supply"
Ardmore Daily Times, Ardmore, Oklahoma

"Dairies Accused of Using Powder"
New Ulm Peoples Press, New Ulm, Minnesota

"Milk Withholding Action Continues Amid Truck Hijacking
    Charges"
Hamilton Tribune, Hamilton, Ohio

"Canadian Milk Shipment into Ohio Reported"
Bellefontaine Peoples Press, Bellefontaine, Ohio

"Capper-Volstead Members in Steele County Dump
   32,500 Quarts of Milk Here"
Owatonna Examiner, Owatonna, Minnesota.

"Hogs Enjoy Hold Campaign"
Dickinson Daily, Dickinson, North Dakota.

"Incidents Increase in Milk Withholding"
Stevens Point Standard, Stevens Point, Wisconsin

"Dump 17,000 Pounds of Milk A Day"
Knoxville News, Knoxville, Iowa

"424,000 Spilled in Area Counties"
The Winona Star, Winona, Minnesota

And if there were not headlines, there were photos: $26,547 worth at
the grocery price going on the snow at Ellsworth, Minnesota; 100,000
pounds in Faribault County; 57,500 pounds on the ground (in color)
in the *Worthington, Minnesota Journal.* And there were others, for
example, "Poison Scare Boosts Powdered Milk Sales."

The person who wrote a threatening note and mailed it to Madison,
Wisconsin may never be known, but it was the greatest boost to
powdered milk sales in recent memory. The Wisconsin Cheese Exchange
downplayed the strike. It was a tempest in a teapot, an official said.

Jim returned home after a half day run to Parsons for a rally. Xander
met the pickup. "Daddy, Daddy, we've got three new calves." The little
fellow almost bowled Jim over with a pint-sized shoulder block and hug.
Heidi was right behind him. She already had names picked out, classical
names. She liked Xanthippe for girl calves, and seemed to name at least
one calf Xanthippe each season. She also liked Socrates, Plato, Aristotle,
Xerxes, Darius and Jezebel.

"How did Jezebel get in the roster?" Jim wanted to know.

"I heard the name in a sermon at church," she said.

Each night Heidi and Xander helped their dad assemble stories from
newspaper clippings that came in from all over the country. The press
was a nebulous entity that conveyed opinions and prejudices that every

American capable of voting took to heart. An Ohio newspaper seemed to echo H.L. Mencken's writing in the 1930s, "The Alliance strikes terror in the hearts of mankind. Nothing elicits sympathy like the cause of unwed mothers, poor farmers' sons, or Methodists. Without these categories, our public would never have been blessed with its greatest legislation, namely: price supports, the Mann Act or Prohibition. No more selfish, self-centered and dishonest mammals exist on planet Earth than those who claim to be the backbone of the free enterprise system. No organized group in America has supported the government handout, the unearned dollar, the something for nothing gimmick more than our farmers. These people who have us by the hind teat with products absolutely vital to our survival have twisted and warped the whole concept of free enterprise until it is neither free nor enterprising." An Appleton, Wisconsin paper editorialized, "It has become apparent to farmers that they are the sacrificial lamb for this country." Jim read with abject disbelief and disgust. The import gates were wide open. The General Agreements on Tariffs and Trade, first initiated into being by Harry S Truman in 1948, were pursuing their agenda in support of world trade, one world, milk in orders at prices certain to close out dairies, family farms, finally the dairy industry itself.

"Today milk, tomorrow typewriters and cars," Jim said to himself as he put clippings in chronological order. Farmers liked to think they were exporting products, they failed to discern the reality that enough imports arrived on schedule for the purpose of bringing American commodity prices down to the world level.

The slogan then current had it that the U.S. would make products for the world. If a few million farmers had to be sacrificed to keep the game afloat, well, that was a small price to pay.

"It is a disgrace that farmers must take such drastic action," noted one newspaper, the *Times of Three River Falls,* Minnesota. Jim stacked them up: pro, con, ambivalent. In terms of copy inches, the pros won hands down. In terms of circulation, the metro dailies tore the scales off the wall. The Russellville, Kentucky paper came to the point. "We're not going to waste space joining the metro papers crying against violence. We don't condone the rough stuff. What we're more concerned about right now is relief for the dairymen whose situation is so desperate that they're willing to jeopardize bank and stock credit by destroying their milk in the hope that someone will listen to their case."

An Idaho newspaper wrapped it up in one whiplash line. "We can expect some of the big city press to be just as provincial about the economic plight of farmers as much of Idaho is about the Justice Department sending operators into Wisconsin and Minnesota, and then into Michigan, Indiana, Ohio, Illinois and Iowa."

They reported back that Alliance members were intimidating non-members, that there was violence afloat, that the Capper-Volstead Act was being violated across the board, that the holdback action illustrated an attempt to "unduly enhance" prices.

A federal marshal, the very picture of Matt Dillon, presented himself at Alliance headquarters in St. Joseph, Missouri. He had papers which were duly served on Billy Jon Poole. It was a very courteous encounter. Billy Jon thanked the lawman, who was ushered out politely. Then all hell broke loose.

Lawyers who had been waiting in the back room filled Billy Jon's office. Knute Rockne never delivered half as much coaching as the lawyers unloaded. They were all due in federal court in Kansas City on the next Monday morning. The government was asking for a restraining order, and threatened to jail all those in non-compliance.

Monday morning the courthouse was loaded with marshals, uniformed cops, and well dressed men who just about had to be plainclothes detectives or secret service. It was an awesome spectacle when a half dozen Alliance leaders, most of them in work clothes, were admitted to the paneled courtroom. Jim Neff made the trip to Kansas City and gained admission to the spectator's section after checking his briefcase and tape recorder at the door.

"There will be no tape recorders," the court clerk announced. "There will be only one record by the stenographer." When the proceedings got under way, the sheer boredom of due process became self evident. Justice Department lawyers turned detectives read their affidavits into the record.

Alliance attorneys made the point that any break in the withholding action was tantamount to breaking the action, leaving an inequitable policy system in command of the field. The entire proceeding lasted about two hours. Jim Neff wrote a note in the back of his checkbook. "It's like a Greek arena. The tragedy happens off stage."

Just then the judge summarized, "It won't hurt to pause a bit." The temporary injunction was ruled in effect immediately. Continuing arguments would be heard in two weeks.

The word went out to twenty-five states, and the milk stopped pouring. When Jim returned home, little Xander echoed the words children were being told in school. "Daddy, why are farmers dumping their milk? Why don't they give it to the poor?"

He could not explain to the boy that it cost more to give it away than to dump it or use it as a liquid fertilizer. He caught the boy in his arms and rubbed his nose with his own. Then he said, "because they are the poor." The poor were forever an abstraction to the bureaucrats. Farm and other raw material production as a formulation for factory and service employment simply did not resonate with people who could not empathize with poverty and loneliness, much less make the connection. Once there was a glass of milk, it should not be destroyed. Very well, but what if no one bothers to maintain a cow, milk her, and make available that glass of milk? When Jim Neff sat down with Xander, Heidi, and Jake, the explanations came easily. In the main, children understood. Other students faced the atmosphere of intimidation under which classroom fare is generally processed, so they said nothing. "Forget your college BS and equations about supply and demand. All of it comes down to two things: production of goods and services for human use, and the price of goods at the consumer level. Multiply production times price, and you generate income, which is the monetary measure of value. This income delivers the ability to exchange the product produced. If, along the line, you fail to generate enough income from production to utilize it, then the gears drop out of sync. The equation points up what is wrong. Either there is not enough production to generate income, or not enough price to enable exchange."

That was what the milk action was saying to those who had the wit to understand it. Corn at ten cents a bushel contains as much energy as corn at $2.50 a bushel. Milk at $2.50 a gallon has as much food value as milk at $8 a gallon. "If the price is too low for the initial producer," Jim said, "then it moves through trade channels without generating an adequate income for the exchange economy." Little Xander looked puzzled, but Jake said he understood. He tried to lay it on one of his teachers, who was scoffing at the milk farmers, but she moved off to something about the paramecium and flagella.

Except for officials, the farmers stayed home for the next three months. Even organizers paused to put in soybeans, corn, grain sorghum, edible beans, and the miscellany of row crops, which Eisenhower had once characterized as "political." Hog producers were farrowing all year long in order to even up supply with actual demand. It did not seem to matter. Ever since Ezra Taft Benson had invoked the sliding parity formula, prices seemed to go down. There was little on the chart, but the long-term direction was down. Jim began home schooling the children, and Nora, first to sharpen his own understanding, was second to confer the orientation that had seized his life onto the entire family.

"If a price falls off 10%, then your income equation is 100% production times 90% of the income required to consume the production. How short are we?"

"Ten percent," said Jake.

"Right. If you try to cut that by cutting back production 10% to balance with your income, then your income equation becomes 90% production times 90% price, so that only 81% of the income will be generated to utilize the production created in the first place. Any questions?"

Nora said, "I think I see what you're saying. When you reduce production, you destroy the physical production required to employ the labor force, is that it?"

"Bingo!" said Jim.

"Jim, do we create unemployment by underpaying agriculture?" she asked.

"To the head of the class!" Heidi giggled, and Xander tried to pinch her.

Jake asked, "Is there going to be another milk strike?"

"I don't think so."

"Then you'll be home?"

"I hope so. I want to do something revolutionary with the herd."

"Can I help?" asked Jake.

"I wouldn't want to try without you."

245

Calving was easy that spring. Of the entire herd, only one heifer had a bit of difficulty. Jake saw the problem in motion, and called his dad. The two of them effected a delivery, a sound looking bull calf. As they entered the house for breakfast, the news on WIBW told of federal marshals patrolling Wisconsin, Minnesota, Iowa and Michigan. The informed source had it that the government was about to ask for a consent decree to stop the withholding actions. It was a Thursday. By late that day Splinter Glass told reporters it did not matter what some fellow on a dais in a Halloween costume said, the hold would continue.

"What does it mean?" Nora wanted to know.

"It means a moment of truth. Either farmers stand their ground, or they cave in."

"Which?"

"I don't know. At Le Mars, Iowa in the 1930s, Milo Reno's Holiday Movement people went to court. When the judge came in, a few did not remove their hats. The judge told them, 'Take off your hats, you hoodlums!' That did it. Most of the farmers had been pushed beyond endurance. They vaulted over the rail, seized the judge, dragged him out to a crossroad, and proceeded to hang him. The smartmouth judge fainted dead away, which probably saved his life."

"Jim, we're not going to have violence?"

"No, no! Everyone knows what happened back then. The Guard put all those fellows in a barbed wire enclosure under machine gun guard. Then they scared the hell out of them and paroled them out with a 'go home and milk your cows' gesture."

"Has this been considered?"

"Yes. I suppose I'm not a militant. I argue passive resistance. Martin Luther King brought Alabama to its knees that way. We can fill those jails for them."

"Jail!" she said with horror.

"It would be good company. Don't worry! I can take care of myself."

"You don't need to get involved."

"No, But I probably will."

By Friday night the word was out that the Capper-Volstead Alliance was ordered into a Kansas City court early Monday morning. The government was seeking a consent decree.

St. Joseph was swarming with Highway Patrol troopers, cops and plainclothes people who just about had to be federal marshals.

"They must think we're going to make a run for it," Splinter Glass told Jim.

"Or rush the bench," Jim responded.

27

The word was out even before the papers had been hand-delivered to the St. Joseph headquarters of the Capper-Volstead Alliance. On the basis of affidavits filed by federal marshals who had toured Michigan, Wisconsin and Minnesota, the Alliance was to be taken into a Kansas City court in one week to answer the government's request for a consent decree. On the basis of these reports, Splinter Glass's PR office stood ready to activate the telephone tree. Each contact was organized to call ten other members. Each set of ten was to relay the call until the entire membership had been notified. It took ten delegates acting as a board to order up a special meeting, the proviso being that no special meeting could be called to order in less than twelve hours after notification was started.

Jim got his phone call late Friday night. Nora made the ten calls he had been assigned while her husband packed for the four hour trip on Saturday. The meeting was to be gaveled open at 9 a.m. Sunday morning. There were other calls that came. Howard Espy of Fargo, North Dakota, Eddie Brushbreaker of Mt. Pleasant, Michigan, Carlos Santos of Sapulpa, Oklahoma, and Jody Heston of the Little Rock, Arkansas area all called to set up a rump session on Saturday. A few other dairymen were being invited.

"I'm not a dairy farmer," Jim protested when the first such call arrived. "Makes no never mind," the man from North Dakota said. "You'll be the only non-dairy farmer there, but there's a reason. We want to discuss this consent decree business in advance. If we don't, Billy Jon will slam dunk protest before it gets started."

That was it. A protest was afloat. For several years and throughout the holding, criticism of Billy Jon's leadership rolled in over Capper-Volstead like a fog. Fully half of the Board was employed by the organization. This fact was unsettling to the non-employed members who often did not even claim expenses for their services. There were rumblings that many of the test actions over the past several years were set up to stroke Billy Jon's ego. One hog action was called off, the decision being made in secluded sessions, when the packers involved were about to cave in. One grain action delivered a whopper of a loss to Capper-Volstead because Billy Jon could not make up his mind on the hedge to be applied, and the loss ran into millions. All through these milk dumping days, the leader had been sheepish over standing his ground.

"You think Billy Jon will cave in for the government?" Jim asked Carlos Santos when he called.

"You've got it, buddy! Let's talk!"

The motel selected for the meeting on Saturday had a conference room. It was off Highway 69 a mile or two, away from the loop that now routed traffic going north and south. When Jim arrived, a few dairy farmers were already present. Jim knew the Fargo man. Howard Espy looked to be about fifty, well wrinkled, with hands that gripped like a vice. He milked eighty Holstein cows with the aid of two sons and old milking machines, always frustrated by a debilitated cashflow and rising input costs. He was an original dollar day member of Capper-Volstead, a reluctant delegate because of his workload, but he made the sacrifice when monthly meetings were called because he believed in collective bargaining. He was damn mad at the President of the U.S. because he had helped deliver the votes for that man during the last election.

Jim also recognized Carlos Santos, but that was about all. Carlos wore a big black Stetson, a dark shirt with a Western cut, and Tony Lama boots. His hat was brand new, having been picked up at the St. Joseph Stetson factory that day. Carlos milked forty cows. He knew he was not much of a factor in the withholding action, but his heart and soul for Mexican inclusion was up. He had been recruited by Espy, and the two paired off as best friends. Calvin Waldo, a medium-sized dairy farmer from Red Oak, Iowa was there when Jim came. He was nursing a Coke. Calvin was a throwback to the Milo Reno days. His dad was one of the farmers who had pulled the judge off his bench back in the 1930s. He was sorry that Capper-Volstead declared itself nonviolent. "Some of those bastards need a good buggy whipping," he would say this to shock and awe his listeners. He was forty, a Jersey aficionado and closet Socialist.

That was Capper-Volstead, mused Jim, half to himself. We have room for Catholics, Jews, Protestants, Democrats, Republicans, Socialists and Libertarians, all under the same roof. Those who joined could get along. Why would not the other 80% join? The door opened and a man known as Brushbreaker entered. His name was Eddie, and he milked about a hundred cows in Michigan about halfway between the town of Midland and Lake Michigan. Brushbreaker was half Irish, half Chippewa Indian. He called all his non-Indian friends members of the Wannabe tribe. He was articulate in a small group, but froze in front of a crowd.

Three or four more members spilled into the overcrowded conference room after that. The introductions came on like grape shot. Jim had met them all at one time or another, but he was overwhelmed by names at times. He shook hands with Art Kane, Kentucky, Rudy Smith, Michigan, Ford Handy, Illinois, and then the names started to run together.

Brushbreaker led off, "Mr. Neff, some of us know you better than you know." A chorus of agreement echoed that statement. At first, each man reintroduced himself when he got the floor, but this idea faded soon enough, and Jim soon started recognizing each of the dissidents by state only. "Hell," said Kentucky, "we've gone this far. I can't see knuckling under to some guy in a black skirt who sits on a platform a foot higher than the rest of us in a courtroom."

Iowa reminded everyone of the Depression era judge at Le Mars, Iowa.

"Forget that stuff," Jim counseled. "The question is: what can they really do? The answer to that depends on the way the farmers stick together. They haven't got enough jails to hold everyone for very long."

"Yah, but if the National Guard is called out, we get creamed," reminded Illinois.

"Our problem ain't the government. Hell, the government is a paper tiger. Look how Washington caved in on the blacks. Martin Luther King stood his ground, and by God they had the President chanting 'We shall overcome!' by the time he was through." It was Nebraska, Jim noted.

"That's right," Oklahoma said. "The people who ruled in World War II wouldn't recognize Oklahoma now."

The exchanges went on that way for fully an hour. Finally, the non-official session got down to the problem of the hour. It was agreed that Billy Jon tried to be a Kingfish. He talked tough in front of a crowd, but he was a real trembler in personal confrontation.

"I'm going to tell you something," northern Wisconsin said. "If we don't get a resolution absolutely telling Billy Jon to tell the judge to chuck it, he'll go yes, yes, and comply with whatever Washington wants. That much is a given."

Jim asked for the floor. "What makes you think he'll act on direction from all those who'll be there tomorrow?"

A chorus came on. "He'll have to. If he don't, he's automatically out. That's in the by-laws." Jim could not identify the speaker. Actually, several were speaking over each other. "OK," said Jim, "I'm just here as a member. All who attend will have a vote, but I'm only one vote and not even a dairy farmer."

"That's not why we wanted you here," a man from Colorado said. He was a mountain of a man who had a dairy herd in the San Juan Valley. Colorado was a newly organized state, and Jim could not recall his name. The man went on. "We've heard you speak. You're the only one who knows how to speak worth a damn. We want you to be our spokesman."

"You know what that means?"

"We hope it means an order to Billy Jon requiring him to confront the government. If that don't happen, we've just poured away a lot of milk for nothing," Colorado said.

"What do you think, Brigham?" a voice asked. Jim did not know that Brigham Young of Twin Falls, Idaho had slipped into the room. "The man's right, Mr. Neff," Brigham Young said.

"Boys," Jim said, "I hate to turn you down, but the fact is that Billy Jon will never recognize me. He doesn't have to, according to the by-laws. Even assuming that you cleared that hurdle, well, you know how vindictive Billy is. It will cost me my membership."

Illinois grabbed the floor. "If this action is put down, do you know what will happen?"

"I think I do," Jim said.

"My brother is an attorney. He says we'll get let off the hook if Billy Jon signs a consent decree. Do you know what a consent decree is?"

Jim said he did. Illinois went on, "It's a straitjacket. The organization is through. Oh, it'll continue to exist in some hole in the wall office, like Jack London's Wobblies, but it won't amount to a damn!"

Jim did not put up much of an argument against this thesis because, unfortunately, the man was right. Wilson, Armour, Cudahy and Swift were cut down by a consent decree in the 1920s. Oh, they're still around as specialty packers, but the monopoly ball has been passed to the likes of Tyson and upstart packers near the feedlots who'll end up driving red meat producers to the wall now occupied by dairy farmers. At length he said, "You want me to make the case on your behalf?"

"That's the long and short of it," South Dakota said.

"How will you get me recognized?"

"Leave that to us," Nebraska said.

The meeting went on another hour. It was speculated that there was at least one turncoat in the motel, and that the full design was being heard and carried to Capper-Volstead headquarters. Two very quiet men in the conference room caught Jim as everyone left. "You just be ready, Jim," they told him. "We have until morning to do our part."

"Our part" was an eat to the fill supper in the Rhubi Dioux Hotel with a chicken fried steak dinner for Spangler Drew of South Dakota and Kansas City steaks for Fred Paul of Muncie, Indiana and Carl Rippen of Dillsburg, Pennsylvania. The target was Carl, a very loyal follower of Billy Jon, who had been exhibiting cracks in his armor lately. The two worked on Carl, a steak and four bottles of beer, and Carl was good as gold and a little gullible, for which reason he had followed in Billy Jon's wake for so long. Billy Jon could abuse Carl with snide remarks, but Carl had not a comeback when Billy Jon made an offcolor remark about a member's wife. Carl could not abide raunchy stories or swearing. He was not at the meeting because a few of the boys were certain to forget themselves and say "Hell" or "Damn," and this offended Carl Rippen. One thing was certain: if Carl asked for the floor, he would get it. By the time the dinner was over, the two farmers had Carl's word that he would ask for the floor. The rest of the move was as choreographed as a stage play.

In public meetings, the Alliance had come to ape the protocol of lawmakers in Congress. They did not refer to each other by name. It was always, "The Chair recognizes the distinguished cotton producer from Mississippi," or it was the "distinguished wheat grower from Nebraska," or the "prize winning dairyman from Wisconsin." The Chair had dictatorial power over the meeting in any case. The Chair was Billy Jon, and Billy Jon had selected and oriented the speakers he was prepared to recognize. Thus, Article 5, Section 8 was made a part of the by-laws as eyewash. Billy Jon never expected ten delegates to invoke its provisions to require a spur of the moment meeting.

All right, so the dissidents had had their meeting. The troops had their marching orders. He knew who would be recognized and which mic to kill dead. It was all a part of having an orderly meeting. Billy Jon left little to chance. He knew the rebels and finks by sight and smell. He would get fooled once in a while, usually when a delegate or board member had a change of heart three hours into the meeting, but all speakers ratified exactly what Billy Jon was doing. Not one wanted an order of direction to hamper the leader in court or in negotiation with the Justice Department.

"Mr. Chairman," came the plea from microphone #6, which had come into life in the person of Carl Rippen.

"The Chair recognizes the distinguished dairyman from Dillsburg, Pennsylvania. You may take as much time as you wish." Carl Rippen had always been a Billy Jon stalwart. In his home county, some of his detractors called him Rubber Stamp Rippen. "Mr. Chairman, under Rule #11, I now yield my allotted time to the distinguished researcher and red meat specialist, Mr. Neff of Kansas." Billy Jon recognized microphone #2. "Switch it over!" he shouted to the engineer. Microphone #2 came alive. The speaker was a real Billy Jon running dog lackey. He had been thinking of revolt. Now he had his chance, and the issue was point of order.

"Mr. Chairman, I feel Rule #11 is clear, and under Rule #12, I ask the parliamentarian to rule and reverse the Chair's order."

"Out of order," was Billy Jon's gaveled response. Pandemonium broke out. The microphone was still open when the delegate from Colorado demanded division of the house.

Secure in his rule, Billy Jon allowed a voice vote. The thunder from the audience annihilated the Chair's authority. The parliamentarian ruled, and Jim Neff was allowed to speak "for as long as he wants." Jim refused to speak from the floor. He demanded a microphone on the stage. The buzz of voices continued while the proxy for the dairyman traveled the long aisle. Atop the stage, he fidgeted with the microphone until it was adjusted just right. It was a one directional mike. Jim measured the distance by eye, then he started slowly, like a latter day Will Rogers, first sweeping back a shock of his blondish white hair.

"You know," he said, "even a dog knows the difference between being stumbled over and being kicked." Some of the tension was broken right there.

The dairy states knew Jim. His straight talk had reoriented several of them and his messages in the *Common Sense* publication of the Capper-Volstead Alliance resonated with even the most skeptical. "When I came to the organizational meeting of this Capper-Volstead Alliance some years ago I stopped by to ask along a neighbor. I was too late. By the time I drove into his yard, he'd seized his shotgun and gone to the barn. I myself heard the shotgun go off as I got out of the pickup. We found him between two bales of hay. He'd left a note: 'I did this to myself.' Well, he didn't do it to himself no more than 2,399 others didn't do it to themselves that week. All of those others had also left agriculture, not necessarily with a shotgun, but they left. When I came home from the service at the end of the war, we had a prosperous agriculture. The farm was free and clear for most farmers. The banks could hardly find a market for all the money they had in their vaults."

Jim worked the assembly through the several steps taken by government to reduce farmers to penury. He restated his thesis that the income withheld from agriculture can throw the country into a 1930s depression. Why has not it done so? Because the shortfall is being made up by debt expansion, public and private.

"I ask you, why are our sons dying in Vietnam? Why? Because the farmer isn't being paid. The nabobs of privilege in glass towers back east have used war as an engine of credit and debt, so we are being removed from the land by the banks. As families are removed, the great holders, the corporations, and the so called 'strong hands' take over. The powers that be, figure that production will keep coming. But you and your families are superfluous. Go to the cities. Go to work pushing iron in a factory. Ladies and Gentlemen, there is no mandate for dissolution of the family farm. It is bad science to take a biological procedure and turn it into an industrial procedure." Then Jim Neff got down to earth.

"We started getting wooed, screwed and tattooed in 1950. By 1955 a machinery salesman started Capper-Volstead. We've been thirteen years getting organized and arriving at our moment of truth." Jim took a swig of water, then continued.

"We've been holding back cattle from the vultures at the sales barn. Some of our members have been suggesting shooting hogs and rolling them into lime-dusted pits. You say that these things are ineffective, and you may be right. What good does it do to hold back kumquats and asparagus? The government measures all of agriculture in terms of the political commodities, all the grains, wheat, corn, milo, soybeans, oats, crops from 80-82% of the harvested acres. Those crops went into bondage in the 1930s. They were sacrificed in The Farm Act of 1948 and screwed and tattooed by Ezra Taft Benson in 1952.

"The focal point of the present action is milk. We've caught the attention of the country, so now they're taking us to the woodshed. We will be told to cease and desist. They're not offering to do a thing about last week's 2,400 lost farms, no moratorium on rigged debt, no management of import invasion by the traders, no hint of debt cancellation except we are to cease and desist. "Our leadership will be asked to comply with a consent decree. This means go home, milk your cows, deliver the milk, and keep sinking ever deeper in debt. The government says that this must not happen again. Your leadership will be offered a consent decree. You will be asked to give a sixty-day notice if you intend to strike. You will be given hoops to jump through, the best one being to lie down and play dead. If you don't, you're going to jail. That is the question. Are we prepared to go to jail?

"Our leader, Billy Jon Poole, does not want to go to jail. He's told you that he says that we have to obey the law." Jim's voice now picked up and packed a measure of emotion.

"Whose law?" he exclaimed. "We have our law: 7 U.S.C. 601-602. It mandates parity for those basic storable commodities that govern the general price level for all of agriculture. But that law isn't good enough for ADM and Cargill and Continental and Dreyfus and Bunge and Born. So they crafted a new law in 1948, and they decided that you needed to give the banker a cut from everything you do.

"Did Martin Luther King lose his cause because negroes refused to honor Hitler-style oppression? No! Did John L. Lewis assume a craven posture during the Detroit sitdown strike of the 1930s? Hell no, he didn't! The governor called out the Guard. 'You're not going to dodge the law!' he told Lewis. Now the governor was an Irishman. His grandfather had been a revolutionary during the bad times. John L. Lewis reminded him of that. 'When the British took your grandpa, they hung him by the neck till he was dead, dead, dead! Was he dodging the law?' John L. opened his shirt. 'Shoot right here,' he said, 'and be damned!'" Jim paused for emphasis. "Had he been shot, I have no doubt that those workers would have taken Willow Run apart. The Guard was withdrawn, and the workers prevailed. We won't prevail if we cave in now. If the leadership won't take the direction of this body to refuse a restraining order, to refuse a consent decree, then a requirement is in order, and that is to appoint a leader who has the sand to make good the sacrifices already made."

The silence that followed lasted for fully half a minute before scattered applause took over. The Chair gave itself the last word. It took Billy Jon forty-five minutes to tell the delegates that he needed a free hand to negotiate, that this was impossible if he was to be burdened with "instructions." He was not afraid of jail or the negotiators. He had faced them before, not just over theory, but eyeball to eyeball.

"I am humbled by the task before me," he said. "I've been there before. I've endured almost twenty lesser withholding actions. Believe me, I know when to hold 'em and when to fold 'em."

He concluded several times, finally making the conclusion real by ordering ballots. The delegates and members were to vote between "a free hand" and "instructions." It was an orderly ballot, each delegate passing an identification test before dropping his ballot in a box. In less than half an hour the result was announced. A bare majority had voted to give Billy Jon a free hand, to use his best judgment.

Jim did not notice the Phineas priest as he fell in behind him as he strode toward the door. "Multitudes, multitudes in the valley of decision," the man quoted.

Jim turned around. "Phineas priest!"

"One and the same. Before you bolt for freedom, can I have a word with you?"

"For your research?"

"Yes. For the archives."

"Let's go sit in my truck."

The two crossed the parking lot, walking rapidly. Jim started the motor. The weather was not really cold, but it was not comfortable either. Jim cut off the radio and let the heater to do its work. The professor said nothing. Finally Jim met his eyes.

"Where were you and your lance when I needed you?"

Professor Phineas priest chuckled. "My friend, you need to read the Bible carefully. The official charge given me is dependent on identifying the transgressors. Well, Mr. James Neff, I have that identification. It isn't Billy Jon or the packers or the dairy processors, none of those people."

"Who then?"

"Fortified by infinite wisdom, the Creator didn't allow a Darwinian demon on the planet."

"What's a Darwinian demon?"

"It would be a biological animal that creates itself, eats the way a shark swims, meaning constantly, has an abbreviated gestation period, and never dies until it has totally plundered the planet. Clearly an impossibility, right?"

"No, I don't think there is a Darwinian demon."

"Ah, but there is. It's the world's financial structure. It creates money the way God created heaven and Earth, out of absolutely nothing. It has decreed that your farm organization is to be put down, *verstehen sie?*"

"You mean we really didn't have a chance?"

"Not really. You probably could have gained some concessions, like you said. Maybe some of the foreclosures could have been restructured. Maybe then there would have been less shotgun suicides in Oklahoma. But you didn't have a chance, not with less than 20% organized."

"I picked up that vibe from that colonel you squired into the organizational meeting a few years back. Whatever happened to him?"

"He's passed to his reward. I think they were trying to take away his pension before he choked to death on a big bite of filet mignon."

"OK, what is it you want to research?"

"There have been some 400 farm organizations once characterized as national that have passed from the mind and memory of man." The professor walked through history with Jim so that he could comprehend what Jim knew about the Capper-Volstead Alliance. When he had finished picking Jim's brain, he changed the subject.

"Where do you go from here?"

"Back to Banyon Place, back to tending my own garden, so to speak."

After a long pause, Jim added, "Back to the business of survival."

"James, James, James, survival is not a worthy objective for a man who just took on Billy Jon Poole. You should seek to prevail." "Very fine for the classroom, but out here on the firing line, you have to have clout."

"No, you have to have innovation. You have to do what the Darwinian demon can't do or compete against."

"And what might that be?"

"James, that has to be quality. Ultimately, people will get tired of that garbage from the feedlots. If mental acuity isn't taken away completely, *vox populi* will demand clean, wholesome fare."

The two stayed on almost an hour exchanging their knowledge of tragedy and hope. Finally, Phineas priest cranked open the door, then extended his hand to Jim. "Don't look for a metaphorical lance to put God on your side. You have to do that yourself."

The professor promised to be in court. He would monitor the proceedings and, if possible, record them.

Jim digested the words Phineas priest had loaded onto him. "Professor," Jim said. "I've agonized trying to understand cause. What causes what? We see each cause fade away to reveal still another cause. I've tried to explain our dilemma."

"Well, explain it to me. I don't know whether I understand 100% this thesis of yours, this pricing of agriculture. If you can make an evolved Phineas priest understand, then you ought to get a Nobel Prize." Jim half laughed. "Self deprecation will get you nowhere. Every farm is a bio-factory for milk, meat, grain, vegetables, fruits, nuts. These are the farmer's manufactured products. How does he do this? By means of chlorophyll and photosynthesis combined with water, soil, and his capital, this farm production produces fully 70% of all the raw materials used to operate the economy. The farmer really precedes the rest of the economy, by say, sixteen or eighteen years. This, for the simple reason that the products of the farm have to feed labor from the time of birth to teenage before the new human being goes into the labor supply. The national income is nothing more than raw materials times the sale of the national multiplier. Efficiency determines this multiplier. In 1787 most of the people were farmers. By 1850, only half the people worked the farms in order to feed the people. This last created a multiplier of two." Jim paused for a minute. "Are you still with me?"

"Proceed," the Phineas priest said.

"In 1910-1914, the multiplier grew to about five. That ratio still holds. It's sort of a rule of ratios. Once the level of raw materials has been estimated, the rest is merely cash flowing from one product to the next, each time nurturing national income. The festival comes to town, buy a ticket. The national income goes up, but I have created nothing to pay the promoter. Except for raw materials, each transaction is a wash. Man debited, man credited. With farm raw materials, the equation reads: man debited and nature credited. But nature is not paid back."

"Exactly! Well said!"

"Yes, but I couldn't get even half the membership to understand." The professor figured he might as well be the smart aleck for the evening.

"Jimbo, it's like Einstein said, 'the only thing infinite on planet Earth is human stupidity.'"

28

There was a time when all of eastern Kansas was grass. Features ran out as you moved west of the Missouri line. Emigrants could walk alongside their wagons until they ran out of people, then set their markers with impunity once the trail herds were gone. Weeds previously unknown to the plains, the High Plains, made their appearance with traffic. For the earliest settlers, and later for the Volga Germans, these undulating acres were beautiful. They retained their beauty during the months of spring calving. Jim Neff's paddocks were well east of the isohyet, this meant 34 to 36 inches of rainfall a year. The sky had a pale blue brilliance. At his latitude Jim could grow pecan trees and maintain a grove of fruit trees, cherry trees included. Where grazing animals had not taken them away, there were carpets of wild flowers, buttercups, Indian paint brush, and sunflowers when the season was dry. The colors came on according to the season. In the fall Nora created dining room centerpieces from sumac, bull thistles, and maple sprigs. A running creek bordered the farm. During the last years of the depression, a deep pool had become a swimming hole with a Tarzan like rope tied to an overhanging tree, arcing skinny dippers well away from the bank.

However, Xander and Jake could not use the pond. Runoff from neighboring farms had so polluted the water that it was unsafe. During the late 1930s, the stream had been full of edible fish. With plenty of habitat, there was never a shortage of cottontails. You could feed a family on wild game in those days, Jim mused as he entered his own driveway. Yet all this has been erased in no more than three decades.

The place was a paradise then, he thought, and it remains a paradise. Yet for most farmers, living was paper thin. Few of the luxuries found in urban homes could be found on the farm. Electric lights did not arrive until after the war for many farms, and the telephone, usually a rural party line system, awaited the 1960s before it became marginally adequate. After the convention, Jim replayed the moment he came home from the war.

"Nora, sweetheart, I'm home."

"For good?"

"Yes, absolutely for good." The two did what people who have been married almost twenty years do. It was a mild embrace at first. Then it dissolved into a passionate kiss.

"We lost," Jim said.

"I know. I saw it on TV." She did not ask for particulars. She knew instinctively that he did not want to talk about it. Nora vanished into the kitchen to make coffee.

"The calving?" he asked.

"All done," she said. "Xander helped, and Jake was always around on weekends."

Jake was a student at Kansas State, studying animal husbandry. He was alone among his classmates in having delivered calves. "Last week," Nora said, "he came home and said, 'Ma, they teach so much that isn't so.'" Nora's hazel eyes twinkled as she recited the happenings around the farm.

"Jake has become quite a botanist. He collects weed samples, row crop succulents, pasture weeds, and forbs."

"Well, what is he doing with them?"

"He has a system. He classifies the weed and learns how to recognize it. He's studying the literature to find out what the weed is saying. Xander tags along. I think the boy is going to become a master gardener. He has his own plot for beans, and he harvested excellent peas, shelled them all. The boys were so proud of you on TV."

"I haven't seen my little Heidi."

"She isn't so little anymore. She'll enter nursing school as soon as she finishes high school. She didn't ask me. She told me," Nora said. Without a word, Nora handed Jim a letter postmarked from West Germany. It had been addressed to the Capper-Volstead Alliance in St. Joseph and forwarded to Banyon Place. Jim studied the stamp, then slit open the envelope. The letter was obviously from his older brother whom he had not seen in thirty years. He read:

Dear Jim Bob,

I haven't seen you since before the war. I saw your name and a good part of your talk in *Der Spiegel,* and this now prompts me to tell you what happened to your older brother. You were a kid when I joined the army. I ended up in Patton's chicken shit outfit, the 10th Armored. I was in combat 144 days, didn't get wounded. I am now a German citizen. I didn't figure it was worth coming home after we left the farm. I have a German wife and a son, Johannes. We call him Hans. I was never able to get a job in the States and I didn't want to return to riding the rails. My wife's family has connections, so when I quit the army I got on with *Neustadt Aisch,* the *Besammungs Verein* Genetic Program. I have become acquainted with what you call line breeding because I am working for an artificial insemination program. You see, at the end of the war West Germany under U.S. occupation had few animals except scrawny cows, goats, pigs and horses. The judgment was made to control breeding. It didn't matter how well you liked your herd, if it didn't measure up, it was condemned. All sires to be tested. That's what we do here.

I know I haven't seen you since you were a kid and I feel bad about that. I didn't hear about Mom's death until after the Battle of the Bulge. I don't think I've ever heard from our older sisters since they entered the convent. Jim Bob, I have often thought about you. It's a shame our family broke up. I understand Joe Sam lived in Los Angeles, retired, and is now in a nursing home in Santa Monica. He and his wife never did have any children. Now for the real reason I'm writing. Some of our staff people visited your Capper-Volstead Alliance headquarters. They brought back those ten papers you prepared for your outfit. I think I can be of service to you, especially if you can come here or send one of your kids. Let me explain. For now I merely want you to come over. We have a lot to teach. I know you probably can't leave your place, but why not send one of your boys over here for a year? I've talked to the institute, and they would welcome him. He can stay with us. I have a nice house with an extra room. I think if you learn what we do over here, you'll be a leg up on all cattlemen in the U.S. I know how you feel about the U.S., and I know you wonder why I would take out German citizenship. Well, this is the best place I've ever gotten employment. Dr. Bonsma intends to visit the U.S. He has agreed to stop in on you while visiting ranches in America in the next few years. Write when you have time. Let me know about your son getting a real education by coming over here.

My respects to your family,

Your brother, Roy Lee

Jim read the letter several times. He had fond memories of riding Brenny bareback with Roy up front. They shot rabbits together when Roy was not on the bum or hunting work.

Maybe Roy would come once for a visit. Jim decided to tell Jake about his Uncle Roy and the invitation to study with him in Germany. He thought of this when he went for a walk with Jake. The letter opened a barrage of questions it took half the afternoon to answer. Jim explained that the innovator ultimately demolishes the existing order. "We have to do something here that the bigs can't accomplish or compete against. When you get back, Banyon Place is going to be the Cadillac of genetics."

Nora waited until the next day to ask, "What happened, James?"

"Jake thinks he would be happy to be on Banyon Place the rest of his life, but he finally got excited about meeting his real uncle and studying in West Germany. He understands he could learn from the mistakes that were made and the results of experiments that are saving the animal world and livestock of Germany and Europe.

"I think we're living through one of the great blunders of history. The industrial farm is going to produce crops at world prices, and the government is going to subsidize the big holders. The rest of the farmers can hang on, take care of themselves, maybe even make a little money if they're innovative enough."

"What about the Alliance?"

"About half walked out. California is gone, so is western Kansas, Oklahoma, Texas, half of Nebraska and the Dakotas. I expect I'll just let our membership contract run out."

"Well, aren't we making it?" She already knew, she kept the books.

"Yes, after starving for twenty years, for which I apologize."

She waved off that comment. "It's been a great starvation," she said.

"Seriously, Nora, I'm going to make this place tick. I was thinking all the way home. I'm thinking fully 80% of the cow-calf operations do spring calving. You've heard me say it a hundred times, what most people do has got to be wrong. I'd like to try a small amount of fall calving."

Fall calving had been called into question, ratified, and repudiated by the experts. Jim figured he would do his own experiment. She knew he would have a reason. A little silence would drag it out of him. It came in a rush, a veritable treatise on why the mother cow should nurse her calf through the winter with weaning taking place exactly when the spring grass delivered its greatest nutritional load. The business of a calf leaving a body temperature womb to be dropped in often sub zero temperatures was debilitating. His excitement was furbished and refurbished by the fact that he had sold three bull calves from the Xanthippus line sire. All answered linear measurements required for excellent pre-potency. Further, he had sold half the straws of semen in storage from Hard Rock Charley, a descendant from one of the calves Grandpa Xander Staab had willed him as WWII got underway.

Jim invited Jake to join him on a pasture walk.

"Look at those cows, look at their mouths, what do you see?"

"They're all eating grass. They must think it's good stuff."

"What do you see around their nostrils?"

"They all have beads of sweat."

"Well, son, you'll have to listen so you'll know their side of the story."

"I suppose."

"Sweat? Let's say it's an exudate, a culture. Do you know what I think is happening?"

Jake said he did not know.

"That culture is passed to the grass just about every time the animal rolls out its tongue and brings the grass in over the cutting edge of the lower teeth. Of course, the bovine has no upper teeth."

Jake did not want to admit that he had never noticed, so he maintained a discrete silence.

"Here's what I think," Jim said. "That culture inoculates the grass. Dew and rain take it into the soil. Nature says to the animal, 'I'll give you grass, but you have to pay out the stimulant I need.' That's why I believe animals create good pasture just as good pasture creates good animals. Don't feel bad when you find how slow we learn. I learned that off an old fellow in Minnesota. He harvested some of that culture and had a fellow in Montana dilute it with distilled water. Then he sprayed the solution on test plants. He maintained the usual controls."

Jake's interest jumped, maybe triple time. So what! became "My God! What were the results?" he asked.

"About a 50% growth response."

They walked in silence for a while. The beads of exudates loomed larger than life on every cow. Jake said to himself, "Nature has some funny ways."

"You'll have a hard time learning much on your own," Jim said. "Son, pay attention to wise old men. Guys who have lived seventy or eighty years are founts of knowledge that you won't find in most textbooks. Real knowledge comes out of the field. Old men, like Xander, your great grandfather, taught me more than I've ever learned from Extension and that swayback shelf of books in the den. The best grass, native grass, doesn't grow in a single year. It develops over centuries. We don't have much of that. Early settlers plowed it all under."

"Well, we have seeded some."

"Yes, when I didn't know better," Jim said. He said he would explain that later. They came to a neighbor's field full of weeds, Canadian thistle, knap weed, volunteer corn and soybeans. "I just bought this field," Jim told Jake. "It's 120 acres. Mr. Tally plowed under some very good prairie grass to raise corn and soybeans in rotation. Prices for the crop being what they are, and costs being what they are, the bank sold him out, machinery and all. I tried to help him, but he wouldn't listen. He consumed his capital for years until he was broke."

Jake had heard that story a hundred times. He dismissed it. "Are we going to plant grass?"

"No, we're going to divide the land into paddocks. We'll turn in as many cattle as my computations allow, usually a half day at a time, and let them have what they want. They'll leave their manure full of seeds behind. I expect we'll re establish pasture in a couple of seasons at no cost."

"All of it?"

"No, we'll have control plots, tame pasture, a mix of legumes, the name of the game is to 'control costs.'" He emphasized the last two words. They walked the newly purchased land, noting its deterioration. Hard clay rose to the surface here and there like sour milk. The nutrients were there, albeit imbalanced. How could plants structure their internal hormone and enzyme systems when insulted once a year with unbalanced salt fertilizers? Jim said this to himself, then he laid it on Jake. It is the role of grass to take up micro-nutrients in sizes beyond the ion or angstrom. The herbivore functions best on grass. You can not finish them quite as fast that way, but you cut your costs in half. I guarantee you that old Xander made more money on grass than cowmen do today sending their critters to the feedlot at about eight months of age."

"That's not what the university teaches," said Jake.

"I know what they teach, that's why I wanted you home now and then to un-brainwash you."

The two smiled and laughed a bit before Jim continued. "Animals force-fed on a high-carbohydrate diet is a flawed procedure. Even a switch from open-pollinated corn to hybrid is dangerous. Hybrids do not pick up the trace nutrients. Open-pollinated pick up 85.7% more copper, 34.5% more iron, and 20.5% more manganese."

"Dad, how do you expect me to remember all this?"

"Do you remember when you played Willie Loman in *Death of a Salesman* during high school? How did you remember all those lines?"

"I memorized them."

"That's what you'll have to do now. Memorize. You can't run to a notebook or textbook every time you need to know something. What I'm telling you: memorize. Just keep asking till you have it, OP corn contains 400% more nutrients than hybrid. Right now I'm working on the data for genetically engineered corn and its effects on sexual development and breeding."

"The core of vitamin B_{12} is cobalt," Jim went on. "A lack of cobalt causes brucellosis, your Bangs disease. Do the professors see to cobalt in the ration or pasture?" Jim answered himself. "Nope. They kill whole herds to get brucellosis-free acres. They write a law to make vaccinations mandatory. I tell you, Jake, Bangs is about as infectious as the stomachache." They came to a fresh paddock, one the animals had entered the first thing in the morning.

"I figure a cow needs 3% grass on a dry matter basis in terms of her body weight if she's lactating, a little less if she isn't. You have to take that little hand held computer and make the calculations. For instance, to have a fifteen-day rotation, it's two days to a paddock. Grass means forage. A good pasture will have, say forty or fifty species of grass, forbs and weeds. Pastures need fertility if the grass is to nourish. I have a small test going. I'm using a high dilution of seawater on an acre to see what it will do."

"Won't the salt kill the grass?"

"Not with the proper dilution. That water has at least 92 trace elements. We need those traces, otherwise our grass will be as worthless as grass in Mississippi or Florida."

The several paddocks revealed several stages of growth. "I don't want an animal to have to walk more than a quarter of a mile for water. With this plastic pipe, I can have a water supply from our deep well pumped to each and every paddock. I got this system finished last year."

"What about silage?"

"No way, Jose," Jim said. "Preserved feeds lose their vitamin A content. In fact, almost all vitamins are degraded by the silage process. Let's move on. I just want you to pick up on the fine points. So far you've moved cattle only occasionally, with all those high school and college activities. If you want to follow this profession, and it is a profession, you'll have to educate yourself. I wish I had another dog like Rover. She does most of the cattle moving nowadays."

They walked down the transfer patch toward Hard Rock Charley's pen. "You seldom have a sick animal if you have good grass. Believe me, Jake, it's goodbye to vet bills."

As they walked, Jim summarized. "I'm the gadfly. I guess I produce seed stock in a humane way. The university says no, no you're supposed to send cattle to a feedlot, stuff them with corn, antibiotics, hormones, protein bypass, cattle cake, and so on. The end product has about as much taste as cardboard, get the picture? This business of taking a calf from 80 pounds to 1,200 pounds in fourteen months means tasteless meat protein. It's all part of the low profit scenario public policy has installed in the countryside."

"What's the economics?"

"I'd say the average grain producer is able to make maybe $80 an acre in a 36 inch rainfall part of the country. I can make $300 per acre, often $500 per acre with grass. I know some dairy farmers who make $600 per acre on grass."

Jake made a few mental computations, and they all canceled out the claim by soybean pushers that plowing under pastures to grow the estrogen laden bean was good economics.

"Put this into your mental adding machine," Jim said. "About 400 pounds of dry matter per edible inch on a per acre basis is a reasonable expectation. Plug that into our paddock system and you have the basis for figuring that 3% per cow requirement. Of any given inches of forage, cows will eat about five or six inches. Five inches times 400 pounds, and so on. You know more arithmetic than I do! The non-lactating animal needs only 2% in terms of body weight each day."

They stopped for a long look at Hard Rock Charley, one of Jim's favorite semen producing bulls. "I should have named him Cash Register. That's how well his straws of semen sell."

Pasture maintenance is an art. So is bull genetics. The conventional ignorance has it that expected progeny difference based on lots of statistics is the signal to buy or reject a bull. Jim Neff scoffed at the idea. Oh, he registered animals, but he really believed that the first order in achieving improved beef herds is to burn the registration records. EPD was that much of a loser.

Hard Rock Charley was sculptured perfection. The hair on his head coiled in clock spring ringlets. Every sign said pre potency. Certainly this bull could sire fifty sons and daughters a season and still pose for Michelangelo. When Hard Rock Charley was six months of age, Jim knew what maturity would bring. Jim found his insight warehoused in the minds of wise old cattle breeders. Nowadays, commercial cattlemen could not care less what kind of meat protein they produce. "All they want is gain; four, five, six pounds a day. The faster an animal gains, the sorrier the meat." Jim went over the bull for Jake's benefit. He had numbers. He did not expect Jake to have total recall, for there would be many pasture walks, including the one from Jake's remodeled home a quarter mile from the home place.

"It all comes down to this, a 1% increase in weaning rate is twice as important as a 1% increase in price. This means a 1% greater calf crop in a hundred-cow herd is ten extra calves. The reproductive rate is 50% of the economic value of the farm." Jim was on a roll, and his recent college graduate found that his degree in animal husbandry was merely a visa to start learning. "Low maintenance and high fertility go hand in hand," Jim went on. "One reason so many farmers don't make it under our present conditions is high maintenance, too many toys, too many inputs."

Hard Rock Charley seemed to appreciate his visitors. He seemed to say, look at me, I'm exceptional. He was. "I tested Charley at seven months of age. He had a scrotal length of 5.5 inches. He was not a bull calf in gender only. That's where you start. If the scrotum does not measure up, the grown bull will never settle all the cows. He might just as well have a game leg." Jim ran down the anatomical chart and explained what the pituitary has to do with semen production, that the epididimus has to be the size of a pecan, no larger, no smaller.

"This farm has always practiced ruthless culling, will not sell a bull that doesn't measure up, that doesn't have the right sperm count. You build a reputation on honesty, and you destroy it by charging a sire's price for a defective bull."

Jake was jolted back to reality by his father's statement of policy. He knew that most farmers not only undercut their neighbors for a quarter's difference in price, but they also sold sick animals before they fell down dead. Bulls that could not perform were mongrelizing the herds of the country, and exotic imports grew to ponderous sizes for lots of cuts of meat that delivered too few good eating experiences.

The hypothalamus regulates the pituitary. The pituitary regulates the testicles and ovaries in offspring, as well as the liver, the adrenal, the pancreas, the thymus, and the thyroid. The bull should be able to settle cows at twelve months of age.

Jim pulled out a tape measure. He measured the bull which stood still and invited the attention. "Thirty-nine centimeters in circumference, perfect!" said Jim. "He routinely settles about 90% of the cows in the first 21 days of the breeding season. He'll even impregnate a marginal cow if you let him." The two returned to the kitchen to share lunch with Nora and Xander. Heidi was not there, but Nora had a letter, and she said that their daughter would soon be home. It was not the farm that was a problem. The farm knew how to operate. Some 80% of the cow-calf operators were small, maybe 25-30 head. A lot were part-time farmers, lawyers, doctors, businessmen, some with decorator herds in the corner pasture that faced traffic. The Longhorn was a favorite for this crowd.

Most of the cow-calf people were serious farmers under the pressure of public policy. Some of the high tech people wanted cows to produce litters like goats or rabbits.

Seated with Xander and Nora listening, Jim told Jake, "Here's the bottom line: the school people want to have cows twin. You'll never get a good sire from freemartins or twins. There's something more sinister afloat. The big money, I mean the money they create out of thin air, is banking on a takeover of cow-calf operations the way it took over poultry. This means contracts, so the cow-calf man no longer owns his own calf. They'll come out, inseminate the cows, any kind, then own the calf when it's born. The contract farmer will do the work. The pay will be slimmer than those Arkansas poultry growers get for cleaning up chicken litter."

Jim's pronouncement was ominous. Outside, the leaves of the big oak tree rustled in the wind. Birds that were chirping their blessings a few minutes earlier either fell silent or were drowned out. The temperature outside the kitchen was falling. The dog barked as if to announce an intruder. There was nothing dysfunctional afoot. The Neff family was unique in holding together. The farm was solvent in a sea of insolvency. Neighbors were still leaving the farm, and the work of the Capper-Volstead Alliance seemed to have spent itself, leaving debilitation in charge of the scene.

29

Flushed with victory over the matter of "direction," the Alliance board met that Sunday evening and voted an all commodity hold. It was a futile gesture in the face of a court order that the same board had voted to obey when it came.

Mr. Miller, Jim's old history teacher, was gone, dead at the age of 83. He had deeded his ten acres to Jim Neff for value received and services rendered during his fading years. The house on the place was a comfortable bungalow that now stood empty. In many rural areas such facilities ended up as storage for feed and hay. Jim and Jake figured they would remodel the unit so Jake could move in with the young lady he intended to marry. He had met Amy during his last year at Kansas State in Manhattan. Jake lost no time in courting, and now the wedding was imminent. She was a stunning beauty from Garden City, Kansas, the daughter of a successful wheat farmer. She was an athletic girl with track and field talents and a love of horses. She had always wanted to marry a farmer, preferably a cowman, and it was clear from the start that one or two saddle horses would soon grace the Banyon Place complex. Even during his college years, Jake had become an indispensible part of Banyon Place, especially when Jim was away on Alliance business. When Jim came home with news of the vote on the matter of a pending court order, there was general dismay. Nora had patience on her side, and really wished to be done with the Capper-Volstead Alliance. She did not nag or contest Jim over the matter because she knew he felt deeply the departure of so many farmers, so many in Oklahoma repairing to the barn for the shotgun release from life.

Three men phoned one evening. They were Alliance members from North Dakota, Tennessee and California. Jim had encountered them at Alliance headquarters and barely remembered them.

"Can we come over?" the voice at the other end of the phone said. After answering, Jim turned to Nora with the news.

"Will they be eating?" she asked. It was merely a rhetorical question. She knew her husband would never expect her to serve up a meal on an hour's notice, although Alliance families were used to doing just that.

"No," he said. "We'll go to Eat." Eat was the name of a small restaurant better known as The Greasy Spoon.

"We'll leave the light on for you," she said.

"We may end up in the library to talk," he added. In the journal he had kept on and off during his life, Jim simply referred to his visitors by state, North Dakota, Tennessee and California.

"This ain't right!" Tennessee opened.

"There's corruption!" added California.

"How's that?" was Jim's laconic question.

"Let's start with that court matter," California said. "Suppose Number 1 had the guts to stand up and be counted."

"And go to jail for contempt!" threw in North Dakota.

"Like you said, Jim, go to the lockup like Martin Luther King. With thousands of farmers hangin' tough, well, hell, you said it all with that John L. Lewis story."

"They, meanin' the newspapers, really had their Ludlow typesetters working overtime with those violence headlines!"

"Violence!" chimed in Tennessee. "Violence! Violence!" Patrons in Eat took notice. The waitress, a lissome girl with dimples and a smile, came to the table, filled the coffee cups, then departed. She figured they would leave a quarter, no more, when they left, and that would be when their kidneys revolted.

They discussed a few of the incidents that clouded the milk hold. Someone in Wisconsin had thrown a section of harrow spikes in the path of an eighteen-wheeler. There was a report of dye contaminating a tanker full of milk. Other than that, there were a few picket lines at meat processing plants. Over all, the strike was really quite peaceful.

After hamburgers and more coffee, Jim and the visitors repaired to Banyon Place for more conversation. It was then that California came to the point.

"I understand you're not going to the annual convention?"

"That's my idea," was Jim's reply.

"You're going to let your membership lapse?" It was Tennessee, the same Tennessee who had once invited Jim to talk sense to some very hard headed people.

"I think it has come to that," said Jim.

"Just because Billy Jon ain't got no balls." Tennessee started, but he did not finish the sentence.

"Have you heard of kickbacks at hog collection points?" California asked.

"I've heard," Jim said. He said no more.

"Then you must know," California added, "that this all commodity hold is bullshit. Christ, you had think we had the oranges and kumquats organized, or the nut groves and rice farmers. Hell, there's 400 commodities produced in California alone. And what about cotton in the South?"

"Or rice in Texas and California?" added Tennessee.

"It comes down to this, a little organizing in the corn and hog belt, a little foray into Texas, and wheat in the High Plains."

The conversation added hogs and cattle, and the conclusion was reached that the all commodity hold was merely a grab for headlines, and that headquarters was going to knuckle under to the government from now on.

"Billy Jon will issue a lot of talk about processing the processors, and farmers caught in their credit trap will go on sale, having decided to quit farming." Tennessee was on a roll. "Why the hell doesn't anyone tell the truth? The banker, having cut the legs out from under me. I've thrown in the towel. I'll end up on the assembly line at the atomic plant."

"Gentlemen, there was a mandate for a milk action but the leadership gave up."

"We read your papers. We've heard you talk. Those papers you prepared on key commodities, why hell! They're first rate." One by one, Jim's papers filled the bill for exposition and analysis, and the clock chimed 1 a.m.

"I think this decade we will see the greatest expropriation of property in the history of the country. They haven't missed a lick since 1948, and to tell you the truth, the Capper-Volstead Alliance will not be able to do anything about it," Jim Neff said.

"Isn't this a hell of a note?" California spat, striking a match on the heel of his cowboy boot, lighting a cigarette. "A bankrupt agriculture in a nation headed for bankruptcy itself. Everyone wants a one-world economy. But the leaders don't want a world currency, or a world minimum wage law!"

It was obvious in 1965 that the President removed the gold reserve for Federal Reserve deposits. In 1968 the gold backing for currency was removed. The gold window was about to come down. After that, debt would double and redouble every ten years or less. This much was a given that any producer of commodities could understand.

"What does it all mean? I'll tell you what it means," added California with emphasis. "Right now I can buy a top of the line Chevy for $3,000. By the end of the century, only thirty years away, that Chevy will cost up to $30,000. Do you know what rice and corn and cattle will bring by then? Something less than what they bring right now!"

Jim closed down the meeting. The three visitors needed some sleep. Jim knew what the three wanted. They were waiting for him to ask the appropriate questions and lead them down the path of questioning that would see him stand for president.

"We'll be back," they said almost in unison that next morning. Monday morning was destined to explode like a pea-sized atom bomb across rural America.

An Indiana hog grower called a press conference. The TV cameras were sure to be there. Hog farmer Spike Olson warned reporters to have plenty of flash bulbs. He promised to shoot hogs and roll them into a lime dusted pit as a protest. The Alliance knew nothing about the decision or the resolve. Billy Jon did not know whether the killing would resonate with the press. He expected a revulsion would fill the front pages of the metro dailies. The inner circle at St. Joseph was up all night trying to frame a response. At 4 a.m. two inner circle people were flown to the scene. One made a short statement that perhaps these hogs would better fulfill their purpose in a pit than by going to market at prices sure to bankrupt the producer. Maybe government and consumers would then re-examine the disastrous food policy being followed. The rifle shots reminded one journalist of the coordinated rifle shots over the caskets of fallen farmers, fallen by shotgun to escape a debt dilemma. It was over in less than an hour and on the nation's screen before the court opened its session at 10 a.m.

For several days Alliance members prepared pits and shot hogs. They really did not shoot very many, yet each demonstration was like a nail in the national political coffin.

There were visits to Kansas City by federal officers. Billy Jon was taken into an empty judge's chamber. He assumed the room was wired, for which reason he said little beyond the demand that his attorney be present. The Justice Department had their good guy, bad guy program. These were not sophisticated people. Billy Jon could have argued that Smoot-Hawley was still the tariff law of the land, or that no court order of any kind was in force, but he did not. He listened. One Justice Department man stepped out while the other spoke. They would never confirm or deny what was said to the farm leader. Under deposition, the phrase "I have no personal knowledge of that statement" repeatedly made the transcript. The Farm Act of 1948 was still public policy, and GATT (General Agreement on Tariffs and Trade) was off and running, and the Kennedy Round was all but law headed for WTO (World Trade Organization). All of this meant that farm prices were headed for the floor or depression levels, whichever was lower. Nasty guy told Billy Jon that no stink foot was going to embarrass the President. The term "stink foot" was a favorite of the bad guy. The good guy lawyer re entered the chamber now and then. He addressed Billy Jon as Mr. Poole, and referred to the hog shooters as colleagues. There seemed to be a united effort to protect the President, and no stinkfoot dipshit could set aside the law. Word of the chamber conference seemed to penetrate the courthouse walls, and a murmur filled the halls. Good guy left to have a look.

"Get it straight!" bad guy said. "No shit kicker of a farmer from Iowa is going to upstage the government. Poole, your farm is all but broke. You have a few hogs and some corn and alfalfa, a few cows. Technically, your all commodity action violates what your own lawyers have agreed upon."

Billy Jon was sweating bullets when he heard the next open threat.

"It's you personally who goes to jail, Mister!"

Billy Jon started to speak. The heavy cut him off. "You'll get your lawyer. This is but a friendly chat. I didn't want to Sunday Punch you." Billy Jon protested that the hog killing was a spontaneous demonstration.

"Cut the crap!" the heavy agent said. "I've seen you 'spon' your spontaneous demonstrations. I'm just telling you it has to stop." With that the lawyers were summoned. The government wanted Billy Jon to issue a statement commanding Capper-Volstead members to cease and desist. The statement also chastised militant members for abandoning a peaceful demonstration policy.

The rest of the day in court was perfunctory. The court had its temporary restraining order. Before the day was over, Billy Jon signed a consent decree. "Anything less," he was told, "and you go to the crowbar hotel."

Leadership had taken its toll on Billy Jon. He was at least fifty pounds overweight. His suit, especially under the armpits, exhibited the stains of copious sweating. The threat by the heavy bad guy rang in his ears. "We know you can make bail. This will run for years, pleadings, motions, interrogations. I doubt your kids will end up going to college. We'll own your farm. If we have to, we'll take your members to court one at a time. Get it out of your head that this dipshit of an organization is going to bring down the government!"

When the last release went out that day, it was represented that the Alliance had initialed a tough agreement with the government, that two withholding actions would be the wave of the future, except that each would have to be announced thirty days in advance. It was all legalese chloroform in print. The hog killing and milk dumping had to stop. In the days to come the temporary order was made permanent. The Capper-Volstead law was considered to be operative as long as farm prices at the tailgate were not unduly enhanced. The word went out that the Alliance had spent itself, leaving the old institutional way of big business in command of the field.

When Jim heard the word, he recalled the words of Professor Wade Phillips, "The ten years were up!"

By the time the annual Capper-Volstead Alliance convention came around in December, Jim's earlier visitors, by mail, phone, and personal visits, had convinced him to attend the convention and to renew his membership. He expected a dying spasm to be played out in the big municipal auditorium in St. Louis. The rhetoric was positive, and the consent decree was paraded like a trophy of accomplishment, when it was really a badge of defeat. It was an insurance policy against any organized escape from the role agriculture had been handed ever since full parity was struck down. The annual show went smoothly until a Board member brought up the matter of corruption among Board members, kickbacks at collection points. It became impossible for Billy Jon to wash the affair. At one point a delegate asked for credential verification and audit of the upcoming election. For a time, a fist fighting tension prevailed. In the end, a motion by Vice-President Vincent prevailed. It was agreed that there would be an internal investigation.

Tomorrow would be the time for election of President. In its ten years of life, Capper-Volstead had elected Billy Jon each year, always without opposition. The opening gavel was scheduled for high noon. On the way to his hotel room, Jim Neff was startled when a taxi pulled to the curb where he was walking. The three men in the back seat were the three men who had come to the farm after the "direction" meeting. "Boys," he told them, "I'm too tired for this." But he got into the front seat. The drive was short. The hotel to which they were headed was not Class A, but neither was it seedy. The conference room had plenty of coffee.

Several Capper-Volstead members were already assembled. Jim knew the six minority

Board members there. Most of them were well dressed, wearing high-priced western clothes, Stetson hats, and string ties. Two wore blue jeans. Tall or short, all were very comfortable in their roles. Almost all exhibited a farmer's facial tan with an untanned forehead guardedly covered by a cap or hat.

California made the introductions, moving around the big conference table. Each man was given a blue plate special. They were all substantial farmers who had so far survived the eclipse of commodity prices begun during the Ezra Taft Benson administration.

California was a rice producer. He had joined the Alliance a year ago, after the organization had explained the economics of the nation and its impact on the family farm. His granddad had made the trip around the Horn to settle in Colusa County. Much of California was in the hands of great holders. He saw the whole of California being supplied by capital created out of thin air by banks, all with the blessings of an industrially oriented government.

Tennessee was a milk producer. He stood five feet five in his cowboy boots, but he was a giant of dissent in contrast to the leadership that had caved in on the milk strike. He was solvent because he stayed out of debt, and he vowed they would not get him off his land until hell froze over. He fairly crackled with energy and spoke non stop if given a chance. North Dakota came to the Neff farm to sound out for himself whether Jim Neff was linked to headquarters. When he found that this was not the case, he repeated for himself the words of Alexander Pope, that "Hope springs eternal in the human breast."

The two Texans seated next to Jim were both six footers, and both sported belt buckles the size of a saucer. One was a cotton grower, one a range cattle operator from the hill country west of Austin. Both gave their taciturn greetings and said no more. They were there to listen on behalf of their Texas friends, and then to act accordingly.

Arnold Olson, Oklahoma, grew wheat. Over a lifetime he had assembled seventeen fair sized wheat farms under one operating roof. During harvest he had combines going around the clock, but debt was pulling him under. When he ran into the Capper-Volstead Alliance, he learned all about the national income, world trade, and how he had been lured into debt for the purpose of paying interest, period. Now he was losing his capital at the rate of 3% a year, interest swallowing him like a worm on a hook. The industrial model of getting bigger and more efficient proved to be a scam. He did not figure he would be around long enough to get him out of his land commitment.

Ted Albright was called Washington because he operated a diversified farm near Quincy, Washington. The nut producers were organized, but they had a lot to learn from the Alliance organizers. Even so, the diversified end of the farm needed help. Frustration economics troubled this man, but charges of organizational corruption troubled him even more.

Ohio, hardly anyone knew his real name, Cass Webster had a cow-calf operation not far from Youngstown. The wife and kids milked a few cows for local consumption, and Webster was forever fighting with state gumshoes who demanded pasteurization and homogenization. He saw great potential in organization.

Directors from Iowa, Colorado and Nebraska rounded out the group assembled. Nebraska said, "Mr. Neff, the Alliance is gone. I think we all agree on that."

There was a short murmur of assent.

"We mean it's gone! Kaput!" It was Colorado who added his word as an apostrophe of confirmation. He added, "When we stuck with the leader!" Jim listened. He wondered what they were leading up to. Jim did not need to be told the state of the organization. He had always refused a Board post, but he was considered a driving force by many because of the ten papers he had written and because of his insight regarding the big picture. He had worn out a mimeograph machine circulating his papers with well-reasoned pieces they had all used when trying to convince their neighbors. He could not figure out what he would do now. Nora had not been entirely silent about his many absences during the past ten years.

"Let's run Banyon Place," she had suggested. "The whole of agriculture is a bit too much for this country girl."

Well, it was too much for Jim, too. He knew that he would make a good Secretary of Agriculture, but the fact was that he did not have that job. He did not have the job of running the Capper-Volstead Alliance either, and that fact was a deal breaker. In the theater of his mind Jim saw this as his last meeting, and he was not quite sure why he had allowed himself to be talked into coming.

Someone said something about Billy Jon's lack of comprehension of issues and official policy, and another, was it Nebraska?, added that the big man's continual occupation of the saddle was slow or fast, he was not entirely sure which.

"Do you think he understands a Milk Marketing Order?" asked Tennessee.

"He probably doesn't," admitted Ohio. "But he's tolerated as a leader. Even if he quit now, he would be considered a hero. He could go on working the farmers into a frenzy."

One of the men from Texas surrendered his role as one of the strong silent types by injecting, "That two million he lost at the Port of Houston because he couldn't make up his mind on the hedge," and the sentence dropped uncompleted because Texas knew the refrain and so did the others. "You can't organize on the basis of half truths and lies,"

Iowa added. "Hell, he hasn't had an original idea since he first leered at some girl in high school."

A short roll of laughter seemed to close down the Rorschach of comments, each falling on the blotter paper like a drop of fresh ink with capillary action free to take the comment in any direction prescribed by physics.

The statements continued to roll around the big conference table, one trumped another. They had all been in Billy Jon's office at quitting time: 5 p.m. Often, Billy Jon commanded them to stay on. Most of the men had been on duty since 6 a.m. They were "dog tired and skunk hungry" was the way Tennessee put it. "Then Billy Jon would send out for a steak and all the fixin's, and he would eat it in front of the salivating staffers." It was true, and it was commemorated by a fragment of doggerel taped to the men's room wall.

I met them early,
And I met them late.
I watched them hunger
While I ate.
I licked my chops
As was my manner,
Belched and farted
The Star Spangled Banner.

The poem became the breaking point, or rather the catalyst that brought the meeting to that point. California brought the assembly to order. "We're all of one mind, Jim. If the present leadership continues, the Alliance is history. Oh, it'll go on existing, like Jack London's Wobblies with some hole in the wall office, but it'll never amount to a damn. Agreed?" There was a murmur of general consent.

"Well," said Jim Neff, "I tend to agree with you, but what are you really saying?"

Everyone looked at California. "Jim, we want you to stand for President."

"Not a chance," said Jim Neff.

"We agree with that," Duke said. "At least not much of a chance. But we might as well go out, T.S. won't mind if I say, with a bang, not a whimper. We have to try and we need some ideas for a fresh start and new programs." The three who had sounded out Jim's real thoughts and attitudes recaptured the scene for those now present. Jim marveled at how correctly he was being quoted.

Duke turned to Jim again. "Jim, most men are afraid to stand on a platform with raw hostility seated behind them. Billy Jon has a college degree in church ushering, I think. You don't. But I know you can mop up the floor in a debate with him."

Jim Neff suddenly found himself engulfed as in a whirlpool. He saw no dust clouds, no rabbits being herded into a circular fence, but the collective of farmers he faced was as resolute as a pack of wolverines. What California proposed took him back to a conversation, indeed, a confrontation, with Nora. "You're not the Christ," she had said. "You can't take the sins of the world on your back."

The men kept talking and Jim kept thinking, there is not a chance in hell of defeating Billy Jon. Well over half of the Board members, state officers, and field operators were on Billy Jon's payroll. Even the rank and file members looked on Billy Jon as both the Prophet and the Messiah. Few were exposed to Billy Jon the champion except at a convention where every move was choreographed. Billy Jon demanded worship, and he got it. Jim Neff reasoned that it would take three or four years of solid work to take him out, and the strife involved would likely reduce the membership to small splinter group status. He counted off these points with a resolute one, two, three and four. "Maybe so," said California, "But we have to make a stand. We win or we lose. If we win, we try to recruit Billy Jon as an organizer. He probably won't do that, but the movement goes on. If we lose, it's the status quo for Capper-Volstead. Under no circumstances do we want a long sustained knock down, drag out fight."

Ohio put in his comment. "Mr. Neff, we want you to represent the dissenters."

"You're the only possibility," Colorado said. "I wouldn't be here if I hadn't gotten the Capper-Volstead message straight from your lips. We can't just walk away without making a statement."

Jim had a hard time seeing himself as a rural Don Quixote. In less than twelve hours the election exercise would be gaveled into existence. If the dissident election move leaked out, civility would suddenly cease to function. Recognition for placing a name into nomination would be drowned out in confusion and futile cries of "Mr. Chairman! Mr. Chairman!"

"We've thought of all that," California said. "I'm fairly sure Number 1 has a list of all of us. I'll not say more at this time except to assure you that we're on top of the situation. We'll get a motion made. We'll get it seconded, even if we have to get physical. Don't worry about that!"

"Boys," said Jim Neff. "I need to get some sleep. If you get a motion made, I'll be genuinely surprised. I'll be honest with you. I don't expect to win. Maybe in a few years new leadership will arise, but by then we'll all be out. In fact, you can expect a star chamber procedure over the issue of this meeting as soon as the connection is made. You do understand that?" They understood. In fact, a phone survey conducted by an anonymous, albeit erudite, dissident figured the vote was 50-50, too close to call. Jim digested this information. Was there really a chance? Then he said, "Well, if we really have a chance, we have to take it."

"Do you mean we can go ahead?" California asked.

Jim threw up his arms in the posture of a man being crucified. If the symbolism was lost on the farmers, the meaning was not. Jim left the group to its deliberations. He walked several blocks to his hotel. He was alone when he walked into the lobby. He was alone when he entered the elevator and alone until he closed the door to his room. It was a little after 1 a.m. Even before Jim Neff had excused himself, one of the latecomers quietly left the big conference room. He found a telephone in the lobby and reported to one of Billy Jon's associates. This caused the noon election to be postponed two hours.

Jim Neff was in his seat at high noon when word came down of a delay. Two hours later, with six hours of sleep under his belt, he called home to Nora. There was a long silence after he revealed that he was standing for President. He assured her that he had to seize the opportunity. If he came off with a Truman win, she would have to come to St. Joseph to be with him. "I'll always be home for calving," he said, "and besides, I think I can depend on Jake to handle the herd."

When the gavel fell at 2 p.m., the usual parade of hired help placed the name of Billy Jon Poole up for nomination, it being understood that there would thus be no change in vice-president, secretary or treasurer. The speakers that followed the nomination retraced the history of the organization, how it had been started by a machinery jockey, how it was rescued from oblivion by Billy Jon Poole's inspired leadership, and how Washington had been shaken in its boots. When the perfunctory "Are there any other nominations?" came on, one microphone after another went cold. New Jersey seized microphone #6. New Jersey was a recognized Billy Jon supporter. The chair's assumption was that a motion for election by acclamation would be forthcoming.

"Mr. Chairman," came the mic amplified voice from #6. "The organization owes eternal gratitude to Billy Jon Poole. He has guided the Alliance all these years. He has sacrificed his time and treasure for the welfare of the organization."

The Chair interrupted. "We appreciate these kind remarks. Does the gentleman from New Jersey wish to make a motion?"

"No, but I have a nomination. I nominate James Robert Neff for President of the Capper-Volstead Alliance."

Instantly, South Dakota stepped up to microphone #6. "I second that nomination."

Cries of "Second!" came from the balcony, even from the floor, where the most favored delegates were seated, newsmen from the Associated Press and two dozen newspapers, including the *St. Louis Post-Dispatch*. Due process could not be denied. The election committee was not prepared for this. Ballots would have to be mimeographed while speeches were being made and the business of auxiliary posts being attended to. Billy Jon could use the time to refortify his position. As sitting president, he was entitled to speak last. That was his choice.

Accordingly, James Robert Neff walked across a stage full of hostility to take the convention mike. You could hear a pin drop even in the far balcony, the silence was that deafening.

Jim saluted the members, the Board, the officers, finally President Poole. His talk was military tough, meaning it contained no sarcasm, no double entendres, and no mud whatsoever. He recalled for the packed house the tragedy of the Great Depression and the lessons of World War II. He explained with discerning detail how the public policy had decided to cash in its farmers for an industrial model better suited to international trade and international finance.

"Congress dabbled in socialism while it crafted the opposite blueprint. The Employment Act of 1946 set up a Council of Economic Advisors so that we might know the drift of the economy. The very first report by Edwin Nourse and Leon Keyserling told all who wished to see that agriculture was the flywheel and balance wheel of the economy. That is why, in 1948, the people Truman called the worst Congress in history passed a farm law that struck down parity. By the end of that decade, farm prices were headed for the floor, and they have never stopped."

Jim Neff said, "History does not draw its nourishment from the heights, but from the valleys. When farm prices fell to a depression level in 1955, a trade salesman stepped forward on behalf of agriculture. The Capper-Volstead Alliance was born. Now, ten years later, we are required to audit our decade long battle."

The audit James Robert Neff presented would have annihilated the defendant in any jury trial. Organization delivers not only members, but production, and it was this production that was proffered for collective bargaining. Jim recited just enough details to make the case, never too much to become boring.

"The Founding Fathers," he went on, "were astute enough to realize that the nation would be served by good leaders and by bad leaders. They also were astute enough to realize that leadership cannot be a guidepost of the past because it has to change with the times. It cannot dig in its heels and refuse to consider the future.

"In a few days, or even over the next year, every person in this convention will better understand why my name was placed in nomination. Unfortunately, tomorrow will be too late. The decision has to be made within the hour. I will not detain you.

"I did not seek this honor. But I can't refuse to shun participation in the events of out times. Great questions have been put before this convention, and the answers have been found wanting. It should be the role of the Alliance to put everything on the table. If errors have been made, then let's correct them." There was a murmur of approval and scattered applause.

"If we have a problem, let's deal with it." Again, scattered applause.

"We have not made our case where it matters most, with the consumer. We have achieved headlines, but these are always ephemeral. Our purpose is not to chastise the past, but to assure the future."

A smattering of applause followed the pause. When that was over, the press people took note of quotable lines. Tape recorders captured every word. Cameras were running, stabbing out with tortuous spotlights. "If I win, so be it. If not, perhaps the leadership will remember the legacy I now leave. One, we must comprehend completely the industrial bondage that our land grant colleges and Extension have foisted on us. I have met very few of those gentlemen who wouldn't be broke in six months taking their own advice. Two, it is up to us to understand the anatomy of every community, the nuances of the trade, and the mechanisms by which our economic enslavement is achieved."

Jim saw that he was getting a bit esoteric. "Get to the point," he told himself.

"In the 1950s, Roger Babson founded a college at Eureka, Kansas. Fittingly, it was named Utopia College. I believe it was his objective to teach rural America that most of the wealth of the nation is located in the farm states and in states with farming, but we haven't exhibited the wit to control it. I recommend that we establish and support a school dedicated to training our young people in economics, biotechnology, history, and the requirements for human health, in the range of knowledge geared to getting justice for the nation's biggest industry, and to refuse our children to those who seek their help in the undoing of their farmer parents. I recommend short courses at first, a few dozen students a year, and in ten to twenty years, a full course college. In decades to come, I would expect our graduates to be county commissioners, town council members, USDA staffers, and so on. Our bread and butter can no longer be providing cheap commodities for the international absconders. Without strong support for the future, our efforts will come to naught. We can no longer expect to convince. With our consuming public friends, we have to become the government." Even the Billy Jon true believers blanched with that statement. The applause was heavy and sustained.

At first, Billy Jon fidgeted, then he relaxed. It had always been his policy not to let any of these self educated spellbinders rattle him. "All right, boy," he said to himself. "You've shot your bolt." What he saw and heard merely confirmed the genius of his policy. This Neff fellow had never been allowed to speak in all territories, so he does not have

285

too much of a following. Billy Jon relaxed appreciably as Jim Neff concluded.

Jim picked up the few notes he had set down on the podium. "The state of the arts has conferred efficiency on industry and agriculture. Labor is being paid for that efficiency. Agriculture is expected to deliver that efficiency at low prices." In a few whiplash lines he ran the gamut of issues being used to liquidate private enterprise. With sledge hammer blows he annihilated unregulated free trade with its contradictions. This was too much for an electorate that expected miracles this week, this year.

As a parting shot, Jim figured he might as well unload what was really on his mind. "Finally, I suggest that we never again kill hogs and roll them into lime dusted pits. Instead, we should tell the Alliance that we'll take the lead in giving the nation chemical-free food. If we do not supply the nation with citizens capable of thought and reason, we have no future at all. I leave it in your hands. May I quote St. Paul? 'I have fought the good fight. I have finished the race. I have kept the faith.'"

The response was electric. Seasoned observers said it would be a toss up who won. Billy Jon did not see it that way. He had the last word, and he expected to use an hour and a half delivering it.

He was a picture of humility as he started, almost whispering his words into the microphone. He even referred to himself as a dumb farmer. He did not know much about market econometrics or highfalutin' words, but by God, he knew how to farrow hogs and grow corn, and by golly, he was not being paid by the processors. He was not worried about those people in Washington. The problem was right there on the farm, in the silo, in the calving barn, and the answer was collective bargaining because collective bargaining meant farmers joining together and selling together. Once the farmers were all joined together, the show would be over. Two or three decades down the road, why hell, we'll all be dead and gone by then.

Billy Jon settled down. He relived the test actions one at a time. He told how he faced down the enemy within, who did not believe in collective bargaining. He took the several presidents since Truman apart and put them back together again. He told about the farmer who tried to change horses midstream, a story first made famous by Jack London.

Billy Jon went on. One of his sentences, transcribed from a tape, comprised 216 words. Quotable quotes were so rare that some newsmen literally tore up their notes.

"OK," Billy Jon concluded, "let's vote."

The election committee made a big show of credentials and ballots.

When the result was announced near midnight, Billy Jon Poole was named the winner by 46 votes. Although a recount was started immediately, Jim Neff conceded, extending his hand to Billy Jon Poole. Poole refused to take it. The refusal of that handshake defined the future and division of Capper-Volstead. Jim did not stay on for the rally his friends expected. He walked so briskly that his steps nearly erased the slight limp left over from that afternoon on Jolo Island. Banyon Place beckoned. In the future, he would be most reluctant to leave it again.

30

The Capper-Volstead Alliance convened a special meeting at headquarters. Troublemakers, one of whom was James Robert Neff, stood accused of conduct contrary to the best interests of the organization. In a trial presided over by vice-president Vincent, the board, acting as a jury, found all twelve members guilty and ordered their dismissal from the organization, the unused part of their dues to be refunded.

When news of the dismissals became known, the last of California, Texas, Colorado, Washington, Oregon and Idaho left the organization. Parts of Kansas, Nebraska, the Dakotas and Oklahoma simply ceased to function.

Membership dropped perceptibly across entire networks. Professor Smythe, the self-declared Phineas priest and researcher of populist movements, came by. Jim took the afternoon off. Nora served up coffee, cookies, and joined what was sure to be an intellectual feast. Jim opened, having exhausted the usual pleasantries and having talked Capper-Volstead to death.

"Have you ever found that single head on which to deliver the lethal blow?"

"I think I have."

"Does this mean you're headed for the battle?" It was Nora adding her insight. She had often remarked that in this society you can't kill people even if they deserved killing. It comes down to those multitudes. 'Multitudes, multitudes in the valley of decision.' Joel, remember? The multitudes will never prevail. And that's why our Capper-Volstead organization can never prevail."

"Phineas priest, you escape me. You once said that civilization draws its nourishment from the valleys, not the heights."

"Ah yes, it does, but it rules from the top. You supply the bread, they take it away from you. Why is this so? Look, you do your studies, you print the findings, then what? A few thousand copies? The absconders hire the professors and colleges to spin their message, never mind how absurd it is. Their stuff goes out in billions of images. The multitude is tickled by your message now and then, but it is simply mesmerized by the serpent's lure." Nora picked up on the Biblical priest's assertion.

"Dr. Smythe, haven't there been instances in which egalitarian voices prevailed? At one time, the Populists took the governorship of Kansas, and the House, and the Senate!"

"They didn't know how to use their power and they promptly lost it. Why? Mostly, dear child, money. Once the absconders managed to privatize money creation with the Federal Reserve, they had it made. They can create capital out of thin air. All they need is management. With that in place, they can take over poultry, cattle, hogs, soybeans, wheat, whatever. In the mind's eye of the absconders, the ability to have a private lending institution creating money out of thin air is wealth. You talk about raw materials, and you're ignored. But the absconders recite their mantra in the face of its absurdity because their money backed voice out shouts you, *verstehen sie?*"

"But can't they see," interrupted Nora, "that debt doubling and redoubling and inflation will ultimately cut the legs from under the accumulators of the wealth of the country?"

"That's the dilemma. These people are grown men and women, yet they write the public policy of imbeciles. I am afraid that the really bright people are often really quite stupid."

"So you don't figure Capper-Volstead is going anywhere?" Jim asked.

"Not a chance," the Biblical one said, backed by his modern intelligence. "With a purchased Congress, reform becomes impossible. There is hardly even a contest in the several Congressional districts. The House itself has less turnover than the House of Lords, a hereditary body. The people allowed to run for President are mere Pygmalion products of ad agencies, all suitably trained to adhere to the public policy, a policy drafted by the money power. There's the rub! It was decreed that the policy of Lincoln's broad spectrum agriculture be appropriated. You know the drill, Jim."

"Conspiracy?"

"No, no, no! Each step was published, put on library shelves, openly sold to the public like so much toothpaste or popcorn. They even make movies out of the stuff Ayn Rand wrote."

"Ayn Rand!" Nora said. "Are you talking about *Atlas Shrugged?*"

"Verily, her book had it that a few masterminds run the country, that if they deprived the country of their guidance, the whole place would fall apart like an overripe avocado. So they all holed up in Colorado and let the country go to hell. It was a parody on Roosevelt who was perceived to be helping a lot of losers. Well, Rand writes a good potboiler, but quite the opposite is true.

"The great leaders never grow a crop, farrow a bunch of hogs, raise cattle, or build a building. But they know how to merge, consolidate, use predatory methods to cancel out real producers. They can always divide and conquer a farm movement."

Nora could not let go of the idea that the producers had the hole card and only had to use it.

"But the fact is: they haven't any cards at all, not once the money creation power has been privatized and taken out of the hands of the legitimate government."

"I suppose that's why we can't get anti-trust enforcement against the packers and the grain cartels," Jim added.

"To the head of the class," the Phineus priest said. "You see, it is quite simple to control the multitudes they see as the great unwashed. They allow the *vox populi* to vote on two people who are carbon copies of each other. The Senate is made up of millionaires who wouldn't jeopardize their job by serving the people even if you put a gun at their collective heads."

"Then the public policy is for all of us to consume our capital, albeit producing to the bitter end," Jim said.

"Hell, yes!" Then The Phineas priest added, "But wait! You must remember that the best laid plans contain the seeds of their own destruction, and the innovator puts his genius and insight on the other side of the equals sign. It is the innovator who annihilates the existing order."

"Doctor," Nora said, refilling an often emptied coffee cup. "You drop your ideas like ink on blotter paper, then you watch to see which way the innovator's capillary action takes them. What exactly do you mean by *innovators?*"

"The thing that pulled down England's dominance over the U.S. was one seldom observed fact: innovation. Look at history, the great innovators, the steam engine, the automobile, the airplane, even the computer, pardon me, Pascal, go on and list them. It will be the innovator who annihilates the monopolies, the obscenity of the feedlots."

The professor went on to discuss his professional work on populism with special attention to what was left of agriculture. There was a resistance in the countryside, he said. Fully 75% of the remaining farmers are out of debt and will stay out of debt even if they have to resort to subsistence farming for their own survival. Fully 80% of the cattle are owned by farmers with no more than twenty-five head.

After almost three hours of such conversation, Nora still looked radiant. She wore little makeup, and yet her eyes had a sparkle that told all who wished to see that she considered herself the top of the pyramid. She was never a prude, but she had style and manners. She would never tolerate tawdry jokes or crude expressions. She had the uncanny ability of seeing through phony people, and was only slightly hesitant in giving her opinion. When she first met Billy Jon Poole, she maintained a discrete silence. Only after intimate encounters with her husband did she speak. "He's a pretender. He pretends he knows what he doesn't know."

During a break in the afternoon session, and just before the children arrived looking for supper, Jim asked Nora the fatal question, "What do you think of the priest?"

"I think he's right on. I suspect he rarely finds anyone in academia he can relate to."

Nora found the man so interesting, she invited him for supper and even offered the priest one of the spare bedrooms in Banyon Place. The professor priest accepted because he had formed a new thesis in his mind and badly wanted to run it up the flagpole. It was after supper, with Heidi and Xander trundled off to their rooms, that the Phineas priest made his suggestion.

The professor, Phineas priest, did not mention his earlier comment about a Darwinian demon. Instead he indicted bad science and big business for containing the seeds of their own destruction. There was a move afloat to take red meat production away from the independents, as was the case with poultry a few decades earlier. Governmental functionaries were on the take, not directly, but indirectly via the mechanism of rubber chicken and hard peas served at the campaign dinner. Agriculture was the anointed patsy and it would require quite an innovator to rise above the carping mediocrity in and out of office.

The professor was working on his magnum opus dealing with populist movements, especially farm movements. It was much too early to assess the lasting value and the damage done by the turn of events in the Capper-Volstead Alliance. As the professor saw it, the nation was well on the way toward carving out a modern version of empire. This one would rely on military power, scientific bullying, and a great deviation from the norms of civilization that so far had characterized the U.S. and its instruments of government.

"I don't know where this will stop," the professor said. "I do not know whether a family farm such as yours will be allowed to survive in the brave new world our betters are crafting for us. I told you the world finance masters were the Darwinian demon of our times. Now I have to correct myself and tell you that the military is in charge, not only of the President, the Senate, the House, but also the courts who seem powerless to rein in the CIA and the terrorists that teach torture to the world's absconders and their lackeys. I'm concerned about those bases in Okinawa, in Germany, England, and just about every corner of the world. I'm afraid there won't be much room for the Bill of Rights in the world that the real power will permit."

The word "permit" caught Jim broadside. He had "permits" coming out his ear. Experts were constantly telling him how to handle manure, whether he could dig a pond or burn brush. Experts were after his hunting rifle. Experts would like to inspect the water heater he had installed and the underground electrical services because a neighbor had complained of stray voltage, this, when no one had a clue about the cause of stray voltage. There was legislation coming down to close deep wells and force farmers to rely on chlorinated and fluoridated water via rural water district pipes. "Permit the farm itself?"

"Read your Committee on Economic Development report," the professor suggested.

"They may not even permit a hobby farm before this is over."

31

The hulk of a cowman parked his brown Stetson atop the jukebox, gave his belt a hitch, exhaled cigarette smoke in nice little concentric circles, and sat down. The screen at the front door fenced out angry blowflies trying to get in. Back at the counter, young Caleb Watkins took notice, which is to say his antenna went up. You could pick up a lot of scuttlebutt listening to unguarded conversation in the Cowboy Cafe in Canyon City, Texas. Some of that information was worth knowing, the kind of cutting edge information that Caleb liked to pass on in his struggling newsletter. The cowman with the brown hat must have known the other two fellows at the table.

"Mind if I sit down?"

"You're sittin'," came the reply from one of the men.

"The name is Card, John Card, Amarillo."

"William S. Hart, Fort Worth." He stuck out his hand.

"The silent film star?"

"In name only," William S. Hart said. "This here is Josh Albert, Canyon City."

The obligatory handshake followed.

The young man at the counter strained to listen. The hustler always starts with a contract. That way some of the top cattlemen are roped in, even given a good deal. It takes a decade for the trader to take over the way big money was taking hogs and had already captured poultry. The young fellow nursing an over the hill cup of coffee was a journalist trying to get a little newsletter going. He needed hot items to lure subscribers, and so much of hustle, he liked that word, was slam dunk stuff careless talkers let out of the bag. The drift of events since the war, the Vietnam War, was bringing on the monopolization of the American cowherd.

"I figured you were the guys I was supposed to meet," said Amarillo.

"Ok, let's have the skinny," urged Hart.

"I'll get to the point. I represent Plus Genetics, Inc., headquartered in Washington, D.C. I won't give you the details now, but I'm authorized to tell you that we have front burner dairy connections."

Josh Albert just listened. He did not want to sound off and carelessly betray the fact that the lenders wanted his hide right now. He wanted any kind of a deal he could get. They came right to the farmer these days, often once a month, all of them worthless. Maybe this one would be different. Hart was a little heavy for a man aged fifty, a consequence of overeating due to worry. He was worth a lot of money on paper, but today he was in a liquidity bind. He too was prepared to listen.

"The objective of this exercise, gentlemen, is to take Piedmontese cows from France and harvest the embryos off the ovaries. This is called *isperation*." He pronounced the word carefully.

"Go on," encouraged Josh Albert. Now here was high science! Albert figured that much from the delivery and from the authority with which the novice hero spoke.

"We use ultrasound to identify the target area. Our technicians then stick a needle in that ovulated sac of the ovary. They suck out the ovum. This goes to the lab where a patented process prepares the egg for fertilization. Fertilization is achieved at that time."

"Where do we come in?" Hart wanted to know. He saw a contract coming, but the financial gendarmes were also on his case. "We need inspected and reliable ovaries of Holstein heifers to receive implants. We take the calf when it is born. After a colostrum feed, we'll raise the calf on a bottle."

"Why?" Josh Albert forgot himself and asked, "Why?" a second time. "This produces a specialty meat for a specialty five-star market. We expect to make 'Piedmontese' a household word."

Caleb Watkins at the counter took it in. By the time he got to his car, he started having the shakes. Had he been lured into a hoax? He retraced his steps. He needed a piece of pie and a position at the counter a little closer to the billingsgate. The newsletter writer told himself, they can't make it work. It's too scientific and costs too much. More listening did not deliver much.

294

After the papers were put on the table, the journalist left again. Caleb was an innovative youngster just out of college. A journalism school graduate, he had opted to go the entrepreneurial route, having consumed an ample amount of beer with one Jacob Neff, the son of seed stock line breeder Jim Neff, now well known because of his former support of the Capper-Volstead Alliance.

Caleb Watkins, class of '70, was the publisher of *Cowboy Arithmetic*, a newsletter for cowmen and breeders, especially line breeders. *Cowboy Arithmetic* was now in its eighth edition, barely alive and ever on the hunt for paying subscribers.

A week later he related the incident to Jim Neff. There were stops along the way, but finally he arrived at Banyon Place. He met Jim Neff in the yard halfway between the barn and the carriage house which was being repaired. "The lab," said Jim, nodding to the half finished job while shaking young Caleb's hand.

"I'm a friend of Jake. Is he here?"

"No, Jake's in West Germany."

"Germany? What's he doing there?"

"I suppose you could call it post-graduate work on the job." Jim went on to explain the German installation that was fast making Germany the center of gravity for animal genetics.

Caleb was invited into the library. There he ran everything he knew up the flagpole.

"It's probably not a hoax," said Jim. "They'll probably do it. Just remember, those guys selling the package are not cattlemen. They merely have access to a bunch of money, lots of it. This isn't any different from half a dozen other scams and schemes that come down the pike every year, like chickens and hogs, not self-sustaining. Rent- a-uterus has become state of the art, if you listen to the professors. Wrecking cattle is what it is. Wrecking cows, putting embryos in surrogates with the promoters getting the calf, and slowly crowding out the farmer seems to be the name of the game."

"Listen," Jim Neff told the reporter. "There are things happening. If the farmer doesn't stay on top, there will be outfits like Tyson, Cargill, and Con Agra that will tie up cattle to where it will be against the law to own a bull unless the monopolies supply it or the semen. Don't laugh.

They did it in Germany. I'm in the crosshairs and I know it. Yes, it is doable."

"How long?" the reporter wanted to know.

"Ten years, maybe twenty! Ah, yes, the hook is out. They'll treat the first participants very well. In seven, eight, ten years a lot of cow-calf people will want to get aboard. That's when they pull the rug out from under them. Just like the hog boys."

Caleb Watkins knew the rest, how most of the so called advances were being hatched on the drawing boards of professors at Pennsylvania and at other places too. The cow-calf man gets market plus a dime price when the calf reaches 500 pounds and becomes feedlot fare. It's the chicken hog equation all over again.

Ever since Jake left for Germany, written reports had been coming home. Jake told his family that the Poirot Company, 62% owned by French investors, was methodically buying up pre-potent bulls in the U.S. They hoped to accomplish in the U.S. what reconstruction Germany had accomplished in the wake of WWII. They wanted all genetics licensed, with the investors owning the licenses. Legislation to this effect was being drafted for transmission to well compensated legislators the minute the terrain was right. Jake was picking up knowledge about sires that Jim didn't know even after years of study.

The family always gathered together at the dining room table for the reading of Jake's near weekly letters. He would be home in a few months, and he missed Heidi. "Tell my little sister that I love her and not to dare go away to school before I get back."

In fact, Heidi had made up her mind to go to nursing school, the entire tab to be paid for by the U.S. Army. She had her career all mapped out. Short courses, college work, and a second lieutenant's bars together would give her credentials and security as a surgical nurse, public health nurse, and administrator, all in the fullness of time.

Jim tried to persuade Heidi not to become a professional military nurse. For the first time in his life he suffered pangs of guilt over the lives wasted in the South Pacific.

"I joined the army several months before I was to be drafted," he said. "I saw a film, *Why We Fight.* I bought in to the proposition that the U.S. was fighting for pure and high ideals. Now it's clear as the nose on your face that this wasn't the case."

"What is the case?" she asked.

"Most people still think of the Germans and Japanese as Satan. This doesn't fit into the fact that a few companies can order up a war in order to drum up some business. It took me over thirty years to figure out that I shot down Japanese soldiers like dogs to make the world safe for a few international corporations. Heidi, now I see war as a substitute for the maintenance of a sound agriculture. I really wish you wouldn't make yourself a part of this killing game."

Jim went on to explain the films used to brainwash boys into hardened killers. *Why We Fight* made it sound like 6% of the world's population had a duty to wet nurse the world, fight the wars, keep it on relief, and do this by extinguishing broad spectrum distribution of land and resources. He paused to let all this sink in.

Heidi started to protest. When she did, her father connected the dots. "These people we really fight for, they know where the earned income comes from. When they started closing down agriculture in 1948, they also started closing down America."

"But, Daddy," she protested, "I can't do anything about that. You can't either. I can at least help human beings. Isn't that what mother did for you when you got hurt?"

He had no answer then, and he was not sure he had one now. Heidi was a baby boomer. That generation had little real knowledge of the world. Very few had any comprehension of economics or geopolitics. What tormented her father was the propaganda used to enable the killing and stealing. *Why We Fight* was a fraud. Under its auspices, unseen forces were set up to consume agriculture first, then industry, both abstractions the education machine did not qualify most people to handle. Those who ran public policy in the 1940s demanded, and relied on, the gullible to accept the proposition that Stalin was really a good guy and that Roosevelt embraced the pint-sized dictator in order to keep the Soviet Union free. By that time Stalin had murdered at least ten million, and the filmmakers knew it.

Finally, Dad Neff said, "Heidi, your mother and I gave you life. It was a blessing from which I still haven't recovered. We just want to give our best counsel." He waited to see if his remarks registered. No one said anything, so Jim picked up the conversation again.

"Do you know what your mother has put up with all our lives together?"

"I think I do," Heidi said.

"You don't. I almost lost all my sight in the Philippines. My head needs constant attention to keep inflammation away. I still walk with a limp. I'm the surgeon's best friend, I've had so many operations. I still expel small bits of shrapnel now and then, usually accompanied by a little bleeding and an infection. This is stuff from WWII. Do you have any idea what war does to human beings?"

Heidi started to answer, but thought better of it.

"They have weapons that would make King Arthur cringe. cluster bombs, radioactive atomic dust, poison gas, flame throwers, artillery that can obliterate a city block, and guys two miles high dropping bombs, and they're out of rifle range." He paused without finishing his sentence. "I shot Japanese with no more thought than I gave to clubbing jackrabbits in western Kansas."

Nora came in on the scene. She listened briefly, then she entered the verbal fray. "James, I ask you to let her follow her star. I did mine, and I think it was the first really correct move I made."

Jim met Nora's look with complete meltdown. She was so breathtakingly beautiful, and his daughter was a look alike except for the tint of her hair. Both of his women used makeup sparingly. Heidi stood an inch taller than her mother, but otherwise only family and close friends could tell the difference. She is probably right, Jim told himself. Maybe she could help some poor bastard on one of the killing fields our leaders have scheduled down the track a way.

On the day that Heidi left for nurse's training, Jim and Nora brought home a Tandy Corporation computer. The objective was to computerize the records and have fingertip recovery of data. Since the last of the withholding actions, Jim had drilled into his memory bank the adage that the Phineas priest had delivered, the innovator ultimately demolishes the existing order. The absconders might take over most of agriculture, dragging producers into bankruptcy via mindless expansion and unwise borrowing, but there were innovators who survived, even prevailed. Fully 75% of the farmers still on the land the day the gold window came down and the Washington crowd set sail into the Never-Never Land of inflation received no subsidies at all.

Cow-calf and seed stock producers were considered exempt from the effects, but Jim knew they weren't. Most of them had been talked into feeding bovines grain, in effect turning a herbivore into a ruminant hog. The feedlot system had closed down collective bargaining, but it had not closed down ranchers who relied on grass.

Just the same, a new clash of wills was shaping up. University researchers hoped to do for cattle what they had most assuredly done for poultry and stood ready to implement for hogs.

Wisconsin was the scene of the first volley fired in this struggle.

32

Jake's letters continued to come home at regular intervals. He was lonesome, but he was thrilled. "Uncle Roy has turned out to be a hale fellow. He spends a great deal of time teaching me all about genetics. He himself has taken university courses on the subject and, of course, has spent over two decades in the laboratory."

At the end of World War II, hoof and mouth disease was running rampant in Germany. The cattle herd had been consumed by the war, both by starving soldiers and surviving citizens. "They tell me," wrote Jake, "that few livestock animals survived the war. Many of the zoo animals were consumed, especially by the Russians. Most people honor General George Marshall for his Marshall Plan." The Marshall assist to West Germany had an uplifting effect on agriculture. Heino Messerschmitt was the German Under-Secretary of Agriculture when *Neustadtisch des Verein* was developed. The first order of business was the pooling of animals for artificial insemination use. An all-out program was developed to prevent transmissible diseases. It was in this program that Roy Lee Neff found the first job in his life. The claim was that West Germany indeed had developed a surefire system for disease control and, further, had refined the art of artificial insemination. In one letter Jake got quite clinical. "They have a probe that is ten inches long. It goes into the rectum. Two electrodes fit on the prostate gland. The instrument goes to work. The animal gets an erection. In a minute the bull delivers semen. In the old days simple massage was used." Jake told his dad how a bull was encouraged to mount. "This done, his penis is deflected into an artificial vagina filled with 115 to 120 degree water. When the animal feels that 120 degree temperature, he thinks he's in the vaginal area of the cow. He then thrusts and squirts his semen into the collection vessel."

The laboratory at *Neustadtisch* processed the semen. "It's all a count of sperm cells per cubic centimeter, the live count, the norms, the donors, and how many straws each collection makes. It looks like we'll have to buy a microscope," Jake wrote.

A cow cycles every 21 days. If in heat, a simple pipette with sperm can enable sperm to fertilize a ready ovum. A cow knows exactly when she can invite a bull. Human intervention is less certain. The window of opportunity is narrow, for which reason the art of AI often fails.

Except for one letter, Jake left business out of his letters. He missed the family, he missed Heidi and Xander. But in a few months he would be home. "Dad, you can cut this out and paste it on your shaving mirror. You can never achieve superb genetics unless you line breed, measuring and matching male and female."

As the communications came back and Jake literally champed at the bit to implement his new found post graduate knowledge, a new line was drawn in fast drying concrete. It was feedlot genetics vs. grass genetics. An unrecognized trend revealed farmers attempting to grow out calves on forage alone. This trend was more than matched by entrepreneurs supplying farmers with semen, artificial insemination expertise, or even a bull, then taking the resultant calf at a nickel a pound above the thoroughly rigged market. Control of reproduction is the name of the game. Jim wrote back, "Here's the problem, son. If you've got a big farm and you have enough money to keep it debt free, and you have 500 or 1,000 cows, and you have a big sale each year and feed everyone barbeque and put on a straw sale, it doesn't seem to make much difference how good the cattle are. After all, they're feedlot cattle, and the feedlot admits the lowest common denominator as trend setters. That's the problem in the countryside. People have their hands out, saying, help me, feed me, show me, tell me what to do. I was in on this, and the quality goes down and down. Maybe that was what was wrong with Capper-Volstead. We claimed parity for junk." Jim's point was clear. The country Svengalis were leading people away from cows that could thrive on grass. Yet all a farmer has to sell are grass and sunshine. To sell grass he had to have the right kind of cow. The cow needs to finish on grass.

When Jake returned from his yearlong stay at the institution, he talked day and night for a week.

One of the visitors at the reproductive center in West Germany was Jan Bonsma, a Ph.D. professor from Pretoria, South Africa, the very same Bonsma who had served as consultant and guiding light to the fledgling German livestock industry at the end of the war. Now Bonsma had been invited to the U.S. to lecture and visit, taking in a number of western ranches. Bonsma assured Jake that he would visit Banyon Place.

He arrived at Banyon Place a few months after Jake's return, landing at the municipal airport in a single-engine Cessna with a rented pilot. He turned out to be a tall man, this Jan Bonsma, well tanned, as muscular as a wrestler and not at all the picture of a professor. Bonsma had correlated the wisdom of the horsemen and the cowmen. His findings assured all who chose to listen that the key to genetic excellence was seated in the measurements. "Progress," he told Jim now, "is never achieved by putting evolution in reverse. Your cattle industry is so far gone, it can't be saved without an infusion of new blood."

"Well, maybe," said Jim. "Let's walk the place. I think you'll agree that Banyon Place isn't headed for the feedlots."

Jim explained to the South African that the feedlots sprang up like magic in the 1950s when it looked like organization was coming via Capper-Volstead. "Pretty soon they had traincar loads of pipe being disgorged on the High Plains. They built those pens rapidly while farmers organized slowly and ineptly."

Jake tagged along with his dad and the wily South African as the trio went through the first of many gates. The herd bull was Xerxes, a fifth-generation descendant of Pericles, the bull calf Grandpa Xander had willed grandson James Robert Neff at the end of the dust bowl days. The South African eyeballed the animal and took a few quick measurements. "Outstanding!" he said. After some urging, the professor agreed to return to Xerxes, this after seeing what thirty years of herd work had accomplished. "This farm has a carrying capacity that is expanding" Jim Neff opened. "The venue is grass. All our animals are horned Hereford. All have been line bred since the 1920s."

"Very good," the professor said.

Jim and Jake explained non stop. Grandpa had this vision with no one to follow. He took a shine to Jim as a young boy, and when he died, he left correspondence to connect his grandson well enough to enable a line breeding operation.

Nothing happened during the end of the Depression or during WWII or during the recuperation period Jim required, except that the herd increased and multiplied, all on grass. From the start, herd bulls and dams were matched to maintain the line breeding norm. As a consequence, Banyon Place produced cattle that were constantly graded Choice Grade #1 carcasses. "The best to the best," Bonsma interjected.

Jim went on, "Grandpa said that line breeding preserves and builds. This assures a true line that puts the life span of the breeder in harmony with herd development."

Over the years Jim, and now Jake, exchanged knowledge of genetics whenever a suitable source could be found. The opportunities were rare because the colleges never ceased touting the feedlot system and the so called "industrial model."

Among the several breeds in the public eye *circa* 1970s, the Hereford was best suited for maintenance on grass. It came to the West for grass, indeed became the dominant breed while Grandpa almost alone shunned wheat in order to make his way via grass. Even before Grandpa grew his Xanthippus bull, the bloodline of a champion sire named Socrates went back 22 generations. Selective mating of bull to dam, not EPD (expected progeny difference) was the name of the game.

The trio walked past fenced paddocks one at a time and as clusters. Jim and Jake, speaking in tandem, seldom talking over each other, explained the brand of rotational grazing being used. Banyon Place had only one machine, a tractor with a post hole digger. The tractor also had a reel attached to one wheel for drawing up and reeling out barbed wire or electrical wire. "We have dozens of paddocks, each a product of experimentation, development, and care."

Without explanation, it became clear to this visitor that monoculture had been rejected. There were no row crops, there was no simplistic N, P and K fertilization. This James Neff, Bonsma told himself, relies strictly on management of grasses, with variety as the objective, the mandate. Soils at Banyon Place ran the gamut, and yet this farmer managed to grow grass on clay soils as well as on silt loam. There was even a stretch of wind blown loess covered with native grasses.

Jake explained, "Dr. Bonsma, it takes up to fifty species of grass and forbs to hold these soils together."

Many cow-calf operations are absentee owned, often by dilettantes who have a lot to learn about the bottom line. Most like brightly painted tractors and enough equipment to satisfy a showroom display. Many seem to follow the model of taking a high-priced calf, stuffing it full of high-priced ration, opting for high-priced vaccines, then selling at a loss. Jim Neff still had the Depression era attitude that "a penny saved is a penny earned." He had not wormed a cow since he came back from the Sulu Archipelago wounded and half dead. He relied on forbs and grass in the pasture to ward off bacterial, viral, and fungal health destroyers. Using genetics and grass, Banyon Place hung on to one herd of cows that are related, using the best bulls. Sale of bulls had become a mainstay, cash cow, in fact.

Jim told how he stayed within the 50% rule decreed by the line breeding model. Some few years ago, Jim Neff had well over several hundred animals on grass. But economics requires adjustments. At one time he raised the herd size drastically.

"We raise our own replacements," Jim told his guest. "When cowmen do not raise their own replacements, the whole year is focused around weaning and selling calves. Grass management calls for a difficult sequence," the dust bowl boy turned rancher said. "After all, the cow's condition dictates the weaning date, and grass dictates the stocking rate. Grass should put enough tallow on the cow to make low level feeding conditions less debilitating. Further, such adjustment cancels out the expense of most supplements."

Jim did not patronize his guest or avoid points in question. He said, "Many ranchers simply do not know how to grow animals on grass. They stuff a lot of feed into them. They believe it is cheaper to buy replacements. As a result, the genetic integrity of the herd is compromised. That is why they can no longer be sustained on grass.

"I like to wean my calves on the hot fence. This means I put the herd in one paddock, let the cows out into another paddock, then put the calves in the adjoining paddock. This lets the calves selectively graze grass. I keep moving them. You see, the calf is always grazing near its mother."

While the Kansan explained, the whole show fell into place. When a need to cut the stocking rate becomes evident, short or long term, calves already weaned on grass were available for herd reduction, all with minimum stress. Calves can be sold off without a sickness surfacing to sour the situation. "What you see here is merely one Kansan's idea on how to grow cattle on grass," Jim said. "The selection process makes the determination."

"There was a time when the Hereford built its dominant position during the first part of the last century on grass. It can still finish on grass. That's not the concept being lionized by the college experts. They want to feed an animal full of corn and cattle cake and bicarbonate of soda. They produce the wrong kind of fat. Cows on grass have the right kinds of fat. Their omega 3 to omega 6 ratio is 1 to 1, not the 1 to 20 you find in feedlot fare." Bonsma listened with interest. His whole career had been dedicated to quality. Now in the twilight of life, he saw a nation's herds beyond repair, possibly irreversibly. Without his knowledge, his findings squared well with the "innovator" thesis of the prophet professor who believed himself a lineal descendant of the Biblical Phineas priest. For now, the South African admitted that the industrial arrangement for doing business does not accommodate the producer of quality. The innovator who can reach the consumer with this kind of quality is the wave of the future. Bovine that can thrive on grass is only half the equation. There has to be grass management planning to keep a supply of grass available at all times. The nemesis of the Kansas cowman, indeed the cowman west of the isohyet meridian at Topeka, is drought.

"I like to wean my calves early just in case of drought," Jim Neff told the world's greatest bovine specialist. "I always have a drought plan. The critical dates are based on the equinox. Without moisture by those dates, adjustments have to be made. There always has to be enough forage to meet the feed requirement."

"What are your dates?" Bonsma wanted to know.

"If it doesn't rain by June 20, the stocking rate has to be adjusted. July 4 is too late."

The men compared notes all afternoon. The professor took note of this Kansas man who had shaken off the poverty of the dust bowl, reclaimed his herd after the war, and rejected the mandate of his

305

government that he give up the farm so that big capital can create monopolies and take control of the food supply. This young fellow talked about feeding the soil and in turn the soil feeding livestock. He was even trying to colonize dung beetles so that his unpaid workers could redeem and use the full economic value of the cow manure that hit the turf eight to ten times a day per cow, a billion times a day for the American cow herd.

He had seen the devastating effect of overstocking around the world. Grass fades into oblivion during drought and becomes susceptible to erosion. Yes, indeed, the livestock in the soil has to have its fix of carbohydrates or perish. If the underground task is not accomplished, there would not be enough grass to feed the animals. Manure can never be replaced with factory acidulated fertilizers. In Eastern Kansas it usually takes a paddock a day to keep a herd in ecological splendor. No college scientist has ever been able to genetically modify a crop or animal to withstand starvation. Starving an animal is an absurdity, as is stuffing an animal with feeds designed for non-ruminants. Jake broke into the cowmen's reverie. "Mom will be waiting," he said.

Can we continue with some real food in front of us?"

The South African mentioned that he had seen a dozen herds on his present trip. Most of them, he said, were in a race for the floor. Feedlot fare was mediocrity. It looked like meat, and with factory taste enhancers it might even taste a bit like meat, but it was commodity meat, substandard meat, meat without natural taste.

Before supper was over, the South African had dropped off his manual for linear measurements; the shoulders, the length, the scrotum, the location of the various glands, and two dozen measurements that could tell a cowman whether a bull calf could become a suitable sire, measurements being taken at six months of age.

Before the great consultant left, he made a pronouncement, "People, I've been all over the world, and I know how hard it is to keep a farm together. This is so because modern life finds it difficult to keep a family together.

You've done both, but I urge you to look beyond survival." Jim mumbled to himself,

"Yes, you should seek to prevail." It was a philosophical declaration that stretched Jim Neff, challenged his uncommon good sense.

The South African went on, "Your people are importing big cows, not matching them, and opting for commodity beef. It is not fit to eat, but no matter. The food specialists that line the freeway in New Jersey can make a rubber tire taste good, never mind what it does to people. These mammoth animals are high maintenance. They don't deliver the testosterone and estrogen that confer taste. Your Herefords are a natural grass animal, but I think you need a smaller cow, genetically built to live on grass. If you put the feedlot cattle out on pasture, they would perish."

Jim thought back to the day when the army corporal, the self-ordained Phineas priest, unloaded his insight that "the innovator annihilates the existing order."

It was well past midnight when the consultant and the farmer called it quits. Early the next morning Jim drove his visitor to the local airport where a single engine Cessna was running and ready to take Bonsma to a ranch in southern Oklahoma.

It was dry that year. Jim and Jake weaned calves early. They cut numbers to be in compliance with forage availability. Cowherds have a top third, a middle third, and a bottom third. Jim always cut out the bottom third, the least capable of making money. Under conditions of drought, maintenance of the bottom third can be ruinous. They have to be moved out. The idea that a certain number of cattle be maintained did not resonate with Jim and his son. In a manner of speaking, Jim and Jake Neff had taken on the role of innovators. They were seed stock producers. Their basic product was top-quality bulls, bulls that complied with all of Bonsma's measurements. Banyon Place sold bulls at a premium, measured bull calves, and declared them future sires at seven months of age, or ruthlessly culled them out, and earned premium dollars on the rail, meaning dollars three to six times the price of EPD seed stock.

EPD meant "expected progeny difference." It was a bookkeeper's idea of what a sire should be. Banyon Place bulls, thirty years in the making, had a reputation that could settle 85 to 90% of the cows during the first thirty days of the breeding season.

On the way home from the airport, Jim turned to his boy.

"Jake, I'm hatching a real innovative idea."

"What is it, Dad?"

"Not now, it'll have to wait until Xander is finished with school." It did have to wait, but in the meantime Jim Neff's research would take him halfway around the world.

33

It was the boy Xander who called Jim Neff's long-term program for preservation of the farm and his family into question. Jim pegged the boy as a real scientific type. Even during grade school days, the boy collected weeds, as had his brother Jake. When he left for college, Jake had turned his own weed collection over to Xander, who promptly enlarged it. He preserved each specimen in a plastic envelope created for the purpose. Each was taped with its several common names, common according to the area of the country, along with its botanical Latinate.

Xander, with Jake's counsel, found that almost every weed manual written during the 20th century had the same outline. This is the weed, this is how you recognize it, this is the poison you put on it. Xander dismissed poisons as frustration science. Soon enough, he developed a new entry in the weed book outline. What is the weed telling me? became the rhetorical question. When that one question was answered the young scientist was well on the way to having a new paradigm.

Xander never found foxtail in his dad's pastures. That nemesis of the grain farmer seemed to like plowed soil, soil compacted by tractor tires. A little more investigation told Xander that foxtail germinates in the presence of carbon dioxide and in the absence of the planet's usual air. The poison spray route could not be correct, the boy reasoned, because atrazine seems to bring on a vicious weed called fall panicum, a weed that loves drought. Xander's mother often helped him catalog and file his samples, which numbered 400, as he made ready to enter college.

His very favorite weed was the common dandelion: *Compositae Taraxacum officinale.* This denizen of the lawn had its role assigned by the Creator. Since calcium likes to migrate down deep into the soil, the evolutionary process decreed that the dandelion root go deep to return calcium to the top.

During his last year in high school, Xander became interested in an issue that was spawned by committees from coast to coast. Fluoridation of the drinking water had become politicized by then, meaning an atmosphere of intimidation had installed itself in the lexicon as settled science.

Young Xander did not think so. He submitted a term paper, and was astonished when it came back with a grade of "C." A note was attached: You show unusual zeal, but when you attack settled science, you tend to follow the dictum "This is the case on which I base my facts."

Just the same, Xander's paper prompted him to enter the University of Missouri at Columbia. Although the great professor mentioned in his paper was retired, Xander figured he would make contact. The boy learned all about cation-exchange capacity and trace nutrients in his soils courses, but when he came home during semester breaks, he agreed with Jake, "They teach so much that isn't so!" There seemed to be too much emphasis on the holy water of agriculture: nitrogen.

Xander was a tall lad, over six feet. His build was his father's, but his face was his mother's. He did not like boxing, although he tried it. Nor was he interested in that college stuff of cross-country running or streaking. However, he shared his mother's love for gardening, plants, and the soil. What was not so was the myth they had at school about the natural nitrogen cycle and the natural carbon cycle. In fact, biological activity in the soil hardly figured, as professors and teaching assistants hammered home lessons about nitrogen, phosphorus, and potassium. It was a chemical feast, this higher education and industrial farming. Lore from yesteryear hardly mattered when agriculture could literally dial a yield and cause nature to perform on signal and on demand.

Xander and Jake had always been thick as fleas while growing up. There was a time when a local bully picked on Xander, usually by distorting his name into "Neanderthal." Once the bully caught the boy alone and beat him into the ground. Jake figured the thing to do was to set the hulk up for his own chastisement. Xander would lure the bully with his bicycle down the main drag of a nearby development. Jake trailed at a comfortable distance. When the hulk struck, Jake came up in an instant. The two, acting as one, gave the bully a good thrashing. Xander was never bothered after that. Jake was Xander's mentor, and the two figured they would end up ranching if, indeed, the ranch could support that many families. Two years into college, Xander questioned the possibilities. By then, he had developed a more than academic interest in statistical analysis. Xander figured the answers were in the numbers. Was not science merely a matter of statistics? LD 50 by then had become holy writ. It meant that such and such a dose of poison at such and such a body weight will kill 50% of the test animals.

What if the poison did not kill at all, but merely deformed or sickened?

Dad had never allowed poison on the place, and Dad, now in his sixties, was a pretty astute fellow. Poisons meant cellular damage, damage quite like atomic radiation. During his third year in college, Xander raised an objection to toxic genetic chemicals, which he had first heard about from his dad. The professor gave Xander's revelation a put-down, and most of the class laughed. Was the professor pandering to the firms that slopped a little gravy in the form of grants to the department?

Xander took up the matter with his brother and dad. After all, Dad knew such malfeasance firsthand. That's why he had opted for grass. He wanted to preserve the soil, not create a new round of dust bowl erosion trouble with N, P and K fertility, and reliance on rescue chemistry. Those dust storms came because the soil was lifeless. In time, the soils left their imprint on the animal and human populations. The environment became so out of balance that the jacks took over, and after that, the poisons took over.

A confrontation in the classroom became inevitable.

"Dr. Storm," Xander queried, "is it true that in the cell, whether plant, animal or human, there are chromosomes that carry almost all the information needed to direct that cell's growth, life, and reproduction of chemicals such as proteins?"

"Well, yes. Do you have a point?"

"Is it true that these chromosomes are composed of information bearing genes?"

"Great, so far," Professor Storm said, as he finger combed his mustache. Xander stood almost a foot taller than the professor. For a moment, one could read distress in the learned one's face. Usually no one questioned the professor, but his bland assertion that farm

311

chemicals are perfectly safe if used as directed somehow got under Xander's skin.

"Is it true that farm chemicals are radio mimetic, meaning that they ape the character of radiation?"

"They have been characterized as radio mimetic."

"Doesn't radiation, and do not the farm chemicals, injure the chromosome either by altering the chemistry of a single gene so that the gene conveys improper information, or by breaking chromosome called point deletion."

"Mr. Neff, you have fifteen Swiss seconds to make your point." Professor Storm liked that expression. He used it at least three or four times a day. Some of the class took to expressing themselves for so and so many Swiss seconds.

"Isn't it true," Xander continued, "that the cell may be killed or that it may continue to live reproducing its error? As I understand it, some cell damage causes genetic misinformation which fosters wild proliferation, or cancer."

There was no answer, at that moment. But there was a response at the end of the course. It was not a failing grade, but one next to it: C. A "C" grade could not annihilate the settled scientific fact that malnutrition, like radiation or chemicals, delivers the damage Xander mentioned, and ionized farm chemicals in, around, and on the food supply did just that. "Still not a problem, if used as directed," Professor Storm said, as a final benediction.

Dr. Cardiff Cadwallader proffered an assignment in the third year of Xander's college career. It was a sociology course entitled *Myths: Their Anatomy and Endurance,* and *How They Square with Scientific or Historical Facts.*

Nineteen myths were placed in a #10 coffee can. Each student was required to draw a myth. They were an interesting lot, these myths: that Jesse James survived to reach age 100; that Roosevelt lured the Japanese into attacking Pearl Harbor; that Amelia Earhart survived a crash in the Pacific only to die in a Japanese war camp; that the fallen regularly build campfires at Gettysburg; that fluoride is a Communist plot; that John D. Rockefeller survived to a ripe old age on human mother's milk; that the dead walk in Haiti; that a ghost ship once roamed the Caribbean; that stigmatics relive the passion of

Christ; that a white buffalo foretold the Custer debacle; on and on. Dr. Cadwallader roped in every available myth and required his students to write a paper "no shorter than fifteen pages, no longer than twenty-five." When Xander pulled his assignment from the #10 coffee can, it asked for the origin of the fluoride myth and a clear cut refutation of the Communism connection "if this was the fact." Xander took the assignment home to the Banyon Place library in consultation with his dad. In short order, books were spread on the great conference table, dozens of books and journals. With that, Xander started sorting his materials and constructing an outline. He found a few transcripts of disc jockeys making sport of a certain colonel who claimed that fluoride in the drinking water stunned the minds of the citizenry. He found no direct connection to Communism, but such a connection could be implied because, at the time, a Communist was thought to reside under every rock.

As Xander continued to explore the subject, it came to him that the Food and Drug Administration made great demands on the pharmaceutical industry whenever their laboratories wanted to market a new drug. The protocols demanded were draconian as well as budget wasting. At the same time, the agency was demanding that sodium fluoride, or stannous fluoride, be added to the drinking water of all cities in America, effectively making fluoride at 1 ppm a combination drug with everything in the medicine cabinet. As Xander lined up his materials, he felt certain that he would blow the entire myth out of the water. His twenty-five pages became one solid syllogism of proof. The foundation for the fluoride myth was first reported in the *Journal of the American Dental Association* as a survey of dental health in Deaf Smith County, Texas in August, 1952. The children involved had the lowest inventory of dental cavities recorded in any civilized nation. Next, the U.S. Public Health Service claimed that this was due to the high fluorine content in High Plains ground water. This was from "The Town without Tooth Decay," Hereford, Texas, a small town south a ways from the Kansas High Plains where Dad and his Granddad Xander had lived.

The idea that fluorine in the drinking water affected the apatite crystals in teeth was embraced by the aluminum and phosphate industries. Xander realized that there was a myth afloat, but it had to

313

do with the presumed efficacy of the halogen, and that the danger of the element as an enzyme poisoner was no myth. The fallacy of the fluoride myth relied on misinformation.

"Son," said James Neff, "consider your chemistry an element at a time." Xander did just that. There was that calcium and phosphate bearing apatite in those Texas and Kansas soils which was putting more calcium and phosphorus into the food. Decomposition of the apatite puts halogen into the water as fluoride, that most subtle of the table elements. It has only a single valence. It departs from the soil easily and penetrates into wells and underground aquifers. Calcium has a double valence, phosphorus a triple valence. As fluoride departs from the apatite, it leaves behind the calcium and phosphorus to contact with each other, thus making both more readily available to crop plants. Mineral-rich, high-protein crops accounted for sound teeth, not the discarded fluoride.

Xander was up to page fifteen by the time he made his sledgehammer blows slam home. Now, what about the Communist myth? The boy puzzled his way through some twenty-four papers, a sampling of 50,000 in the literature. He invited his dad, an omnivorous reader, in on the study. Jim Neff pointed out that those who favored fluoride and those who opposed cited the same studies. Both sides were using the same material. They couldn't both be right. It did not seem possible that science, the arbiter of such controversies, could not furnish an answer.

"Follow the chemistry," Dad Neff advised.

Xander found that fluorine is a potent enzyme poisoner. There are several reasons for this. In the table of elements, fluorine belongs to the halogen family, sharing chemical properties with close relatives chlorine, bromine, and iodine. As halogens reacting with other elements, they all carry one negative charge. As a halogen having the smallest atomic weight, fluorine is the most active. It is extremely active in combining with any element or molecule having a positive valence. It bonds with water to form hydrogen fluoride, which readily melts glass. It actively bests its sibling halogen, chlorine, in any solution, including hydrochloric acid in our stomach or chlorine molecules in our blood, or inter-cellular fluids.

Could fluorine trump iodine, thus inhibiting the formation of thyroxin by the thyroid, thyroxin being needed to metabolize sugar?

Was this not one reason for the pandemic scale of diabetes in the country? Xander made phone calls, recorded the answers, and footnoted the results. Two physicians said they thought he was right.

Xander ran out of space. He had to delete some of his favored passages in order to stay within the twenty-five page limit set by Dr. Cadwallader. The origin of the Commie myth was spewed by propaganda serving the aluminum phosphate industry disposal problems, he felt sure. "Dad, can we afford a phone call long distance?" Xander pleaded. "I have a study from the International Institute for the Study of Human Reproduction at Columbia University that I need. I have the study by Dean Berk and John Yiamouyiannis on the cancer connection, but what I need now is the brain connection. The only real study seems to have disappeared from everywhere except the footnotes."

The call was made to retired U.S. Army Colonel Lindegran. It was this colonel's testimony that disc jockeys and wise cracking TV announcers relied on for their on air prattling. Lindegran told Xander that in the 1930s Hitler had his scientists hunt out an odorless drug that could be unobtrusively administered to the German people to make them more docile and open to suggestion. I. G. Farben came up with sodium fluoride. Lindegran said, "In the rear occiput of the left lobe of the brain is a small area of tissue responsible for the individual's power to resist domination. Repeated doses of infinitesimal amounts of sodium fluoride gradually reduce the individual's power to resist domination. By slowly narcotizing this area of brain tissue, sodium fluoride causes paralysis. Minute doses cause loss of the will." Xander watched the fading light on the recorder. He had the message and the title of the House hearing and one of the citations from the exact same source. He said to his dad, "I think I can go to press." He worked the computer keyboard, and during the next class session he presented his paper, neatly done on a laser printer.

Both James and Nora thought it was a brilliant paper. Professor Cadwallader said he was not impressed. He used the term "pseudo science," which infuriated Xander. To his dad he said, "Science is now politics instead of science. They can kill over 100,000 a year with prescription drugs taken correctly, and call it science. But if one person overdoses on vitamin A, all holy hell breaks loose."

315

Xander graduated on schedule, and then he dropped a bombshell. He wanted to get his master's degree. One of the professors who took a liking to his gadfly approach managed to lay a fellowship on him. He was interested in making a statistical evaluation of the freemartin phenomenon in cattle reproduction.

Graduate degrees are usually awarded on the basis of directed study, a thesis, and evaluation by an examining board. The examination board, in this case, would be composed of five professors, three of whom had been involved in the candidate's study program leading to a graduate credential. That two of the examiners did not like, actually hated, each other was a plus. They argued among themselves a good deal of the time, thereby excusing the candidate from much heavy grilling.

For reasons Xander didn't discern at first, Dr. John K. McCune exhibited open hostility.

"What's your thesis, young man?" was McCune's opener.

"That significant statistical support suggests that freemartins are the consequence of malnutrition of the dam during the gestation period, possibly supported by genetic damage to previous generations."

"I can't see that you've supported this thesis statistically."

"Well, he has eight tables that seem to provide significant correlations," Professor Jones said.

"And jumbled together to support a prejudiced conclusion," McCune rebutted.

"Wait a minute, John," Professor Foster Philips, a DVM instructor said.

"That's a little heavy."

"It may be heavy to you, but what do you make of slams like 'sexual preference?' Right here on page sixty-four. That's code language for anti-gay prejudice. The Supreme Court of the United States has ruled for gay rights, and I can't see putting the stamp of approval of this university on poppycock scholarship designed to humiliate our gay and lesbian students." Dr. Philips said to himself, "and professors."

In fact, no one said anything. The silence could have shattered glass.

Xander tried to salvage the situation. "May I say a word?" Four of the professors mumbled their permission. Dr. McCune maintained a silence.

316

"This study was conducted because of an interest in twinning at the University of Wisconsin. Tables 11 and 12 codify all available information. You can see by the numbers that the attempts to fertilize two ova at the same time were only partly successful. The health crisis of the resultant animals, and the hardship on mothers, in the opinion of the numbers, if numbers can have an opinion, cancel out the economic benefits expected. That's all." Dr. McCune mockingly read from Xander's manuscript. "Milk processors know that plastics give up plasticizers while the product sits on the shelf. They calculate the economic benefits of longer shelf life even if it means slowly embalming the losing consumer." Finding more fuel for his fire, he continued, "Case University researchers have found that 40% of the mice in a controlled experiment had chromosomal damage. The effect telegraphed the probability of Down's syndrome." Paging on he paused, then read, "40% of chromosomal damage became the consequence of using detergents in cages made of plastic." Visibly irritated, McCune slammed the pages down, "One, two, three. He attacks the plastics industry to make assertions prejudicial to gays in our student body."

Xander's director of studies said, "Hold on, McCune. You're on the border of being out of control. Let me read a few pertinent passages in what I consider a remarkable thesis." He did not wait for approval, but began reading.

"Page 82: Lab workers washed the cages with a harsh detergent. As a consequence, the plastic in the cages started breaking down. The chemical BPA used to make the plastic affected the mice. BPA is known in the laboratory as 'bisphenol.' It mimics the effect of sex hormones. It is now a matter of record that plastics containing BPA can alter sexual development of wild and domestic animals and human beings.

"He cites here frogs with both male and female reproductive organs, this after exposure to BPA. He cites alligators with stunted reproductive organs and a low mating success in the wake of DDT spills. He cites calves achieving freemartin status after using plastic drinking cups. Let me continue." No one could stop the master defending his student.

DTA leaks, especially if the plastic is scrubbed with detergent. "Mr. Neff cites forty studies of low doses of BPA including insects, fish, frogs, mice and rats. The result is accelerated puberty, decreased sperm count, and changes in gender behavior."

McCune was back. "Changes in gender behavior! Little digs all the way!" The only lady professor on the examining board interrupted. "I think the candidate should defend his thesis. Don't you agree, Mr. Neff?" Xander agreed. He was prepared to answer questions, reasonable or otherwise.

"What you're saying seems to refute the concept of LD50," Dr. Philips said.

"This thesis holds that the preponderance of evidence annihilates the LD50 concept of toxicology. Low dosages often support that concept."

"Meaning you're ready to reject settled science?" was McCune's retort.

"Not settled science, if it's truly settled," Xander Neff said. "May I continue?"

Xander received a general nod to go on.

"I have a footnote to the effect that California studies reveal the presence of BPA in the umbilical blood of fifty newborn. Low dosages of BPA are lethal because they confirm that low dosages, like fragments of pesticide drift, are often more dangerous than massive doses certified in LD50 studies. In my opinion, the saw that the dose makes the poison is Stone Age science. I think I have proved as false the idea that below some threshold level there will be no biological effect."

"How long has BPA been around?" queried Dr. Phillips.

"It was developed in the 1930s. It was replaced by DES: diethyl stilbestrol. BPA was shelved as an estrogen mimic when its role as a plastic polymer was discovered."

"You are saying that reptile eggs, human eggs, mouse eggs can be disturbed causing a sexual dysfunction?" It was Dr. Phillips, passive as a statue.

"That's the assessment this thesis makes."

"Then BPS, like DES, causes genetic misinformation in the formation of sperm?" The passive look did not change. "And the consequences are being visited on generation after generation: calves, test animals, human beings?"

"Agreed."

"And anonymous molecules interchange wherever plastics touch food, heat, and detergents that disturb the composition of plastic containers? And that's where your sexual development remark, so offensive to Dr. McCune, comes in."

"With this modification, I'm talking about calves, not humans. This thesis has to do with livestock husbandry, not human genetics."

"Thank you, Mr. Neff." It was the clarion, and the interview was over. Drs. Jones, Phillips, and Carlos could hardly believe what was taking place. Dr. McCune was reading into the boy's thesis, not out of it. "You have statements about the estrogen level in soy," McCune said, shattering the stony silence that had developed. "And then there is a gratuitous remark about the amount of soy texture in fast-food hamburgers. Now, if that isn't a left-handed suggestion that our food ultimately is impeding the sexual development of young people, then I guess I'll just levitate and walk out of here two feet off the ground."

"John," Phillips said.

"Don't jive me," came the defense like a rifle shot.

"Gentlemen, lady, we're here to pass on a very fine student. Let's stick to business."

The examination proceeded without incident for fully thirty minutes. Then came another explosion. Professor McCune's hand came down on the table with silence shattering force. "Dig, dig, dig! What you see here is a prejudiced young man trying to carve up the gay population by inviting comparison to some half-assed studies that pretend to be scientific. We're to draw the conclusion that our food industry is creating homosexuals, that somehow we're to go back to the Dark Ages and burn people at the stake."

Again, that leaden silence.

Xander stated, "My thesis speaks for itself. I won't add or subtract. I do not believe that I should be held responsible for what some people want to read into it. Tests and database reveal that the mercury in five-way and seven-way vaccines disturb the estrogen testosterone balance in a sire. On a scale of 100, estrogen content should be 25. The testosterone should be 75. If the balance levels are disturbed, then the bull won't settle the cows. Moreover, he'll assume feminine characteristics. I make no assertions. That's all I'm saying."

Except for the forty minutes of uninterrupted examination, there was no further discussion of the master's thesis. The chair thanked Xander Neff for his cooperation, and then went into executive session.

"Executive session" is a euphemism for having done with intellectual honesty and academic freedom. "A little hard on the boy, weren't you?" the DVM said.

"Let's get something straight. We're not going back into the closet."

"That's not the issue," Dr. Philips said. "The issue is support of this institution. That stadium out there is paid for by soda pop. Hinky Dinky Hamburgers keeps the food lab going. Do you have any idea how much money in grants the Soils Department gets from agribusiness? What'll happen is this: some newspaper person will get hold of this if we pass it. The next thing you know we'll be on the shit list of every gay organization in the country. I can see *The New York Times* bringing out the hammer and nails for our crucifixion. It'll be the creationism versus evolution argument all over again, and so we end up looking stupid."

The vote was 3-2 against accepting the thesis, which would be salvaged 535 by deleting any reference to freemartins, eliminating the aside about plasticizers in baby formula, and sticking entirely to the issue of twinning in cattle reproduction.

Xander made the deletions, but his heart was not in it. Professor Carlos tried to comfort him. "The art of the possible," he said. "But that's politics," said Xander.

"I guess so. That's science."

Xander did not go back to the farm. He had to sort things out, he told his dad. He had a two-year gig at the Centers for Disease Control if he wanted it, and he did.

Those two years went fast, with one study after another rejected for very specious reasons. Figures did not lie, but liars figured. Data were malleable, especially when they indicted the powerful chemical and pharmaceutical industries. The very idea that only drugs be used when dealing with illness failed to comply with the rule of reasonability. If this were true, then food would not matter, and the degenerative metabolic diseases sweeping the nation should be allowed to happen so coal tar derivative drugs can get a whack at them.

Xander came home in time for Jake's wedding. Jake got more out of college than Xander. He had met Amy. The two continued to court via mail, and often traveled between Banyon Place and Fort Scott. Jake had remodeled the old Miller farmhouse.

Amy was a vision in her ankle-length wedding dress and pearl studded tiara. Nora welcomed her with open arms, having missed Heidi all these years. The five; Jim, Nora, Xander, Jake and Amy, paused for a toast after the cake was cut. Each took a turn with sentiments suitable for the occasion. When Xander's turn came, he lifted his glass, his face aglow as though favored by God with a revelation, "Dad, I have an idea." With a measure of home schooling, Jake and Heidi had made it through high school without a ripple. Not so with Xander. He turned out to be a gadfly, a Socrates who delighted in plumbing the depths of an assignment, usually annihilating the conventional wisdom. At college he astonished his professors, causing chagrin if not permanently altered facial expressions.

34

Xander's idea became a high priority session in the library at Banyon Place. By the time the meeting was called to order, Jim had visited an attorney, corresponded with and telephoned New Zealand, and discussed the idea in depth with Xander and Jake, at least once over lightly with Nora, and by long distance telephone with Heidi, now Major Heidi Neff, United States Army. Jim led off. "This farm is no longer my farm," he said. He waited for this to sink in. As he did so, he seemed to scan and examine the classic room that the once sprawling living room had become over the past forty-plus years. Floor to ceiling shelves covered the entire north wall. Similar shelves covered the part of the south wall not needed for filing cabinets and Nora's computer desk. Jim's executive desk commanded the east end of a room that could easily seat two dozen people, classroom style. The open wall featured handsome blown up photographs of Xanthippe, Paracelsus, and Xerxes, three of the bulls that had put Banyon Place on the map.

Jim continued, "I have deeded the entire property to a trust. I have named myself as one of the five trustees. The other four are your mother, Xander, Jake and Heidi. Heidi has promised to make all meetings. I expect once a year will do. Any questions?"

Jake fidgeted a bit. He was probably the best cowman in six dozen counties, but when it came to legal ownership, he was still a long way from understanding.

"Amy would like to know why, " he said.

Jim nodded his appreciation. "Good point. As you know, Mother and I are getting up in years. Should this property become part of an estate, fully half of it would have to be sold off to satisfy taxes. As a trust, it can operate in perpetuity. When one trustee dies, the remaining four name a replacement. Some day it will be one or two of your children,

322

Jake. The rest is bookkeeping, and I think we're smart enough to keep books."

It was a good time to examine the books, and this was done with the assistance of a bookkeeper who was called in for the purpose. On the shelves next to Jim's desk was a collection of *Hereford Journal,* all editions between May 15, 1910 and the present. Recent editions carried pictures of the Banyon Place bull Xanthippus, and each year Jim had paid the association registration fees because buyers demanded credentials and, when possible, expected progeny difference statistics going back to old man Xander. The herd had been line bred for almost a century. The Hereford became famous as a grassfed animal from the end of the frontier days to the present. It had even survived the harsh treatment of the feedlot. It was a low-maintenance animal when not force fed, as had become the custom among conventional cowmen.

"We should continue line breeding," Jim said, and he laid out the rest of his proposal. "I want, with the Board's approval, to split the farm in two. The Snyder property is ours, if we want it. John Snyder is 92. He has no family.

He's in a rest home, and he wants us to buy his equity." The metes and bounds of the transaction were discussed for half an hour before Jim said, "Xander, you have the floor."

Everyone considered Xander an expert. During his stint at Centers for Disease Control he had put together numbers on every important cattle breed in America. The exotic breeds imported during the early 1970s and before were high-maintenance animals. They produced marginal product to a point where some restaurateurs said, "Only two out of ten expert diners had a good eating experience." Color meant nothing when it came to taste. The ability to make testosterone and estrogen required for meat protein taste was annihilated by feedlot procedures.

"In short," said Xander, "a cow has to have grass. Yet the cows being fattened in the feedlot can't survive on grass because, as Dad puts it, they've become ruminant hogs."

Jake took the floor. "Is it the objective to create a line-bred herd like the one Great Grandpa Xander had?"

Jim knew there would be a lack of comprehension to some degree. "Let's back up a minute."

They all shifted in their chairs. If Dad was going to lecture, it was time to listen.

"Before 1870 there were as few as half a dozen Hereford herds in the country. But it was a start at replacing the Longhorns. You know about the Industrial Revolution and the growth of population. Well, those stringy range herds were no longer acceptable."

Young Xander said to himself, "Come on, Dad, we know that stuff." Out loud, he said, "What about Shorthorns?"

"By 1870 they were vastly dominant. Angus? Maybe 10 or 11%. Herefords were hardly noticed."

Jim went on, counting off eras and reciting details. "By 1880 Hereford importations started pouring in as a flood tide. So great was the export out of England that a move developed to stop it. A fear was expressed in the House of Commons that the breed would vanish from its native land. "By 1900 Shorthorns were down to 30 or 40% of the beef cattle. Angus remained in the 10 to 12% range. By 1900 the Hereford breed dominated. That's where your Great Granddad came in. He got started with a son of Anxiety and built around Xanthippus."

Young Xander asked, "That's where you got your start?"

"Right!" Jim explained that between 1900 and 1960 Herefords became 80% to 85% of the beef animals.

"Then what happened?" Heidi wanted to know.

"Two things. Hereford breeders went to dwarfs because the school men who did the judging took a shine to dwarfs and freaks. Next, they endorsed the size of the exotics, Charolais, Simenthal, Limousin and such. Hereford breeders were crossing into Canada, buying semen from Simenthal bulls, and smuggling it back in, all on the QT. They recorded resultant calves as from American bulls."

"You've never showed in the ring?" young Xander asked.

"No, not at all. That episode came to a halt in the 1951 explosion." No one asked about the explosion because all those present knew the answer would arrive framed by revelations.

"I was just out of the army five years at the time. Your mother was pregnant with Jake. But I went to Kansas City for a day. I couldn't afford any more. Someone from the country put together a revolt the likes of which we never had before or since. The bull on a stick and the new Association building was up. About 1,000 breeders forced resignations, fired people, and set up a lab to smoke out the dwarf genes. They even took on the Xanthippus line and others like it, but it was quite late."

For perhaps the first time the passage of events made sense to Heidi and Nora, and even to Jake and Xander. The Hereford breed put a premium on the Xanthippus blood line because it was one of the few uncontaminated lines in the country. It, of course, linked back many generations to the famous Anxiety bull.

"No", said Jim, "we can't create a new line with a magic wand. It takes more than one lifetime to do that. But we have to try. The Hereford is still the best grass fed bovine, but we need a smaller animal, one totally grass fed and unsuited for the feedlot. That's the only way we can break the tyranny of the lots.

"Homozygosity means the breed is controlled by a dominant gene. Heterozygosity means strong recessive genes are in control. Our objective is to have the dominant trait preside. All breeds on Planet Earth were developed with line breeding. When you complete 14 generations in a herd without outside blood, you have a homozygous state. That blood will breed through in perpetuity if incestuous breeding is avoided, meaning no more than 50% of the blood of an ancestor."

Jake spoke up. "Dad, can you tell then how to calculate the bloodline through generations?"

"Well, the best generation parents are 50% each. Second generation, 25%. Third generation, 12.5%. Fourth generation, 6.25%. The next generation, 3.12%, etc. It halves as you go back. Spread over the generations, an animal may appear twenty times. Whatever generation it appears in, multiply that percentage times the number of appearances, and add to the total. The influence can't be over 50%. Our computer program takes care of the computations. Every animal we have has 25% of the Xanthippus bloodline, and it can't be any different as long as we stick to Grandpa Xander's program. "There you have it," Jim said to summarize. "Open range to stock pen, to freaks and dwarves, to runts. And then the exotics. It all has to do with downgrading grass and feeding subsidized grain!

"The biggest industry is no longer agriculture. It is war material sales, airplane sales. Expensive airplanes were first used in Kansas, but that wasn't enough. The military now occupies the globe. No one can get us to go home. Well, when we lose, we go home, as in Vietnam. But they can't get us out of Korea or Germany or a dozen, maybe two dozen places. Why?" Jim held eye contact. "Why?" he asked again. "Because they're there to protect American interests, meaning business interests. They can import enough cotton, soybeans, wheat, and milk to break most farmers. But they can't break the farmer who goes organic and develops a market the bigs can't service or compete against.

"Organic beef? Absolutely. You told me vaccines sap a bull's prepotency, that vaccine contains mercury, that it disturbs the balance between estrogen and testosterone. I think hormones and antibiotics are sapping the mental acuity of our people. I'm afraid my Phineas priest lance may have been blunted with a less complicated line."

Xander had identified one breed nearly extinct that could rescue red meat and failing farmers. Only about 2,000 such animals remained in the U.S. They were known as the Red Devon, or just plain Devon. This smaller animal thrived on grass and grass alone. The problem, though, is "There just aren't any satisfactory bulls."

"Satisfactory" to the Neff family meant compliance with the mandates of linear measurement.

"The man who thinks he can look at a bull and tell within an inch or two the required shoulder measurement is a fool," Xander said harshly. Jim turned to Nora. "One thing is certain, our boys know that you have to know the inside of a bull before you can validate outside assertions. That's why I want Xander to go to New Zealand. I want him to pick up as many straws of semen possible."

"The Devon," said Nora.

"Correct. And I want him to buy six calves." He turned to Xander. "The ovaries and testes. You can rely on linear measurements." Jim Neff's new insight arose from a document called the profit and loss statement in the old days, but was now known as an income statement. Until Nora had pointed it out to her husband, he hardly paid attention to the fact that his line bred bulls were commanding prices three and four times what other breeders were getting. They were line bred, true, but also they were measured meticulously to comply with the norms imported from South Africa via the connection with Roy, the soldier who hadn't come home. "This is going to cost money, so I don't want any mistakes," Jim told his family. "I ought to send Jake to New Zealand, but he can't be spared right now."

This meant that Xander was elected. Using the references available to him, Jim created an itinerary. Xander was to visit the various ranches. He was to select the finest Devon bull and purchase as many straws of semen as possible. He was to contract for no less than four calves and order up the paperwork for quarantine, all in compliance with the goal of bringing to America the great genetic potential of a breed all but extinct. The family seminar lasted half a day during Jim's explanations.

"The Hereford is a good start. The line has been kept secure ever since Grandpa's day, but I want an animal with a smaller frame size. I want them smaller so they can work on grass entirely."

"You mean cross breeding?" asked Jake. "What about registry?"

"From my point of view," said Jim, "you can take those registry books and burn them. Burn them all, and on the basis of breeder satisfaction, I'll still outsell them all."

Nora spoke up. She had listened intently, but she still did not understand.

"Go through that program again!"

"A Herbataurus is any kind of a cow, Brahmas excepted, mainly a British breed, that is bred to one of the full blooded Rotokowa Devons I hope to get out of New Zealand. We will use a line bred Devon bull on, say, a Hereford or Angus or mongrel, whatever kind of cow the farmer has. The product will be the beginning of the Herbataurus. The standards are still to be set. I want a small cow. It'll be a half blood, and we'll use the name Herbataurus. The Devon goes back on the half blood. Then we issue papers on any female that complies with the linear measurements we require. Same for males."

"A minimum relationship test," supplied Xander.

"A breed self sufficient in forage, one that can compete with the force-fed feedlot animal! This is the only way we can help the farmer sell grass on a sustainable basis," said Jim.

"But the breeding line has to be kept line bred?" It was Jake quietly reiterating what he was learning.

"Yes," Jim said. "Paternally line bred."

Xander caught a flight out of San Francisco on Qantas Airlines, and was met by the proprietor of the sprawling Rotokowa Ranch on the North Island. Even by eyeball, Xander could tell that the broad shouldered bull called Captain Cook more than met expectations. As he measured the animal and noted the signs denoting pre-potency, testicular excellence, and virile maturity, he became a convert to his own idea, now raised to new experimental heights. The scene before him was a grazier's haven. It invited a pasture walk and envious scrutiny at a breed far from extinct in New Zealand, yet the salvation of that same breed in America. The Devon did not thrive during the feedlot era. Consuming carbohydrates laced with bicarbonate of soda did not produce the expected bulk that the feedlot game required, so the breed was wasting away for want of genetics. Xander was not a novice. He presented his letter of credit at an Auckland bank, employed the solicitor needed to execute bureaucratic paper work, and, not least, shelled out $100 a day for calves in quarantine until the law permitted them to be shipped by air to Kansas City. To confirm the correctness of his transaction, Xander visited three other graziers. All had superb sheep and cattle, but nothing the likes of Captain Cook at Rotokowa Ranch. Even before Xander returned from down under, the word went out. Jim Neff had a mechanism for the grass farmer to become sustainable. Sunlight, water, photosynthesis, all had a value that would crowd the high-expense feedlots to the wall.

Xander brought his prize to his mother, an Australian Blue Retriever pup. It was a case of love at first sight. The pup loved Nora, and Nora positively glowed when the pup nuzzled his way into her affection. She did not know why, but she had a feeling that the pup was a harbinger of a great decision to be made one day.

"His name is *Vlieger,*" Xander said. "That's what the Dutchman who sold him said. It means 'Flyer'."

"Can we call him *Flyer?*"

"Oh, no," said Xander. "It's bad luck to change a dog's name."

"The Herbataurus is an open-ended breeding program," Jim elaborated, noting that Nora was paying more attention to the pup than to his explanation. Jim went on. Never very talkative, he of late bubbled when he calculated what the program could do for the family farmer. "Nora, we're doing what the Capper-Volstead Alliance could never do. We used to have to go down the road trying to convince farmers to come aboard. Now we have a waiting list for semen or a calf." Jim was excited about the Herbataurus as a dual-purpose animal. "A lot of small farmers want a family milk cow. It's simple to produce a dual-purpose cow. The Devon is dual-purpose. Most dual-purpose cows can't give all that much milk, but they're high in other fats. Kids lacto intolerant on grocery store milk suddenly are no longer lacto intolerant on fresh, raw milk."

As the months packaged twelves into yearly twelves, and new crops of calves hit the ground, the herd rapidly grew. The almost vanished Devon with its line bred bulls now spawned a smaller red meat animal. A new axiom reached the far flung corners of the farm country. Farmers were talking about three-quarter bloods when the second calf hit the ground, many three-fourths Devon, three-fourths the bull's blood. Such a bull is dominant, not the pansy type that was causing cattle breeding to deteriorate into mongrelism. Dominant bulls were all but unheard of as the 1970s folded themselves into the 1980s.

The dominant line bred bull can settle forty to fifty cows a season, or hundreds if artificial insemination is used. The Jim Neff objective was to encourage farmers to take their own bull out of their herds and breed half brothers, uncles, cousins back to their own sire. Thus, the gene pool continues to be condensed.

Soon enough, Jim Neff and his sons were faced with the curse of the innovator. Farmers like to have someone hold their hands when setting out on a new adventure. The Herbataurus brought prosperity to Banyon Place, but it also annihilated free time.

Banyon Place stood like a prairie Taj Mahal, with trees planted twenty and thirty years ago defining the property and confirming the proprietor's dedication to good maintenance. The 14x20 foot laboratory building replete with microscope, flasks, scales, refractometer, and La Motte soil testing instruments was still serviceable, albeit a bit cramped. Five years into the Herbataurus program, it became necessary to give up Banyon House as a residence. Two ranch style houses were constructed under sycamore trees planted when Jim and Nora first settled in. Jake's two children were growing up, and Xander brought home a stunningly beautiful redheaded girl to announce their engagement, and Heidi wrote home that after Kuwait she had decided to leave the army. By the way, she was coming home with a Captain boyfriend, and "Would Dad like to walk down the aisle with me?" she wrote. Banyon Place became a base for short courses on artificial insemination, soil science, pasture management, and, when Heidi arrived, on human nutrition.

The non-fighting soldier from Biak who called himself a Phineas priest came back to Banyon Place the year the Berlin Wall fell. He had met Royal Lee Neff in Germany and came to report to Jim. "Your brother is quite interested in your Herbataurus. Is it a breed?"

"It's on the way. Unfortunately, the human lifespan isn't long enough to see it to the end, but some of our younger farmers will see the benefits."

"You know," said Phineas priest, "I've honored the Bible all my life. My heritage says I'm the blessed slayer if I ever find the place to tip the lethal lance."

Jim merely smiled. He enjoyed Phineas priest Smythe and he had quit blaming him for not shooting Japs during the late unpleasantness. "You're the real Phineas priest," said the visitor. "I do believe you're the one who will slay the absconders with your ecologically sound breed. I mention this idea of cattle finishing on grass, and the ag boys laugh out loud."

"Well, look around you in the countryside. The cows are too big, too long, and there is little meat on their bones. All the feedlot cattle average 1,200 to 1,300 pounds. We need cattle that'll finish at 900 to 1,000 pounds. Now. So we're going to create them. This animal will be fed out at eighteen months of age with balanced omega 3 and 6. The feedlot cow is finished at sixteen months. We're allowing a man to sell his grass. If you have grain genetics, you can't get cash for that sunshine."

Xander followed a post graduate plan for a time, but in the end it was his own father who turned out to be his best professor. During mellow moods, his father told his son of dust bowl days and taught him that dryland weeds do not proliferate in the Rainbelt. Set grass, iron weed, tumbleweed, and all the wild sages made it into Xander's collection as gifts from Western cattlemen who got to know the boy. Weeds that thrive in heavy rainfall areas will not grow in the desert west. Xander made such observations a part of botany course papers, raising the eyebrows of some professors when the boy started naming broad leaf weeds; lamb's quarters, pig weed, Jimson weed, buttonweed, spurge, where there is moisture, irrigation or otherwise. Grassy weeds invade both paddocks and swards when land suffers depletion, for which reason corn farmers often become custodians of more weed samples than they care to enumerate. To have a junior point out defects in classical farming caused professors to blanch and seek advisement in marking grades.

"Your language is picturesque, but it isn't scientific," Xander was told.

"Where's your database? Where are your proofs?"

Xander did not get around to presenting the data he had on rye grass, wheat grass, cockleburr, barnyard grass, and not sedge, ragweed! When Xander presented his paper, the word was thumbs down. Xander moved on through his university coursework while noting how many courses were "fluff" courses designed to relieve parents of excess cash and expand the time it took to get a degree.

Freemartins have biological problems that push nature's envelope, Xander found. In his paper he stated that the hormone of the male is released first. In other words, testosterone gets into the uterus, then affects the development of the female reproductive system. The complete reproductive system with elements missing is often the consequence. It is impossible then to settle female twin calves. Most of the time the female will be sterile, which is why it is called a freemartin. The business of a freemartin having a preference for their own sex is usually a consequence of the ovaries becoming septic. A septic ovary produces the male testosterone. Such an animal becomes an aggressor in riding females in the paddock. "This condition continued long enough to allow estrogen to metabolize into testosterone. That cow will take on male characteristics."

Xander's research expanded into nutritional support, again pushing the envelope. He assembled statistics produced by Wisconsin research on twinning. He then supplied data assembled from the records at Banyon Place. One footnote delved into plastics because the agent often used acted as an estrogen.

Most of America's remaining farmers raise cattle. The public usually refers to cow pen operators as cattlemen. Nevertheless, the greatest common denominator in farming is cattle. Fully 80% of the calves are born on farms with no more than twenty-five head of cattle.

35

In barely a dozen years, Herbataurus cattle broke from a time-honored tradition common to cattle country while obeying the Biblical injunction to increase and multiply. Vlieger had equally as many years to his credit moving cattle from paddock to paddock. Lately, the Australian native spent much less time on the Herbataurus than resting comfortably in the doorway. Vlieger, always dependable to a fault, missed his call, starting when he acted out of sorts.

"Come here, boy," Xander called, and then he noticed the obvious. Vlieger had developed cataracts in both eyes. They must have been coming for some time. A few signs might have been noticed earlier, but Xander didn't make the connection for nearly a week after he returned from one of his trips. "Easy, boy, easy," he said as he held open one eye. In a minute, Xander was on the phone.

"Heidi, I need you as soon as possible." While he waited for Heidi to travel across the yard to the farm laboratory, he assembled the properties he would need, hydrogen peroxide, bottled water, and eyedropper. He mixed one drop of H_2O_2 in 35 drops of distilled water creating approximately a 1% solution.

"Heidi, I want you to hold Vlieger. He's tranquilized so it shouldn't be difficult."

"You're putting that in his eyes?"

"You got it."

"Doesn't it sting?" she asked.

"Like a driven nail. With three or four treatments he'll be able to see. I learned it from a native doctor in Iquitos, Peru."

"It works?"

"Yes, it works," Xander replied.

"Then why don't doctors do it?"

Xander broke out with laughter.

"My dear sister, do you realize cataract surgery costs $800 to $1,500 an eye? This costs a penny and a half. Now you don't expect practitioners to shut down a cashflow like that?"

Vlieger looked up as if to ask, "What are you doing to me?" But he endured the treatment and endured it a few more times until the cataract disappeared.

When Heidi came home after twenty years of military service as a trauma nurse, she brought along her also retired army doctor husband and two daughters. She had not walked down the aisle on furlough as planned because bureaucracy had gotten in the way. She had served briefly in the Gulf War. She had been with troops in Grenada, Lebanon, Panama and Iraq. It was in Kuwait that she and her physician colleague were married by one of the rare Catholic priests operating in the city. She had been home on and off since the Gulf War. She had gotten from her dad a quit claim deed for two acres, "where I intend to spend my retirement years." The husband was Jason Layton, an athletic young man who had joined the army to see the world and get a free medical education.

"Just as you get near the retirement age," Jason said, "you realize that protecting America really means protecting the interests of the industrial companies that have an American address." Just before retirement, Jason joined Doctors Without Borders. He and Heidi agreed that he would spend some time on foreign missions. Heidi had her own plans. She wanted to start a foundation for nutritionists needing advice.

She had only half listened to her father and Xander. She wrote letters about her experiences in Iraq when soldiers became ill without apparent cause. She corresponded with her brother, Xander, by letter. His advice was short and exact. "Follow the rules."

The rejection of her report from the field received the same rejection of reports from the Gulf War.

"What happened, Sis?"

Heidi paused, then smiled. "I guess I got on the wrong side of the General," she said, almost laughing. "Can you believe it, a lowly nurse causing Cheney-Stokes palpitations in a high and mighty General?"

"What did you do to have such an effect on a General? Talk back?"

"No, worse than that, I wrote a letter. It failed to get even a first endorsement. Then I resubmitted my letter as one directed to world agencies. The letter went as far as the company commander. No one would print my letter, so I constructed a new copy promptly." Xander asked Heidi to show him her article. She found it soon enough in a box of her papers she had transferred into the laboratory.

Vlieger was still out of sorts but much calmer.

"I ran across a report in an Israeli medical journal. This report pointed out that service personnel were required to take an untested and unapproved drug under threat of court martial. I suspect that the mentioned drug was delivering metabolic mischief. I know some 7,000 service people had died by the time I saw the medical report. This was after a three day war with less than 200 casualties. The medicine we gave troops was pyridostigmine, a synthetic version of physostigmine."

Xander had started to ask, "What is that?" as she continued. "Physostigmine was isolated from the calibar bean by British scientists in 1844."

"Go on!"

"The botanical physostigmines were amended or synthesized," she said, pausing as if to catch her breath. "I got the researchers to call up documents that said the stuff was even more dangerous in connection with other vaccines. After taking the pill for 67 to 100 days, servicemen became ill. An estimated 100,000 will die. The rest of them expect to die with infections that medicine can't cure. This was swept under the rug, like Agent Orange in Vietnam. The only recognition of any substance surfaced in Senate hearings held in 1994."

Xander put Vlieger outside before he returned to Heidi and her decision to leave the service from what was a soldier's job.

"It's a nerve agent, worse than an overdose of fluoride given African children without nutritional support." She passed Xander her original typed article.

Xander read it out loud.

"Israeli scientists have revealed that a chemical ingested by Allied soldiers and airmen during the Gulf War in fact authored the unhappy consequences. The preparation dispensed as a tablet and ordered taken each day under penalty of court martial was a synthesized physostigmine called pyridostigmine. GIs who escaped the holocaust, it seems, were the ones who threw away the pyridostigmines that military experts figured would defend servicemen against chemical warfare."

Heidi came home to the U.S. with enough service time for a pension. Heidi and Jason lived in Banyon House while their place was being built. The little girls, Heather and Holly, had the run of the place, and Heidi had her foundation off and running within six months.

Over the last half dozen years, Heidi had assembled no less than 800 books and magazines on healthy nutrition and recovery from degenerative diseases. After the ex-military family moved out of Banyon Place, Jim paid a postponed visit to the doctor. When he came home late in the day, Nora knew something was wrong. She knew the American Legion wanted to honor him. He had always been stoic about his pain and Nora did not realize that the suffering had increased exponentially. For fully an hour there was barely a word between the two.

"Jim, there's a magazine that wants to do a story about the war and you."

Jim shook his head. "No."

Since he came home from the Springfield hospital all those years ago, Jim had endured recurring pain, especially in his left foot. Steel fragments started to work their way out of the body. Usually there was a drop or two of blood and then he would feel the expulsion of a small splinter of shrapnel with his fingertip. As recently as a month ago shrapnel had worked its way out of his neck. He did not mention it to anyone. After supper Jim took Nora by the hand.

"Look," he said, "The doctor says I'm full of cancer." Nora gave a gasp. She squeezed his hand as the tears formed in her eyes. "He said there is nothing they can do."

"What about cancer therapy?"

"He said it would only make me miserable. He recommended chemotherapy and radiation. Surgery is out of the question."

"James, we haven't had a second opinion."

"He suggested that, and gave me the name of an oncologist in Kansas City."

"We can do nothing? Well, I don't think we can accept that." Nora went with Jim in total desperation runs, first to Kansas City, then to the Mayo Clinic. The story did not change. Jim decided to do nothing, meaning no radiation, chemo, or surgery.

"We'll have to tell the children," Nora said.

"No," Jim said. "I'll tell them one at a time." He started planning things in writing.

"Take care of your mother, keep your promises, and mind your own business."

Heidi came up immediately from her retreat house when she heard the news. Xander caught up with Heidi just as she was about to comfort the family.

"I don't know much about human medicine," Xander told his sister. "But I do know you don't build immunity with cold hard drugs, only with nutrition and immune cells. In a herd of Herbataurus, you have essential fatty acids, trace elements, and live nutrients that impart and increase enzymes, that's the building of immunity."

For the next two months Jim prepared a special alert expected for September. He worked with statistics for Allen County, Kansas. The end of an old century and the start of a new one seemed appropriate for a report period. Jim assembled data for the crops: wheat, corn, soybeans, and milo. He noted the prices they brought at market and extended those data to prices they should have sold for at parity, assuming the farmer should be paid as much as a floor sweeper. The numbers were all computed by the United States Department of Agriculture. The difference was a shortage of income. In the year 2000 Allen County was short.

"That's not even figuring livestock and specialties," Jim told Jake. "There are over 3,000 counties. At least 2,500 of them are basically agricultural. It's a job. But one of you boys will have to figure each county." After Jacob left his father that afternoon, he said, "Good God, he doesn't pay a bit of attention to the fact that he's dying."

But Jim knew that he was dying. "Death comes to everyone," he told himself. He repeated it to Xander when he came in off the road two days later.

Nora said, "Xander, he won't take chemotherapy. He told the doctor to take his data and chemotherapy and stuff it."

"Good for him," Xander said.

"You're the chemist here," she reminded Xander. "Isn't there anything we can do?"

"Mother, we're not going to let Dad die from cancer. That's a given." The urgency in his voice brought Nora to attention.

"The oncologist gives him three to six months, maybe a year or more."

"The following is not proven, but it's got to work. There've been terminal cancer cures with nutrition at the Gerson Clinic in Mexico for years. So the first order of business is hope without any reservation."

"But the cancer wouldn't stop. What are you going to do?" Xander knew that cancer wasn't really definable, for which reason it was the most defined condition on earth. Was it caused by farm chemicals as warned by Rachel Carson? Probably not, since Jim had not allowed chemicals of organic synthesis on the place; first, because he could not afford them, second, because he found out that they were the alter ego of atomic radiation. Xander doubted that heredity had anything to do with it. And it probably was not malnutrition, that much misunderstood business of a mineral shortage or marked imbalance thereof. No, it was probably some of that wartime shrapnel that cysts could not contain. He would feed it out of his dad the way he had taught a few neighbors to feed Bangs out of a Banger before inspectors found it.

"First, we'll have to hydrate Dad with plenty of green tea and Jason Winters tea."

"Is that all?" asked Heidi, who was also present.

"No, no," Xander came back, "Get your pencil and a pad. We'll have to hit this with stuff not many practitioners even know about. We have some of these in inventory. The rest" he waved his hand at a row of supply catalogues, "Heidi, it'll be search and order."

Heidi sat at a small desk. Sunlight stabbed through the Venetian blind to fire her blond hair with a golden touch. As Xander started his recitation, he said to himself, "My God, Sis is a real beauty." She had been gone so much he had never really noticed.

"Let's go," she said, "Dad needs us now."

"First," said Xander, we need selenium, magnesium and iodine, you know the kind we'll need. N-acetyl cysteine, your NAC, OK?"

"Got it."

"Chlorophyllin."

"Got it."

In rapid succession came names and products she was quite familiar with: cilantro extract, calcium d-glucarate, cucurmin, indole-3-carbinol. Xander said, "Jot down milk thistle, chlorella, garlic extract, alpha lipoic acid." Heidi interrupted, "Boy, oh boy, this is more complicated than nurse's training."

Xander did not break pace, "Trimethyl glycine, astragalus extract." That was enough for an opener. Tomorrow he would recite a list of vitamins, minerals, enzymes, materials that would be essential or helpful for digestion, and goods to be eaten, and foods to be avoided, especially red meat. Pharmaceuticals did not figure too much in Xander's equation, herbal medicines did. He had picked up on many of these in Peru. He had studied alternative therapies in health, and he knew that most of what he proposed had been well researched, including the shocker he was about to unload on Heidi.

"What's next?" Heidi asked.

"I'm going to make Dad a smoothie. But it'll take a couple of months. Now listen," Xander repaired to the laboratory. He punched in the numbers on the phone. "Heidi, over here on the double, right now, please!" When Heidi arrived, he explained his objective.

"I need a 10 cc sample of Dad's blood right now. You're a nurse, he always gives in to your requests." Heidi picked out the appropriate syringe. She was back in a few minutes. Xander had a Herbataurus with two months of her gestation period waiting. He infused the tube into her udder. "When she freshens I will take the first four days milking and freeze it. That's eight or ten milkings. The colostrum has the immune factors, the enzymes. When that cow is with antigens, it's going to produce a whole array of immune factors. Antibodies are just one. Other factors provided are commander molecules known as antitoxins. These are also known as transfer factors. When the patient consumes the smoothie, that Herbataurus's immune system creates antibodies and antigens in the blood. Immunity is infused into the blood by transfer factors. In effect they augment the circulatory system of the patient. Coconut oil confers your triglycerides, microbial factors, and anti inflammatory factors, anti-fungal, antibacterial, readily absorbed and easily processed by the liver. The eggs have yolks making complete amino acids, fatty acids, and carotenes, emulsifiers. The eggs are an amazing food rich in fat soluble vitamins A, D, E, K, cysteine, and other amino acids. Heidi, this stuff has been well researched. This is heavily documented as an insulin provider. Human beings are unique. The human body is able to correct malfunctioning genes 90% of the time, usually within twenty-four hours. Mice as test animals are able to do it only 13% of the time. This is nature's answer to cancer, the correction is the immune apparatus.

"Heidi, do you remember when Jake was collecting weeds and marking each with information on why it grows? Jake was thinking in terms of fertility. Now I look at them for their DNA blueprint. What do they accumulate, and why?" Xander's older sister literally glowed when infected with her brother's enthusiasm.

"What is that?" she asked.

"That's Japanese Knap weed or bindweed. Heidi, there's magic in the roots of that plant. It contains a substance that protects the plant from insects and disease. That's the short version."

"Does it have use for human beings?"

"Listen." The long version followed. "It blocks the progression of estrogen related cancers. It inhibits metastasis and spreading of cancer to organs. It maintains normal estrogen activity. It kills cancer in all three phases: initiation, promotion, progression. It is effective against the analoid beta protein, which causes Alzheimer's Disease. It increases nitrogen oxide to relieve the blood vessels. It cancels out abnormal blood clots and blockages. It inhibits COX-2 inflammatory enzymes. You've heard of COX-2 Inhibitors, Celebrex? Well, one of the best COX-2 inhibitors is in grapes and in ginger."

"I think I see what you're getting at. You see pharmacology in weeds. I remember Daddy telling us about the tumbleweed in the dust bowl."

"Heidi, I think half the weeds have medicinal qualities. When you match up medicinal qualities with the known propensity of the human body to repair itself, there's your answer to cancer. Unless the American Medical Association comes down on me, I'll have Dad setting up electric fencing within six months, and not a funeral."

The next morning, the oncologist was on the line, "You better get in here and start chemotherapy," the second opinion oncologist stated. "No, thank you," Jim Neff said.

"You're not being reasonable," the doctor responded like a shot.

"Look, I know about your bag of tricks. I'm not buying. I know what your historical data are." The oncologist on the other end of the line hung up. He was about to say "stage 4."

With life and death hanging in the balance, Heidi and her mother were troubled. Suppose Xander was wrong? But how could he be wrong when the only alternative was certain death? Xander hit the books at Banyon House. Follow the research, Xander kept saying to himself. Research told him to put his Dad on large dosages of live foods with live enzymes: organic carrots, wheat grass in the smoothie, AEI-10 (hyper-immune colostrum extract), N-acetyl cysteine, low-dose Naltrexone, DHEA 25 mgs, resveratrol 20 mgs, melatonin, antioxidants A, E, D, and C, cod liver oil, pro-boost thymic hormone, co-enzyme Q-10, selenium and zinc, and antimicrobials, iodine (Lugol's solution), Lacto-Ferrin 300 mgs, cilantro extract and Maitake mushroom extract.

Nora replaced coffee with green tea. Xander ordered up organic vegetables, especially brassica, kale, brussel sprouts, broccoli, asparagus, garlic and onions, carrots, beets, arugula, mustard greens, endive, dandelion, radish and celery. He included any sprouted grain products, and began sprouting mung beans himself. He started to provide more fresh fruits such as blueberries, strawberries, cherries, and tropical fruits but only certified organic to avoid the toxic, cancer-causing preservatives and pesticides. Totally forbidden was sugar, which feeds the cancer cells and destroys the immune system, and all vegetable oils except olive oil, all processed foods, and all processed dairy foods and meat.

Heidi knocked on Xander's door. His wife, Amy, answered. "We better not take a day off," Heidi said. Xander knew what that meant. He had seen Dad the night before. He was slipping away. He was dying of cahexia, wasting disease. The cancer lives on glucose. The cell takes glucose via insulin. Cancer cells have up to fifteen more receptor sites on the cell than healthy cells. Greedy for glucose, they starve the body cells, ergo the patient. When the smoothie was ready, Xander handed it to Heidi. "Get him to take it," he said. "If he says no to his little girl, it'll be the first time."

Two months into the deathwatch, Jim was sleeping in the living room and spending most of his time in the reclining chair. One after another the smoothies went down, and Jim got up out of his bed. The funereal pallor left his face. Heidi consulted with Xander. "You'd better infuse another Herbataurus," she said, "or you'll run out of colostrum." Jim no longer felt like dying. His natural processes rose above the basics of survival. A new breed was assaulting the ground defenses of those who had the provider of food and fiber in thrall.

As Jim gained back a measure of his strength, he pondered the demise of something bigger than himself, the American family farm. The United States Department of Agriculture ordered up death with its policies and subsidies that prescribed non production. The few who produced the political crops, corn, wheat, soybeans, cotton, grain sorghum, and those who withheld land from production so others could produce corn, wheat, soybeans, cotton, and grain sorghum could produce the amount required for State Department use. The family farmers were being destroyed in the name of progress.

Now that something taken from a cow's immune system was doing something wonderful in his body, Heidi noticed that her Dad was wonderfully alive. He was weak, but his mind could write volumes, and he wanted to get it done. Two nurses were really more than a man could hope for, Jim told himself.

Nora saw to it that he had his resveratrol, the extract from the grape skin. The specialists at the University of Chicago were on record claiming this extract was one of the most powerful cardiovascular agents in existence. Xander did not know it, but the French have fewer problems with their hearts as a result. You can not get their cholesterol levels in record volumes, of course. Nora followed Xander's instructions to the letter. Some were out of his laboratory.

"Don't worry, Mom. It's well researched and extremely effective in managing cancers, people who have terminal cancers. Mom, it's profound."

"How much of this do oncologists use?" Heidi wanted to know.

"They don't use any of it," Xander said.

"None of it?"

"None, even though the research comes out of their own peer reviewed journals. You'd think they'd have respect for Johns Hopkins, Sloan Kettering, places like that."

Heidi appreciated what her brother was saying. He had agreed to redo his master's thesis, but he had never gone back. He left the Centers for Disease Control to be a Herbataurus breeder for mostly the same reason, but he had never put his mind on hold. He knew that several hundred million dollars had gone into researching cancer, the only real result being the maintaining of the status quo. There was an alternative arm to research on the leading edge, most of which was ignored, as it takes years, sometimes decades, of research before it is recognized and approved. The reason was simple. More people were making a living out of cancer than were dying from it. Nora and Heidi brewed a quart of green tea for Jim's daily intake.

"A very powerful liver detoxifier," Xander explained.

To drink eight drops in fruit juice buffered the nasty taste, but Jim agreed because after half a dozen smoothies he had complete faith in Xander's alchemy. "DHEA is the preeminent hormone of all the hormones that real research has validated," Xander said. "Its role in the adrenal glands, well you can't make any cells without DHEA." Xander prescribed fifty milligrams per day. Heidi wanted to know why this information was not available to the public for the immune system and all health problems.

"Sis, you can't annihilate a cash cow, a billion dollar cash cow." The supply of colostrum lasted for several months. When Heidi reported a faltering inventory, Xander selected a gestating cow and started all over, 10 cc of patient blood infused into the udder exactly the way he did it before making the natural smoothies which did what raw milk had to do. Between reading the results of Xander's research, the patient took to reminiscing. He remembered the bums who scratched their initials on a corner of Banyon House, designating the place as a good place for food. Dummy Ortman's quarters in the back had been turned back into a tack room so that the grandchildren could have their ponies.

"Banyon Place, super rich? But they've never met my accountant," Jim revealed. "I have a bit of parity to build a herd without debt." A neighbor came by. "I don't understand this parity business you talk about."

"How much was the postage stamp in 1946?" Jim asked.

"Four cents?"

"How much is it now?"

"Really, I don't know, I only fax or e-mail my copy, what? 38 cents?"

"If farm prices had increased on par with the postage stamp, the red meat on the ranch would be worth nearly $4 a pound. Anything short of that, the farmer gets short pay or consumes his capital, or goes into bankruptcy. Any questions?"

He went on, "The costs vary, a nitrogen tank, a truck, fencing, a posthole digger, but most of all the interest that holds the farmer in thrall." As the months sped by, the terminal patient seemed less terminal. The oxygen tank ceased being used. Two years to the day after the patient received his death sentence, those dreary hours were all but forgotten. Looking back, Heidi believed that one of those shrapnel shards, microscopic in size, had finally inserted itself into the long division process of the cell like a chemical intervention and caused the cell to go into wild proliferation on the hunt for its sustaining glucose.

Maybe that's the way it is with tiny splinters from a grenade assault on the human body. The doctor said Jim was losing control. Chemo would merely have tormented him the rest of his life. Jim's family did not want to subscribe to it at all. Heidi, Jake and Xander brought their children to see Grandpa as often as possible, and each visit seemed to make Xander's smoothies more palatable. All the Neff and Layton children were home schooled at Banyon Place during the early grades.

"Most of the time their schooling was a riot," Grandpa Jim once recalled. Jim did not hesitate explaining his take on life. Even the children seemed to understand that most farmers were merely interest paying patsies, conduits between the government and the banks for deficiency payments. They could not be organized because they thought only in terms of production. "Very well," he said, to all who would listen. "Then let's make them producers of quality." The Herbataurus producer wasn't after the Wal-Mart customer. Their kind of quality was boutique quality, attractive to five-star chefs and health food stores, and holistic health centers. Small processors, one for every six or eight counties would spring up in time."

He scribbled ideas on his note tablet during the long days he waited for the boys to come by. He told the older grandchildren the Crazy Ivan story. He told it the way Grandpa Xander said it happened when he was eleven years old. He explained it all to the children who were nearing adolescence. There were hundreds of acres, but only the few that accounted for 82% of the harvested 575 acres need apply. What it meant to farmers was subsidies. They were held to a unit price level by a market based on unregulated free trade. The Smoot-Hawley Tariff was still the law of the land, but it was ignored. World trade was eroding prices to the level of third world producers. Cheap world prices, in fact, subsidize these commodity fields and deliver substandard fare to the consumer.

Heidi called, Nora listened, even the talkative children listened. "Well, by God, we're going to collect parity for our production. Get the picture?" The picture was so clear it might as well have been painted on the broad side of a barn in the colors of Van Gogh. "Why don't they make the American price the world price?" Earnings at the raw materials level would erase these buildups of debt, inflation, and poverty.

"They tell us that when public and private debt gets too heavy it has to be repudiated. If they repudiate debt there will be so much surplus you won't know what to do with it. You'll have repossessions terrorizing the nation. You'll see production in complete chaos! Worse than the 1930s. Why not make the American parity the world price?"

"I can't buy into this Rhodes Scholarship crap. Send out help via competent people to upgrade the world's agriculture! There's a fellow in California who wrote a book called *The End of Agriculture in the American Portfolio*. He wants to import food and use the land for better purposes, probably suburban sprawl!"

Heidi was learning things never brought up at army conferences. "Back in World War II when I was getting cut up by razor grass, the professor Phineas priest found that 40% of the profits of New York bankers came from international transfers of credits and money. They made their profit on international trade. Did you ever wonder why, if they wanted a one world economy, they didn't create a world currency based on raw materials?"

As the second year of the fatal diagnosis came and went, it became apparent that the end was a long way off. The oncologist found no sign of cancer. "I don't want to know what you're doing," he told Nora and Heidi after they brought Jim in for a visit. "Just keep it up."

"It isn't a problem," Nora said, "I can tell you." The doctor remained silent. He really didn't want to know, and yet he did. Nora broke the silence. "I'll tell you." She affected a big pause and a stance to fit the issue. Her eyes had a sparkle and her voice was infused with dignity, awe, and reverence. "Prayer," she whispered.

Some Capper-Volstead cronies came by and stayed past the official visiting hours. Billy Jon Poole was dead. "I think he ate too much. He ran into a telephone pole and totaled his car. Deader than a door nail," was the fragment of a sentence the visitor left as an epitaph.

On the day that Nora insisted they return to the oncologist for a blood test, her James said, "I don't feel any worse than I did ten years ago." A book came by mail. It was Homer Smythe's historical study of farm philosophy entitled *Old Men Dream Dreams, Young Men See Visions*. The inscription read "To the best damn soldier I ever knew, on or off the battlefield."

News clippings were enclosed telling about Capper-Volstead Alliance moving to a storefront in Sioux City, Iowa. The organization was still operating in a few states. As Jim thumbed through the book his mind took him back to the old farm in Ness County not far from Grandpa Xander's place.

"My Dad figured he was a failure, but not because he lost the farm," he told Nora. "He knew what caused wheat to dip from $4.00 a bushel to 17 cents a bushel. That wasn't it. I think he came to realize what a terrible thing they did when they plowed up the steppe." Jim paused to see if Nora wanted to insert a comment. Her stare was his answer. "Dad figured himself a failure because he couldn't keep the family together. I don't think I saw my oldest brother J. Samuel a half dozen times in my life. Royal, not since before the war. Imagine that, a brother who forgets other relations and then becomes a German citizen. Nora, I have two deceased sisters, both nuns I've not seen as long as I can remember." Nora started to say, "Well, James, we have our family," but she left the words unspoken. Her James did not often read these days and he was thirsty for words. She said, "I guess I'm the luckiest person alive."

Jim nodded and smiled. The look on his face said more than a thousand words.

"James, do you realize what you have done? You built a farm when most people were going broke. You've held our family together, helped them understand the earth's rapport, helped them feel responsible, 'their brother's keepers,' when many kids are rebels without a cause.

We're solvent, out of debt, and I do believe you've conquered cancer. Do I thank St. Jude, or Jesus, Mary and Joseph?"

"All the above," he said.

36

The barefoot boy of the dust bowl who had soldiered and then turned cowman retired when he reached the age of 82, only to become a political activist. "How did we get here?" he asked himself and the other old timers who came by for a little socializing and perhaps a free night's lodging in the carriage house above the laboratory.

The politicians talk freedom and the people vote for pure and high ideals, but the public policy of closing down farms continues administration after administration, and bureaucrats subtract freedoms as if the invasion of a fungus was taking over.

He remembered that long ago *sotto voce* utterance by his mother, something about "a beast of muddy brain." Later on he had stumbled across its source, a poem by Tommaso Campanella he had found in a well-thumbed volume of Will Durant. Were the people really "a beast of muddy brain," and therefore destined to "stand loaded with wood and stone?" He pondered how they vote and vote, and each administration carries on as before "because they have the guns."

Or was there a Darwinian demon that governs the affairs of men? Phineas priest saw that myth as a metaphor for those who discovered the miracle of compound interest and the creation of money out of thin air. They ruled, the nabobs of privilege, and they recruited lesser men and women to manage people, those beasts of muddy brain who count cadence when told to march, who ask "how high?" when told to jump.

Jake walked in one day with a bulletin. Starting almost immediately, all farms were to register with the government and supply global positioning coordinates for the land, its buildings, and its landmarks. Hardly a week later both Xander and Jake came to their dad.

Xander led off. "They have a computer chip the size of a grain of rice that is to be implanted under the skin with a code number so they can create a national registry down to the pound of what red meat there is.

They want us to put that computer chip in all animals: birds, ponies, dogs, everything."

"It's supposed to be a health measure," Jake added.

Jim thought this over. "But there hasn't been an epizootic since the hoof-and-mouth outbreak of the twenties, except a little Bangs trouble in the 1950s and only sporadically after that."

The news literally pulled Jim Neff out of retirement. The President bragged about democracy and pushed it down the gullets of the Iraqi people, but at home individual privacy was slithering away a foot at a time. Jim wanted to get out news releases and go on the talk shows, but what good would it do? The bureaucrats were God Almighty! They no longer even telegraphed their moves. They simply dropped them like the proverbial shoe. A few days later, another bomb came screaming to the scene. The Food and Drug Administration had given its blessing for the use of the rice sized computer chip on human beings. "A health measure, of course," Jim said to himself. While he was analyzing this modern Mark of the Beast as foretold in Revelation, Jake returned for a second conference in less than a week. "Pop, we have a bigger problem than ID chips," Jake said. He handed his dad an official looking piece of paper. Jim read it over. In stilted legalese it told Banyon Place that four of its animals sent to slaughter in a federally inspected facility were Bangers, Bangs being the common name for brucellosis, or infectious *brucella abortus* to academia. "That can't be," Jim said. "We've never had a Banger on this place since I started ranching. Your great granddad Xander Staab never had one either. What happened?" Jim asked Jake.

"I started to send our culls to Clean Beef, as usual, but they were overloaded, so we had to go to Up To Date in Missouri. They're federally inspected. It's as close as we can get to getting grade and yield, but a little further to go, of course. Dad, I always get the top of the market." Jim was not interrogating Jake. Both knew the procedure. Each sale was covered by a ticket that recorded each animal's tattoo numbers, one in the left ear, one in the right. Tattoos were made as soon as possible after birth. Banyon Place used a consecutive calf number in the right ear and the year of birth in the left. Records were kept on an annual basis, including pasture rotations, the identification of the attendant sire, and the breeding group commingled. Jim had constructed the record system shortly after he had been discharged from World War II.

The computerized record enabled him to follow the individual animal through its life cycle. It told what cow an individual animal was with, what bull presided, and what calf was delivered. Jim could look back over fifty years and construct an individual animal's biography. The practice was to write the tattoo number next to the traffic tag provided as the animals were unloaded.

For several decades Jim had sent breeding sires and dams into most of the states and Mexico, all of them Bangs tested, and never a reactor from this closed herd.

The mailed notice was followed by a phone call. The anonymous voice said that a veterinarian would arrive to bleed the herd. It would take three bleedings to get the quarantine lifted.

Jim was military firm as he spoke to the bearer of bad news. "You have no right to quarantine us. We have a closed herd, never an abortion on the place." He demanded that the vet come down and start bleeding the cows immediately, none of this next week business.

The vet duly arrived. Jim asked him to describe a Banger cow. The man of science told how a cow could lose a calf and drag placenta all over the pasture.

"OK," said Jim. "Let me show you our records." Jim then pulled up the records of the cows in question. All were old cows, all earmarked for slaughter under Banyon policy. Not one had ever been vaccinated before it became mandatory. The production records were outstanding. All except one of the so called reactors were sixteen years old. All had weaned a 14th calf. None had ever aborted or lost a calf. All had raised their 14th calf. "Do these look like Bangers to you?" Jim asked. The bureaucrat vet scratched his head and started to shuffle his feet. Jim pushed hard. He closed the space between himself and the vet.

"You have a flimsy case. Your quarantine is tantamount to putting this operation out of business for the year. I can't buy into the proposition that sixteen-year-old cows with calves to their credit, each of them having raised their calves, are Bangers." Jim added a codicil. "I'm not taking this. I will sue your pants off."

"You can't sue a federal or state employee."

Jim bristled. "I have a very smart attorney. He'll find a way to sue you personally. So you might as well figure out what you're going to do after you leave the service."

"Let's not get hasty," the vet said. He put the bleeding on hold. That record troubled him. He admitted to himself that there was something wrong here. He knew Jim Neff's reputation and he also knew that both of the boys were straight shooters.

"Look, Mr. Neff. I'm going to do some checking. I need to talk to my bosses. So we'll put everything on hold, OK?"

The veterinarian never returned. He called to say that the quarantine was being released.

"That's fine," Jim said. "I'll have to have that in writing."

"That's not our policy," came the response.

"It is now," said Jim Neff.

"Well, I'll look into it," was the restrained admission. "Look hard," Jim said, his voice friendly yet firm. He hung up the phone and turned to Xander and Jake. Both had been listening to that particular phone call. "Boys, you have to stand your ground."

As Jim returned to the issue of a mandatory computerized chip identification, he admitted to himself that there really was no way to be firm when a government unloaded oppressive measures. First of all, the national animal identification system was a fraud. The only reason for such a concentration camp ID system was to hand off to the likes of Tyson and Iowa Beef an inventory to the pound of all the beef on pasture and in the pens, so the commodity speculators could further rig the markets and so government could have the "correct number" of farmers to be put out of business this year. Each time a fast food victim takes an ambulance ride after eating an *E. coli* hamburger, it will be possible to trace the burger back to the primary producer for delivery of blame.

Jim encountered the veterinarian again at an Extension meeting. Here he was addressed as Dr. Grant Rudd, now Chief State Veterinarian. He took Jim aside during a break in the evening presentation.

"Mr. Neff, thanks for refusing to accept our finding."

"Not a problem," Jim said.

"I don't want this to go much further, agreed?"

"I'm listening, but if you tell me, the information becomes my property. I'll decide."

"That's OK with me. Jim, we had a little trouble at that facility. One of the inspectors was catching blood in a dipper and filling the test tubes. We had a lot of Bangs cases from the run that day, that's how we put it together."

"Can I have the name of the culprit?" Jim asked.

"I'm afraid that's against the rules."

"Is he still employed there?"

"I can't answer that. All I can say is that all of those so called reactors that day were clean as a whistle."

Jim thanked the veterinary doctor. He assured him that he would not condemn the service because of the incident. To himself, Jim admitted that he had lost most of his confidence in government programs, and he had even less in the animal marking system as a health issue. National identification and a Dark Ages approach seem to go together, he mused. They claim high science, but the eradication approach is more of a Dark Ages device. Jake asked his dad, "Why isn't our own ID system good enough?"

"Money," said Jim. "It's a multi-million dollar expense that the cattlemen will have to pay. I'm sorry to tell you that it probably can't be stopped. If we had a Capper-Volstead Alliance, maybe. Disease control is the spin." There was a feeling of impotency afloat. The people said to be "a beast of muddy brain" were merely pawns in the hands of the Darwinian demon and its even muddier brain. All were required to express fealty to that demon, that demon of a government! And the last of the farmers' valued freedoms were going down the drain.

The long code tells most of what there is to know about the rancher's private affairs. Applied to human beings, the code starts with blood type and ends with the Biblical Mark.

To a radio audience, Jim Neff explained that even the Black Death was not infectious to everyone. Debilitated, undernourished animals, animals fed according to the science of the universities invite transmission. Animals with a healthy body ecology can walk into a pen of mad cows with no chance at all of contracting disease, which in any case has no settled etiology. Infectious *brucellosis abortus* denotes a shortage, or a marked imbalance, of magnesium, manganese, cobalt, copper, zinc and iodine.

Jim contacted the many cowmen he knew. He met with the apathy of a stunned ox.

"Nora," he said to his wife, as she folded her dish towel.

"Yes, James."

"I think we've seen it all. Since Capper-Volstead folded, we've seen tractor drives to Washington. We've seen co-ops come and go. We've heard talking heads this and that. But the one thing that won't fail is the quality clean food movement. You know why?"

"Why?" was her echo.

"The Darwinian demon can't digest clean, wholesome food. It's really a vulture of sorts."

It was twilight as they talked. Nora tried to excuse herself.

"We need to get some supper going."

"Let's put a hold on it for a bit," James said. He did not want to make a speech to Nora, but his thoughts were churning his stomach. In over fifty years he had raised his sights above the mundane albeit exciting business of seed stock production. He remembered the colonel at Oink Smith's restaurant in St. Joseph. "You have about twelve or thirteen years to put your act together if you're going to stop the country from sliding into oppression," the soldier had said. The years had come and gone. It was like gangrene creeping up on you, this nibbling away at small and large freedoms.

"Democracy," he told Nora. "We vote on the lesser of two evils. A club of millionaires and a House of talking heads vote enabling laws, and half the losers in society get jobs lording it over the rest."

Nora had seldom heard such cynicism from the mouth of her James.

"But we have Banyon Place," she reminded.

"For now," he went on. "But I see a debilitating wasting away of personal freedoms, economic freedom. Nora, we fought the good fight thirty years ago. Then we went back to tending our own gardens. So now we're being told to line up like sheep and take a concentration camp number on a computer chip electronically read by faceless bureaucrats."

"James, I don't know what to say except that the demon dies while we live on through our sons and daughters."

"True, but will they see the soft fascism and the hard lies?"

"Enough of them will."

"I did not think there was such a thing as a Darwinian demon," James said. "Then Phineas priest convinced me there was. It's the financial structure that robs the farmer, pretends security, invents weapons of mass destruction."

"But there were no such weapons," Nora interjected.

"Oh, yes. There was one. Iraq wanted to go off the dollar and onto the Euro. Now Iran wants to do the same thing. So here comes another weapon of mass destruction, and a terrorist under every rock. At every turn the farmer gets squeezed. The next thing we'll hear is how all land has to move into monopoly hands so we can create bio fuel from cheap corn. Nora, what do we tell our boys to do?"

Nora took a moment to respond. She smiled.

"James, we tell them to outlast the absconders. When the rich get too rich, they are engulfed by a human tsunami. They couldn't stand that. They may even have to learn how to feed themselves. That's what I propose to do right now, feed us both."

37

As Jim Neff moved toward his eighty-third year, he became acutely aware of the fact that his grandchildren were adults. He measured this against the norm he had been taught as a child and by a culture that measured maturity at the age of reason. His mother said that this was age seven, no ifs, ands, or buts. When Heidi's twin daughters, Holly and Heather, asked Grandpa whether they could cite one of his diary pages for a class assignment, thoughts came back of Big Chief pulp tablets full of his neat cursive. They were all in box files in the library, and the girls became curious. They had turned up an entry dated April 14, 1935 Black Sunday.

"Grandpa, how old were you on Black Sunday?" The girls spoke almost in unison.

"I would have been just turned twelve."

It was easy to answer children. Jim did not like to talk about the war, and did not like to be reminded of the dust storms either. But when grandchildren asked, that was something else. He examined that yellowed diary page. The date was clear enough.

April 14, 1935 Just came home from church. Beautiful weather. No wind. Mom is calling. I'll write later. The rest of the page was blank.

"Grandpa, we're supposed to write an undocumented report for English class." The two girls talked over each other, and Jim listened. My, these were beautiful children, he said to himself. The spitting image of their mother, and Nora. They would be graduating from high school before he knew it. To stonewall these kids would be a slap in the face for both Heidi and Nora. "OK, I'll tell you what I would have written if I had taken the time," the children's granddad said. "When Mom called that Sunday just before Easter, a black cloud from as far as the eye could see had risen in the north. Dust storms there had been aplenty, two to four a week during the early part of the year, and now a new phenomenon arose to hunt and hurt. Static electricity had already stopped the 1928 Dodge hardly 100 yards from home. Dad harnessed the two work horses to bring the car in, and was attaching a drag chain to a rear spring so that the problem wouldn't happen again. He saw the cloud and alerted Mom, and Mom called for me. The cows had to be sheltered in the same barn as the horses. Chickens were invited into their stone house, and the wind came on."

"There had never been a duster from the north. Usually the scouring winds trailed the jet stream, finally sweeping north through the Texas and Oklahoma panhandles . . . " He paused to remember. "usually" had come to an end as the dust bowl grip on the High Country tightened and squeezed. Now the dusters arrived around the clock and calendar, summer, fall and winter. The death squeal of jackrabbits was amplified by the shooting of cattle and horses, for there was no food. "It was so thick you couldn't breathe," the girls were told. "We hunkered down, swallowed muddy water, re-wet the washcloths over our faces, and your grandmother prayed, not for the storm to stop, but for all the babies dying of dust pneumonia."

He paused as if in a trance. What he was telling the girls was a composite of the dozens of black blizzards the family had lived through for the last four years. It was the newsmen who gave April 14, 1935 its sobriquet, Black Sunday.

More cows died on that day than ever before, and on the day after. He had helped Grandpa Xander perform necropsy examinations on four prize dams he had lost that day. Their stomach chambers were packed with mud. Their lungs were sacs of damp soil. The whole herd seemed debilitated. Animals in the open did not fare that well.

Jim went on as the girls took notes. "On Black Sunday, the roads . . ." He stopped. He did not want to tell the girls about an aunt who had suffocated like a mud-clogged cow, or the funeral that followed with still another storm threatening. But he stayed on to make a point.

"There are events," he said, "that change history and civilization. One was the war. But before that there were the dust storms. Black Sunday enlarged the dust bowl to 200 miles wide, Texas to Canada, and looped in the rest of the country. They got their taste of dust in Washington, and so they voted to help the farmers." He stopped. The girls were too young to understand that too many farmers were simply ushered off the land. It was that terrible calm before the storm that haunted Jim even more than the ordeal on Biak and Jolo Islands. There was such a calm right now. Even while young men were being sent to foreign battlegrounds, the nation was as calm as institutionalized poverty could make it. No one was hungry even though many were starving. But civilization would change just as surely as a big paddock gate swings on a small steel pin.

Jim's concern with cattle genetics was morphing itself into a similar concern for people. He was troubled by the national stem cell debate, and young Xander, in from a trip to Brazil and Argentina, provided him with what he called Genetics 101 dialogue.

"Dad, you can't deny the potential. We may be able to grow an organ the way a salamander regrows a missing limb."

"But this Dolly the sheep thing." Jim started to say. "Isn't that a bit like having an underclass for the purpose of harvesting organs and limbs?" Heidi, then Nora, joined the conversation quite by accident. They were passing through the library of Banyan Place in order to refine arrangements for an upcoming seminar.

"May I join in?" asked Heidi. She was a mature beauty, a daughter mother look alike, and the invitation to Heidi was equally an invitation for what had become a family ruckus. Jim mocked formality. "Resolved," he intoned, "that stem cell research and cloning are being designed to put the herd bull out of business."

"That's an angle," Xander said. "Let's go back to Dolly the sheep."

"Yes, Dolly the sheep," Nora added. "You'd think that blessed event was like the second coming of Christ."

"Well," joked Xander, "to settled science it was."

"Settled, my eye!" Heidi and Nora agreed in unison, the unison befitting identical twins.

Xander asked for the calm that a fresh cup of green tea could bestow, and Heidi was on her feet in an instant to comply. When she returned with the tea, Xander was well into the promised 101 course.

"It all started even before I worked at Centers for Disease Control. The word is 'genetic engineering.' I don't care whether we're talking about plants or animals or microorganisms or human beings, alien genetic constructs are put into the seed or the developing embryo. The problem is, we really don't know what happens in this genetic roulette.

It may get into the germ line so that these traits are inherited. Are you still with me?"

The nods and sounds were affirmation enough.

Xander continued, "When it comes to crops, a good example is using the cauliflower mosaic virus to infect the plant embryo. That virus carries the genetic construct that the designer thinks they want in that plant. That virus carries the construct to every cell in the plant's body. If the genetic construct is a toxin to ward off an insect, the herbicide is retained in the plant."

"And we eat the plants!" It was Heidi, not with a question, but with a statement of fact.

"Yes, yes, indeed. We, or the animals, eat it, and it is released to damage intestinal bacteria, etcetera, etcetera."

"And we deal with all this by creating hundreds of names for new diseases," Nora supplied.

"Yes," Xander said, "for cats, dogs, horses, cattle, and humans." Jim remained silent for a time, for here was a point that asked for an explanation. "Is there anything to govern how much of this strange genetic stuff the plant expresses?"

"No, not really," Xander said. "Dad, they're finding so much expression that genetic foods are causing kids to climb the walls in classrooms. That's a fact. The worst case scenario involves sheep dying, cattle debilitated, and reproduction canceled out for hogs and man and woman. So, what does FDA say? They say that these GMO foods are substantially equivalent to Nature's foods."

"They're really not safe?" Jim suggested.

"No, but you can eat them and still make it to the door for quite some time." Xander did not sound impatient, but he really wanted to return to Dolly the sheep and the presumed future, or lack thereof, with reference to Banyan Place and the Herbataurus breed.

Heidi did not want to talk over others, but when she saw an opening, she stepped right in. Her interjection gave Xander, Dad and Mom time to sip more now cooling green tea. Outside, the roar of trucks punctured the calm, and the voice of Jake rose above the engines' revving.

"Roll 'em!" was all he shouted. Banyan Place was no armchair operation. Hired hands moved cattle into and out of paddocks, and the laboratory measured and computed the grass component in each grazing cell. Heidi held the floor, not because she failed to comprehend what Xander was saying, but because she wanted to refine grist for the seminar mill come Monday.

"GMOs are causing systemic damage, especially to the immune system, liver, spleen, stomach, you name it! Fact is, we can't handle foreign proteins."

"What you're saying," Jim interrupted, "is that Nature is kicking us in the butt the way it did when USDA told farmers that soil is indestructible. So they plowed up the High Plains prairies and created that dust bowl blunder."

"The blunders haven't stopped there, Dad," Xander said. "The bovine concentration camps are Petri dishes for some pretty exotic diseases, and I'm afraid they'll outlast most cattlemen."

"Will they outlast cow-calf breeders?" It was Jim speaking, and clearly he still had that dust bowl blunder in his mind.

"Well, Dad, let's look at test tube breeding cloning style, and then you answer your own question."

The question that needed answering was whether the dust bowl survivor had really survived to prevail, or whether Jim Neff's heirs would be cut down by bad science and big business. Right now, the feedlots were surviving, and delivering amply infected *E. coli* meat protein into the market. The country was full of cattle, but not cattlemen. Government programs had become a laughing stock, as had the Food and Drug Administration scams and grafts that had come and gone since Jim Neff had claimed his heritage, four dams and a prize bull. But the very wise men in the university now claimed that the bull will not be a factor in the brave new world of settled science. It bothered Jim, the reluctant patriarch. He knew that history turns on blunders, things like the High Plains blunder, or the extension of Wilson's War called World War II, or the apparent public policy of war, empire, and insolvency. Previously, the blunder machine had left Nature's design alone. But now, daring designers were rewriting the Gospel according to St. John.

"In the beginning was the gene,
And the gene was with God,
And the gene was God!"

The gene came first, but breeding with all 46 chromosomes from one parent was barking at the heels of the cowman. The suitcase wheat growers of the High Plains were merely greedy men who left on the day the storms came. The wristwatch cave dwellers in city apartments lasted hardly at all as that blunder reshaped agriculture. But now, men in lab coats pretended to be geneticists, and they exhibited apparent success. The trees that Jim had planted on both sides of the quarter mile run from the county road to Banyan Place were mature long before the century had turned, but beyond them the soldier cowman saw a cloud as dark as the pall on Black Sunday. "The blunders called CAFOs are expanding," Jim mused half to himself. He thought of the grandchildren and their ponies, of their cherished rural life, and, as the images danced across his mind, again he saw that single sheep, a harbinger of what?

"Dad," Xander said, as if to read the old cowman's mind, "cloning is to replace the herd bull. They hope ultimately to replace sexual reproduction the way our forbears hoped to replace High Plains grass, and" he added as an afterthought, "the way feedlots expect a herbivore to become a ruminant swine."

"Are they talking science fiction?" Jim Neff seemed a bit irritated. Heidi and Nora excused themselves. "Piano lessons for the twins," Heidi said. "There's more tea in the pot. We'll be back in an hour." It would take Xander at least that long to detail his assessment of the situation. Funny thing, the old cowman already knew the answers, but he felt more comfortable whenever he could corner Xander long enough to get maximum confirmation.

"The dream is, if you have a super cow or a super racehorse, to have a whole herd or flock like that. All they have to do is take a cell, not even a stem cell, from any part of that animal and put it into an empty egg of another female of the same species. This calls for lots of eggs being harvested. In Dolly's case, it was from a sheep's ear. They use electrical fusion to activate that cell in an empty egg to start the cell's multiplication in a Petrie dish. The idea is to put lots of cells into the wombs of many surrogate mothers, hoping one or two will take. At term, Dolly the sheep! Right now, only a few cells take. If this gets rolling, big capital hopes to birth and feed out all the red meat animals" Xander did not finish. Jim closed out the sentence with, "And the consumer gets the full load GMOs, subtle toxins, and all the rest. You know it won't stop there."

"Oh no," Xander came back. "If you have Parkinson's and you had the foresight to save umbilical cells when you were born, the stem cell engineers hope to grow a new you, so to speak, especially what's ailing you. It takes a real match to do that. So if this guy surrenders an uncommitted cell, and some donor hands over a few eggs, then fertilization in a dish might create a synthetic pregnancy in that dish. It can't live there, of course, so it's transferred to a uterus. At some point before term, they harvest the fetus or a part thereof and have a perfect match. Presto, a cure! No, Dad, they're not kidding."

Jim did not want to ask the next question, "Can this succeed?" He was not a Luddite, and he knew that the world changed. His family would always end up on their feet, he knew that. But this attempt to clone or even install parthenogenesis in a cow herd, he shook his head and let out a long, low whistle.

"I don't know how it happened," Jim told Xander and also Jake, who had entered the old library with a fresh cup of coffee in tow, "but the Irish came to have a sexless potato in about 1845 to 1850. It worked like a champ until one day the spuds fell apart. They rotted overnight. The people starved by the thousands, even millions. Nature just plain revolted. I don't know of any complex life that reproduces by parthenogenesis. It's Nature's own cloning tactic for aphids, yes. Sheep and cattle, no. Boys, I think this college smart stuff will backfire. Heidi thinks it's already backfiring in terms of the general health profile. Telling sexual reproduction to go away is a bit like Xerxes beating the ocean with bull whips to enforce compliance with the wishes of a come lately designer. God, what a waste!" As the years of the twentieth century replaced each other, family jam sessions became Jim Neff's passion, almost his reason for being. He started preparing for get togethers between Jake, Xander, Heidi, and Nora. His rejection of cloning also became a passion, and his willingness to explain the difference between legitimate stem cell research and embryo stem cell research was just as passionate. Fellow ranchers did not listen very well. It was a characteristic of the Midwesterner to remain ignorant and indifferent, and this created the spawning ground for mendacious corruption and breathtaking blunders. Quality did not mean much to most people.

Jim took a pasture walk one June day, with no less than five grandchildren tagging along, neighbor children included. Usually he walked alone or with Nora. He dreamed dreams on those walks, and, like the prophet Joel, he saw visions. The children asked children's questions, and he enjoyed his role as elder statesman. He knew they all had to live their own lives, but his concern for their welfare never wavered. He had not worried about the future while cowering in the cellar during dust storms, but he worried about it now. Robber barons could steal money, and fools could make war, but damn fools were a class all their own.

The children asked, "Where does it come from? Where does it go?" They named calves, then forgot the names. They wanted Grandpa to see a bird's nest, a robin in the tree, a tadpole in the pond. Jim did not really worry about their nourishment. Nora had banished junk food from the place long before any of them were born. Now, Jim was showing the children dung beetles, and wondered anew about other people's children.

"Well, Dad," Heidi had invited, "come to our seminars." Jim had always been a good student, but never a good pupil. Before Heidi knew it, he was telling her classes that when Dolly the sheep was born, her cells as a clone were the same age as the donor's cell. Dolly died of a form of cancer related to a totally collapsed immune system. There had been an attempt to clone an endangered species. It was a success. The clone was born. It lived a few days before dying of overwhelming infections. It had no immune system.

He dreamed of whole herds of pigs and sheep, clones, all of them. The public prints told of animals cloned to be heart donors, blood donors, everything except sperm donors. Science or science fiction? "Neither," Jim the pupil told one class. "I call it genetic parasitism." He questioned their arrogance, their state of mind, their sanity, their religion. "Dad," Heidi cautioned her father, "I know you can entertain, but I do have an agenda." She smiled the smile to which he had never said "No." She did not have to say any more.

His dark mood started to evaporate a few days later when Caleb Watkins made one of his somewhat frequent calls. Caleb covered most of the United States now that his *Cowboy Arithmetic* newsletter had become a sprightly, well managed monthly that pulled no punches in reporting cow cult news.

361

He had a manager and the usual platoon of computer operators, proof readers, and ad salesmen. But he himself liked to report the cutting edge news, and James Robert Neff was on a roll about cloned herds. That meeting became his epiphany.

After the obligatory cup of green tea, pasture walk, and look at Xanthippus IV, Jim Neff poured out his soul. He recalled his mother's charge, "Keep your agreements, and stay out of other people's business." He did not say this to Caleb Watkins, but he thought it as a prelude to what he did say. "Nature has only two rules, balance and fecundity. Rob her of her balance, and she revolts." He had heard about it when palefaced Easterners turned their bonanza farms of the Red River Valley of the North into a bankrupt wasteland, into a raped landscape. He had seen it firsthand on the High Plains when half assed empire builders turned a grass wonderland into a dust bowl Hell.

Nature is not alone in demanding balance and production. The economics of a people demands the same, with balance including distribution of land and income to people so they can consume their own production. At Capper-Volstead, "without balance the nation would dismantle itself" were words that flowed like a clear spring, as Jim's stream of consciousness thinking became quotable language for the scribe.

"We've committed blunders before," Jim told the *Cowboy Arithmetic* founder, a younger man of now near fifty, as old as Jake, his old school chum. Tall, well tanned, as slim as Slim Pickens when he was slim, Caleb pulled out his tape recorder and "fired 'er up," as he put it.

"Cloning herds of cows for those bovine concentration camps," Jim went on, "makes my blood boil." He paused a moment. "You know what? We railed against it when bank loan money set up those feedlots, but we assured ourselves that crowded feeding would fail, so we set back and watched feedlots eat up cattlemen and deliver *E. coli* to the dinner table. We sat still, except for Capper-Volstead, while the money lenders ate up the farmers, millions of them, because it was more economical using Enron-style accounting. Caleb, you can recite the rest, chapter and verse. But did you ever think they would muck around with genetics, marrying different species to each other at the molecular level?" Then he spat out the word "cloning." "Now they want to take sex out of reproduction. Do you know what will happen?" Caleb Bingham had an idea, but he said, "Go ahead!"

"At some uncertain point in time, it'll be the Irish potato famine all over again."

That needed explanation, so Jim told the journalist about the sexless potato that had collapsed as a species, taking the Irish population with it. Jim was enjoying himself. "You have to laugh to keep from crying," he chuckled. Caleb Watkins knew what was coming. Over the years, James Robert Neff had literally memorized passages from a famous speech by a famous Kansas Senator, John J. Ingalls, an orator in the William Jennings Bryan mold. "What a man, a community, a nation can do, think, suffer, imagine, or achieve depends on what it eats. The primary form of food is grass. Grass feeds the ox, the ox feeds man." Jim could almost entertain when he quoted prose or poetry, and now he recalled lines about how meat protein eaters are the kings of men, not to be compared to mush eaters nor identified with the diet of slaves, the impoverished, the tribes of civilization forever undeveloped.

The visiting journalist was not always a docile listener. "But, Mr. Neff, we figured the feedlots would fail, but they're expanding as we speak. State legislators are crafting laws that make it impossible for townships and counties to protect themselves from CAFOs. Hell's bells, they could put one within smelling distance from you and make Banyan Place impossible. I know that feedlot beef isn't fit to eat, but people are eating it." When Caleb paused, Jim allowed silence to take over. The two, Jim and Caleb, took turns watching bluebirds scold each other at Nora's feeder out the window. Well within view, cows were taking their diet of grass. These are scenes peculiar to Kansas, the sweep of bluegrass over swale and dale, Nature's triumph and benediction.

"'All flesh is grass,' said the prophet," and Jim added, "not soybean meal, cattle cake, or protein bypass. Dealing with feedlot bloat by shoving a garden hose down the throat of a bovine in confinement is an abomination to God, the capital letter God who blessed the animal and ordered it, like Nebuchadnezzar, to eat grass. No priest ever baptized bluegrass or gave it that name, but by any other name it couldn't be greener, more succulent, more digestible. Once, its failure would have depopulated the Earth, but now the alchemists delete grass as bovine feed in order to turn base protein into gold. Fields plowed by cannon, soaked red with blood, then stolen by uncompromising winds, have been planted green with grass, 'Nature's constant benediction,' as Senator Ingalls once orated. 'Grass is immortal!' he said. Is it? There are parts of the dust bowl that have yet to recover, the kiss of the desert is that severe. But there is not a square foot on Banyan Place that is not directly or indirectly protected by grass, while neighbors endure drought and dust devils that portend what they will. Yes, Nature is offended and man is offended, but Nature will prevail all in her own good time. The clone will vanish like the sexless potato because without DNA finding correction via sperm and ova, errors will grow exponentially and cancel out what evolution has ordained.

"I know what you want to say," Jim Neff said in measured words, "but waiting for the ultimate truth to win out is like asking others to do the fighting."

"Mr. Neff, I think we've both been fighting for a long time." Long after Caleb Watkins and Jake's family had held their obligatory barbeque, and Banyon Place had settled back into a working mode, Jim asked his bride to climb up to the widow's walk. "James, you're getting romantic," she smiled. He smiled back. "Let's take along a beer."

He liked the view from the widow's walk. He could see every paddock, every sorted group of animals, and the blanket of some few experimental grasses. There it was, the biography of the life the two of them had made for themselves. No doubt about it, the farm was prosperous because Jim understood genetics, especially bull genetics. What happened elsewhere did not seem to matter. Xander could sell superior sires faster than Nature's own good time and Jim's genetics could produce them. It was not a "What'll ya give me?" market. The sales were premium, but Jim saw a cloud on the horizon that towered higher than Mount Everest.

"I hope I haven't oversold the boys on the cow business," he said, holding Nora's hand as he had done so often during their young lover and young married years.

"I don't think so. You actually didn't sell them anything. You romanced them into it. I don't think I've ever seen middle-aged men happier with their jobs. James, they have a passion for this business."

"But will they when cloning makes bull calves a boutique business?" Jim simply shrugged his shoulders.

Suddenly they stopped talking business, and Jim kissed her as he had so many years ago in a hospital chapel. They stayed there on the widow's walk, she with her head on his lap, enjoying the warm Kansas breeze, listening to the night sounds, the bawling of an unhappy calf somewhere in its newly assigned paddock, and an owl in a sycamore tree issuing a nocturnal call to its mate. It was getting late when Nora decided to go back to their smaller house. She did not say, "Let's go home." She said, "James, I want you to hear what Heidi has to say, what she told me about her dad." A calving session intervened before Heidi, Nora, and Jim found a closure to his black cloud concern. "Unless you can show me a society that has eaten a certain diet for five generations, we have no proof. Nor do we have proof that people can retain health eating GMOs, feedlot beef, or cloned beef or lamb or pork."

Jim said simply, "Proof? At Iowa State, one of the professors told Capper-Volstead that, for $100,000, he could prove anything." Heidi simply smiled her dad's remark into oblivion. She cited chapter and verse of the Pottenger study with cat test animals that had lasted five generations. As long as the cats could still reproduce, they could be regenerated. But once the reproduction ability was lost, no miracle of diet or medicine could reverse the loss.

"James," Nora supplied, "Heidi means the imprint of perfection remains even after debauchery. You haven't had backslider cows, so you may have forgotten how debilitated animals were just before the war." "What's too far?" Jim was persistent in his interrogation. "If it hasn't gone beyond fertility," Nora said, and Heidi nodded agreement.

Heidi picked up the exchange. "Dad, it took two to three generations to lose fertility."

"They couldn't be regenerated as a breed after that?"

"No." Heidi explained that males lost fertility first, then females. "Well, Heidi, where are we going?" Jim was really addressing both of his women.

"We're going to extinction based on estrogen in foods, junk foods, cloned meat, bovine somatotropin milk, and many aisles of processed foods in chain grocery stores."

"We've lost fertility in 50% of human males." Nora was almost pontifical in her pronouncement.

"You know, Dad, I never heard of a fertility clinic when I was going to nursing school at St. Francis hospital. Now it's a growing industry. Now we're fertilizing five and six ova at a time as a stop gap. The reason is, women can't get pregnant, and the blame belongs to the farmer and the food processor."

"James, Heidi is saying what you know pragmatically. When you have a non-performing bull, you excuse him from the herd, sure! But before that you look at the diet. You know you love grass. You hate hormones in feedstuffs. You keep a chemist's count on selenium for the sire. Now get this, Human sperm count has gone down tremendously in twenty-five years. So they answer with Twinkies and Ding Dongs."

Heidi was really laying one of her seminars on her dad with the aid of her mother, for which reason their sometimes interrupted séance lasted two hours.

"I think I get the picture," said Jim. "Man or animal, a lot of things happen on an unhealthy diet." He started to count them off on his fingers. "Skeletal malformations, hair loss, lack of fertility, same sex attraction, problems with teeth." And the count went on. "And this is based on five generations."

"James, we don't know, and we don't talk about it. It's taken us fifty years to talk about what caused the dust storms, forty years to talk about the fight that Capper-Volstead made." Nora was speaking, and she sipped on the tea cup that had been refilled once too often, then rejected the brew that had become cold. "We can't deal with what can't be put on the table." Heidi was as effervescent as a glass of vintage bubbly. "Dad, you and I will be gone long before the clone fools run their course. But when it happens, you'll be there. You were there when the government used war to raise farm prices, to cut loose money, and to lift the country out of depression. You witnessed the folly of plowing under good green grass before I was born. So I know you'll be there when all this comes to fruition. We're only in our first and second generation trying to re-invent Nature. Folly has a way of running its course."

Nora took note of Heidi's intensely personal salute. What was it that James sometimes quoted? "The people is a beast of muddy brain, a mere child guides it with bit and rein." In the twilight of their lives, she and her James would reflect on this, pass the lesson on to their children and their children's children, and, in the end, the gates of a finance hell and a Pentagon hell would not prevail.

38

Outside her kitchen window, Nora heard birds chirping their blessing each spring. South near the alfalfa field, Jim listened to the frogs goaded to life in the farm pond. Spring dealt kindly with the Neff tribe. Now age eighty-three, Jim Neff could reflect on his trip to Germany to bury his brother, Roy Lee. He met Roy Lee's son, Hans, a biologist with a professional reputation, a professor at the University of Bonn.

Jim extracted a promise from Hans to visit Banyon Place in the near future. A year later it became his duty to handle the affairs of his brother Joe Sam, who had passed away quietly in a nursing home. Joe Sam's wife had preceded him in death. Joe Sam left his estate to Jim's nieces and nephews and to all of Jim's grandchildren. Jim picked up a few of the artifacts of a bygone era that survived in his brother's papers, including the receipt for the box car used to move the family out of the dust bowl. Almost six years to the day after Jim Neff was pronounced a terminal patient with cancer, he was investigating crop circle activity, one of his post-retirement interests. Jim believed the circles a natural phenomenon, a hybrid occurrence somewhere between a dust devil and a tornado. A circle was found not ten miles north of Banyon Place. Jim realized that background radiation escaping the earth in spring and summer was being exacerbated by the presence of farm chemicals in the absence of carbon. The farmer to the north was what Jim called "poison crazy." Ever since 2,4-D herbicides had come onto the market, this farmer had applied the stuff with reckless abandon. "As background radiation escapes the earth in the spring and summer, about 75 clicks on a Geiger counter and it locks in on the 2,4-D and sets up a spin," Jim reasoned out loud. The evidence was there. A circle with radioactive grain, totally dehydrated, singed about the edge, was created in a vacuum, hence no fire.

"Of course," Jim Neff reasoned, "in the absence of oxygen there could be no fire." The crop circle on the farm up north had made its pattern in a wheat field.

On the afternoon that Jim made the scene, the sky was dark. The weather bureau people had a funnel cloud warning out, but, as usual, farmers, and forever Jim Neff, paid little attention. At 3 p.m., a twister came close to Jim's pickup. As he left the vehicle to seek shelter in a culvert, a slab of debris caught him on the right shoulder and in the back of the head. It was a small twister that left the ground in less than a quarter of a mile and jumped skyward.

Jim got back into his truck and drove home. His head hurt, he rested on the couch in the cottage. By 6:30 p.m., Heidi and Nora ordered up an ambulance on 911. They kept Jim in the hospital overnight. "He'll have a headache," the doctor said, "but I think it will pass." He was dismissed the next morning. By mid afternoon, his blood pressure had dropped drastically. More sirens, more white-coated attendants, more of everything followed except relief for the soldier turned farmer. Jim remained in the hospital for one week and then his wife and daughter, both nurses, insisted on bringing him home. The physicians figured the swelling had to go down before they could even think of operating, and one doctor speculated that when it went down, it might not even be necessary. Jim was resting on a hospital bed in one of the cottage bedrooms with either Heidi or Nora in attendance.

An unexpected phone call came to Nora's cottage.

"This is Dr. Smythe," the voice said. "May I drop by?"

"Please come. I'm not at the big house. I'm staying in the first cottage." When Dr. Smythe arrived, Nora asked, "Whatever happened to Phineas priest?"

The professor chuckled. "That was Jimbo. I don't think I've told that to too many people in my life."

The picturesque professor accepted a cup of green tea. He took Nora's hand. "What happened to Jimbo?" he almost whispered. Nora related the facts almost clinically. It took a couple of minutes. "When he came home, he laid down. There was an eighteen-wheeler on the gravel section road. It was very dry and a really heavy cloud of dust rolled across the pasture. I saw it coming, so I raced to close the window. You know James does not like air conditioning, so the window was open. I heard James say, 'The dust storms are coming back.' At that point I noticed his blood pressure was dropping rapidly."

They talked about the past, the present, and the future.

"The university has archived your husband's ten white papers in a bound volume. They wanted you and Jim to have a set." She accepted the now retired professor's proffered volume with a gracious "Thank you."

"Are you up to a few questions I can tape?"

Nora agreed. "Yes," she said. "Some of the old Capper-Volstead Alliance people came by over the years. Glass Splinter, the PR man, was the only official. They, James and Glass, talked for two hours. Glass came around to the position James held. He realized that with the closing down of so many farms, America's great hope is no longer for solvency and peace."

"And how has Banyon Place been doing over the decades?" He knew the answer, but he wanted it down on tape.

"Ten years after James left Capper-Volstead, we all of a sudden tasted real prosperity."

"The sale of sires?"

"Yes, that, and the start of the Herbataurus breed."

Banyon Place was now headquarters for the Herbataurus breed registry, a breed well represented in forty-seven states.

"James always quoted you. 'The innovator will upset the existing order.'"

"Are the boys following in his footsteps?"

"Phineas, I have been married to James over fifty years. I wish more people could have the life we've had. Our sons are looking beyond tomorrow. You know how Jim wanted to have Capper-Volstead start a college to teach parity, structural balance, and ecologically correct farming? Well, we have a start. Xander teaches. Jake teaches. I teach. We have a laboratory in the old carriage house and professors come in for lectures. We have laboratory courses on artificial insemination and economics, and, well, Heidi has her courses on nutrition and health."

"What happens when they graduate?"

"They go back home. We expect some to become town councilmen, county administrators, and successful farmers. James always says the country has to be reeducated and resettled. He thinks the organic movement will ultimately prevail because it's innovative and will upset the existing order." Professor Smythe, the Phineas priest of yesteryear, turned off his tape recorder. "You know," he said, "back when Clinton went into office, we had no Internet, little real software. All we had was a fast track to globalism. The smart operators found ways of relying on cheap labor from poverty pockets of the world. No one gave much thought to people who talked about anything except Wal-Mart and a race to the floor."

Nora excused herself and went to the kitchen. When she returned, she had a tray of cookies and a fresh pot of tea. She settled herself comfortably near the tape recorder. As she started with, "My husband." Heidi entered. "He's sleeping," she said. "His heartbeat is regular and temperature normal. Do you want me to stay, Mother?"

"No, I'll check on your father regularly."

"I'll send over some supper," said Heidi.

Nora stood up and thanked Heidi, who gave her a kiss on the cheek. She introduced Heidi to Dr. Smythe with a short biography of his connection with her husband.

"Your father and Dr. Smythe served together in the war," she said. "They met again during the Capper-Volstead Alliance days I've told you about. He's a Phineas priest. Do you know what that means?"

Heidi said, "No, I don't."

"He's traced his family genealogy back to the days of King David, how many generations?" she asked, turning to the professor. "Thirty-six," said Dr. Smythe, but Heidi did not really understand, and closed down the conversation with a bow and a "Nice to have met you" as she left.

"Now, where were we?" recommenced Nora.

"I think we were about to discuss your husband's philosophy and wisdom."

Nora took a sip of tea, one of many during the taping session. "You know, James is a life-long student. He can hold his own with any Ph.D. in economics, politics, cattle breeding, you name it. First of all, he's a cattle breeder par excellence. He learned it from his grandfather, and his grandfather learned his art from his father who learned quite a lot from a Kirghiz tribesman, but you probably know about that." Nora did not wait for an answer. "James knows what it is like to be homeless. He knows what it is like to be a young man in Kansas without a future, and with a war pending. He was rescued with a legacy of four calves and a bull when his grandfather Xander died."

The tape cassette was spinning. The professor stole a look now and then as Nora continued.

"Jim reads a lot. He picked up on what was happening to farmers in 1955 when our second child was born, Heidi."

"The beautiful lady I just met?"

"Yes, that's our little Heidi. In 1955 corn dropped to ten cents a bushel, hogs about the same per pound. The cattle market swan dived. That's when James joined Capper-Volstead." Nora smiled. "I think you know that story."

"Some of it," the professor said.

"You're probably correct. What you don't know is how often James tried to stop evictions in at least ten counties. I think he said we were losing 2,400 farmers a week during those Capper-Volstead years. James saw well beyond the personal tragedies. He saw the emptying of the countryside as the opening gun for free trade governed by the poverty areas of the world. He explained it this way. Each year the gross domestic product goes up, and each year the number of people participating in the benefits goes down. Either their wages are cut, or their buying power is demolished." She turned away from the tape machine and made eye contact with the Phineas priest. "Do you know how seriously my husband was wounded in the Philippines?"

"I've been told," he said.

"Well, I do," continued Nora, almost ignoring his answer. "I helped nurse him back to health. I saw a thoroughly beaten young man regain his health, go home, take over a cattle farm, and grow it into prosperity, completely against the tide. He never once lost sight of the fact that the vast agricultural machine was pulling the country down because the absconders, his word, were canceling out earned income. I think James understood more than most that the military and war were being used as engines of credit to feed the rich and damn the poor. James read *Progress and Poverty,* and he often remarked that Henry George at least got the title right." There were pauses during her long discourse. She checked on her husband, observed vital signs, and reported back to "Homer" Phineus priest "Smythe." "He's doing fine. He's sleeping."

"What happened to your husband after Capper-Volstead went dormant?"

"James came back, as he said, to 'tend his garden.' He wouldn't go to reunions of his army outfit because everyone he knew was dead."

"Everyone except me, I think," Phineas priest said.

"He spent lots of time with the boys and Heidi. He saw Heidi off to the army and the boys off to college. He did not browbeat them into becoming cattlemen. He reasoned them into it. He also home-schooled them in animal husbandry."

"The draft was dropped after the Vietnam fiasco, so the boys didn't have to go. James didn't want Heidi in the army, but finally she followed her star. She's home now, retired with a pension. You should consider her our militarism expert. She was on standby when Bush, the elder, invaded Panama and killed some 2,000 civilians. She was in Iraq for the first Gulf War. I think it's pretty clear to her how war, so-called prosperity, and the demise of agriculture fit together."

While Nora reached for a cookie, the academic priest changed the direction of the discourse.

"I'm writing a paper on what makes a prairie rebel tick. What makes James Robert Neff tick?"

Nora hardly hesitated. "His family first, last, and always. James lost his family during the Depression and the war. He rescued me and I rescued him. We both wanted a family, and I think James literally dedicated his life to holding our family together.

"Number two, the herd. He takes pardonable pride in line breeding the best meat protein possible. He strives to get genetic improvement, and I know he's distressed by the fact that the beef herd of America has become mongrelized. What makes him tick? Beyond the farm, it's the plight of other farmers who aren't surviving. That's why he took part in the revolt against Hereford dwarfism. That's why he joined Capper-Volstead. He saw organization 'Martin Luther King-style' as the only way to correct public policy and the drift to globalism and free trade. Dr. Smythe, do you remember that ruling by Federal Judge Coleman in North Dakota in the '80s? He told the leaders and other judges to stop driving farmers off the land without due process."

The professor priest nodded that he remembered.

"In 1988 ASC and the rest delivered a package of papers to debt-heavy farmers. The thing was about an inch thick. It required lots of signatures. It said that successful applicants might get their loans restructured. Well, James read the package. He discovered a quit claim deed in it. My husband blew the whistle. All of us at Banyon Place got into the act. We lectured, we wrote letters to the editor, we got on the radio and TV. As I recall, about 80,000 packages went out. The agencies had already determined that only about 10,000 would be restructured. The rest were to be sent packing. James told everyone, 'Don't sign, don't sell, don't walk away.' About 7,000 refused to sign. As far as we know, they're still out there. The rest were whistled off the land in a heartbeat. Then the bureaucrats gave each other certificates suitable for framing for closing out cases. My husband was really excited when those 7,000 refused to sign."

Nora was on a roll as she retold her life's adventure with the soldier boy she came to know, whose suffering she shared, and whose life she complemented. But the greatest credit, in her way of thinking, went to one Phineas priest.

"You told my husband that the innovator annihilates the existing order, did you not?" She did not wait for an answer. "You know about Herbataurus? James came to realize that the feedlots could be defeated by grass fed cows. The Hereford was destroyed as a natural grass feeder by the lots and subsidized grain. That's why he and our son, Xander, came up with the Herbataurus idea. Herbataurus can't make it in a feedlot. They're the right size, they're grass feeders, and they'll never be feedlot animals."

"Jim Neff once dropped an idea I asked some of my colleagues to ferret out. It's equity of trade."

Nora was interested. "Yes," she said. "James often talks about the exchange prices being dropped to poverty levels instead of raising them to the high market level via equity of trade."

"Exactly," the professor said. "No commodity, no production should come to the U.S. at less than the American parity. But the adjusting tariff does not belong to the U.S. government. It belongs to the nation that exports into the United States as special drawing rights. Those rights extend the privilege of taking any American production they want at an American price."

"You have it all worked out?" Nora asked.

"Our economist colleagues do."

The professor suddenly came up out of his chair with a start, he realized he should be taping the conversation, all of it. Checking the tape, he found it used up and inserted a new tape in the machine.

"What does he believe about the future of the farm?"

"James believes the country will be resettled. We'll do what we've always done, we'll survive, and as James puts it, we'll probably prevail."

"Did he ever explore that structural balance idea? Mainly that a society has to create the money required to consume its own production?"

"Oh, yes," Nora said. "You can find all that in his papers and published articles. He believed a few strong hands in agriculture would collapse. I've heard it a hundred times, those boys are a sunset operation. They're mostly technically bankrupt. James believes good food has to return because the nation's mental acuity requires it. He doesn't believe it's possible to grow all of the beef with a mongrelized herd. I think you know all about line breeding, don't you, Doctor?"

"Did your husband ever tell your boys to join the army?"

"He did not. James thinks that war is a racket. The military exists to kill people and destroy property. Our boys went to college and became highly qualified, Jake in animal husbandry, Xander in biology. I shouldn't quote him, but I will. One day he said, 'Why don't they let us farm and stick to what they know best, killing and stealing?'"

The professor next asked, "What about Heidi?"

"She's a registered nurse. She joined the army and became a major. She was in on some of those adventures, Panama, Lebanon, and Gulf War #1. We killed about 2,000 in Panama, mostly innocent civilians. God knows how many we've killed in Iraq. So when Heidi retired, she started a foundation teaching nutrition. You met her a while ago. Right now she's helping me with her father."

When the professor ran out of tape and darkness was closing in, he asked Nora, "Would it be possible to see Jim for a minute?"

"No, I'm afraid that's not possible according to the doctors. Well, go on in, but don't wake him. If he wakes up, two minutes only. In any case, I gave him a sedative before you came. But I can assure you he'll

374

recover and be as good as new. He's tough. I know the rumors you hear. My husband terminal! Don't be foolish!"

"When do you expect an national epiphany?" he asked.

"When people get sick and tired of perpetual war for perpetual peace. When they get tired of using war as an engine of perpetual debt creation and inflation. You'll know when this WTO and NAFTA and CAFTA have finally run their course. As my husband put it, 'When globalism finally declares bankruptcy or runs out of oil, or incubates another world war.' The professor opened his brief case and pulled out a sheaf of papers. He proceeded to read a few choice passages from his book on populist movements. It took an entire hour to capture the essence of the short discourse. He refused an invitation for supper, which was brought in by one of Jake's boys. No, he was just a retired professor who did not want to drive too far in the dark.

"Heidi was finally lecturing on the evil of war," Nora said. "She was calling attention to the destruction loosed on Iraq because of radioactive steel used in tanks, contamination found to affect children for generations. Her classes were literally standing room only when she held conferences." Off tape, Nora told the professor, "We had our fiftieth anniversary celebration right here in the yard. Probably a dozen old Capper-Volstead Alliance people came by. They didn't scold James and he didn't scold them. I think they all knew they had missed an opportunity, and James made it clear that a newer opportunity was here. I don't think James realized he was being seen as an organizational hero."

As Nora and Phineas priest closed down their discourse, they talked about ethical ballast, the culture of religion and foibles of mankind. Nora fired the closing shot. "One question," Nora asked. "Do you really believe that business about being a Phineas priest?"

"Of course," he said. "It's my heritage. And you and Jim? Much of the country sees religion as more of a cultural matter. Are you two *cultural* Christians?" He paused, then asked, "Do you really believe in guardian angels, the communion of saints, the forgiveness of sins, and life everlasting?"

"Of course," she said. "It's our heritage."